Joshua Humphreys was born in Melbourne in 1985. He was miseducated at La Trobe University where he read Modern and Ancient History. He spent two years writing and performing in comedy plays and doing stand-up before deciding that he should be writing novels. So he has spent the last few years gallivanting around Europe, America, and Southeast Asia. In 2015 he published his first novel, *Waxed Exceeding Mighty*. For six weeks he smuggled copies of it into London bookstores and exhorted his social media followers to steal them. Thus was born #stealthisnovel. He is extremely fond of watermelon. The ferocity of his tap-dancing is unrivalled, except in China, where his style is derided as only semi-ferocious. His favourite films are Lethal Weapon 2 and Dragonheart. He is currently writing the screenplay for Armageddon 2—Liv Tyler's emotional journey in learning to forgive Ben Affleck for leaving Bruce Willis on that asteroid. His favourite band is Limp Bizkit and yes his Fred Durst impersonation is astonishing. In 2009 Humphreys travelled to East Africa, where he was one of the first white men to see an ostrich eat nails. In 2012 he went to the Holy Land where he, like fellow monarchs Edward VII and George V before him, had a Jerusalem cross tattooed on his forearm; he brags now about how good his hummus is. He was for a brief interlude in 2013 the wolfcatcher royale to His Highness The Duke of Bavaria and later that year went to Capri, where he assaulted a woman in the forehead with a crayfish. In 2014 he travelled through Central America—in Belize was taught how to make rice wine from a donkey's unhappiness and in Guatemala learned that wearing weasel's testicles as a necklace is more of a superstition than a contraceptive. He is fluent in Armenian, Cherokee, and Gibberish, and can read Latin, though he does not know what any of the words mean. He may or may not work for MI6 and can run really, really fast. He is a qualified mahout. He is very happily banned from France. He has not ever lost at paper-scissors-rock. And despite his own frequent assertions he is neither Mel Gibson's son nor Hugh Jackman's nephew. He currently divides his year between London, Italy and Vietnam. *Exquisite Hours* is his second novel.

Also by Joshua Humphreys

Novels

WAXED EXCEEDING MIGHTY
BOONDOGGLE
HIRARIOUS: THE FIRST NOVEL IN CHINGLISH
BOLTOK THE RAPIST
IN THE SPRING WE'D MAKE MEAT HELMETS
REARRY REARRY HIRARIOUS: THE SECOND NOVEL IN CHINGLISH
THE GIRL ON THE TRAIN WITH THE DRAGON TATTOO WHO IS GONE
WELCOME TO COSTCO. I LOVE YOU

Non-Fiction

PORANGE: THE WORD THE WORLD NEEDS
THE 3.75-HOUR WORKWEEK: ESCAPE 9-5, LIVE ANYWHERE,
AND JOIN THE REALLY REALLY NEW RICH
HANKIES
JUDEAN PEOPLE'S FRONT: WANKERS
MEL GIBSON: A MOST BELOVED UNCLE
DRAGONHEART: THE MAKING OF THE FUNNIEST MOVIE EVER MAKED

History

THE LATVIAN ORTHODOX CHURCH
BLOODY DESERT ISLAND: A HISTORY OF MUBJHERUDA
BUNS, PERMS & PEELS: THE FATES OF BEAUTICIAN SOCIETIES
A HISTORY OF THE WORLD IN 100 SCHMOHAWKS
POTATO BLOOD IN MY VEINS: A HISTORY OF MALTESE AGRICULTURE
A HISTORY OF THE WORLD IN TWELVE WORDS THAT
START WITH D AND ONE THAT STARTS WITH A SILENT
P, AND TWO THAT, THOUGH THEY DO HAVE FOUR OR
MORE CONSONANTS, HAVE NO OTHERWISE
REMARKABLE OR NOTEWORTHY FEATURES
TATTOOS, GENOCIDE & YOGHURT: SERBIAN STUPIDITY
A HISTORY OF BOREDOM
HOW LEONARDO DICAPRIO FOUND OUT ABOUT GRAVITY

EXQUISITE
HOURS

A COMEDY NOVEL

JOSHUA HUMPHREYS

#296

Dear Sarah,

I hope this book finds you
exceedingly well in Oregon — I always hear
Oregon pronounced in Al Pacino's voice from
Scent of A Woman. Thanks ever so much
for your perceptions and your support.
Buy these pages anyway
welcome to the resistance

[signature]

ISBN: 978-1-519-64599-9

Exquisite Hours first published in 1901

Japanese translation first published as *Zetsumyona Jikan*
by the samurai-poet-shitkicker Ishikugo Mayazaki in 1910.
For four decades the English version was thought to
be lost and in 1964 the book was re-translated
from the Japanese back into English as
Time Units That Are Very Nice

In 1985 a draft manuscript was discovered in a
priest hole in Berkshire. With the collaboration of
Bob Dylan and Art Vandelay this version of
Exquisite Hours was published by Joshua Humphreys in 2016

It is banned in Thailand and Battersea

Cover artwork by Samuel Humphreys

joshuahumphreys.net

CONTENTS

I.	*What Place For Our Repose Assigned?*	11
II.	*To Pursue Thy Better Fate*	65
III.	*Et In Arcadia Sunt*	123
IV.	*Dare Not To Such Thoughts Aspire*	163
V.	*That Happy Shore*	196
VI.	*To Return, And View The Cheerful Skies*	244

As universal a practice as lying is, and as easy a one as it seems, I do not remember to have heard three good lies in all my conversation.

SWIFT

'The thing is, I've been living a lie.'
'Just one? I'm living like twenty.'

COSTANZA

The liar's punishment is, not in the least that he is not believed, but that he cannot believe anyone else.

SHAW

Exqvisite Hovrs.

EPISODE 1

What Place For Our Repose Assigned?

I

'Miss Spencer, as special gift of Cathay Pacific Airline we would like to offer to you free upgrade for business class in your flight today. Is that OK for you?'

An horrendous day redeemed instantly of its horror. Vivaldi, trilling between the distorted announcements in Cantonese and English, became now a perfectly fitting accompaniment. Things like that always happened to Anaïs Spencer.

'That's very OK for me! Thank you so much.'

'You are welcome,' he said and blushed. 'You are very beautiful,' and he looked childishly down at his keyboard.

'That's *so* nice of you to say.'

'Miss Spencer, do you have a check luggage?'

'Just carry-on.'

And she was told where she could find the business class lounge. She took her boarding pass and her passport and the ivory-white suitcase which contained every one of her worldly possessions and hastened down the concourse. Beneath the halogen panels of the long departures terminal she felt a sequence of emotions born distinctly of liberation and relief.

A young woman in a red skirt and jacket stood at the end of a crimson carpet which led to a conveyor belt and walk-through metal detector.

'An-a-ïs!'

Horror resumed, Vivaldi interrupted—three very distinct and very loud syllables called from the distance behind her. In Hong Kong airport, on that day and yelled in that accent, the voice could only have been that of one person. His confession of eternal love, purported by its confessor to be unsurpassed in the exhausting annals of modern love, came after the week of apparent normality which was the calm denouement to her month of absconding from prolonged Parisian solitude—to Copenhagen, to St Moritz, from Salzburg to Shanghai to Singapore. A surprise, a major inconvenience, yet another imperative to flee. So Harry Fuggle had wept as Anaïs packed, had genuflected in the elevator and begged her to stay, had paid for her taxi before sprinting after it screaming. He could be ignored again. Anaïs lengthened her stride and quickly reached the young woman.

'Anaïs! … *Anaïs*!'

A lowered head and a smile, and her outstretched hand took Anaïs' boarding pass and opened her passport.

'Welcome, Miss Spencer.'

'Thank you.'

'Anaïs!' As Harry Fuggle reached the carpet. 'Anaïs, thank God. Did you not hear me? I was screaming your name as I ran down the concourse.'

Her eyes closed with unmasked frustration. 'I had headphones in.'

'You told me you hated headphones.'

'No, I said I hated pet loans. Why would you take a loan out to buy a pet?'

'But you weren't wearing headphones.'

'What are you a cop?' She was entirely impatient of him. 'What are you doing here?'

'I had to see you again before you left for Uganda. I'm so glad I made it.'

'Yes, we all are.'

An announcement buzzed in Cantonese, and then: 'Flight number ... CPA eight nine zero ... departing at ... fifteen fifty-five for ... New York City ... is now boarding. All passengers please proceed to boarding gate number seven.'

'Harry, I really have to go.'

'Your flight's at seven o'clock you said. You have four hours.'

'Yes but you never know do you? Security, immigration, duty free, massages.'

'Oh, be safe in Kampala, Anaïs.'

'I'm going to Uganda, Harry. I told you that.'

'Kampala's the capital city of Uganda.'

'Oh, Kamp-*ala*. Yes, that's where I'm going. Well, a little village just outside of it.'

'I have a surprise for you.'

'Oh not another one.'

'I spoke to my editor. He can give me time off in June. I can come and visit you!'

'That is a *very* bad idea, Harry. Very bad. You'll be raped. Repeatedly. Shamans in Uganda teach that sex with a blonde man cures every one of the countless, *countless* plagues and illnesses with which Ugandans have daily to contend.'

'I'll dye my hair.'

'Harry. I've had four years of medical training and three military. A dainty civilian like you wouldn't last a minute in Uganda.'

'You inspire me so much.'

'You keep saying that.'

'I don't want you to go.'

'I know you don't,' she sighed, speaking now to a repetitive child of whom she was thoroughly tired.

Harry Fuggle, this slightly overbitten bastion of Englishness, his family for more than a century British pillars of the imperious temple of international finance—himself a sprout of journalistic weed at the Hong Kong office of The Financial Times—was reduced now by this voluptuous blonde Australian girl's softly spoken simpering to a blubbering mess. 'But you have to.'

'Yep.'

'Before… Oh God.'

'I'm just glad the doctors here found the cancer.'

'So am I,' he said, almost weeping.

'You're glad I have cancer?'

'No, no, no! No, no, no, no, no. No! I mean what you meant. That now you can live your last few weeks to their fullest. Helping others. Oh, I won't cry again.'

'Good,' said Anaïs, very brightly. She was almost laughing. It was an aloofness at which she was singularly adept, though for her a relatively new distance. A year previously she would have been feigning the profound return of Harry Fuggle's limitless and unconditional affection. But she had done as much to an American with whom she had lived for two months in Amsterdam and a week later was accused of leading him on. True falsehood this, and she would not have it levelled against her again. She now kept very far from boys and men, even when they were at slightest advance, and had arrived at a level of attention beneath which would have been to ignore them entirely or to converse with the person beside them. It was a disinterest which she was able to maintain amid all her inventions and inconsistencies simply because love, which came to her in frustrating abundance, while blinding men to most things blinds them most conveniently to truth.

'I bought you this.'

'No,' she began to say, the word quickly subsiding into a sigh of amused repulsion.

'You'll think of me? At least until it dies?'

'I shall think of you very briefly when it is dead. Goodbye, Harry.'

'No! Let's not say goodbye. Let's say… I'll see you soon.'

'As you wish.'

'I'll see you soon?'

'Goodbye.'

'No! You'll see me soon. I won't let you go.'

'Please let me go.' Anaïs extricated from his fingers her forearm.

'I'll see you soon, Anaïs.'

'Yes, you said that.'

And, watched by a long and winding serpent of dishevelled, now aggrieved, travellers, Anaïs strode unhindered down the vacant carpet and she and her ivory-white suitcase, and not the pink orchid, cleared security.

Harry yelled from behind the barricade of the young employee's raised arm, 'Be safe in Uganda!'

And very swiftly Anaïs boarded a flight to New York.

II

At the formidable door to apartment 5A of The Majestic, 155 Central Park West, Anaïs Spencer put the first of three keys to the lock. Far too wide a thing. The second went in but would not turn. And she turned the last twice in the wrong direction.

In darkness she reached in and patted one wall to find no light switches. She patted her hand up and down the next and found three brass protrusions. In a bare white hallway of a room which led at one end to a smaller hallway and to her left a kitchen Anaïs unhanded her suitcase and went into the beige-carpeted living room which looked precisely as real estate agents' listings for Upper West Side apartments do look. A low and long white sofa rested against one wall between two matching cube armchairs, all facing a gigantic mounted television above a gas-powered fireplace. Two mahogany bookcases took up the remainder of this opposite wall at whose far end hung two olive-coloured damask curtains. She drew them and saw instantly that she did not at all mind the place. The Manhattan sky was purpling with dusk, streaked long and high with the ashen clouds of just-fallen night. The soaring East Side twinkled and was beginning to rise white and yellow. The green of the park's leafy masses dulled with the light and seemed as low rolling clouds across the earth.

Anaïs exhaled quietly and joyfully to herself, 'Thank you,' and flicked a light at the wall beside the window. Amber lights came up on the art-deco balustrade of a terrace. 'Ahh yes. There we are.'

Then she went to discover the rest of the apartment. There was a note on the kitchen bench; she read and recoiled from and overturned it. The bathroom was tolerably modern—the fixtures stainless, the showerhead wonderfully large, the bathtub clawfoot and enormous. There were innumerable tubes and sticks and bottles and containers of and for a superfluity of gels and lotions and treatments and scrubs and cleansers and balms—all resting around a sink on a large bench of dark marble. There were two bedrooms, a master, (she for a time jumped on its bed, then drew its curtains to find another, larger, terrace) and a smaller, used for storage (a power tower, an empty fish tank, a life-sized plastic goat and an almost-life-sized rhinoceros). Anaïs inspected its wine rack. French reds with mould-spotted labels, brand-name champagnes, non-vintage sweet German whites—and, nestled and dusty in the bottom corner, a 2002 Bollinger R.D.. Immediately she went to the kitchen and put it in the freezer. The refrigerator had a shelf of rewrapped cheese. Rustling through the plastic bags she found her favourite Camembert and her most beloved Gouda. Things like that always happened to Anaïs Spencer. She envisaged her dinner, and yes!, there were Medjool dates in a container in the door and some ludicrously expensive water crackers in the pantry. It would take half an hour for the Bollinger to get to temperature—just enough time for a bath.

She returned to the kitchen in a very soft bathrobe and with a very regal-feeling towel around her head she searched the kitchen for cutlery and for a wine bucket, then for a champagne flute and a cheeseboard. This she bedecked with two knives and a feast and frolicked to the living room. She spun an armchair to face the park and fell back into it and drank from the champagne's foaming neck. She poured a glass and sipped and shuddered. She put her head back and her feet up; placed the first marvel-laden cracker into her mouth and her eyes closed with sumptuous joy.

When the champagne ran dry and the cheese was rind and crumbs she curled up in the armchair and prepared for the coming of sleep.

Shortly her eyes opened with fright. The jangling of keys without, their resounding entrance into a lock, the front door opened. It was the coming into his apartment of Martin Pringle.

'Hello?' he called from the hallway. 'Hello? ... Oh, my, God,' he said, appeared at the living room doorway. 'This is *so* magical! I can't *believe* you're here.'

Draped in towel and confounded, Anaïs stood.

'I can't believe *you're* here,' she said, half-laughing, half-lamenting. 'You did tell me you were going to be away for three weeks didn't you?'

'I cancelled my trip! I couldn't bear the thought of being in Hong Kong knowing you were here.'

'Could you really not?'

'And now we're here in New York *together*!'

'Together, yes. Martin, you should have told me you were

17

going to be here.'

'Why?'

'Well I don't want to be in the way.'

'You couldn't possibly be in the way! I am just so happy to have you here! I never expected to hear from you again after you said you had to go to Uzbekistan. It's so magical that you're even here! How was it?! Tell me everything!'

'Everything?'

'Everything.' Martin slowly made his way around the armchair. Anaïs negated his small steps with her own.

'No, well there are so many details aren't there? Most of them horrific. They're sterilising farmer's wives, Uzbekistan's Got Talent, they're trying to get everybody to change hats. It's a human rights nightmare. And I'm very very tired. And I think I have PTSD.'

'Get them to change hats?'

'The Uzbek hat, the traditional one. Made out of newspaper, looks like a sailboat. Their dictator's paranoid and he thinks the Uzbek hat's being worn as a form of surreptitious protest. Now his police are forcing everyone to wear train driver's hats. Ridiculous, really.'

'Is this…' said Martin, raising the champagne from the bucket. '…is this my Bollinger R.D.?'

'It was de-licious.'

'Hmm.'

'All good?'

'I was umm… I was saving this, for my sister's nineteenth birthday.'

'Oh, I'm sorry. You should have written on it. But nineteen's not really a big birthday though is it?'

'She has Down syndrome. There's a fifty percent chance she won't make it to nineteen.'

'Ah. Well you know you shouldn't give them alcohol anyway, they're prone to becoming unintelligible.'

'Could I try some? Now that it's open?'

Anaïs threw her head back and with it the last little mouthful. 'That *was* the last of it. I am sorry. It wasn't bad. No Boërl & Kroff. Your cheap taste is at least a discerning one.'

'So you hungry? You wanna go out?'

'No,' she sighed. 'So much camembert.'

'You wanna stay in! I'm definitely good with that.' Martin, by a cunning with which Anaïs would not have forecredited him, had cornered her between the bookcase and the window. 'I changed the sheets for us. Pure Egyptian cotton.' And he moved to kiss her.

'What? Martin, no!' she yelled, ducking past him when his eyes closed. 'There is no us! I'm just not like that. I'm sorry.'

'Not like what?'

'Like *that*, Martin. You don't even know me.'

'But I wanna get to know you. You seem so magical.'

'And really I was practically asleep when you came in and woke me up.'

'Hm.'

'Yes. … Well I'm going to go to bed now. Goodnight.'

And she left him, a week's worth of filthily erotic expectations completely and abruptly unfulfilled, alone in his living room.

In the morning she was woken by a deep change in the balance of the mattress, wrought by the sitting of Martin Pringle at her ankles.

'Good morning,' said Martin, very annoyingly. He placed a dinner tray across her legs and put his hand at her calf. She kicked and said, 'Itchy.' Golden light was pouring onto the outside of the curtains and made the room glow. 'What time is it?' said Anaïs, instantly concerned.

'It's ten.'

'Shouldn't you be at work?'

'I took the day off!'

'You did not.'

'I wasn't going to fly you out here and then leave you all alone for your first day in New York City!'

'Were you not?'

'Hell no, girl!'

Then with a look which, had she any friends, would have been renowned among them for its powers of enchantment and acquisition Anaïs said, 'An incomparable shame.' So it still went that Anaïs Spencer's devilishly thick eyebrows, her permanent pout and wide dark eyes, her high cheeks and notoriously immaculate skin—and her generous everything—allowed her to say anything she wished and still be met with infatuation. It had been said, behind her back by a colleague, that no man ever cared about anything Anaïs said, only that she was talking to him.

'And look, I made you breakfast. We got a *huge* day ahead of us.'

'Huge?'

'We'll take a stroll through Central Park. Then we'll do Top of the Rock. Then Times Square and M&M's World. That'll be *so* magical! The Empire State Building, Wall Street. The Nine-Eleven Memorial.'

'Nine-Eleven?'

'Oh yeah!'

'What's nine-eleven?'

'September eleventh.'

'Is that your birthday?'

'Are you joking? You're joking with me aren't you? Yeah you are. Ha ha. And then the Staten Island Ferry for the Statue of,' and he sang the word like Oprah: 'Liberty!'

'I don't much believe in liberty. Do you?'

'And then we'll come back to Midtown for dinner and a show. I've got reservations at Malaspina's. A magical restaurant. Venetian food. My work friends can't *wait* to meet you.'

She waited for him to break into laughter. Nope. He was being serious. 'Your work friends?'

'Yeah! Come on, eat up. We got a huge magical day.'

He patted her on her blanketed thigh as he rose to draw the curtains. Upon the tray which spanned her legs was an enormously burdensome hot and cold breakfast.

'Oh, Martin, I'm really sorry, I should have told you.'

'Told me what?'

'I can't really eat any of this stuff. I'm gluten-intolerant. And lactose-intolerant. And avocado-intolerant, fructose-intolerant, sixtose-intolerant. I can really only eat snozberries for breakfast.'

'Snozberries?' he laughed. 'You mean like in Willy Wonka?'

'Willy what?'

'Willy Wonka.'

'What's that?'

'Willy Wonka!'

'Wonka? What a stupid word. What is it?'

'Have you not seen that movie?'

'Which movie? I don't really watch movies, I think them frivolous.'

'I don't think snozberries are real, Anaïs.'

'Of course they're real, I have them for breakfast every morning! Every other berry has sixtose in them. I'm allergic to sixtose. Do you *know* what sixtose does to me?'

'What?'

She said, as though it were very obvious, 'It makes me grow an extra toe.'

'Where do you even get snozberries?'

'Is there an organic supermarket around? They've always got them. And then we can go out and do all those magical, magical things you went on about.'

'There's a Wholefoods at Columbus circle.'

'Is that *very* far away?'

'Twenty blocks.'

'Mmmm,' she moaned. 'I'm *so* hungry. I haven't eaten since that cheese, and there was so little of it and then you came home and interrupted my dinner. I feel faint. And *so* jet-lagged. I may fall asleep right…' and she yawned and closed her eyes.

Martin leaned down to her cheek and whispered, 'I'll go and get you your snozberries my little snozberry,' and when he reached just a little too far in Anaïs rolled over and put a pillow on top of her head.

Keys were picked up from a table and the front door closed. The apartment fell perfectly silent and Anaïs' eyes sprung open. An hour to shower and breakfast and be out of the house— plenty of time. She ate Martin's breakfast on the living room balcony and sang along jubilantly in the shower to *Travellin' All Alone*.

She left a note confirming their dinner plans and in torn black jeans and a white silk camisole set off across Central Park. She told the effete hipster at the ticketing desk of the Metropolitan Museum of Art that she was an architecture major all the way from Australia and had visited yesterday and just wanted to pop in very quickly to have another look at a frieze before she flew back. She was bored by amphorae and by Roman bowls and for a long time was entranced by a painting called *The Meditation On The Passion*, partly due to its vibrancy of colour, its curious structure, its richly rewarding detail; partly because the information plaque said that it was by a painter called Carpaccio who lived and worked in Venice.

She was thoroughly repulsed by the looming concrete and tourists of Fifth Avenue and at Malaspina's asked if they had a reservation for a Martin Pringle.

'Pringle... Yes, Martin. Five-thirty, for twenty.'

'For twenty? Good Lord. Have you got a pen and paper? Please.' And she wrote Martin a note and asked that the *maître d'* get it to Mr Pringle as soon as he arrived. Then she was unimpressed by the High Line and hated neither Greenwich Village nor Little Italy. At Katz's she told the two suits who would not stop talking to her that she had come to New York all the way from England for a single business meeting ('I'm in adult entertainment.') but all she had wanted to do all day was to get out to try the sandwich for which they gladly paid.

At six-thirty a taxi took her back to Midtown.

'Are you feeling better?'

'Could you pay the driver?' she asked Martin. 'I got mugged. They took all my American money and my bank card.'

'You what?' said Martin, passing cash through the drivers' side window.

'Two Mexicans on the subway. They were very nice about it all. Explained everything to me and it actually seemed reasonable for me to give them some money.'

'You poor thing. You've had a horrible day.' He tried to put his hand at her back as he walked her under the white lights of *The Book of Mormon*. 'I got your note at the restaurant. How was the psychiatrist? You're not still having the terrors are you?'

'No, they're gone. I just... I've never even been to Thailand, Martin. Why would I picture your house as a dilapidated Thai fishing dock?'

'That's really strange.'

'Isn't it?'

Martin Pringle said his name to the woman in the will-call window and was passed an envelope.

'My father's one of the biggest set-builders on Broadway,' said Martin. 'I can drop my name at any will-call in the city and there are two tickets waiting for me. How cool's that?' (This Anaïs had not known. Though it certainly would have, it played no part in her decision to flee Harry Fuggle's constantly occupied Kowloon penthouse for Martin Pringle's allegedly vacant Upper West Side apartment.)

They drank champagne in the interval and left feeling thoroughly entertained. Martin said he wanted to show her Fifth Avenue on their way home and he expounded upon and pointed out almost every one of its buildings and its stores. They turned into Central Park and shortly, to the sparkling polka of a carousel organ, Martin Pringle halted and turned Anaïs by the arm to face him.

'Anaïs.'

'Yo.'

'I love you.'

'Hm?'

'I love you.'

'Nnnn... Ha ha,' she cackled. 'Ohhh, no you don't. No, no, no.'

Either the boys were getting on and becoming uniformly clucky or Anaïs was and they were all inferring from her age a desperation. It was becoming her far too common experience to be proposed to, to have her unconceived children named, her house designed, her future decided. Simpletons and dreamers (not for nothing is any distinction between the two seldom remarked upon), they were with increasing rapidity mistaking her mere presence for her unquenchable and everlasting affection.

'I do,' said Martin. 'I love you. I fell in love with you in Hong Kong.'

'You didn't.'

'I did.'

'Well, Martin...' Then she sighed.

'You love me too?'

Anaïs rubbed her forehead and said with perfect ambiguity, 'Nnnnnn...'

'I knew it.'

'You didn't.'

'There's just something about you. You've got a look in your eye. I feel so alive when I'm with you. You're magical.'

'You call a lot of things magical, don't you?'

'A lot of things *are* magical. Do you want to ride the carousel together?'

'No. Martin, I've not been entirely honest with you.'

'Tell me everything.'

'No. But, I will tell you that I was in Uzbekistan, Martin, but I wasn't working for the Red Cross. I work for a government, Martin. A government agency. Do you understand? A very secret... government agency.'

'A government agency?'

'Nobody likes a parrot.'

'You're a...' Martin mouthed the word and Anaïs raised her eyebrows. 'Wow. I had no idea.'

'Why would you have an idea?'

'True.'

'And they're probably listening right now.'

'They?'

'Mossad has more enemies than any other intelligence agency on earth.'

'Mossad?'

'I should *not* have told you that. Come on.' And she took Martin by the arm and hustled him through the park. He failed to describe her revelation as magical but did refer to it several times as amazing. Then he told her what they were to get up to tomorrow. His to-do list had been neither emended nor shortened. Remembering photographically the contents of Martin's freezer Anaïs said that she felt like some ice-cream. 'Let's celebrate tomorrow today.'

'Oo, no! I have a bottle of Dom Perignon that I was saving for my next promotion. But this is a way more magical moment! Can we drink that?'

'But I really do feel like ice-cream.'

'Ice-cream? ... I don't have any.'

'Oh, do you not? Would you go and get me some? What's the *best* ice-cream in town?'

'The best ice-cream in town? Ooo, Emack & Bolio's.'

'Uptown or downtown?'

'Uptown.'

'Is it far away?'

'Sssseventy-ninth.'

'Twenty minutes?'

'Half an hour.'

Plenty of time. 'Go and get me some? Peppermint choc chip. Or coffee flavoured.' She pouted and looked out beneath her eyebrows. 'I'll wait for you upstairs?'

'Upstairs?'

'Upstairs,' she repeated, nodding. And Martin bounced once on the spot and jogged happily uptown. 'Oh, please don't run,' she murmured.

Upstairs Anaïs closed her suitcase and hurried to descend The Majestic. She walked very hastily downtown and among the motley statuary of Columbus Circle meditated upon direction. She took in Broadway and the lights and glass of the Time Warner Centre, the darkness of Hell's Kitchen, the park; finally she wheeled her little white suitcase through the leaping waters and went down fifty-ninth street.

III

Anaïs passed the jumbled porticos of half a dozen apartment buildings and the entrances to several car parks before stopping at the restaurant windows of Essex House. It was sparsely littered with diners and drinkers and sufficiently upmarket and was attached to the lobby of a hotel. A tubby man with puffy clamshells for eyes and curly black hair was drinking from a tumbler at its second window. Anaïs caught his eye—or rather did several reliably seductive parts of her body—and she turned about and crossed the hotel's art-deco threshold into its wooden and marble lobby and asked to be seated at the bar.

She drank Soave and ordered soft-shell crab and linguine with clams and stared, first at the ceiling of shards of mirrored glass, then at the dining area's partitions—also of shards of mirrored glass—then beyond the ageing foreign bartenders to the copiously stocked liquor shelves. The stocky man was in front of Anaïs before was her dinner. He wore a black shirt stretched over a taught belly, tucked into blue jeans above cowboy boots.

'No one ever tell you if you sit at a bar by yourself you're gonna get creepy rapist perverts comin' up to ya?'

'Oh many times.'

'And you seem to be all right with that. Very fucking cool. I am a creepy pervert but I am not a rapist.' Finding his introduction hilarious, he deeply and sincerely chuckled. 'Chuck Wilf. What the fuck is your name, cutie?'

'Anaïs.'

'What the fuck kinda name is that?'

'I believe it's French.'

'You French?'

'No.'

'Good.'

'Agreed.'

'You're not American though are ya?'

'I am not, no.'

He leaned in to bring his menacing grin very close to her face. 'Not everybody can be perfect can they? … Where the hell ya from?'

'Rhodesia.'

'Where the fuck is that?' he chortled.

'Africa.'

'Africa? You black?'

'You're fantastic.'

'Yeah you're pretty fucking fantastic yourself. Like a toothless blowjob on a Sunday. Can I buy y'a drink?'

'Soave,' she laughed, delighted by his entirely unconstrained virility.

'Whatever the fuck she said, amigo. And another one o' these things. So what the hell brings you to New York, I can't pronounce your name?'

'Anaïs.'

'A-niece?'

'Close enough.'

'Well this would not be the first time that I have tried to have sex with a niece.'

'*That* is amazing. On so many levels. I get cold sores, Charles.'

'So does my niece, now! Ha ha. I'm joking, I never... No. Never. But I do get cold sores. It is a terrible affliction.'

'On my genitals.'

'Me fuckin' too! Ha hey! You're ten kindsa perfect. You stick around and I don't have to go on those herpes dating websites no more. Those chicks are psychos. *And* they have herpes.'

'So are you.'

'I know I do but so do you!' he said, almost exploding with excitement. 'This is fate!'

'It's probably not fate.'

'It's fucking old school destiny, Africa. What are you doin' here again?'

'I, Charlie, have made a terrible mistake.'

'Yeah,' said Chuck Wilf, and looked wistfully into his bourbon.

'I moved to New York for a boy and this evening, an hour ago, I arrived back at his place to find his wife showering. A wife to whose existence he had alerted me only insofar as he had detailed to me the prolonged nature of her death.'

'Holy shit.'

'Yes. And after throwing various items of her own furniture at me she threw all my cash, which was actually her cash, over the fifth floor balcony. And I only have one other friend in all of

America and she lives in Massachusetts. She's leaving her three fatherless children to drive down now to come and get me. She only just left. I hope they let me stay in this bar long enough for her to get here.'

'No! Uh-uh. That is *not* happening. You call your friend.'

'To tell her what, Charles?'

'Call her now. Tell her Chuck Wilf's taking care of everything.'

'Is he?'

'Yo, villager, get me a bellboy.' One was got him. 'Señor, listen in English and very carefully. I want you to take all my stuff outta room 1201 and put it in another room. OK? That's gonna be for me. Then you take Miss...?'

'Spencer.'

'Miss Spencer's shit and you put it in 1201. Comprende? Here's twenty bucks for your troubles. Don't spend it on drugs. That's what I was gonna spend it on. But you have it now. Be wise. All better?' he said, turning to Anaïs with his palms to the heavens like a saviour descended.

'But how can I ever trust another man?'

'You can't trust me. But you can take advantage of me. You call your friend.'

Anaïs pulled her phone from her handbag and tapped at it and then put it to her ear.

'Doritia? It's me. ... No, you don't need to come to New York to pick me up. ... No, a nice man has offered to get me a hotel suite for the night. ... Yes. ... No, I don't know if he is. Are you married?'

'Fuck no.'

'He said, Fuck no. ... No. ... Yes I'll be very careful. ... Well he introduced himself as a creepy pervert but he said that he's not a rapist, so I'm assuming he won't be one. You're definitely not?'

Reflexively Chuck Wilf began to say no but stalled. He mumbled and eventually shook his head and said, 'Nnn-no.'

'No definitely not he said. ... All right, I'll see you tomorrow. ... Yep. ... Love.' And Anaïs blew Doritia a kiss and put her phone away. 'Oh, I'm so upset. Would it be all right if I took this up to my suite and ate it there? It is a suite isn't it?'

Suite 1201 of Essex House felt remarkably like apartment 5A

of The Majestic. The ceiling was slightly lower, the walls slightly darker, the wood panelling a little lighter, the view over the park greater because the floor higher; but in all vitals of style and individuality it identically lacked. Anaïs kicked off her shoes and popped from the minibar a miniature bottle of champagne and twirled her fork into her linguine.

She changed into a bathrobe and after taking in fully the view leaped onto the bed and turned on the television. Not ten channels into a surf there came a knock on the suite door. In a Mexican accent there sounded: 'Room service.' Anaïs attached the door's chain.

'Who is it?' She pulled back the door.

'Don't worry, it is *not* a Mexican,' said Chuck Wilf's voice. 'But I am here to service you.'

'Oh God,' smiled Anaïs. 'How happy I am that you know which suite I'm in.'

'Heh, heh,' he chortled. 'Hell yeah I do. Now open up and let's get to know each other.'

'There's really not all that much to me, Charlie. And you're clearly not complicated.'

'Oh I am complicated. Sometimes I spend whole nights just cryin', makin' poetry. And I don't show it to anyone 'cause it's too personal and sad.'

'You are too much, Charles.'

'Too much fucking fun! Ha ha!'

'If I let you in, Charlie,' she laughed, 'do you promise to stay on the opposite side of the room to me?'

'No I do not.'

'Charles… I've already had a very traumatic evening.'

'How 'bout this? I promise not to touch you at all… until you ask me to. Which you will.'

Anaïs laughed and shook her head and closed the door to unlatch the chain.

'I see you're taking advantage of the minibar?' he said as he charged in.

'Precisely as you told me to.'

'You always do as your told?'

'When it doesn't cost me anything.'

Chuck chuckled again. 'So what now?' he said, taking a beer from the minifridge.

'What could you mean?'

'Here we are.'

'Yes?'

'Just two very single people. Unattached, you as of today. And we both suffer from the terrible affliction that bullies call herpes. Let's have some fucking fun you and me!'

'Do you mean you want to flirt with me, Charles?'

'If by flirt you mean making sex to one another, then yes, yes, I fucking do.'

'Well I never flirt, Charlie, without a glass of champagne in my hand. And this bottle…' She finished it. 'Is empty.'

'Hm. There was champagne in here this morning but I threw it out the window at a God-damn horse that wouldn't shut the fuck up. I got another one in my new room though. I'll go and get it.' And he did. Then he heaved himself onto her bed and stretched his legs and put his arms behind his head. 'So this is it, uh?'

Anaïs was looking out over the park from an armchair. 'What's *it*, Charles? You're very conclusive.'

'I got the champagne, even though I don't drink the shit. Let's get a-flirtin'.'

'A-flirting? *Why* do you want to flirt with me, Charlie?'

He scrunched up his nose and squinted at her. 'There's something about you,' he said, aggressively. 'You got a look in your eye. I feel alive just starin' at ya. Now get drinkin'. Let's get drurnk!'

'Oh but Charlie, one ought never to drink champagne without strawberries. Everybody knows that.'

'But Charlie,' he said, mocking her, 'one ought never to drink strawberries… I'll go get some.'

'Where from?'

'I got some in my room.'

'You do not.'

'Hell yeah I do.'

'Why?'

He chuckled and said, 'I don't know. My gay uncle sent 'em to me. He's some kind of farmer.'

'A strawberry farmer?'

'Pft. I don't know, probably. I'll go get 'em. *Then* we can get to know each other.'

'Can we though?'

'Africa, this suite is seven hundred and fifty-three dollars a night. Hell yeah we're gettin' to know each other,' and Chuck jogged out of suite 1201.

Anaïs took from her purse a packet of little white pills. She popped two from their blisters and put them on the bedside table. She poured two glasses of champagne, drank one and repoured it. She was staring at the tablets when Chuck threw a wooden basket of strawberries onto the bed immediately before splaying himself across the duvet and putting his hand at her waist. She returned hastily to the window.

'Ho ho! Is that ecstacy?' The clamshells withdrew into his cheeks as his eyes became even wilder.

'For one of us.'

'Fuckin' hell yeah. I'll take one.'

'Not yet, Charlie. Slow down.'

'You're right. We'll do it first, then we'll do the E, then we'll do it again.'

'Do what, precisely, Charles?'

'Flirt,' he said decisively.

'Oh, Chuck,' she said holding up the bottle. 'I can't drink this.'

'God damn it! Why the fuck not?!'

'It's Taittinger.'

'So what? Is that shit?'

'On the contrary. It's what my grandmother used to drink. And she was an incomparably elegant woman. But one shouldn't ever drink Taittinger without white-gold stilton, the rarest cheese in the world.'

'You're shittin' me?'

'Decidedly not. And my grandmother was my closest and dearest friend in the whole world. I couldn't possibly drink this without it.'

'I got white gold stilton in my room.'

'You do not.'

'Fuck yeah I do! I told you this shit was fate! My uncle owns some kinda fancy-ass cheese shop here.'

'The same uncle?'

'A different one!' He chuckled. 'He sent me a hamper when he found out I was in town. Gay if you ask me, fuckin' cheese. I'll go get it. Right after you give me a kiss.'

Anaïs slunk to the other side of the room and was stridden

after. 'Chuck…'

'Africa…' Looming, he was barely taller than her. His belly presented the greatest physical obstacle to the granting of his cupidinous wish. 'Just a little one. No tongue. Give me a little taste o' that dark continent.'

'Chuck, I've been very patient with you. I'm very grateful to you for helping me out but I'm *not* going to sleep with you.'

'Yeah you will. You'll see,' and he winked and backed down and went to fetch his obscurest of cheeses.

Anaïs sat over the bedside table. She picked up the white pills and put them at the rim of Chuck's untouched champagne and stared into its feverish bubbles. 'Dear Lord. Grant me the strength *not* to rufie this man. Make him show himself to me wiser than his mouth and his stupid chuckle appear. Of thy mercy please make him deliver himself from me and cause him to hear the trumpet of my desperate warnings.'

Then the phone rang. Anaïs put down the pills and answered it.

'Hello?'

'Who's this?'

'Who's this?'

'Where's Chuck?'

'Chuck's getting cheese. Who's this?'

'This is Chuck's wife you little—'

And Anaïs hung up the phone and shook her head and loosed the pills into the Taittinger. She sighed: 'I thank thee, Lord, for this rohypnol my strength. Do make my foe fall quickly, to sleep, and grant him complete and utter forgetfulness of his complete and utter stupidity.'

'I can't get this damn thing open,' said Chuck, flicking impatiently at the stilton's foil wrapper. 'I think it needs a woman's touch. I just touch women.'

'Let's get drunk,' said Anaïs.

'About fuckin' time!' and Chuck was handed and then made disappear a glass of champagne and two immaculately dissolved rohypnols.

'Hello, is this reception? Yes, my husband has had a little too much to drink and I can't move him. Could you send two strong boys up to help him to his room? … Thank you.'

Anaïs plundered Chuck Wilf's wallet and gave the bellboys each a hundred of his dollars in exchange for their own adopted amnesia. She wrote him a note explaining with very little accuracy what had happened last night and invited him to buy her breakfast in Prospect Park at ten o'clock.

She gave a sigh of relief and finished the champagne and ate half the stilton and soon fell to sleep.

IV

At nine Anaïs had breakfast sent to her room and then spent a purgative hour in the hotel's steam room. She had a massage and a body scrub, a facial and a manicure, and, feeling fresher than any daisy had ever dreamed of, went back upstairs and put into her Givenchy make-up bag all the little bottles of bodywash and shampoo and a larger one of moisturiser and the complimentary safety razor. She packed into her ivory-white suitcase a hand towel and a sewing kit and the water bottles and diet cokes from the minibar and the packets of potato chips and peanuts and sachets of instant coffee and sugar and the bars of chocolate from above it. Then she stepped out onto the Manhattan sidewalk.

Two blocks downtown she came across a lump at rest between a sleeping bag and some cardboard.

She kneeled down and poked it and said, 'Hi.' Its blast radius stank of urine matured for decades in barrels of cabbage, and of donkeys. 'This is for you,' Anaïs whispered, handing her fifty of Chuck Wilf's dollars.

'Thank you!' said the woman, ecstatic. She sat up from the pavement to with putrid fingers count the money.

'Can I ask you a question?' said Anaïs in an angelic voice.

'Anything!'

'How did you get to be… the way you are?'

'What do you mean, hun?'

Anaïs turned from the woman's breath and put her hand over her mouth and coughed. 'I mean, how did you come to be… to *be*, how you are?'

'Sexy?' she said, snapping. Her eyes went from being wide open to being closed to a tight squint. Her frizzled grey curls were matted in most places and her deep wrinkles had rolled the earth's dust into tiny double figurados within the lines of her face.

'No, not sexy,' said Anaïs. 'I mean… I meant homeless.'

'Who's homeless?' she snapped, her voice cracking from its height.

'Are you not?'

34

'What are you a cop?'

'No, I'm not a cop.'

'Or you a drop?'

'Hm?'

'Or a stop? A flop? A hop? I was once Somalian, d'you know that?'

'You were what?'

'I used to sniff the wine. Sniff the wine and tell it to people. Somalian.'

'A sommelier?'

'No, pirates, you remember. Somalian pirates.'

'Pirates?'

'Johnny Deep. Deeper than the oceans of life and death. We beat on against the current, born again Christians into the past ceaselessly. Ceaselessly, leaflets. Do you know what I mean sometimes? I like that word. Can you go get me some, lady? Get me a leaflet. Go. Get me a little leaf. Know what I mean? Big leaf, not a little one. But of paper. Like a Chinese restaurant. Or a Somalian food! Yyyes!'

'Aaaand you're mental,' Anaïs concluded.

'Oh!' said the woman, inaccurately affecting the Queen's English. 'How atrocious of me. *I'm* a mental just because I want a leaflet. I suppose they come easily to you, don't they, blondie?'

'Thank you.' And with no enquiry at all into the process of their destitution Anaïs gave fifty dollars each to the next nine homeless people she came across on her way to forty-eighth street. At the will-call window of the Cort Theatre she said Martin Pringle's name and saw the matinee of *Fish In The Dark*. Then she walked down to Battery Park and looked out over the Hudson and that statue and pouted and wondered, really, what all the fuss was about. Then she headed back uptown. Soon she was watching people take photographs of themselves in front of a large golden bull. Then she was looking up at a church. At dusk she was reading the tombstones of its graveyard. She stared longest at a small lopsided mossy slab of slate, a winged skull at its voluted top. It was the headstone of John Goodenough, born 15th March 1768, died 14th March, 1796.

'That's my great-great-great-great-great-great grandfather.' The voice sounded mellifluously at her shoulder.

'It is not.'

'He was a ruthless slave-owner.' The accent was smoothly Southern.

'Had he no ruth?'

'Murdered or had murdered over fifty of his own slaves. Used to hang them from an oak tree overlooking his farm. A great man.'

'Undoubtedly. And all that by my age. *My* great-grandfather was a Nazi.'

The young man's face shot excitedly towards her. 'Was he really?'

'A very prominent one.'

Golden-haired and tanned and in a tieless blue suit, this young man reached across to introduce himself. 'Paul.'

'Paul Goodenough?'

'Paul Polenmeister.'

'That's quite a name.'

'And yours?'

'Anaïs. Spencer.'

'I believe it to be a pleasure, Miss Spencer.'

'Do you often meet girls in cemeteries, Paul Polenmeister?'

'The good ones.'

'Good girls or good cemeteries?'

'You tell me.'

'Ha. And do you often come to pay respects to your great-great-great-great-great grandfather?'

'Great-great-great-great-great-*great* grandfather. And no. I have a coupla hours to kill before I head back to the airport.'

'Where are you off to?'

'Home.'

'Oh.'

'What are *you* doing in a cemetery after dark?'

'I have had *the* worst two days.'

'*The* worst?'

'I was in Bangladesh a week ago, Paul, counselling beaten prostitutes for the World Health Organisation, when I get a call from my casting agent to tell me that the producer of My Fair Lady has seen my demo reel and wants me to play the lead. Eliza Doolittle! No audition, no interview, I've got the part. So of course I up and fly to New York and this producer pays for my hotel and then three days into rehearsals he turns up drunk at my door telling me he wants me to sleep with him, *and* his best friend. I tell him no, and he tells me that if I don't start sucking the right dick, Paul, that's what he said, that I'll be background until I'm old and fat and ugly. Then he tells me that his best friend's on his way up, and then this guy opens the door and pulls out a fake gun and tells me he wants me to run around the room pretending to be scared before we do it. Then the producer put a curse on me.'

'He put a curse on you?'

'He literally said, "I put a curse on you." He said, "I cast thee out into eternal homelessness." Cast. He was making a pun, a Broadway pun, while he cursed me.'

'That's horrible!'

'I know, I hate puns too.'

'It almost sounds made-up.'

'Doesn't it?'

'So you have nowhere to stay in New York?'

'Nope.'

'And no real reason to be here?'

'Not really.'

'I just had a crazy idea.'

So Paul Polenmeister had a car take Anaïs' suitcase from Essex House to La Guardia airport.

The aeroplane was outmoded and rickety, the champagne in business class warm and unexceptional. Paul and Anaïs picked at a platter of American cheese and dried tropical fruit.

'And you've always wanted to live in New York?'

'Oh God no. But for a musical theatre actress it's the centre of the world, isn't it? So I don't really have a choice.'

'Where would you most love to live?'

'Me? Venice.'

'In Italy?'

'Mm-hm.'

'Why?'

She spoke softly and in her gentlest voice. 'In the memory of vanished hours so filled with beauty the consciousness of present loss oppresses. Exquisite hours, enveloped in light and silence, to have known them once is to have always a terrible standard of enjoyment.'

'What's that?'

'Somebody said it once of Venice. And ever since I read that I've wanted to go there. And I've always felt as though I *would* end up there. Do you ever just feel something, and you know it to be true?' Any outward and nearby observer who knew Anaïs Spencer would have quietly whispered into her ear that she had been staring at Paul Polenmeister for far too long, that a boy might get the wrong idea. Paul Polenmeister thought that she had stared at him for precisely the best amount of time possible. He had surmised from her stare exactly what he thought she meant, and he had indeed contracted the wrong idea.

'I know exactly what you mean,' he said. 'I've always known I'd end up back at home. Austin's all right but Missouri's where I grew up and where my family is and where I belong. You'll love them.'

'I'll Love them?'

'I sure hope so.'

'When will I love them?'

'Well we're gonna be spending the week with them. So right away hopefully.'

'We're what?'

'At my dad's place in Independence. Well, Lake Jacomo, just outside Independence.'

'Independence?'

'Jackson County Missouri baby! The Garden of Eden. And then we can look into moving you down there and getting you a job.'

'Ha!' she cackled. She switched into impersonating his accent. 'And gettin' me knocked up.'

'A hundred little Polenmeisters.'

'Sweatpants and mother's clubs and soccer practise.'

'Breastfeeding, and diapers, and screaming.'

'And then of course the next, nine months later. Twin boys, hopefully.'

'We gotta repopulate the world, baby!'

Anaïs cackled again and they clinked glasses. 'But you *hardly* know me.'

'Do I have to? In a digital age do you think people ever meet for no reason? There's something about you. You got a look in your eye.'

Their flight landed at half past eleven. Paul's stepmother was waiting in the dark by a pick-up truck beside a chain-link fence.

'Hi, Ma.'

'Eleven-thirty I gotta drive out here and pick y'up,' she moaned just over her breath. 'Couldn't you take an earlier flight? Or a later one? Or flown tomorrow morning so your daddy coulda picked y'up?' Hers was a very placid moan, like a cow chewing its cud as it complained about having to eat grass. 'I'm out here in the city now in my nightgown and I gotta drive an hour back t'Independence. I'm not gonna get to bed till one now. I'm already so tired. So tired.'

'Sorry, Ma. Aren't you glad to see me? It's been a year!'

'Oh, of course I am, hun. Who's the girl?'

'Ma, get excited! This is Anaïs. Anaïs, this is Debbie, my momma. Anaïs is here to visit with me, Ma.'

'You haven't brought a girl home in such a long time. I guess we gotta squeeze into the truck now. Paul, you sit in the middle please.'

Debbie squinted through square, fluorescent purple glasses and her drawling continued even as she pulled into the garage and shuffled up the drive and into the house.

Anaïs woke, in a mauve bedroom liberally trimmed and upholstered in pastel brocade, to the sound of intemperate machine gun fire. She followed it—downstairs and to the side of the house, out through a little garden of cherry and apple blossom and hawthorn tree and across a sloping lawn, down to a horseshoe-shaped ha-ha. Paul Polenmeister caught sight of her and left his father's side at the next ceasefire.

'Mornin' little lady,' he said, taking off his earmuffs. She took his hand and lowered herself down into the shooting pit. 'Dad, this is Anaïs. Anaïs, Randy.'

'What on earth are you boys up to?'

Randy drew back his grey moustache and his plump bottom lip in order to grin. His eye sockets were deeply and darkly sunken. Thick pallid bags sat on them like two sacs of veiny milk. 'The M4 carbine,' he said with a mellow excitement. Paul handed her a pair of ear muffs. 'Standard issue United States Marine Corps. The right hand o' God. Here.'

'Oh, no, that's perfectly all right. Thank you.'

'Come on! Quick, look, a black guy!'

39

Anaïs smiled and looked away and laughed and said lightly,
'You can't say that.'

'Shoot him before he gets to the women!'

And, not wanting to be rude, Anaïs took the assault rifle and
put it to her shoulder and her cheek to its butt and put four holes
in a straw mannequin fifty yards distant that was, she then
realised, painted in blackface.

'You believe that? A natural shot,' said Randy. 'He didn't even
have time to play basketball. ... Look out!' he yelled, slowly. 'A
wetback.'

Anaïs lowered her weapon. 'What's a wetback?'

'Third from the left, a Mexican!'

'Third from the left?'

'Quick, Obama's gonna give him citizenship!'

Anaïs counted three mannequins from the left, saw the poncho
and the sombrero, and put three holes in its straw chest. 'A
Chinaman!' she said, joining in and shooting to pieces the
mannequin closest to the trees.

'A Yankee gay-lover!' shouted Randy.

'Which one?' yelled Anaïs, and awaited instruction.

'Everywhere! We're surrounded!'

And she sprayed bullets from left to right and back again. She
was laughing by the time she lowered the gun. 'God, that is fun.'

'Paul told me I'd like you. He didn't tell me I'd love ya. And by
God you're white.'

'No, I haven't been in the sun since last summer. Bit stuck in
the northern hemisphere.'

'So white. What's your surname?'

'Spencer.'

'Spencer. That's Norman. Viking. Good. Your mother's
maiden name?'

'Dad, leave her alone, would ya?'

'What?'

'Just leave her.'

'All right,' he mumbled. 'Come, I wanna show you somethin'.'

The three went into the wood beside the shooting pit and
shortly came to a small clearing of fallen pine needles. A riveted
steel door was embedded at the front of a dome of earth and
concrete brick. Randy jangled through an enormous ring of keys
to find that to the steel door. As he pushed it in the door swung

open from the inside.

'God damn it, Lyall,' said Randy to his other son. 'How many times I gotta tell you to stay outta here?' Lyall's friend rebuttoned his shirt as he ascended behind him. 'You and your friends stay outta my bomb shelter, God damn it. Now are you here for dinner? If you are go help your mother cook.'

'Jesus, Dad, calm down, I'm sorry. I was just showing Joel the meat and potatoes. He wanted to see them. And no we're not here for dinner. We're going to a party in Carthage. Is that all right?'

And Lyall with Joel behind him scampered through the forest towards the house.

'God damn kid, always showin' his friends the bomb shelter. I wish he'd get a God-damn girlfriend.'

Anaïs smiled. 'Do you think he will?'

'I sure hope he does, and soon. Kids that age need girlfriends. It's unhealthy to be spending so much time with other boys.' Randy led them down a flight of steps to another door. 'Four metres of reinforced concrete overhead and all around.' He pulled open a foot-thick painted-steel door and they descended again, into a four-room complex—one of bunk beds, one of a kitchen and pantry, one of living quarters, one of weapons. There were shelves of tinned meat and tinned potatoes and containers of water and gas canisters and a stove and cutlery; a bookshelf and games chest and surveillance drone and camping chairs; longbows and tomahawks and grenades and sniper rifles and box after box of ammunition.

'Pretty impressive, huh?'

'*How* long do you anticipate having to stay down here?'

'Five people can survive down here for two years without having to restock.'

'And why is that going to have to happen?'

'You can't feel it?'

'Feel what?'

'The end o' the world.'

'What about it?'

'It's coming.'

'Imminently?'

'All the signs are there. Obama, China, Mexicans, Gays, Terrorists. I might not live to see it, but you and Paul certainly will. I'm just lookin' after my family like every man should. And you're Australian, s'that right?'

'I am.'

'Hmm.' He appeared to think for a moment. 'It's a shame about you guys. You were one of the last ones to hold out.'

'Against what?'

'Third-world immigration. Ruining everything now.'

Shortly after they resurfaced a handgun was fired three times from the back porch of the house.

'That's you, little lady,' said Randy.

'What's me?'

'That's the dinner gun and it's only one o'clock. That means Debbie wants help. Paul you're comin' in with me, right?'

'Anaïs, I gotta go help Dad with some real estate stuff. We'll be back in a coupla hours. You feel like helpin' Ma with some real Missouri cookin'? You gotta learn some time!'

'I don't know what you mean, but all right.'

And they parted at the drive.

Quantrill House was built of cream stone, three-storied with a shingle roof, a front porch balustraded by cast iron. A portico with a pastorally carved tympanum and stone columns and pilasters sheltered a bright red wooden door. The entrance hall was wainscotted and Persian-rugged. The front was a dining room and beyond two plaster Ionic columns lay the ground floor rooms.

'Debbie?'

'In here, hun.'

'Oh, hi there.'

She was chopping celery with morosely sagging shoulders at a kitchen island. 'What's your name again?'

'Anaïs.'

'Anaïs. I was having so much trouble pronouncing it this morning. You missed breakfast.'

'I did. I've flown so much in the last week. I was in Bhutan on Monday and I still haven't really adjusted. Oh and I did need to ask, Debbie, whereabouts is the washing machine? I've gotten gunpowder all over my white top.'

'Oh, we don't have any fancy washing machines, hun.'

'Are washing machines fancy?'

'Yeah,' she lamented.

'Would it not depend on the type of washing machine? I'm sure you can get unfancy ones. They're a pretty standard appliance, no?'

'Appliances are fancy.'

'Even kettles?'

'What's a kettle?'

'You boil water in them.'

Debbie stopped chopping and looked across the kitchen island. 'Do you mean a microwave?'

'No I don't.'

'Then fancy.' She took some carrots hostage. 'How'd you like the machine gunnin' then?'

'Real fun,' said Anaïs in Debbie's accent.

'You know Randy's first wife was just like you.'

'How's that?'

'A gold digger,' said Debbie, becoming calmer with each executed carrot.

'Am I a gold digger?'

'All o' y'all are. Everybody who sniffs at Paul.'

'But I ain't sniffin' nobody.'

'I just hope he can see what I see. I'm sure he can. He's a smart boy. And if not then Randy'll see it and he'll tell him. Anyway,' she said as a perplexing segue into the readying of two sticks of celery. 'A collection of enormous towels is different from an enormous collection of towels.'

Anaïs nodded mockingly.

'How'd ya like to peel these potaytas?'

'I would love ta.'

Anaïs peeled in silence and watched Debbie's hypnotic chopping. She mouth-breathed and was sweating. Her orange beehive was coming loose and sagging from her head like a Phrygian cap. Not soon enough she sighed, 'I gotta go outside and rewater the ham. I know you're only in here helpin' so Paul thinks you'll work for his money but he's not here so feel free to scram.'

And Anaïs happily put down the peeler and went to explore the rest of the house. The dining room had art-deco dining chairs and a table running with a long plate of Christmas decorations and fake fruit. The door to a sunroom was behind the staircase and upstairs three bedrooms were beside her own, each decorated in slightly differing brocade and painted a different autumnal shade. One door was locked and a library overlooked the enormous and distinct burr oak in the lawn at the centre of the circular drive. On this room's walls hung sketches of the house in its first years, watercolours of an unpicturesque lake, fading photographic portraits of men and women which she surmised to be a century of Polenmeisters. There was a sparsely detailed tapestry of a periwigged youth playing a lute as a petticoated young woman sat upon a floral roped swing; another beside it of the same youths overseeing the completion of a Federal mansion; another beside that of—. Anaïs halted her browsing and looked closely at this third tapestry. The young woman was absent and the periwigged young man, previously calm and very content, was stamping his feet and waving his arms in the air with eyes wide from frenzied bliss as he looked up at three black figures hanging from—. Anaïs went again to the window. The burr oak's high branches also barely met, giving it the same untidy and emaciated look.

She crossed vast mowed lawns and ambled through copses of hawthorn and oak and apple and ended up at a lake. She skimmed stones and wandered among the yachts of the marina and when later she set off to return to the house she heard pistol fire and thought that probably it was time for dinner.

Randy carved. 'You ever tried country ham?' he said, smiling down the candlelit table as he sawed through its pink flesh. 'Honey, why don't you tell Anaïs how this piece of southern magic gets its flavour?'

'Well she wouldn't know would she? She only stuck around for five minutes to help with it.'

Paul tapped at his wine glass and rose. 'I'm just gonna say a few words before we dig in, if that's all right. Anaïs, I'm real glad to have you here, and I'm real glad to have met you, and I do hope you're enjoying our Southern hospitality here.'

'Yes, is this an extreme version of Southern hospitality? Or is this the light version? Because I know we're not *very* far south.'

'My daddy already loves ya. I know he's sure never seen a girl shoot like that. And I know my stepmom loves ya.'

'Did she tell you that?'

'And I have to go away again tomorrow night but rather than leave you here with these crazies, Anaïs, before we start our new and amazing thing I have booked you a flight… tomorrow at noon… to Venice.' Bemused, Anaïs turned her head slightly away as she kept her eyes on Paul. 'What do you think?'

'To Italy? … Are you serious?'

'United Airlines flight 4453 via New York,' he announced proudly. 'Dad's finally gonna be allowed to build Quantrill Estates and I'm gonna be comin' home to work as CFO of the Polenmeister Company. Money don't mean nothin' no more, baby!'

'I'm going to Venice?'

'I thought, why not start this right away? I'm going to Austin tomorrow to tie up a few loose ends and you'll be in Venice for two weeks and then… Hell!' He further raised his glass and said, 'To Anaïs Spencer.'

Randy joined the toast; Debbie drank deeply and quickly.

'Thank you?' said Anaïs, not really knowing what else to say. 'I'm umm…'

'You don't have to say anything, baby!'

'You're calling me baby.'

'Let's eat!' Paul sat back down as two bowls of buttered vegetables were given to him.

Randy divulged to Anaïs the day's successes. He and Paul had finally convinced the newspapers to leave him and his development alone in exchange for renaming Quantrill Estate's business park 'The Lawrence Business Park' instead of 'The Lawrence Massacre Business Park.' And in a gesture of goodwill suggested by Paul he offered not to call the artificial lake in the residential recreation zone, 'Bleeding Kansas' but would allow the first hundred residents to by vote name it themselves.

'They're all commy bastards,' said Debbie, spooning marshmallows and sweet potatoes. 'You shouldn't give in to them.'

And Paul spent most of dinner trying to convince his stepmother that it was financially much more advisable to outwardly let The Civil War go.

'Can I show you something, Anaïs?' Suddenly Randy had the same full-lipped grin across his face as when he had been carving the ham and spraying with a machine gun effigies of ethnic pluralities.

'Something *other* than a shooting range and a bomb shelter?'

He led Anaïs upstairs to the locked door. Rich mahogany shelves of leather-bound books, most with golden blackletter titles, and new books, almost all military histories; a large desk inlaid with green leather and gold studs faced out to the rear grounds; along the curved back wall were two long mounted glass cases at waist height.

'This is the Truth Museum,' said Randy, waiting at the glass case closest to the bookshelf of his office.

'That's a Luger,' said Anaïs.

'Mm-hm.'

'And a dinner plate?'

'Aah,' said Randy, hoping she would say that. He unlocked the cabinet and lifted the glass and pulled out the plate. 'Until you turn it over.' Under it was stamped an eagle holding a wreath which encircled a swastika. 'That plate was inside Hitler's bunker. Part of his personal dinner setting. You believe that? Paul told me about your grandfather. How prominent are we talkin' here?'

'My grandfather?'

'The Nazi.'

'Oh, that. Yes. My grandfather the Nazi. Umm... he was um... Well he was a Schindler's List kind of a Nazi. Rescued thousands. And then he was allowed to move to England after the war.'

'Ahh,' said Randy, completely deflated.

'And you can have this back.'

He returned the plate and pulled out the large gold coin beside it. 'Look at this baby.'

'A gold coin?'

'A krugerrand.'

And Anaïs recognised the thing. 'Diplomatic immunity.'

'Financial immunity. These'll be the solid base to your liquid fortune.'

'My what?'

'Yours and Paul's liquid fortune. All liquid fortunes gotta have a solid base. Finance 101.'

'Randy, what exactly has Paul told you about me?'

'That you're ready to help.'

'Ready to help with what?'

'To repopulate the earth. To beat the Russians.'

Anaïs turned her head again and inhaled to say something and then stopped. 'Beat the Russians at what?'

'At everything.'

'At the Olympics?'

'Baby steps. Then at nukes. Then the Chinese.'

'We want to beat the Russians at the Chinese?'

'No, beat the Chinese too! Have I shown you my bomb shelter?'

'You have.'

'Are you sure?'

'Quite. You don't remember today? Australia, immigrants?'

'Where?' shouted Randy and took the Luger and the magazine beside it and said, 'Outside?' and stormed downstairs while loading the pistol.

'What'd you say to Dad?' said Paul, coming upstairs to close the office door behind him.

'Immigrants.'

'Yeah you can't really say that to him.'

'What have you told him about me, Paul? And about you and I?'

'Oh don't listen to what he says. He just wants grandkids, that's all, and for me to settle down.'

'But why has he just told me that he thinks I'm to be a willing participant in the repopulating of the earth?'

'I told him about the discussion on the plane.'

'And which discussion would that be? The joke conversation we had? About sweatpants and soccer practise?'

'Oh, that was no joke to me, Anaïs. What about Venice? What about that quotation?'

'Well that part was real.'

'The whole thing was real to me.'

'Paul, I had long lapsed into hypothetical sarcasm by the time we'd gotten to children. I'm twenty-eight.'

'And think of what John Goodenough had achieved by that age!'

'Yes, about this John Goodenough and the oak tree outside.'

'You're *really* hot when you're angry.'

'I'm not angry, Paul. I don't get angry. I'm just a little confused.'

'Well don't be. Everything makes sense down here.'

'Everything?'

'Everything.'

'Paul, I don't foresee wanting to own sweatpants for a very very long time. And especially not with you. I don't even know you.'

'People don't meet for no reason. You said that yourself.'

'*You* said that. And that reason doesn't have to be so that they can marry and repopulate the earth with white people.'

'Say that again.'

'Say what?'

'White people.'

He stepped into her and pushed her legs back against the desk. She put her elbows up and warned, 'No. Stop it, Paul.'

'Dad won't be back for hours now. Not while he thinks there are immigrants.'

'Paul, get off me.'

'Don't you want to try out the eggs before becoming the incubator?'

'That is disgusting. Get off me,' and Anaïs pushed him as hard as she could.

'All right,' he said, and put his hands in the air and relented. 'We take it slow.'

As Anaïs repacked her suitcase she thought about all the pictures she had ever seen of Venice—the gliding gondolas and stripey-shirted Italian men, the pigeons of black and white St. Mark's Square, the white stone of the Rialto, redbrick spires, reflections of golden arcades in deep blue water, cappuccinos and seafood pasta and glasses of wine overlooking silent canals.

Shortly after sunrise she watched through the bedroom window the setting of a table and chairs under the burr oak and then the laying of a feast. Randy read a newspaper in sunglasses and shorts as Debbie and Lyall brought plate after plate to weigh down the plastic tablecloth. When Paul stepped out onto the lawn Randy waved him back inside. He returned shortly with a shotgun and fired it twice into the air. So Anaïs went down to breakfast.

'Welcome to your farewell and welcome breakfast,' said Randy, sipping virginal punch through a curly straw.

'Thank you,' she said very warily.

'We got Lyall with us, the whole family!'

48

'Dad you remember I said I needed some money,' said Lyall, completing the array of bowls with a vat of sausages.

'That's all you ever say. Take a seat, hun, beneath this here old oak tree.'

'About this tree, Randy.'

'Mm?'

'Has it ever been used for any purpose other than the shading of breakfast?'

'The hangin' tree? Hell yeah it has! Brought all the way from Manhattan when Quantrill House was built by my great-grandfather. It was still on his farm in New York when the Jews moved in. And now we're takin' good care of her. It'll be yours some day. And I have an announcement to make.' He closed and folded his newspaper and began loading his plate with leftover ham. 'Anaïs, I've spoken to the governor, he's a very good friend of mine, and he's gonna expedite your green card for you.'

'My what now?'

'You can't work here without one and I booked you in to take your real estate test when you're back from Italy.'

'Dad, that's incredible,' said Paul.

'Paul, it's not incredible. I—.'

'I only trust family, Anaïs. And once you're qualified I want you to work for me. You'll like it here in Missouri (he seemed to emphasise the first syllable). Friendly people, great food—thank you, Debbie, again. Winter's a bit cold but that keeps you inside with your large white family, doesn't it?'

'Randy, this is moving much too fast. Paul—'

'All good things move fast, Anaïs,' said Paul. 'Cheetahs, racing cars, Operation Enduring Freedom.'

'Paul told me, Anaïs, that you need some order in your life.'

'But this is chaos. I've known Paul less than two days and you've organised for me to move to Missouri to become a real estate agent and to repopulate the earth. First of all, the earth is already extremely populated.'

'Not with whites,' moaned Debbie.

Anaïs upturned her palms and looked down the table at Randy and smirked with disbelief. He lowered his sunglasses to look her in the eye.

'And here she goes,' said Debbie. Anaïs moved her smirk over to Debbie. 'Diggin' for gold. Movin' from the baby bear to the papa bear.' Even here she seemed disinterested in what she was saying. 'Honey just because my husband's an emotional genius doesn't mean you should be movin' on up for him. He's mine. Is my rich stepson not enough for you?'

'An emotional genius?' Debbie made no retractions. 'Do you mean a racist?'

All except Lyall, who laughed, gasped.

'I am not a racist, young lady. I believe exactly the same thing as the rest of the world. Except for the London Manhattan gay-lovers.'

'Blacks,' said Anaïs, casually.

'Where?' said Randy, looking hawk-eyed up to his home.

'Oh no, they're Arabs.'

'Sand-niggers? Paul, get the breakfast gun.'

'I feel a curse comin' on,' said Debbie, looking wistfully into a pile of toast.

'I so love it when you curse,' said Randy.

Debbie poked at and gulped down sausages as she hummed with no enthusiasm: 'You be gone, you bringer of badness you.' She shook her head and chewed. 'You speaker of false words and carrier of darknesses…'

'That's a fine curse,' said Randy, returning calmly to his curly straw.

And Anaïs was cursed all the way into the house. She collected the last of her things from the bathroom sink and zipped closed her toiletries bag. Paul reached her bedroom door just as her suitcase did.

'Where are you going?'

'I'm leaving, Paul. Your house is a house of crazy people.'

'Don't leave, Anaïs. It's such a waste of Viking blood.'

'You're a freak.'

Paul became solemn. 'I think you're afraid.'

'I am afraid. Of you. And your family.' And she pushed past him and took her suitcase downstairs and out the front door and lifted it into the passenger side of the pickup truck.

Randy walked calmly up to the house to join his son on the porch. Anaïs started the car and Johnny Cash came out wailing, '*Soon your sugar-daddies will all be gone, you'll wake up some cold day and find you're alone,*' and she sped off.

'Make the call, son.'

50

'You're gonna cry, cry, cry and you'll cry alone,' and Anaïs drove until her memory failed her. She pulled over and asked for directions to the airport. She parked the car on the blue concrete outside the departures terminal and found the United Airlines check-in counter.

'Hi,' she said to the heavily made up woman behind it. 'I believe I'm on a flight to Venice today. Is there any way I can have an early check-in? I really want to get through and relax. I'm a bit of a nervous flyer.' She was asked her name and the woman tapped loudly on her keyboard.

'Miss Spencer. … Here we are. So, ma'am, your flight has been changed. You were supposed to have a connection to Marco Polo Airport in Newark. Well now that connection's been cancelled. But you are still departing for Newark so I can just go ahead and check you in.'

'Newark?'

'Mm hm.'

'Where's Newark?'

'New Jersey, ma'am.'

'New York,' she sighed.

'If I could just have your photo ID.'

On the other side of the pedantic security checks she took a seat in an empty departures lounge and pulled out her phone. She worked herself up into a panic and called Martin Pringle.

'Is this really you?'

'Martin! I can't talk for long. This line's not secure. I've been a hostage on a Thai fishing boat for two days. You remember that dream? It came true, Martin. Things like that always happen to me. I had to play Russian Roulette! Drug possession, but it was a plant by one of the 'stans.'

'One of the stans?'

Her heels and knees bounced as she raced. 'Kyrgyzstan, Tajikistan, Dagestan. One of the 'stans. We're not sure which yet, but one of the very anti-Semitic ones. They're trying to go nuclear, Martin. Nuclear! I have to come to New York for a briefing and then go out there. Can I stay with you?'

'Tonight?'

'Israel needs your help.'

'I'm in Hong Kong, Anaïs.' At this she looked gratefully to the heavens. 'I just can't cancel another work trip for you. I know this is the life you lead and I suppose I could get used to it. Love really does conquer all, doesn't it? But I can't be rearranging my life at the drop of a hat, do you understand?'

'No hats, Martin. There are no hats to be dropped here. Can I just stay at your apartment for a few nights?'

'There are spare keys at reception. I'll tell the doorman you're coming. I won't be home for another week. Will you still be there?'

'It's too early to say. Probably not.'

'I got coffee *and* peppermint choc chip ice-cream for you. I didn't touch any of it. It's still in the freezer.'

'You're a gem, Martin.'

'And if you're still there when I get home maybe we can talk about things?'

'You do like talking about things. Wait, no!' she said, popping her eyes open and sitting up.

'What?'

'No! No! I won't go with you!' Then she yelled in pseudo-Arabic-Thai.

'Anaïs? … Anaïs, are you there?'

'No!' she shouted, and then mumbled the mumbles of a struggling kidnappee and hung up. She laughed and smiled and fell back into her chair. She sensed a bemused elderly couple at the edge of the row of seats.

'Boys,' she lamented to them.

V

She was herded into economy class and a man in a charcoal mohair suit, his hair greased back over his head, helped her lift her suitcase into the overhead compartment. She smiled and thanked him and when he had finished stowing his own suitcase he took his own seat beside her. After take-off the drinks cart was brought and Anaïs ordered a gin and tonic.

'Actually, could I have two?'

'Two?' said the flight attendant.

'I've had a horrible couple of days.'

'I'll stay close by then, hun.'

And when there were eight plastic cups and eight crushed cans of tonic water on Anaïs' tray table the man in the mohair suit pounced. 'New York, uh?' Umistakably French.

'New York,' she stated in her Chuck Wilf accent.

'I'll drink to zat. First tum?'

'Sure is.'

'And what do you do in Kansas City?'

'I run away from it.'

'I'm sorry?'

'I am a girl without a home. I got no money, no family, nowhere to go. All is lost. I have run away from the circus.'

'From ze real circus?'

'No, from the metaphorical circus.'

'I ate ze metaphorical circus.'

'I ate it too.'

He sipped from his wine cup and soon snuck in a declaration: 'I have somewhere you can go.'

'Oh yeah? And where's that?'

'I have a villa in Du Sai. Do you know where zat is?'

'Nope. Is it tropical?'

'It is very tropical.'

'I'm sold.'

'Palm trees, servants, food, accommodation—all taken care of. I have a villa zere zat is vacant. Right now actually. You can go zere for as long as you like.'

Things like that always...

'As long as I like?'

'You zere will keep ze servants away from my sings.'

'From your sings?'

'From my sings,' he said, and nodded.

'But you don't know me.'

'You don't know me eizer. But I sink you have aaaa… a look in you eye. Zere is somesing about you, no? Oo knows, maybe you will end up working for me?'

'Ha. I have no qualifications whatsoever.'

In a very long glance this French person's eyes went to Anaïs' seat belt and back. 'Everybody is qualified to do somesing, no?'

'A villa?'

'A villa.'

'Is there a swimmin' pool?'

'Zere are sree.'

'What's that?'

'Zere are sree.'

'Hm?'

'Sree, swimming pools. One, two, sree.'

'Oh, three!'

And Ali introduced himself and told Anaïs that if she went to the Biman airlines sales desk at Newark there would be a ticket waiting for her under his name.

At a workstation in the Newark Lounge she went into her email account and opened the email that was subject-titled 'Death Notices' and printed (from a list of documents including 'death_notice_ASIO.doc', 'death_notice_MI6. doc', 'death_notice_CIA.doc') a document entitled 'death_notice_ Mossad.doc' and printed it and signed in pseudo-Hebrew above Tamir Pardo's name and put it in an envelope which she addressed to Martin Pringle and then handed to a lounge attendant.

Anaïs was first to board the plane. The glass of champagne waiting for her in her first class cubicle was so awful that she decided to put on the eye mask from her amenity bag and to try to get some sleep. Passing by her as she dozed, women in saris were directed to their seats by women in saris, Arabs in cheap suits bickered with one another and men in kaftan and topis stroked their long beards and their laptop bags. There was a draped reticulated python and a procession of chickens—some caged, some handheld—and the bringing on of a very mangy rooster. The plane took off; when it was at cruising altitude Anaïs was woken by a flight attendant.

'Miss Spencer? … Hello, my name is Pavi and I will be assisting you with all your needs today. Now we are taking orders for the dinner. You have had time to look at menu?'

Although it was Pavi who had shown Anaïs to her seat only now did her red and golden sari occur as peculiar for a flight attendant.

'No I haven't,' said Anaïs.

From the rear of the cabin came the crowing of that unsettling rooster. Anaïs really started to wonder. She leaned out of her cubicle and looked backwards. No curtain separated first from the other classes. The rooster's owner was scrambling after him over the empty middle row of seats as the male passengers prayed in the aisle. At the plane's rear a plastic bucket was duct-taped to the aisle floor. A calf sawed its chin over the corner of a headrest. Anaïs stared at the back of the cubicle in front of her and then looked around the first class cabin. Save for Pavi she was alone.

'Pavi, where's Du Sai?'

'Du Sai?'

'Yes.'

'It is four hours northeast of Dhaka.'

'Dhaka?'

'Yes, Miss Spencer.'

'Where exactly is Dhaka?'

'Miss Spencer?'

'Whereabouts is Dhaka?'

'Right in the middle, Miss Spencer.'

'Yes, in the middle of what?'

'Miss Spencer?'

'Of what country?'

'Of Bangladesh.'

Anaïs looked everywhere in panic. The mangy rooster eluded still his owner and as a woman squatted to hover over the bucket the men prayed on.

'Oh dear God,' she said and opened her purse and flung two

rohypnols into her throat.

The captain's announcement of the commencement of their descent woke Anaïs. She felt intensely thirsty. Very shortly she realised that she was on an aeroplane. She called for a flight attendant. Pavi came from behind a curtain and smiled down at her.

'Could I have something to drink? Anything. I'm dying of thirst.'

Pavi returned to the galley. It soon occurred to Anaïs that the woman's red and golden sari was rather peculiar for a flight attendant.

'Where are you from?' said Anaïs as a can of Coca-Cola was poured into a plastic cup.

'I am from Bangladesh.'

'Bangladesh,' said Anaïs. 'And they let you wear—.' She became suddenly and acutely aware that the cabin smelt faintly of excrement and strongly of cumin. 'Www—. Where is this plane going?'

'We land in twenty minutes, Miss Spencer.'

'Yes, we land where?'

'In Dhaka.'

'Dhaka?'

'Yes. Hazrat Shahjalal Airport.'

'here is Dhaka?'

'Already I told you, Miss Spencer. Right in the middle.'

'Right in the middle of what?'

'Miss Spencer?'

'In the middle of which country?'

'Of Bangladesh, Miss Spencer.'

'Oh dear God.'

And all too shortly Anaïs' window was barely above a runway in the middle of ochre farmland torn by crevices and covered with weeds. Emaciated farmers toiled obliviously besides the tarmac as the enormous machines flying about them made only marginally worse the already pestilential heat.

Anaïs was despondent. She ignored Pavi's kind-hearted announcements that they had landed and simply stared. Soon Pavi became commanding. 'Miss Spencer you must leave the aircraft before the other passengers. You understand we are giving you head start.'

She pushed her suitcase up the jet bridge and followed the signs in Bengali and English to immigration. There was no queue. Blue-uniformed men in surgical masks stared at her from behind their counter. She smiled and looked around the hall (a dark, beige and mildewy void) and when a good time later they were still staring and had done not a thing with her passport save for ogle its photograph she eyed the document and said, 'Could you?'

It was stamped and she went into another dark and beige and mildewy void. As she veered to enter the 'Nothing to declare' passageway a man in blue uniform and surgical mask stepped out in front of her and raised a rubber-gloved hand towards a door. Anaïs said, 'Are you serious?' and the man nodded and began to shuffle his feet in order to corral her to the door.

Around a steel table were four stained and fraying rush chairs. Three of them were occupied by men in the familiar Bangladeshi airport employee uniform of surgical mask and rubber gloves. Her suitcase was lifted onto the table and splayed as her customs form and passport were handed around the room. Her clothes were lifted by the handful. The seated officers rose to sift through them one article at a time—lifting, unbunching, sniffing. The lining of her suitcase was comprehensively fondled and its zipped compartments opened and peeped at. Then the initial officer raised his arms at Anaïs and said, 'Arms up.'

'No.'

'Arms up. Feel we must.'

'What could I possibly bring into Bangladesh that you could object to, hm? Nutrition? Sanitation?'

'Feel we must. Arms up.'

And Anaïs, shaking her head, slowly raised her arms from her body. The four pairs of glowing white eyes quickly broke into a perverse argument involving much relaying of fingers from Anaïs' to their own chests until one of them, the smallest of the three previously seated, seemed to win. After taking a quick burst of photos with his phone he stepped forward.

'Now touch,' said the man across the table.

'No,' said Anaïs, looking the little Bangladeshi square in the eyes as a mother would her audaciously idiotic child.

'Feel he must.'

'No,' repeated Anaïs. 'No,' she said again, shaking her head and pleading for the little officer's good sense to get the better of him. He looked up at her chest and then further up at her. She shook her head again and mouthed, 'No.'

He nodded his head with a blank face and she shook hers with a very serious one and she said again, as though to an adolescent dog, 'No,' but it was no use. Before she had finished the word his gloved hands rose quickly from his side and came to rest on her chest. He broke into a smirk while looking at her then turned to his colleagues and smiled, a golden retriever proud of how high he could stand at a wall. A burst of photos were taken on a phone and the senior officer said, 'OK,' and the hands were withdrawn from her body before the officers scampered out of the room.

Anaïs repacked her things as quickly as she could and soon emerged into the unthinkable heat of the dark and beige and mildewy arrivals hall. Hundreds of Bangladeshis, abounding in decades-old clothing and pushing luggage carts each with an enormous suitcase and comprehensively taped cardboard box, drifted towards the glass doors at its front. Anaïs walked as slowly as she could. Each time the glass doors opened it was as though somebody opened an oven door in her face. Were her steps any smaller or infrequent she would have been standing still.

Across a short expanse of gravelly asphalt high white gates kept the subcontinent at bay. Gripping at the rectangular bars were hundreds of men, low-browed in kaftan and topi, despondent in fluorescent green shirt and black trousers, wistful and balding in striped polos and moustaches. No vehicle could enter the concrete-canopied drive without passing through a manned security gate. A youth swept garbage into a pile as a soldier sat on a bench and watched the crowd.

'Be careful, woman,' said a kind-looking man in a suit, stopping his trolley beside her.

'Why?'

'Why do you think they are looking at you?'

'Because I have blonde hair?' The man shook his head with pity and disappointment. 'Because they want to rape me?'

'Only half of them want to rape you. The other half want to kill you.' And a car pulled up for him and he was gone.

She scanned the panorama of captive faces with a look sculpted of disgust, fear and warning.

'Where you go?'

A rickety little taxi-van had pulled in.

'Du Sai,' she said cautiously.

'Du Sai I know very well,' said the jolly tiny driver through the open window.

'Thank you,' she said as he lifted her suitcase into the boot.

'You go to Du Sai, isn't it?'

'Isn't it.'

'Du Sai very nice. Where you are from?'

'I'm an Anglo-Argentinian Jew.'

He nodded without comprehension and eventually returned from staring at her in the mirror to the road.

Immediately a cracked and bumpy highway jammed with traffic; a slow procession of old cars and rickshaws and buses that looked as though they were made of wood; of vagrants and amputees and lunatics and ridden elephants. The roadside was of rubble, scrub, and slum, the concrete divider between the six lanes of traffic almost invisible beneath wind-gathered refuse. When they turned off the highway they were on a barely constructed road surrounded by sand and dirt and shacks, the distance one of high rise buildings unfinished or derelict, and palm trees. Beyond Dhaka they passed bogs which varied in size and in shade of noxious colour, each filled with a surprisingly diverse combination of water buffalo carcass, protruding bicycle, dead baby, litter, and sunken coracle. As dusk set in over the housing estates wandering gangs of shirtless youths hurled rotten bananas at the van. Her journey finally opened onto rice fields and swamps and soon the van came to a driveway and its headlights lit up a huge stone placard which read 'Du Sai Villas & Spa.'

The drive was lantern-lit and palm-lined, the grounds lush and trimmed; the driver stopped beneath the coconut-thatched canopy outside reception.

'Now you pay isn't it.'

'My money's inside, just give me a minute.'

'Now pay you, isn't it?' said the driver, inexplicably angering.

'I'm going inside to get your money, little man. Calm down.' And Anaïs wheeled her suitcase through the automatic glass doors.

'Welcome to Du Sai Villas & Spa,' said the young woman behind the high stone desk. It was blissfully cold inside. A huge air-conditioning unit blew a frosty gale overhead. Behind the young woman was a wall of glass which looked up to the teeming tropical grounds of the complex.

'I'm here to stay in a villa at the invitation of Ali Ramadi.'

'Mr Ramadi. Very good, Miss.'

'Could you charge that taxi to his villa? I don't have any Bangladeshi money.'

'Of course, Miss.'

'And could you go out and pay him before he pops a blood vessel.'

'Yes, Miss lady.' And the young girl took a wad of cash from a drawer and gave it to the young man beside her, who went out to calm the taxi driver.

'What name will you be using?'

'Anaïs. Spencer.' She handed the woman her passport.

'Ah, that is your real name, isn't it?' she said holding open the photo page. 'Most girl prefer different name to use. Candy very common. Britney also I think. And now Charlotte because of princess baby. ... Here is your passport, Anna, and a please follow Shuvagata to your villa.'

'What's that?'

'Shuvagata,' she repeated.

'Hm? ... Yes, you too.'

'Shuvagata,' she repeated, extending a hand towards the bony bellboy in mandarin collar and cummerbund who moved to pry Anaïs' suitcase from her.

'Oh, it's a person.'

Shuvagata led Anaïs out of reception and up a paved footpath lined with coconut palms, through an amber-lit succession of thatched brick bungalows, across the slate of a pool area and a jacuzzi and up onto a jungled path which led to the honeymoon villa.

'Stay many girls in honeymoon villa isn't it. This pool,' said Shuvagata, pointing to the pool.

'This is the pool?'

'This pool, yes.'

'This?'

'This is pool isn't it.'

'Is it?'

'Yes, this is pool.'

'This is pool?'

'This is pool.'

Frangipani and bougainvillea floated in pool's still and luminesced waters. Shuvagata slid across the honeymoon villa's heavy glass door and turned on its lights. It had floorboards and a dark timber ceiling; towels were arranged on the enormous bed, two as kissing swans, three as the letter I, a love heart, and the letter U, all scattered with rose petals. There was a living room with two large sofas and a floor lamp and a small dining table. Shuvagata showed her how to operate the television remote and then lit up the bathroom.

'Thank you, Shuvie,' said Anaïs. 'That'll be all.'

'And in here phone for to calling reception need you anything isn't it?'

'Precisely.'

'Many times man become too excited. Sometime angry. We come very quickly.'

'You come very quickly?'

'I come very quickly.'

'You have no idea what you're saying do you?' He smiled and nodded. 'But thank you.' And, chanting like a pungi, Shuvagata left.

'Home?' thought Anaïs, momentarily concerned that she might have been allotted such a horrid place. She stepped out to look into the azure swimming pool. 'No.' Cicadas and birds clicked and whooped in the forest. In the jungle, which Anaïs sensed to be not quite distant enough, monkeys exchanged howls. The night was hot and sticky and there was no breeze. But there was air-conditioning inside and unlimited towels and the bedroom did open directly onto a pool. She could dive straight in from her bed, she thought. She stood in the middle of the bathroom and did a *promenade en arabesque* without touching a single fixture. But there was no city. She would very quickly be bored. She had seen no other guest on her walk up from reception and none of the villas appeared to be occupied. It would be her and the staff, and she had had quite enough of the locals already.

She grabbed the swans by their necks and wrung them and

flung them and swept away the remaining towels and jumped and twisted onto the bed. Then she got up and changed into her bubblegum-red and aqua Triangl bikini. She stood at the bathroom mirror and was taking her mascara off when she thought she heard a door slide open.

'Hello?'

No answer came. She went out to the bedroom and inspected the pool area but found nobody. On her way back into the bathroom she was startled by a large figure prowling towards her in the living room.

'Hello,' said the man, his brow lowering as he unbuttoned and then took off his jacket.

'Hello?' said Anaïs, wary and confused.

He crept towards her. 'Hello.'

'Stop saying hello. What are you doing in here?'

'Ali know exactly how like I them, isn't it?'

'How like you whom?'

'Resisting.' His bulging other chin was lowered as he glared at her. His head was like a scorched marshmallow squished onto a potato. 'Not wanting to.'

'Not wanting to what? That's a bit rapey, buddy. And your eyes are freaking me out. Close them a little bit.' Anaïs backed to the outside door and the man stalked the floorboards after her.

'This fun will be isn't it?'

'Will it? For whom?'

'Run from me you. Then hard on bring to me.'

'What?'

'Then fucking we, isn't it?'

'You sound like a fucked up scary Yoda, buddy. Will you—' Then he pulled from behind his back a handgun. 'Woah. Woah! What the fuck is that?' said Anaïs, now most displeased. 'What is that?'

'Not real it is isn't it?'

'That is a *very* confusing sentence. Is that real or is it not real?'

'But with you me chasing after make to feel me like spy bond.'

'What?!'

'Double double zero seven.'

Anaïs pointed to the amber-lit path behind this aspiring spy-slash-rapist. 'Would you please seriously fuck off. I don't know what Ali told you but you and I are not going to be engaging in any other interaction than this very short and rather frightening one. Fuck off.'

'You run more around isn't it, *then* fucking we.'

'No! No fucking we! Stop saying that.' And when she was again beside the pool and he in the lights of the bedroom Anaïs turned and sprinted and was immediately chased down the path. He growled with delight as he descended after her. In her black bikini she leapt onto the slate of the pool area and ran past the freshly washed sunbeds. One of her feet fell out in front of her and she slipped and banged most of the joints which are associated vitally with the fleeing of rapists. Gaining on her, he pointed his ambiguously authentic weapon at her and told her to stop. She stood, but so painful was her knee that she could manage only to hobble. As she finally reached the path which led down to reception a dark hand was almost laid upon her. Then a figure stepped in from the pigmy date palms behind the shower-wall and hit the pursuant so hard in the face that his legs flew a great deal further forwards than did his head back, it being stopped inevitably by the earth.

Anaïs screamed; a pool of blood ran into the cracked tile. Her new saviour beside her, they loomed over the knockout. 'You run fast,' he said in a peculiar, transatlantic accent.

'So do rapists.'

'A friend of yours?'

'You are now. Thank you.'

'Stanley Felix. How do you do?'

EPISODE 2

To Pursue Thy Better Fate.

I

Stanley Felix's villa was much the same as Anaïs', only it was on the very top of the hill into whose side the others were built and was by far the resort's largest. Two paths led up to it—one at the rear to the guest bathroom, one at the front which opened onto his vast pool area and master bedroom.

'Stanley,' said Stanley to one of his servants, calling him over. 'Stanley,' he called to the other. Both were dressed in the same kind of white shirt and in swimming shorts of the same Hawaiian print as he was. 'I want you and Stanley to stand here and keep watch. Do you understand?'

'OK Stanley Felix.'

'And if you see anybody coming up, you go down to them and you stop them. Yes?'

'OK Stanley Felix.'

'And you translate for Stanley.'

And Stanley Felix had two other of his servants stand guard over the rear path.

'Are all your servants called Stanley?'

'For some reason they've all *decided* that they're called Stanley. And they dress like me. It's very embarrassing. They've had copied, times twelve, my entire wardrobe. They wait outside my bedroom each morning to see what I'm going to wear and then they scurry off and change. It's very weird. Did you see that?' On the slate between the master bedroom and the jacuzzi a statue carved of dark timber stood headless. 'Yes it's a statue of me. I lop its head off and they just put another one back on. I'm getting uglier as they go.'

Behind the blue-lit elliptical bar which stood beside his pool

Stanley Felix prepared two negronis. He was a great deal older than Anaïs, certainly at least fifty, his silvery hair flecked with white and his skin shining and tanned. Anaïs reclined on a sun-lounge with one knee up beside his infinity pool. This cascaded over onto the golden lights and shining green fronds of the resort.

'Now *why* was that man chasing you?'

'If I tell you you have to promise not to tell anybody.'

'Of course.'

'People always say, Of course. Say, Absolutely I swear in the name of Elohim not to tell anybody what I am about to hear.'

'Elohim?' said Stanley, stopping the Campari mid-pour. 'That's Jewish nonsense.'

'That's a strange thing to say. Now swear it.'

'I absolutely swear not to tell anyone what I'm about to hear.' He handed Anaïs' drink over her shoulder and lowered a cloth bag filled with ice onto her knee.

'Do you know about the price war?'

'I can't say that I do.'

'There's a price war going on at home and my family is caught right in the middle of it.'

'Over the price of what?'

'Wheat, wool, cauliflower, the internets, everything. There've been dognappings, character assassinations, dance-floor showdowns. People are smashing avocados all over the place. Nobody's hydrating. My sister's been in a food coma for a month. So my father sent me here to hide until the war's over. I was staying with an Indian family in Dhaka but they turned and tried to poison me with butter chicken. They were bought. With promises of cheap leather jackets. My father bought the protection of this resort, but I think that's been compromised too.'

'You're not a serious person are you?'

'Quite the contrary.'

'Well you're lucky that I *am* a serious person.'

'And why is that?'

'It means I dislike serious people.'

'So you dislike me, Stanley Felix?'

'Hm,' he smiled.

'So what do serious people do in Bangladesh?'

'They languish as international operations managers for very big fashion companies.'

'And moonlight as sleep therapists.'

'I saved your life tonight,' he smiled. 'At least do a boring old man the courtesy of humouring him.'

'Oh I'm humouring you, don't worry. But why *Bangladesh*?'

'I use factories here, and then in Indonesia and Vietnam. A month here four times a year, the same in Jakarta and Hanoi. The job needs someone with a certain lack of attachment. And I'm practically homeless, though my homes are palaces.'

'I knew I liked you.'

'It's hell here. Worse than every country I've ever been to. Not a single redeeming quality. They wipe their behinds with one bare hand and eat curry with the other. They marry thirteen-year-olds. But I used to have to stay in Bangkok, so it could be worse. I have the villa all year round. The Stanleys take care of it for me. And while we're both here in hell we may as well stick together, don't you think? Your place isn't safe for tonight?'

'I wouldn't say so, no.' She handed her tumbler to him.

'You drink fast.'

'I'm *very* thirsty. I haven't run in years.'

'Not a jogger?'

She scoffed and said, 'I wouldn't be caught dead jogging.'

Stanley Felix finished his drink and mixed two more at the bar. 'There are four bedrooms. I take breakfast at six and I'm out by seven. You'll have the place to yourself until I get home from work. And six Stanleys at your service. Shall I get one of them to go and get your things?'

'That would be very kind of you.'

'Which is yours?'

'I think it's called the honeymoon villa.'

'The honeymoon villa?' He again stopped mid-pour.

'What?'

'Did your father buy you protection or did he just go ahead and sell you?'

'What do you mean?'

'That honeymoon villa's used by a prostitution ring. A very big and very international one.'

'That explains it. … I'm not a prostitute.'

'It's interesting that you think you have to pre-emptively

defend yourself against such a claim. I didn't for a second think that you were a prostitute. You are a vaguely more dignified sight than the decrepit Natalyas they normally have in.'

'Are you flirting with me, Stanley Felix?'

'Not in any profound way. It's late for an old man. I'll get a Stanley to get your things.'

'Would it be all right if I took a midnight skinny dip? It calms me down before bed. Can you call the Stanleys off? I feel perfectly safe up here.'

'Are you flirting with me, Miss Spencer?'

'Not in any profound way.'

Anaïs woke and drew the curtains to her very well air-conditioned bedroom and slid open the glass doors which overlooked the northern slope of the hill. A blast of heat nearly cooked her outsides and she turned around and walked through the house calling for a Stanley. She found two in the kitchen.

'Never mind. I was going to ask you if there was a kitchen.'

'This kitchen isn't it.'

'Yes it is.'

'Breakfast, Miss?'

'I'm just going to take a look.'

The inside of Stanley Felix's refrigerator was an Eden. Not a sub-continental foodstuff in sight. Dairy, charcuterie, alcohol—the three earthly delicacies whose presence foreshadows always that of the European divinity—took up all three shelves and the whole door.

'Ice?' she asked of a Stanley.

'How much you want?'

'How much you have?'

'Many ice we have. We get from big kitchen isn't it.'

'Is it?'

'Yes sir.'

Anaïs inspected the wine labels. 'Stanley, bring me many ice.'

'Many ices?'

'Manys.'

'Manys ices?'

'Oh yes.'

'OK.'

When Stanley Felix arrived home later that afternoon Anaïs

was floating on a lilo, shining with perspiration and propelling herself aimlessly around his pool with dainty flaps of her hands.

'Stanley,' she said, her eyes closed behind her sunglasses. 'Cheese me.'

She and two of the Stanleys had spent the whole morning preparing a second lilo especially for the purpose of her uninterrupted relaxation. They had covered it first in ice then laid upon that a towel and then as much cheese and prosciutto and diced cantaloupe as they could fit around an ice-bucket. One of the three Stanleys now standing around the pool bent down to cast this gourmet vessel from the shade of an outdoor umbrella. Stanley Felix grabbed his outstretched wrist and put a finger vertically across his own lips. He took off his trousers and his shirt, and the other Stanleys did the same and watched him slide silently into the pool.

'Stanley!' Anaïs growled, rolling her head from side to side. 'Cheese me, one of you. There is nothing all the wine soaking up,' she said in her Laurence Olivier. 'And of it there is so very much.'

'How much of my asiago have you eaten?' said Stanley Felix, standing beside her. Then he tipped her into the water.

She resurfaced with a gasp and pulled her blonde hair from her face and said, 'Not as much as I have of your Soave drunk.'

'That stuff's expensive.'

'Precisely why I drank it all,' she said, imitating his voice.

'Four bottles?'

'Were there four? I lost count. It has been such a very long day. But the Stanleys and I have had a lovely time. We reheaded your statue.'

'I think I've found a way for you to repay me.'

'Well I won't behead it again, if that's what you want. It took us twenty minutes to carve your face into a watermelon from memory.' She took off her sunglasses and moved her eyes into a very suspicious squint. '*How* do you want me to repay you?'

Stanley led Anaïs up the avocado- and palm-lined brick path which wound its way through the resort. The trees were lit by sunken spotlights, the way marked by little stone lanterns glowing with the shapes of flowers. The night sky was navy blue with late dusk and moist with the hot breath of encroaching jungle.

'I'm about to meet with Manjoo Hossain. He owns twelve factories in Bangladesh, factories that I use, and he's been offered a lot of money by a journalist to let her into some of his more questionable establishments.'

'Your sweatshops.'

'And I want you to kill him.'

'No problem. How?'

'What?'

'Do you want me to send a message? Horse in the head? Horse's head in the bed. What about the journalist? Can I kill her too? I don't like journalists.'

'I was joking.'

'Oh.'

'I'm a businessman, I don't kill people.'

'Now who's being naïve, Kay?'

'Kay?'

'No killing then?'

'No, no killing.'

'You're sure?'

'Yes I'm sure. Now, have you ever pretended to be somebody else?'

'Mmmmmmm…' she said, squinting. 'Mmmmmmm…' she went on in crescendo, redoubling the squint. 'No.'

'One of my factory owners thinks he's about to meet with this journalist but I've made sure that she will not be joining us.'

'And you want me to sleep with him?'

'No, I don't want you to sleep with him. What is your life, nothing but sex and murder? Anaïs, I want you to *be* the journalist.'

'Aahhhh.'

'She was arrested at the airport today on possession of cocaine but the charges won't stick because I made them up. But you're free to be her for the night. I need you to show Manjoo that you're going to use the story on his factories in such a way that in the end *he* will be the one who suffers, and gravely.'

'Too easy, Shtan.'

And they climbed the wooden staircase to the large wooden-framed and thatch-roofed and glass-walled restaurant in which most of the resort's guests conducted their business.

'Mr Hossain!' said Anaïs walking frenetically to their right in order to shake the hand of a suited Bangladeshi man alone at a table. 'I'm sorry we couldn't meet earlier, I've only just gotten in from Strasbourg. The European Court of Human Rights is a procedural nightmare. Have you ever worked with them? You wouldn't *believe*. Shall we order drinks? Mine's a negroni.'

Stanley Felix extricated her hand from this confused man's and said, 'I am very sorry to bother you, sir. … This is not Mr Hossain,' and Anaïs twirled under his hand and followed him to the other side of the restaurant.

'Mr Hossain!' He was sitting in a golden embroidered kaftan and white topi. He had hardly any eyebrows and his gut meant he had to sit at a great distance from the table. 'Or can I call you Manjoo?'

'Manjoo is fine. How do you do, Miss Peckham?' She had instantly delighted him. 'Please you sit down.'

'I'm sorry we couldn't meet earlier. I've only just gotten in from Strasbourg. The European Court of Human Rights is a procedural nightmare. Have you ever worked with them, Manny? You wouldn't *believe*. Shall we order drinks? Mine's a negroni.'

'You're sure a negroni is wise, Miss Peckham?' said Stanley, thinking on those four bottles of Soave.

'You said human rights isn't it?' said Mr Hossain, turned instantly queasy by this most Western pairing of words.

'Isn't it! I wrote a story about a year ago covering the donkey fighting in Mexico. And now the trainer who helped me catch the Spanish billionaire who ran it all, well…' She trailed off, trying to catch the eye of a waiter.

'Well what?' said Manjoo, already beginning to panic.

'Hm?'

'Well what?'

'Well what what?'

'What happened to him?'

'To the waiter? I don't know.' Anaïs called out, 'Stanley!' and waved an arm in the air. A waitress came and Anaïs ordered drinks.

'And what happened to him?' said Manjoo.

'What happened to whom?'

'To the trainer.'

'The trainer?'

71

'The donkey trainer.'

'The donkey trainer? You're being silly.'

'Miss Peckham,' said Stanley. '*Miss Peckham*.' And shortly Anaïs clicked both to her own assumed name and to the inventions at hand.

'The trainer,' she said. 'The donkey trainer. ... Yes. The Mexican one. Well it was him *and* his painter.'

'His painter?'

'You know painting. Paint. Like Leonardo DiCaprio. They paint donkeys to look like zebras and then they make them fight in a pit. They kick one another to death. The donkeys. Not the Mexicans.'

'And what happened to them?'

'To the Mexicans? They're still there. Eating tacos.'

'Not to the Mexicans.'

'To the donkeys?'

'No!'

'To the zebras? They're not zebras. They're donkeys painted like zebras.'

'What happened to trainer and painter, Miss Peckham?'

'Man, I feel like tacos. So! I ran the story in the Western papers and of course the billionaire got off on everything, denied having ever even seen a fake zebra or eaten a taco. I am *so* hungry. Do they have tacos here do you know? Stanley? Manny?'

'And trainer and painter?'

'What?'

'The donkey trainer.'

She looked at him sideways, as though he were having her on and would any second breakout in a grin. She squinted at him and shortly remembered. 'The donkey trainer! He is a *very* nice guy. Talented too. He can stick his whole fist in his mouth.'

'And what happened to him?'

'When?'

'At European Court of Human Rights.'

'Oh there! No, he never made it. He was murdered in custody by the Spanish billionaire. Shot in the back of the neck, Soviet style. Can't prove anything of course. But dead. Ghastlily, horrifically, dead.'

And it was just about that simple. Manjoo Hossain sat through dinner smearing wet food across his mouth with his fingers, hoping that some of it might go in as he listened to Anaïs' implausibly long record of inadvertently imprisoning or killing her journalistic sources. Stanley Felix was in awe of her. In the course of one brief dinner she had invented and smiled her way through more lies than he had come out with in the course of his whole life. By meeting's end he was enamoured. Mr Hossain politely informed Anaïs before the arrival of dessert that the political situation in his country simply would not allow her access to his factories.

'Zebra-painted donkey fighting?' said Stanley, laughing as soon as they were outside and out of Manjoo's earshot. 'You should be doing this for a living.'

'Who's says I'm not?'

'Lying to handsome old men in order to stay in their villas is a very different ball game, Miss Spencer. That golden tongue of yours and that very golden hair could make you a fortune if you found the right buyer. Have you ever considered work as a fixer?'

'What's a fixer?'

'Or a broker.'

'Could I do both? That seems very profitable. To break and to fix. Fix and break.'

Around his pool again, Stanley dismissed his Stanleys and took off his cream tie and made drinks. 'Do you believe in destiny, Anaïs?'

'Stan…' she said, warning him.

'Do you or do you not?'

'Why?' She was squinting again and already disappointed in him.

'I've been alone in Asia for seven years now.'

'Yes, so have I,' she lamented.

'Can't you see what I'm trying to tell you?'

'I can not.'

'I love you.'

Anaïs grumbled and growled and scrunched her nose and made a succession of unladylike movements with her tongue before saying, playfully, 'You absolutely do not, Stan. You're a normal, mature, man. You dress well and you speak nicely, and this is completely beneath you. Don't be so shameful.'

'There's just something about you, Anaïs. I just… You've got a look in your eyes.'

'I'm buying very dark sunglasses tomorrow.'

'I just feel alive…'

'…when I'm around you, yes,' she said, finishing his sentence with him. 'I know all that. But did you feel dead before you met me? No.'

'I didn't know it but when I met you I realised that I *did* feel dead. For such a long time. Three ex-wives and not one of them made me feel the way you do. You're what's been missing in my life, Anaïs. It was destiny that made you run past me last night.'

'No, it was a rapist.'

'I'm not an old man yet and you're old enough to not be my daughter. We—'

'Of all the things to use to try to convince me that you love me, you go and use destiny. Utterly shameful. You don't love me, Stanley Felix. It's either my lips or my chest or my legs or my hips. It's physical. You know that. *Please* tell me you can tell the difference.'

'I've got contacts all around the world. I'm incredibly rich and incredibly powerful. I could get you a job practically anywhere. Where do you want to live? Name your city. New York, Paris, London, Venice.'

'Stan, you have two choices here and now. You retract your confession of love and admit that you are simply attracted to me. There's no shame in it. And we can go back to normal and I will eat your cheese and drink your wine and we can have fun here for a while. Or, I leave. Because if you actually think that you love me then is the world like your statue and has lost its head.'

'I love you. I want to spend the rest of my life with you.'

'Goodnight, Stan.' And she put her drink in his hand and he with extremely wide-eyes watched her disappear around the corner of the villa.

'Have breakfast with me?'

Anaïs rose at five and walked in the relative cool of dawn down to reception and asked the young woman behind the stone desk to call her a taxi. She waited against the cold wall beside the automatic glass doors.

'Going somewhere?' said Stanley Felix, crossing the polished concrete.

'Yes.'

'Where?'

'I can't tell you where I'm going, Stan.'

'I'll chase you.'

'Exactly.'

'I love you.'

'If you love me you'll stop telling me that you love me. It is very annoying.'

'Why does it have to be like this?'

'Because, Stan, I have not been entirely honest with you.'

'I know that. I don't care.'

'You will care. I'm going to tell you why that man was chasing me yesterday.'

'I don't care if you're a prostitute. I'll get you out of it.'

'I am not a prostitute. I work for Mossad.'

'Mossad?' His face washed white with horror. 'You're a Jew? You don't look like a Jew.'

'A black car is going to pull up any minute now to take me to the airport. I should *not* be telling you this. But I like you and you saved my life. Could you hang on a second?' She pulled out her phone and Google-translated into Bengali: *Drive! I pay.* 'That reminds me. I've been undercover here for so long that I don't have any Bangladeshi money left. Could I borrow some, just in case?' He gave her a wad of soiled cash. 'Thank you. And Stanley, it's the Russians. They're looking to take over Trieste and give it to the Serbs. We think their long-term goal is to take Venice and use it as a tourist resort. There'd be Russians everywhere. There is no fate worse. I have to go to Venice to stop them. And Stanley…'

'You're really a Jew?' The revelation had shaken him. The tips of his fingers were at his brow as he reconsidered the depth of his affection.

'And Stan…' A dented and rusting orange taxi pulled up outside the glass doors. 'There it is. I have to go.'

'That's not a black car.'

'It's orange. That means it's a level one emergency. I thought it was only a level B. I had no idea.'

'But Anaïs…'

But Anaïs was gone. She passed her phone up to the driver and he drove on into the morning light and the heat.

In another very much larger dark, beige, and mildewy void, this one propped up by white pillars of plastic which bloomed fantastically to the ceiling, Anaïs studied the departures board. Colombo, Kuala Lumpur, Mumbai, Riyadh. Moneyless she, all departed too soon. But Thai Airways flight 322 departing in ninety minutes—infinitely catchable. She and her suitcase made a lap of the terminal and finally found the Thai Airways ticketing counter. She smiled as she approached the young woman whose diligently downcast head was almost level with the countertop.

'Hi.'

The young woman, moustachioed and monobrowed, looked up from a computer. 'Hello, Madame, how can I help you?'

Anaïs smiled and talked as kindly and as slowly as she could. 'How are you?'

'I am good, thank you. How are you?'

Anaïs caught a silhouette of movement at her shoulder and turned her head. But it was a Bangladeshi man. 'I'm very well thank you. How are you?'

'I am also well. How can I help you today?'

'What's your name?'

'I am called Puja.'

'That's such a lovely name. Mine is Anaïs.' Another passing shadow at her back—she snapped her head around but the man, though a Westerner, had a wife and child in tow.

'Anaïs?'

'I'm sorry?'

'Your name is Anaïs?'

'Yes! Well done.'

'And Anaïs, you have a flight today with Thai Airways?'

Another set of broad shoulders, another quick glance—to a woman, strutting, curly-haired, as large and as ferocious as an upright gatekeeping rhinoceros.

'I do have a flight today,' said Anaïs, very slowly, 'but... I was wondering... if you could umm...' Another shadow wandered in behind her. This one was alone, in his forties, and white. Anaïs turned and greatly raised her voice.

'What do you mean you've cancelled my ticket!?' She lowered it again to say, 'Sorry Puja,' and then returned to yelling, 'How can you cancel my ticket? I paid for that seat six months ago and now...'

But he turned his head only slightly as he passed and did not break stride.

'I'm really sorry, Puja, to be so erratic. Ummm…' Several unsuitable silhouettes passed as Anaïs talked as slowly and with as little content as she could manage. 'But yes, as I was saying… I do have a flight with you guys today… Thai airways… And I was just wondering… ummm… if… there were any chance…' And she broke again into yelling. She startled Puja's elbows to her waist. 'How could you cancel my seat!? I just don't understand. Is it because I'm a Christian? I know how you people love to hate Christians. If I can't get on this flight I will miss the birth of my first niece! Do you understand?!'

The bait was comprehensively taken. He had already passed Anaïs, staring, and now, his head turned to enable him to listen over his shoulder, he rolled his suitcase about and came to her side. 'Do you understand, Puja? My first niece! My sister spent a hundred and fifty thousand dollars on a new uterus and…'

'Hi. I'm sorry. Hi, is everything all right?' He was slightly chubby, olive-skinned and in a suit and spoke with a daft and piercing Australian accent.

'I'm sorry. It's nothing. Where are you flying to today?'

'Me? I'm off home.'

'Lucky you. I *was* meant to be flying to Bangkok but Thai Airways have cancelled my ticket,' she greatly raised her voice, 'because the card I used to buy my ticket, six months ago, is *now* expired. Is that fair?'

'That can't be right.'

'I know! But Puja won't listen to me. Though she's really very lovely.' Anaïs mouthed, 'Sorry,' to her. 'Company policy apparently. And I can't buy a new ticket because the card that expired is my only one. Now I'm going to miss the birth of my first niece. My first niece! Two hundred and fifty thousand dollars my sister spent on a new uterus just so she could have this baby, not to mention the fertility treatments. The first grandkid out of all the siblings. They're all there in Bangkok, waiting in the hospital room. My whole family. Induced labour. My parents. I just… I can't miss this flight. I'm sorry, what's your name?'

'Nick.'

'Nick, I just can't miss this flight.'

And nor did she. Not very long before Anaïs was to begin crying the paltry airfare was paid for her and she wrote on one of Nick's business cards, '04,' followed by a succession of random numbers.

II

Anaïs strolled across the arrivals terminal into the white-lit tranquillity of the fragrance section of a Duty Free store. It was a habit of some longstanding. Amid the rainfall-soaked chiselled jaws and the piercing blue eyes and the unbuttoned shirts and designer stubble she wandered the tightly packed halogen shelves and sprayed the sample bottles onto the white strips of card. There was Calvin Klein—hoodies and pizzas and sundaes and her father's disinterested temper; Polo Ralph Lauren—new freedom and deceit, the bars and nightclubs of Flemington and Kensington and vodka blackouts; and, always last, Acqua di Gio—summer nights on the beach, that smile, the overwhelming excitement of it all, hours laughing in South Melbourne bars, St Patrick's Cathedral at midnight, the tiny St Kilda jazz clubs, youth and in love, and deepest heartache.

'Hello how are you can I help you?' said a bespectacled Thai girl, short, slim, her head slightly lowered.

Anaïs opened her eyes and said peacefully, 'Your sense of smell is the closest part of your brain to the part that's responsible for your memory. Did you know that?'

'Oh,' laughed the girl, shyly. 'I'm sorry, but English I no can very good. Sorry.'

Another blast of pestilential heat and malevolent sun as Anaïs stepped out through the glass doors of Don Mueang Airport. The second-level road was packed with veering taxis and spluttering mopeds and pink buses, all blaring out a panicked and alarming symphony of horns. White-gloved officers failed to conduct it with their whistles and their batons.

Anaïs stopped at the kerb and ignored the unintelligible touts from beneath helmets and through cracked windows. She looked right, to the up-ramp and the growing stream of traffic; left, to the dispersing wave of vehicles; off into the distance where golden naga finials and terracotta gables were baking in the yellow heat among tall palm trees. Right again, left again, temple, heat. Right again—and there it was. Stuck onto a beige pillar a sign with a diagonal arrow giving the direction of the Private Jet

Terminal. Things like that always happened to Anaïs Spencer.

The executive lounge of the Don Mueang Private Jet Terminal was furnished in much the same fashion as apartment 5A of The Majestic, Central Park West. The longest wall was of glass, private jets and chartered Cessnas arrayed on the tarmac. Desk lamps shaded by maroon cloth rested unlit at the backs of pairs of cube-shaped beige sofas set facing black glass tables. Gold-framed pictures of the airport at various stages of its hundred-year existence adorned the walls. Rambutans rested untouched on plates.

And sitting at the bar, Anaïs Spencer, watching and waiting.

Suits leaned in to discuss with little interest what their laptop screens were telling them as waitresses like apparitions moved in and out of their crossed legs to bring them iced coffee and cake. Departing passengers checked their watches and swirled their almost palatable wine and waited for their personal pilots to arrive. A man with a chiselled jaw and soft and combed brown hair sat in the far corner, peering through wayfarers over a wilting English-language newspaper. Every few minutes he turned from his reading as a new suit entered the lounge through the sliding glass, flight attendants in arm, to cross the expanse of the hard-floor and head out into the blazing heat to be driven to the horrible city. Flight attendants Anaïs long knew not to compete with. Only when a very tall Asian man sat unattended beside her did she find anybody worth attempting.

'You're *not* Miguel de Cervantes are you?' she said, swivelling her barstool to face him.

Slowly the man turned his head to her. He barely raised a condescending eyebrow before returning to his whisky.

'Are you sure? Because I've not seen him. He *was* meant to be picking me up here in his jet but nobody's shown up. I thought maybe it was you. You're sure you're not Miguel de Cervantes? Are you tricking me? Is that why you sat next to me? Miguel? It's you isn't it?'

'Do I look Mexican?' he said in contrived and unlocatable American.

'You're Chinese?' He made no answer. 'I was meant to fly to Mexico as Miguel's personal masseuse, but I guess that's not happening now. Stranded at another private jet terminal,' she sighed. 'The life of a topless Swedish masseuse I guess.'

'I'm Hao.'

Anaïs briefly inspected a stone slab in the centre of Hao's hotel's drive. It was a copy of a twelfth century lintel, a sandstone bas-relief of Mara's assault on the Buddha. Then one of two huge glass doors was pulled open by a delicate old man in red silken breeches. As Anaïs came to stand upon the white and green and red marble floor she watched this man put his palms together and close his eyes and bow and mutter something in Thai. She nodded once, sternly, back at him, and her white suitcase was eased from her hand by another man in silken getup with white socks and gold slippers.

The lobby of the Bangkok Shangri-La is a masterful exercise in the concealment of vents, for in Southeast Asia all paradises are immaculately air-conditioned. They are disguised as paired balcony windows beneath Siamese-carved tympanums; as venetian shutters folded back from lofty white balconies of hidden units; disguised as simple rectangular windows with no adornment or sense of arrangement whatsoever. The high lobby is given an empty grandeur by stone pillars and pilasters, their towering capitals carved as lotus flowers. Several large planter boxes of pink marble give the vasty reception hall the teeming verdancy with which all Edens are preconceived; feminine devas stand among them offering pink flowers. Low golden fauteuils and red sofas are scattered around teak coffee tables and low writing desks. A shallow river, a red wooden bridge crossing it to a golden-carved doorway which leads to jewellery shops, runs from the simple shopping mall to behind the elevators.

Hao entered the lobby and put a hand at the small of Anaïs' back. Three Chinese heavies sprung immediately from armchairs and buttoned their jackets as they came to his side. All was observed by a handsome man in white linens and wayfarers who was still pretending to read the newspaper in a sofa by the elevators.

'Where is Pookie?' said Hao to one of the ageing bellmen.

He whispered, 'OK,' and somehow made Pookie appear. She was an inoffensive young woman, heavily made-up to conceal acne and pockmarks, her sheening hair in a bun, she in a black skirt and beige mandarin collar. Her heels sounded over the floor before did her voice through the hall.

'Mr. Kam. So very nice to see you again.'

'Pookie, could you put Miss…?'

'Spencer.'

'Miss Spencer in the suite next to mine? Anaïs, I have an afternoon of meetings but I'll be back in time for dinner. Do you like Italian food?'

'Very much.'

'Good. Eight o'clock?'

'Eight o'clock.'

'Pookie, give Miss Spencer a tour of the hotel and show her Angelini. And reserve us a table for eight.'

'Eight people at Angelini. What time, Mr Kam?'

'No, for eight o'clock.'

'Eight o'clock,' she said and Hao nodded. 'For eight people.'

'No.'

'No?'

'Eight o'clock, two people.'

'Oh, OK. I am sorry. Eight o'clock for two people. Angelini. Thank you, Mr Kam.'

'No, not eight people. Two people.'

'Oh, OK, sorry. Two people. At what time?'

'At eight o'clock.'

'Eight o'clock. Very well, Mr Kam. Thank you.'

'Remember, Miss Spencer. You're *my* masseuse now.'

'I am your masseuse.'

'*My* masseuse.'

'Got it. … Your—. No, wait, whose masseuse am I?'

'My masseuse.'

'I am your masseuse.'

'You're *my* topless masseuse.'

'Are you leaving soon?'

And with his three heavies, one skin-bald and chubby, one very wide and mangle-toothed, one giant—all in black—Hao Kam returned silently to his car.

Anaïs was shown her room. It was not nearly as large as the hotel's pretensions suggested. A gaudy blue bedhead loomed over a big enough bed; silver drapes and modest teak furniture finished out the suite. The bathroom was black marble and bathless and stocked with what are termed luxury toiletries. The balcony was small and convex and concrete and planted with bouganvillea—identical to the four hundred or so others above and below and beside her which gave view over the dark brown of the Chao Phraya river. A dual carriageway bridge of constant and speeding traffic, intermittent skyscrapers, calmingly wafting sampans, a swimming pool and palm-shaded courtyard directly below—an average view which it was too hot to long enjoy.

Downstairs Pookie showed her, between the lobby and the river, the Riverside Lounge, a grand piano its centrepiece, cooks walking among the blue armchairs and teak fauteuils which were its furniture. Floor to ceiling windows gave the courtyard and the river a faint green tint and were being cleaned with long-handled squeegees. Anaïs was led along an outside path between low bubbling fountains of granite bowls, lotus whirling atop their waters. Three guests sunbathed on lounges on the courtyard's grass, a great deal more were entertaining their children in the jade waters of the Krungthep Wing's pool.

'Miss Spencer, you may use all facilities of the Shangri-La wing but guests of Shangri-La wing cannot use facilities of Krungthep wing. Between the two wings are our restaurants. Here we have Salathip, serving traditional Thai cuisine on the River of Kings. … Up the escalators is Shang Palace, our Chinese chef have thirty years' experience. And this is Angelini, with Italian chef, where you and Mr Kam will to dine tonight. I will take care of reservation for you. Over through there is Shangri-La wing of our hotel, which have main swimming pool, Long Bar and Chocolate Boutique. If you want to know anything else about Shangri-La hotel, please you ask. Is there anything else I can help you with?'

'Is Pookie your real name?'

Pookie almost giggled and said, 'No, Pookie my Western name.'

'And what's your real name?'

'My name Poonawithi.'

Anaïs nodded and said, 'Good change. And no, I think I have everything. Thank you so much, Pookie.'

'You are welcome. Have a nice day and enjoy your stay.' And with a bow and a long and soft 'Kop Khun Ka,' Pookie returned to the lobby.

Anaïs looked blankly over the river and then went upstairs. She changed into her bikini and divided an hour between the sun and the pool, tambourines and Nina Simone and *I'm Going Back Home* sounding on repeat out over the grassy riverside, and then had champagne delivered to her room before showering and watching the sun set over a gloomy horizon of grey haze and highrises.

At seven she descended, in a black sheath dress and black heels, to the Riverside Lounge and asked a waiter, who had no idea what she was talking about, for a pink gin.

'Plymouth gin, angostura bitters, lemon peel.'

Without a word he walked off. Shortly he returned with a South African person.

'Hello Miss Spencer, my name is Stephen Gould. I'm the resident manager here at the Bangkok Shangri-La. How can I help you this evening?'

'I just felt like a pink gin, Stephen.'

'A pink gin? I'm afraid our bar here in the Riverside Lounge doesn't have Plymouth, but our Long Bar certainly does. Would you like me to have a bottle sent over?'

'No, don't bother. I have to go over there for dinner anyway. Thank you.'

One was eventually placed in front of her in the martini glass which she had prescribed.

'Could you charge this to room 514, in the Krungthep Wing?' she asked the bartender.

'What?'

'Could you charge this to room 514, in the Krungthep Wing?'

'What?'

'Are you serious?'

'What?'

'You don't speak a word of English.'

'English yes. I speak.'

'I'm afraid you'll have to dumb it down a bit for them.' Unmistakably the interjector was Australian. 'I think they really struggle with sentences.'

'Well I don't expect that I will,' said Anaïs.

The man called for the bartender's attention, 'Warren,' and then pointed to himself and the pink gin and then held up a thumb. 'That drink, my tab. OK?'

'OK,' said Warren.

'Thank you,' said Anaïs, raising her glass from the bright

yellow bartop.

'No worries. Glen's my name.'

'How do you, Glen? Anaïs.'

'What is it?'

'What's what?'

'Your name.'

'Anaïs.'

'That's a strange one. *How* do you say it?'

'Anaïs.'

'Anaïs,' he repeated, slowly. 'I like it though. Where's it from?'

'It's very ancient.'

'And you're English?'

'Australian.'

'Are ya!?' This excited him rather. 'So am I!'

'I could hardly tell.'

'You don't talk like an Aussie though do ya?'

'I've been overseas for some time. You still live there.'

'Yeah, just here on business. Coupl'a days.'

'And what business would that be?'

'Prosthetic eyes.'

'Glass eyes?'

'Yeah some of them are still glass. Have a look at this one.' Glen dug two fingers and a thumb at his eye socket and was very shortly offering Anaïs his own prosthetic ball. 'Pretty cool, huh?' She was transfixed, her mouth wide open, the eye larger in his fingers than she thought it would have been, though precisely as slimey.

'That is so disgusting,' she said, staring at the thing.

'That's how I got the job. Who's the best model to sell a prosthetic eye, hey? A cyclops. And check this out.'

Anaïs wondered what an eyeless eye would look like and then took her eyes off his to satisfy her curiosity. She found him to have a finger buried in his right nostril, protruding from his left eye socket. She spluttered and covered her mouth and broke into appalled laughter and then coughing. 'That is so disgusting.'

'Frightens the hell outta kids, I tell you what. Look,' and he moved his finger back and forth.

'Ah! Stop it! No!' she laughed. 'Glen, that's disgusting!'

He withdrew his finger and reinserted his eye and wiped with a handkerchief his digits and cheeks. He ordered another Tiger and pointed at her empty drink and held up a single finger to Warren and said, 'How about you?'

'Me?'

'Yeah what brings you to Bangkok?'

'Oh I can't tell you that.'

'Whaddya mean you can't tell me?'

'It's very secretive.'

'Come on!'

'Do you really want to know?' she said, still thinking.

'Yeah! Go on.'

She thought for a few more seconds and soon came up with: 'I'm in horsepionage.'

'Say again?'

'Horsepionage.'

'Spying you mean? Like James Bond stuff? Maybe you shouldn't be telling me.'

'*Horse*-pionage, Glen. Polo.'

'Like water polo?'

'Horses and mallets, Argies. Polo. A four-point-two billion dollar industry. And horse trainers and team owners employ all manner of information technologies to spy on their competitors. I am one such information technology.'

Sitting in the Long Bar were two parents trying to get their children to turn their attention from hitting one another to their cokes, a pair of heavily plasticised old tourists in large sunglasses sipping mai tais and complaining that Bangkok had been spoiled by tourists, a young couple of boys on their honeymoon looking through their phones at the day's photos, and the handsome and burly man who had been pretending to read for the larger part of the day. He was now pretending to read an Ian Fleming. He looked discreetly along the bar at Anaïs and smirked.

'That's a weird job.' said Glen. 'How does it bring you to Bangkok? They play polo here do they?'

'Polo is all about the mare, Glen. And the Thais have just spliced a mare's DNA with an elephant's. They have no morals here. Think of the size and strength of that animal. The BPA wants her destroyed.'

The man at the end of the bar was shaking his head.

'The BPA?'

'The British Polo Association. If she falls into the hands of their greatest enemy it'll ruin the sport.'

'The French?'

'No, the French are the world's enemy, Glen. Ours is Argentina.'

'Australia's enemy is Argentina?'

'England's.'

'But you're Australian.'

'Yes, but I work for the BPA.'

'How on earth d'you get into that?'

And three pink gins and three Tigers later Anaïs had come to relay precisely how one does manage to get into international horsepionage. Talking to Glen made her feel strangely comfortable. He was goofy and sincere and had grown up a few suburbs from where had she. He reminded her of her father and of her seldom seen uncles, of her parents' friends who had shared their dinner table on the weekends of her youth—of all the profusely-drinking tepid sentimentalists who freckled her provincial childhood. She enquired of certain Melbourne restaurants which she still remembered fondly, the pubs to which she had first started going out. None still existed. All had either changed ownership and plummeted or had been demolished to make way for high-rise apartment buildings.

'I tell ya, I could eat the crotch out of a low flying duck right now.'

Anaïs spluttered pink gin. Not for seven years had she heard a variation of this peculiarly rooted phrase.

'I was thinkin' of gettin' some tea out at the Thai restaurant there. Do you wanna… do you wanna join me?'

Anaïs reached across and turned Glen's wrist. 'Shit,' she said, reading his watch upside down.

'What?'

'I was meant to meet someone for dinner at eight. Shit. Glen, thank you so much for the drinks. You're here for a few days?'

'Yeah here till the weekend.'

'I'll see you around?'

'I hope so,' he enthused before mispronouncing her name.

She downed the last of her drink and went to cross the inferior lobby but was halted almost immediately by the storming in of the bald and the enormous of Hao's heavies.

'You make Hao wait,' said the bald.

'Yes I've just realised that. I'm coming now.'

'Mr Hao no wait,' said the enormous.

'Mr Hao doesn't wait or Mr Hao has not waited?'

'Mr Hao no wait.'

She pushed through them. From the ground floor entrance she looked over the diners at Angelini. A wooden sort of a restaurant, golden-lit, the furniture white, diners at bar stools, and on sofas and in armchairs. A double staircase of white stone with sheets of clear plastic for banisters led up to a second level overlooking the first. To her immediate right a semi-private room was partitioned from the main dining by large petals carved as simple tracery upon heavy wooden panels. There was a similarly patterned rug on the floor, a couch against the floor-to-ceiling bay window, and two bored waitresses flanking Hao, he scowling through the palm trees at the lights of the river.

Anaïs put her face undeniably into his field of vision.

'I do not wait,' he said, his stare fixed.

'Do you mean you will not wait or you don't tend to wait? Because you have waited.'

'I have waited to tell you that I do not wait.' She expressed with uneven eyebrows her especial condescension towards pedantry. 'Do you think that you can just parade around this hotel with random men while you are my employee?'

'Who's parading?'

'Do you know the Chinese punishment for betrayal?'

Her eyebrows became uneven again.

'I will not be humiliated in front of my colleagues.'

'You're sitting here alone.'

'Sit down, TSM.'

'What's TSM?'

'Topless… Swedish…'

'Marmoset,' Anaïs blurted.

'Masseuse.'

'Oh.'

'Sit down.'

'No thank you.'

'I bought us champagne.'

'Champagne makes me very paradeful, Howie. You wouldn't believe.'

'I have been pig-headed. I'm sorry. Please sit.'

'I don't want to have dinner with you. You're scary.'

'Very well. … I am in meetings all day tomorrow. I would like a topless Swedish massage in the evening, after having dinner with you. Here at eight, Miss Spencer. I will ensure that you are able to be on time.'

'Again, scary.'

'I apologise for my abruptness.'

'Not abrupt. Scary.'

'I will see you tomorrow for dinner.'

'We'll see.'

And, excessively furious, Hao Kam sipped at his champagne and watched Anaïs pass by his window. She wound the path of the jungle-themed gardens which led from the pool to the Krungthep Wing. She turned off, unseen, to the Thai restaurant and found Glen at a table by the window, scrolling at his phone.

'Watcha reading?'

'Anaïs!' he said, avuncularly surprised. 'Fancy seeing you in here.'

'The person I was supposed to meet for dinner turned out to be a psychopath, so I'm still very hungry.'

'Isn't that a stroke of good luck, hey? I've just ordered a pad thai. Should I get you a waitress?'

Anaïs ordered wine and soft shell crab.

'You wouldn't *be-lieve* the news today,' said Glen.

'Would I not?'

'They've discovered a terrorist plot to ruin next year's Anzac Day parade. Abbot's said, "The best thing we can do to counter terrorism is to lead normal lives." And there's a terrorist plot in Italy to blow up the bridge that connects Venice to the mainland. They seem busy don't they, terrorists? How do they get so much spare time? And here in Thailand, look at this… They've interviewed a woman who's been a slave on a shrimp boat for the last year. She said that she watched while one of the other slaves was tied to four separate boats and then he was pulled apart at sea! Bloody horrible isn't it? Makes you happy to be from the lucky country doesn't it?'

'All very modern.'

'So do you miss it, Australia?'

'Not especially, no.'

'No?'

'No.'

'Why do you reckon that is? Where do you live now?'

'Nowhere really.'

'Australia'll always be home though won't it?'

'My home is a spiritual one, Glen. I feel no especial attachment to the place.'

'That's a bit extreme?'

Anaïs sensed that perhaps she was about to break Glen's heart. She smiled as gently as she could. 'I'm sorry. It's a lovely place. Let's talk about something else.'

'No no, I wanna know. Why don't you like it? I've never met anybody that didn't love it.'

'Do you really want to know?'

'Yeah go on.'

'I think it's a frivolous place. An unancient place. Petty. Epicurean in the extreme. Empty somehow. It's a place to exist but I don't think it's somewhere you can live. Not to the full extent of the word. Europeans are not meant to be so far away from Europe, Glen. The twentieth century has shown us that. And we are Europeans, some of us, and so many linger on down there. I don't know how they do it.'

'Hm,' said Glen.

'I didn't mean to become vehement. I'm sorry.'

'No, no. Not at all. Each to their own. Tore me a new one though didn't ya? I friggen *love* it there. It's just home, isn't it?'

'But know that I think that of all people. Groups of people. It's just that Australians are the people I've known best and longest. I'm sure if I stayed here long enough I'd grow to resent the Thais even more. Probably much more.'

When ten minutes after Glen's Anaïs' dinner was brought, the baldest of Hao's heavies appeared at the end of their table. He handed her a gift box. 'From Hao,' he said, and was gone by the time she had opened it. Shining up at her from its grey leather enclosure was a steel Cartier watch, its sides inlaid with, and all of its numbers save for the twelve, diamonds. She began to extract the thing but the box was clomped shut and snatched away. Hao loomed high over their table.

'This was to ensure that you would be on time tomorrow night. But now you cannot have it. I catch you again parading with another man. I told you you are *my* topless Swedish masseuse.'

'Do you know what the word "parade" actually means?'

'I suppose that if I had have left you alone for much longer you would have been topless Swedish massaging *him* this evening?'

'Do you think so?'

The man who had been all day pretending to read had come in after Hao and taken a seat a few tables away. He looked up from pretending to look over a menu.

'In China a peasant's life is worth three thousand dollars. Your suite is five hundred dollars a night. The champagne in the restaurant was two hundred dollars a bottle. The champagne you had delivered to your room one hundred. That watch is two thousand. And you are lower than a peasant. You are a whore, and that is two thousand seven hundred dollars.'

'Excuse me!' said Glen, breathing indignation and rising from his seat. 'How dare you talk to a lady like that?' Hao glanced down at him with little regard.

'This is not your business. ... You have insulted me by not giving me a topless Swedish massage and by parading around with other men even though I own you. You will disappear, Miss Spencer. It is the Chinese way. You will not know where and you will not know when.'

'Oh I hate surprises. I didn't have any of the champagne in the restaurant, Howie. I walked out, remember? And you took the watch from me before I ever got to wear it. And I haven't slept in the room yet. So technically you don't own squat and you're being a baby.'

'The room is already paid for. You have been in it past check-out time. I cannot get a refund. You will not disappear from your room tonight. And I gave you this watch and then I took it away from me so that you knew that I knew what you were doing.'

'You are, you're an idiot baby. A Chinese idiot baby. How does anything function in China with people like you running the place?'

'I will tell you that in Hong Kong babies are very mature. Good night.'

'Disappear?' said Anaïs to Glen when Hao was gone. She said it as though excitement had been added to their evening.

'He's a serious bloke, isn't he?'

'Do you think so?'

'And you're a masseuse?'

'No, it's part of my cover. He's the one we're after for the elephant horse. And I think there's an Argentinian agent in here right now watching us.'

'They're not gonna shoot me in the neck with a blow dart or anything are they?'

'I hope not, for your sake,' and Anaïs looked around the room. Her eyes fell first on the man who was failing at pretending to read. He whipped his neck back down and blankly scanned the appetisers.

Through her own dinner Anaïs was again confined to speaking of Melbourne, he asking if she had been home for this such moral deterioration or that such national embarrassment, Anaïs saying always no or that she must just have missed it. Over a mango sticky rice Glen began to wind their evening down. 'Now what are you doing tomorrow?' He spoke as though he were looking into the camera of the children's television programme he was presenting. '*I've* got a little bit of an excursion planned.'

At eight o'clock the next morning Anaïs wheeled her suitcase out onto the wooden walkway, past the lesser pool and the restaurants, into the Shangri-La Wing's red-carpeted and yellow-lit lobby. She asked one of the young girls at reception if she could leave her suitcase somewhere and a porter in mandarin collar and spiked pith helmet was called over to deposit it for her.

'Excuse me you Miss,' attempted to say a tiny round-faced man in a tropically-printed shirt and loose trousers.

'Mmm,' she grumbled with suspicion.

'My name Anurak. Mr Lobbins say he come in two minute. Today we go to Wat.' About this he was very excited.

'What?'

'Yes.'

'Hm?'

'I take you today.'

'Where?'

'We go to Wat.'

'What?'

'Yes.'

'You're really annoying.'

'What?'

'*What?*'

'Yes, we go.'

'Huh?'

'We go today.'

'Today what?'

'Yes today Wat."

'Yesterday what? What happened yesterday?'

'No, today. We go.'

'We go where?'

'We go to Wat Pho.'

'What for?'

'Yes! We go!'

'What for what?'

'What?'

'What for what?'

'Wat Pho, yes.'

'What for yes? What are you talking about?'

'Today we go Wat Pho!'

'Would you please go away?'

'Hello!' he yelled, seeing Glen at an elevator. 'Mr Lobbins!' He threw an arm towards the lobby doors and goose-stepped thither. The three of them slid up into a silver van parked in the drive and Glen and Anaïs were driven down the razor-wired drive.

Behind the Shangri-La Bangkok, down a filthy and boiling alley of food and baby-clothing stalls and jewellery shops there is a McDonald's with the words in poster paint in one of its windows, 'Happiness Starts Here.' They turned onto the first main road and were stationary and baking among pink taxis and rusting and windowless buses and mopeds and tuk-tuks. The morning was the colour of hot. The locals either wore face masks or had begun a long day of holding a hand across their respiratory orifices. Two-storeyed colonial façades rose above 7-11s and ATMs and juice bars and massage parlours. Overhead a canopy of electrical wires and power lines and Thai and Royal flags gave no shade. They were half an hour stopping and starting on the one short road. Glen asked Anaïs how she had slept and what precisely she had had for breakfast before rhapsodising over what he had had.

They drove north and Anurak began looking down the

93

alleyways which joined the road in front of him. They came to a roundabout with a Chinese archway in its middle. The street beyond it was empty of cars but Anurak slowed almost to a crawl in between dingy alleys. Then the black van for which he had been waiting finally pulled across their path and he braked to a stop. From another black van, pulled up alongside them, four men in surgical masks jumped out, two of whom grabbed Glen through the opened van door and two of whom grabbed Anaïs. She kicked and thrashed as she was lifted and thrown into the adjacent van. Glen, asking repeatedly with uncommitted indignation, 'What are you doing?' was put into the van which had cut them off. Anurak watched the whole thing and thought about the crap he could buy his children with the sum by which his compliance had been purchased.

Anaïs, her hands cuffed to a railing overhead, was driven in silence for an hour. When they stopped she felt light upon her black hood as the van door was opened. She could hear seabirds and the ocean, and could smell cripplingly the stink of fish sauce and of drying squid and rotting seafood. Her hood and her handcuffs were removed and as she stepped down out of the van she bent down to knee the first of her three kidnappers in the crotch. He doubled over and Anaïs was grappled from behind; she mule-kicked the grappler, who fell over with his hands at his groin. The driver, as stunned as a de-familied mouse before a viper, was wary of approaching so large and so accurate of blow a farang. They stood facing each other on a putrid concrete floor, he in full fight stance, she entirely relaxed.

'You kick ball!'

'I do kick ball. But you kidnap woman.'

They were among high, unroofed pillars of crumbling concrete, posters of naked Thai girls and of the King fading upon them. Plastic tubs were stacked on the wet floor. Behind the little driver huge wooden trawlers were docked at a concrete platform. Shortly a faint voice called calmly out in Thai from the distance of an enormous and derelict office building. The driver backed towards the water as down the muddy concrete platform there hobbled an old man, his military trousers and Hawaiian shirt riddled with thorns and burrs, the creases of his arms and face stained with black grease. He had a short wispy beard and leaned heavily on a walking stick. The driver used his entrance as a distraction whereby he might flee, and fled. The old man turned on his stick and looked up at Anaïs. The left side of his face was puckered to conceal the absence of an eye.

'I am to kidnap you.' His voice was weak and oriental.

'Please don't.'

'I,' he said, long and wearily, 'do not like to work for Chinese. Please, you come.' Anaïs watched him hobble off along the platform. When he was distant from her he raised a hand and gave an oddly reassuring beckon of his finger. He went into a ramshackle shed at the end of a pier of dusty concrete and exposed and rusting steel bars.

Anaïs followed slowly. The sea was black and grey and lilting with litter. There was no door to the shed. Beneath a light bulb hanging from a chain was a low plastic table and a dozen tiny plastic chairs. A host of fishermen leaned over bowls of broth less reeking and filthy than they. They looked up at Anaïs, as resentful and as helpless as broken slaves. The shed was the hottest place Anaïs had ever been. In its corners men and women squatted to prepare marine animals, holding long ones and tiny ones and round ones in their hands, going at them with various tools sharp and blunt then tossing them into big plastic baskets.

'Where are you from?' the old man asked Anaïs as she ducked under the sharply cut tin. 'Please, sit.'

She lowered herself onto a stool and a dirty bottle of SangSom was placed on the table. 'I'm English.'

'I like English. Very good history. But now not good.' His shaky hand poured out five shots. 'No longer manly. Country no good when no longer manly.' Those at the table had finished eating and their bowls had somewhere disappeared. They each took a glass.

'To England,' said the cycloptic old man. He put the shot glass at his mouth; in his frail and besmeared hand it quivered.

'To England,' said Anaïs, and he and then she and then the fishermen put away their drinks.

They all watched for her reaction. Her face flinched not. She collected their shot glasses and took the bottle and poured five more. 'To Thailand,' she offered.

'You work for me now on shrimp boat,' said the old man, not overly excited about it as he circled the table.

'I don't really think that's going to happen, Alfie, do you?

Come on, drink up. … There we are. And give 'em back.' And she loosed five more. 'Do I look like I should be working on a shrimp boat? Down you go. … This is *nice* stuff.'

The Thais smiled. Not ever had they seen a foreigner so easily drink SangSom, so willingly, so long before midday. Not ever did they expect to see a female foreigner pour her, and their, fourth shot for the morning and then down it before they did. And not ever did they expect to see her fifth in front of her before they had even sniffed their last. One of them laughed. Then two of them laughed. Then they were all laughing. Anaïs poured her sixth and raised an eyebrow in disappointment at each of their fourths. They scrunched up their noses and waved their hands at her.

'Are we finished?' she said, surprised.

'No,' said the old man. 'If you no work on boat, boss get very angry. You know what he do to last captain?'

Anaïs put her arms out at her sides and snapped them as far out as she could and put her head sideways and her tongue out.

'Yes,' he breathed.

'I'll take care of Hao, Alfie. I promise. He loves me. He'll be happy to see me back. What *is* that man doing over there?'

In the darkness of the far corner an old man was squatting between two plastic baskets. In the basket with the higher and more vertical rim there slithered dozens of snakes, their heads writhing up past the basket edge and falling back down. Between his legs a funnel was inserted into a quarter-emptied bottle of clear liquid. He took a snake, put his tyre-rubber-sandaled foot at its neck and cut off with scissors its head. Then he dangled the limp animal over the funnel and ran his squeezing finger and thumb down its body. Crimson globules diffused slowly through the liquid. He threw the fully drained snake into the other basket and put his sandal at the neck of another live one.

'Snake blood vodka. Make man…' The old man grunted and said, 'Strong.'

'Well come on then,' said Anaïs, downing her SangSom. The fishermen broke into slow and awed banging upon the table. 'Bring me a bottle of that snake blood vodka, Alfie, would you? Let's get manly.'

On the rooftop terrace of State Tower the sun, long red,

disappeared beneath smog before it did the horizon. The clouds washed high and pink across the baby blue gloaming and the lights of the barren and endless field that was the city of Bangkok upon the earth came on increasingly until beyond the golden cauldrons of the balcony darkness fell. In the west, wide and backlit, was the once humbling, now empoisoned and washed-out rainbow of this planet's spheres. A crescent moon rose high and black night fell and Hao Kam and his three heavies, at the end of a long day of crimes against humanity and maturity, ordered oysters and wine and argued in Cantonese.

'Rong,' said Hao, almost pleading. 'I know you like lamb. You always order lamb. And I want to try the lamb.'

'Then why don't you order the lamb?' said Rong in his own tongue.

'He's right,' said Dong. 'If you want the lamb you should order the lamb.'

'But I want duck more. He *loves* lamb.'

'And you should get the tuna by the way,' said Dong to Rong. 'You know you love tuna. And then we have a fish dish that we can all try and the lamb that we can all try.'

'But if you all try my tuna,' said Song, 'I won't get to have any.'

'We'll only take little mouthfuls,' said Hao. 'Just to taste it. And as if you need to be eating full meals anyway.' For Song was by far the fattest of the group.

'So two ducks, one tuna, one lamb,' said Dong.

'I don't want the tuna!' said Song, pleading. 'I want the duck.'

'But then that's three ducks!' moaned Rong. 'And you'll all want to try my lamb and I won't get to have any.'

Rong had a point. 'How about I get the lobster?' said Song.

At the speakers on the terrace above an electric guitar wailed like an air-raid siren; Danzig and Black Hell sounded. And from the ionic-colonnaded rotunda that was the tower's high and golden crown, and down the amber-lit staircase, there emerged and descended Anaïs Spencer, her denim shorts sticky with grime, her mascara slightly smeared by heat and her hair almost untidy, her black camisole dusty and now single-strapped. She had hitched a ride on three songthaews and had walked for almost an hour under a Thai highway. She had been assaulted twice—once by a monkey and once by a Frenchman—and had passed three bags of clubbed rats, two dead bodies, a score of limbless beggars and had seen, in the lobby of the Shangri-La, Pookie.

'Why do you always go for the most expensive thing on the menu?' said Hao. 'I'm not paying for you to have lobster again.'

'There are no prices on the menu!'

'You know it's the most expensive.'

'I don't. What about the Argentinian tenderloin? That's at the bottom. The most expensive thing is always at the bottom.'

'That's not a thing.'

'That's definitely a thing.'

'I think that is athing, Hao.'

'You don't know what things are things.'

'I know what things are things, thank you.'

'How do you know what things are things?'

Anaïs placed from that little tan handbag of hers a fresh bottle of snake's blood vodka on the white tablecloth between these four squibbling Hong Kongese. They showed no surprise but some confusion at her continued terrestrial existence.

'Thank you, Howie, for my cultural excursion to the fishing village. Very fucking informative. Hi,' she said to the waiter who had just finished taking their orders. 'And four shot glasses.' She grabbed a menu from under his arm as he walked away. 'What's for dinner then? Hm? I haven't got a watch, but it can't be past eight can it? I'm not late, Howie, see? Oo, duck. I love duck.' She poured four shots of the disturbingly viscous and vivid solution and distributed them. 'Let's you have a drink, shall we. Snake's blood vodka, Howie. Cheech. Harpo. Curly. Makes a man…' She grunted and thumped her chest and said, 'Strong.'

'Why would we drink when you do not drink with us?'

'*I'm* still sobering up, old cock. *I* had to drink half a bottle of SangSom and three shots of this shit just to convince your cyclops to let me go. He's a nice old man. Mature. You've heard about people like that, I'm sure. *You* can drink, and when you're half way through the bottle I'll catch up with you and make you all look like the little Chinese villager girls that you really are.'

'Could you please not order the duck?' said Hao.

'What?'

'Three of us are already getting the duck. We thought it would be better if we all ordered something different. That way we can try more of the dishes. Why don't you get the lamb?'

In disbelief Anaïs looked around the restaurant, as though she were looking to catch the eyes of some higher, more rational power with whom she could share her bewilderment. Instead she found those of the man from the airport and the hotel, sitting alone at a table with a beer and not doing a very good job at all of pretending to read his novel.

Oysters were brought on a tray of ice over fringed banana leaf. The men took their shots and Anaïs started at their oysters. 'Good?' she asked, and Dong and Song growled and hurried to chase the drink with an oyster. 'One more! Give me that,' she growled and downed Rong's wine. 'So exactly what line of work are you in, Howie? We never really got to discuss that did we? I'm *not* a topless Swedish masseuse, coincidentally. I can tell you that now, now that you've had me kidnapped. Such a special bond we share. And these are your bum buddies, are they? They all like it the same way? Oo! Or do they all *give* it the same way? Howie, you old slut! Here, do you like this stuff? Not bad, is it?' and she poured four more shots and downed Song's wine. They each took another oyster chaser and the tray was taken away.

'You should be careful, Miss Spencer. I don't think you know exactly who you are provoking.'

'Me, provoke? Come on! Never. I parade, Howie, remember? But I never provoke. So are you in drugs as well are you, Mr Dangerous? Shrimp and slavery and drugs? I imagine that's what slavery money's used for. I know some men who are in Rohypnol. Extremely dangerous stuff.'

'What is Rohypnol?' said Hao.

'You'll see.'

The four men, warmed by the spirit and feeling deceivingly strong from the blood, exchanged smug grins with Anaïs as their dinner was placed in front of them.

'I thank thee Lord, for this Rohypnol my strength,' said Anaïs, addressing and quickly confusing the table. 'Grant here my foes very messy faces. And grant unto the world the burning of their souls, if souls Chinese people do have. Burn theirs, and give mercy to whoever's next to them, just for fun. And please hurry up and get me the fuck out of Asia. Years have I toiled in this jungled desert and I am pretty fucking sick of it. Amen.'

And their eyes slowly fell shut and into three servings of duck and one of lamb their faces heavily fell. Droplets of jus and flecks of rillette splattered across the terrace. 'Selah,' said Anaïs and rose from the table and strode to the staircases. The aspirant reader upped and raced after her. He came to stride with her at the first landing.

'I was *not* expecting that.'

'Expectation is the mother of disappointment.'

'Do you know who you've just rufied?'

'A man of very childish peculiarities.'

'You just rufied a world-class people smuggler.'

'Then have I made the world for six or seven hours safe. Though not my hotel room. Where can I stay tonight?'

'How should I know?' He followed her up to the elevators.

'You've been watching me for two days. Either you're a pervert and you want me to stay in your room, which I won't, or you're some kind of spy, in which case you know perfectly well where it's safe for me to sleep tonight.'

'I've been watching Kam, not you.'

'How come?'

'Yes.'

'Huh?'

'What?'

'You've been watching the Chinaman?'

'He's to be indicted by the International Court of Human Rights.'

'I've worked for them! Or I've been pretended to.'

They crowded into a golden elevator and descended sixty-eight floors.

'Every shrimp you've ever eaten probably came through him. And he uses slaves on his fishing boats, as I'm sure you're aware. I'm to negotiate with the International Court of Human Rights to keep him out of prison, but now he's gone and kidnapped you. White slavery is still an international no-no, no matter how much we deserve it. I'll call Interpol and have him arrested. Plus you rufied him. When he wakes up he'll still assume that you're working on one of his boats. You'll be safe in the Shangri-La.'

They crossed the State Tower's almost unlit ground floor and returned to the city heat, untempered by darkness.

'You have a horrible job. What's your name?'

'Johnny. And I have a great job. At least I don't lie about it.'

'Who's lying about their job?'

'Horsepionage?'

'You liked that did you?'

'Very creative. I thought he picked you up at the airport. Now I can see that it was you who picked him up. Is Miss Spencer your real name?'

'Of course it's my real name. I'd never lie about who I am.'

'And do you know who I see when I listen to you talk, Anaïs Spencer?'

'Who?'

'Me.'

'How vain you are, John John.'

'Don't call me that.'

Anaïs pouted. 'John John.'

'And am I correct in imagining that a woman so heavily involved in horsepionage has very little to do during the daytime in this a horseless country?'

They turned off that traffic-clogged street into the filthy alleyway behind the hotel. Spotlights shone white on steaming woks and on diners at low plastic tables slurping over bowls of savoury porridge.

'Is that your attempt at asking me out, John John?'

'That's me offering you a job interview.'

'What on *earth* makes you think I want a job?'

'You'll like this one.'

'I doubt that very much.'

'You travel for half the year and work with me in Melbourne for the other half.'

At the darkness of the alley's corner Anaïs nearly stepped on a huge lump on the ground. At first the lump merely startled her. Then she realised that it was moving, and a man. He crawled on his belly, his mid section caved in, his t-shirt as flat as a cape. Shredded plastic bags were tied at the ends of his four stumps. He prodded along with less than half an arm a hat which contained a single coin. He looked up at Anaïs, his face a canvas for graze and weeping sore, and moaned softly in Thai as he writhed past them.

Anaïs' mouth was wide open with horror, her eyes transfixed with sympathy.

'So what do you think?' said Johnny, passing under the enormous air-conditioning units which protruded from the back of the hotel. 'What's the matter?'

'Nothing,' said Anaïs, shaking off her dread and catching up with him. 'This job's in Melbourne?'

'Home, is it not?'

'It is not.'

They came to the Krungthep Wing's drive and Mara's assault. The glass door was pulled open for them. There was little activity in the lobby. A Korean man was asleep in an armchair with a book on his chest and an aged couple were drinking in silence down by the piano.

'You were having that poor glass-eye salesman on as well then were you?'

'No, I grew up there. It's not my home though. What happened to Glen?'

'He's fine. He was intercepted as soon as he was taken. He's already on a plane home.'

Pookie's heels clomped across the marble.

'Why was I allowed to be taken?' said Anaïs, offended.

'You were followed,' he said as though it were a consolation. 'We wouldn't have let him put you on a shrimp boat.'

'Would you and Miss Spencer be liking a drink this evening, Mr Goodenough?'

'No thank you, Pookie, not tonight. I think Miss Spencer might be exhausted.'

'OK. Goodnight.'

'Yes, goodnight.'

'Mr What?' said Anaïs.

'What?'

'What's your surname?'

'Goodenough.'

'John Goodenough?'

'Johnny.'

'What exactly do you do, John Goodenough?'

'I'm a fixer. A broker, actually.'

'You break and fix?'

'I broker, and I fix.'

'I'll take it.'

'Take what?'

'The job.'

'You haven't got it yet.'

III

Anaïs took breakfast in the Riverside Lounge. After an hour's scorching upon the black slate around the pool with Bechet and Armstrong on *Perdido Street Blues* in her ears, a handwritten notecard was placed beside her beading head—from Johnny Goodenough, instructing her to meet him at Central Embassy.

She charged a taxi to her room and found Johnny waiting, in Prince of Wales trousers and white shirt with rolled sleeves and no tie, inside the main entrance.

'It's the hottest God-damned place on earth,' he said. 'You end up planning your whole day around air-conditioning.'

They walked a short distance through this high hall of echoey white plastic, past a black carpet cluttered with Ferraris, to Bottega Veneta—a dimly lit configuration of hanging wooden poles and handbags spotlit upon shelves like laboratory specimens.

'I've got three meetings left before I leave Bangkok for my Singapore meetings—one tonight, one tomorrow at lunch and then one the next night. You'll observe tonight, assist tomorrow, and you'll lead the last night. If you're as good at this as I think you are you'll be fine. You will need new clothes though. Pick anything you like.'

'Off the rack, John-John?'

'Shut up you.'

She flicked hangers along a clothing rack and draped the clothes she liked across her arm. Johnny leaned against a black pole outside the changing rooms.

'And why me, John John?' said Anaïs from her cubicle.

'Why you? Do you have any idea of the power that bullshit has in the world?'

'I have something of an idea.'

'Business is about making people feel good about themselves. It's not about money. The money makes people feel good. It's one means to the ultimate vain end. I use Bangkok for the sex tourism. Businessmen are perverts, by and large. Their wives hate them and their girlfriends use them for their money. Here I can make them feel wanted again. And there's only one thing that makes them feel better about themselves than does money. Do you know what it is?'

'Seahorses?'

'Love.'

'Ergh.'

'Love makes people feel good about themselves. And whether you admit it or not, Horsepionage, you are a born liar. You notice that people feel good about themselves when they're around you? It's not because of the lies. It's because of how much you love telling them. It's charisma. It has no monetary value. Your love of lying is genuinely priceless. And the charismatic are the only people who can do what I do.'

The lock to the changing room door clicked open and Anaïs emerged, with upturned palms, in a leather skirt the colour of persimmon and a black chiffon top with white sleeves and neck. Johnny nodded.

'And what makes you think I'll work for you?'

'Work for me and your life is yours. You can have whatever you want, wherever you want it. I'll make you rich. Very rich. All you have to do is exactly what you already do—charm and deceive, lie and love—but for me.'

'John John,' she said, returned to the change room. 'Filthy lucre, why on earth would I want to be rich? Everybody around you sucking up to you. I much prefer others to be rich. Poverty is my greatest gift. My poverty is my freedom. When other people are rich I get all the fun and none of the falsehood.'

'If there's anybody disqualified from talking about a lack of falsehood, Anaïs…'

'And just what will I be observing tonight? … John John?'

They were shown to the private back room of a restaurant which felt like the home of a hippie spinster who had spent her happiest years in Osaka. Half the place was decorated with meticulous shab (the daubed walls, the artificially aged Provençal furniture, the pop-culture posters, the shabby chic bird cages) the other half as a clichéd quaint Japanese house (the paper walls, the Hokusais, the teapots, the red lanterns, the open kitchen with three uniformed chefs).

'Feel that?' said Johnny, raising his arms.

'What?'

'The best air-conditioned Japanese restaurant in Bangkok. I told you.'

Very shortly a middle-aged man was led by a waitress into their partitioned room. Johnny introduced him to Anaïs as Cao Nduc Phat.

'Cow and duck fat?'

'Mr Phat works for the Vietnamese Ministry of Agriculture.'

'He does not!' All bodies froze midsit. 'That's amazing.' Anaïs sensed immediately that she had offended their guest and annoyed John John. 'What I meant to say was,' she smiled, 'was that you have a most sonorous name, Mr Phat. It is a pleasure to meet you.'

And shortly a slightly taller middle-aged man in a nicer suit was led in. 'And Mr Wu Yaobang,' said Johnny as all shook hands. 'Miss Spencer is a colleague of mine and will be observing us today.' Johnny seemed to know everything there was to know about Mr Yaobang's and Mr Phat's interests and their families and their personal histories. He pointed out all the common ground that the two men had and enthused as blatantly as he could over their enthusiasms. When the first of a series of dinner courses was brought out he imperceptibly turned things from Mr Phat's grandfather, who had been a renowned pig farmer, to the issue at hand.

'These exploding watermelons. Mr Phat, I feel, and I know that Mr Yaobang must feel, that you're holding on too tightly to the word 'exploding'. It's not as if they explode like landmines, do they? They're not hurting anyone. And forchlorfenuron isn't poisonous. Not at all. You've seen the research. Now we love balloons and they explode too. Do you love balloons? Mr Yaobang?'

'I love balloons.'

'Mr Phat?'

'Yes, I love balloons too.'

'Everybody loves balloons. But balloons blow up, don't they? And we call that popping. You *pop* a balloon. And what I see here is actually a huge increase in profit for Vietnamese wholesalers. Imagine you don't just sell any watermelon, Mr Phat, you sell the popping watermelon. You get your sellers to turn it into a game. You get some monks in on it. If your watermelon pops, seven years good luck. They'll be flying off the trucks.

Imagine a child is given a watermelon on a hot day and it pops in his face. He's sitting there smiling with cool fruit on his lips, laughing. You can see the ads, can't you? This is a product you can not only sell, but profit from massively. It's like gambling on a melon. You can charge triple the price, quadruple the price, four times, because you sell *the* popping watermelon. And Mr Yaobang, how many suppliers do you think you would be willing to deal with in order to get these melons out there?'

'Guangxi Fluit Copulation would feel onry to deal with-a one man, who we already know.'

'You get to choose the sole distributor, Cao. They'll be throwing money at you for the contract.'

And just like that Johnny Goodenough had saved a year's crop of watermelon and ensured the thick greasing of a bureaucrat's pocket. Anaïs had no idea which of the two men he was working for.

Lunch the following day was at a restaurant themed as an American diner. There were buffalo heads on the walls and television screens playing American sport. The waitresses all were tall and in high heels; their tight white tank tops stretched across broad shoulders and concealed no noteworthy chest; tiny orange shorts stretched around their behinds like cling film over Belgian beef. Anaïs was in a light blue sleeveless dress printed with orange Morris-like flowers and soft green vine leaf.

'Are they...?' she asked, pointing to the largest of the waitresses.

'Yep.'

'All of them?'

'Yep.'

'Even her? Him?'

'Minty!' and Johnny called over this the prettiest and most effeminate of the staff. Anaïs inspected her. 'Minty, I'm about to have lunch with a Frenchman. Tall, dark. He'll be on my left. Could you be extra nice to him?'

She palmed the cash from Johnny's lifted hand. 'How nice you want me?'

'Don't touch him, but make him want to touch you. The usual.'

'Of course Johnny boy, for you.'

'Anything for you, Johnny boy,' said Anaïs as Minty left.

They drank beer until their first guest arrived. He was a short man with white hair and tan skin, round-faced and meekly spoken. His name was Samorn Tang, and, Anaïs knew from her breakfast briefing, he was the Cambodian co-prosecutor for the Khmer Rouge Tribunal. He sipped at his beer and asked Anaïs questions about herself before the Frenchman against whom he had for years travailed walked into the restaurant.

'Nicolas Porcine, Anaïs Spencer. I know you know Mr Tang.'

'Very nice,' said the Frenchman as he looked Anaïs up and down. 'Comment ça-va, mademoiselle?' he asked, her hand still trapped in his.

'Do let's stick to English.'

Nicolas grunted twice and sat and looked around the room. 'There is something about these kinds of Thai girls, huh?' he said, abounding in z's. 'Don't you think?'

'Do I sink?' said Mr Tang in flawlessly pronounced American.

'Think.'

'Do I zinc?'

'Sink. T-h-i-n-k. Sink.'

'Oh, think!' said Tang. 'No, I don't understand the fascination.'

'I think that when we love we love above all ourselves, no? We love a woman because of how she make us feel. This kind of Thai girl is just the… form physical, of loving ourselves.'

Johnny called Minty over. She stood between him and Nicolas and smiled down at the Frenchman as Johnny ordered more drinks.

'Minty, uh?' said Nicolas, putting his hand at the small of her back. 'Could you make mine a Heineken, and have a drink for yourself, yes.'

Minty giggled and wrote down his request and went back to the stern woman behind the pine lectern through whom all orders went. Johnny chatted with Mr Tang about his young wife and their child and about Koh Lanta, where Mr Tang took his holidays. Then he and Anaïs chatted with Nicolas about cheese and women. His experience of both was vast. Anaïs was soon unsure as to which he preferred. Minty threw Nicolas a few more smiles and called him handsome and said that maybe they could go out later. Johnny made a pass at discussing the man whom Mr Porcine and Mr Tang were defending and prosecuting. Mr Porcine refused to be drawn into business over lunch.

'Soi Cowboy is only a ten minute walk from here, no?' said Nicolas.

'Soi Cowboy?' said Anaïs, mimicking him exactly.

'You don't know eat?'

'I've only been in Bangkok for a few days.'

'Ooogh,' said Nicolas, raising his eyebrows. 'Zen we have to go. Samorn? What you say, uh?'

'Not in the afternoon,' he said, tiredly dismissing the notion.

'I will not discuss Khieu unless we are at Soi Cowboy.'

Only half the soi's neon lights were turned on, it being two o'clock in the afternoon. Not half the bars were open, and those skeletally staffed with touts. To the others it seemed as though obviousness were screaming at them to be elsewhere. Even the doormen, notoriously thrusting of their laminated pamphlets, ignored them. But the Frenchman's enthusiasm for ping-pong shows was tied to no other thing. Like the sun it shone simply because it was.

'Upstairs, muzzerfuckers!' he yelled after lowering his head at the entrance to Suzie Wong's. He danced a fusty shuffle across its floor.

Johnny paid for the four of them to pass the attended window at the top of the stairs and music was turned on and the daylights off. The corners and the walls glared with red neon as two ageing Thai women took the stage and began to express through dance their disillusion with life. Beers and tequilas were brought on trays to their front-row seats. Nicolas began to chant, 'Peeng-pong, peeng-pong.' Johnny saw that it was in everybody's interest to as soon as possible reorientate the focus of this habitually obdurate lawyer.

'You're up,' he said into Anaïs' ear.

'Nicolas,' she shouted over the music.

'Oui gorgeous?'

Anaïs swallowed her repulsion. 'Nicolas, nous devrions parler de Khieu.'

'Tu parle français?' said Nicolas, his eyes rabidly wide.

'Oui.'

'Aw, très bien. Look at zees.' One of the girls was fiddling with a banana. 'I want to be ze banana!' Samorn was on his phone.

Anaïs spoke at length in French and closed in English. 'Nicolas, Khieu *has* to go to prison. And he has to go to prison in

Cambodia.'

The other performer opened a beer bottle. 'Je pense que non,' said Nicolas as he drank from it. 'Absolument pas.'

'He was responsible for the imprisonment, torture, and murder of over twenty thousand people. He has admitted that and he has to go to prison.'

'He will die if he goes to prison. Especially in Cambodia. He is an old man, a sick man. If the court finds him guilty my client wants to serve his sentence in a prison in Belgium.'

'What I'm suggesting, Nicolas, is that we all rethink what we consider to *be* a prison.'

'Continue,' said Nicolas, his eyes transfixed on the blowing out of candles, the using of chopsticks, the birthing of budgerigars and razor blades.

'Rumduol resort on Koh Rong island. A five-star complex of wooden bungalows on white sand beaches. The Cambodian government has agreed to let the United Nations use it as a detention facility for Khieu if he wears a tracking anklet. Yes he'll be surrounded by backpackers and hippies and Germans, but he'll be free to roam the resort and to take visitors, once a week for three hours. It's a tropical paradise.'

Johnny knew Mr Tang to be a reasonable and humble man. He had laboured under the constraints and compromises of international law for so long that he, like all of modern humanity, now accepted even the most idiotic proposal as long as it was said to have behind it the weight of international opinion. Johnny turned to him and said into his ear that the era of properly punishing war criminals was over. The West no longer believed in the justice of eternal rest nor in anything other than luxurious imprisonment. The millions of Cambodians who lost family members, friends, colleagues, in the genocide, had to rethink what they considered to *be* a prison. If Khieu were placed anywhere that was not sumptuous he would be free within a year, crying in front of a different international court ill-health or maltreatment. And besides, he said, Rumduol resort on Koh Rong was thronged all year round with backpackers, with New Zealanders even. 'Can you imagine? English people, Germans, hippies, dope smokers. Khieu will be just as miserable there as he would be in a conventional Cambodian hellhole.'

Giving his latest in a long and shameful chain of concessions,

Samorn sighed and nodded.

A cigarette was being smoked almost at stage level and a dart readied to burst a balloon. Suddenly overwhelmed by the urge to smoke, Nicolas leaned forward to take the half-burned fag; with deserved accuracy the dart was fired across the dance floor into the bridge between his wrist and his thumb. This amazed him. He stood up and drank more beer.

'Fuck eeet!' he yelled, the dart wobbling like a lubed and landed javelin as he waved his hand in the air. 'Put him in Rumduol! What do I care, uh!?'

And hurriedly Nicolas was left alone so that he could take the stage to have his name written in permanent marker upon his chest.

Outside Johnny apologised to Samorn and hailed and paid for his taxi. He and Anaïs took one to the river.

The sun, blaring low in the afternoon sky, set heavily over the golden prangs of Wat Arun. They sat on the riverside deck of a restaurant and drank mimosas and ate strawberries and cream.

'So you speak French?'

'I lived there for six months.'

'Very impressive,' said Johnny. 'And are you having fun yet?'

'You don't do very much that's honourable, John John.'

'Do you?' They exchanged a serious raising of their eyebrows. 'I do the obligatory work of the only civilized country in Asia. If it were up to those men today an old man would have been tortured to death in prison.'

'Just as that old man tortured twenty thousand others.'

'I know you don't believe that that's the way the world should work.'

'I don't believe in anything, John John. I sympathise.'

'And how have you come to be sympathising with Chinese people smugglers in Bangkok? Or should I ask, where did you meet the Mexican millionaire who was to pick you up from the private jet terminal to employ you as his topless Swedish masseuse?'

'I met Miguel, the Mexican billionaire, at a royal émigré ball in Cape Cod.'

'Do you have an ounce of truth in you?'

'Do you have an ounce of trust?'

'And you were at the royal émigré ball in Cape Cod because

you're a princess, I suppose?'

'I'm a countess.'

'You don't have an ounce of truth in you.'

'I do.'

'You're a countess?'

'I'm a countess.'

'Of my foot.'

'Of Venice, John John, if you must know.'

'Know is a very strong word when listening to you speak. And you expect me to believe even that you're Italian? You look less Italian than him.' He pointed across the deck to a very dark and very pleasant-looking Thai waiter in pith helmet and breeches.

'Everybody knows that all northern Italian nobility are German, John John.'

'Do they?'

'And I'm half Italian. My father was the Duke of Monmouth. A Scot. At least I would have been a countess, until the communists stripped my grandmother of the title. She was the countess Malaspina.'

'You're incredible at this, you know that?'

'What ever could you mean?'

'If she was a countess she would have had a palazzo, no?' Johnny was egging her on. He wanted to be the first person ever to trap Anaïs Spencer in one of her own preposterous webs. He would have been too, if he could pull it off. She could not possibly know more about Venetian palazzi than he, thought he.

'Of course she did.'

'Where?' he said, bowing and then lifting his head.

'In memory of vanished hours so filled with beauty the consciousness of present loss oppresses. Exquisite hours, enveloped in light and silence, to have known them once is to have always a terrible standard of enjoyment.'

'What's that?'

'The writer who wrote that, John John, was writing about staying in the Palazzo Malaspina with my grandmother's grandmother.'

'The Palazzo Malaspina?'

'On the Grand Canal.'

'Yes, I suspected it might be there.'

'All the best ones are. Or were. Until the communists took it from us and turned it into a worker's museum.'

'Where exactly was it on the Grand Canal?'

'Have you been there?'

'I have.'

'Do you know where the Rialto bridge is?'

'Vaguely.'

'Right next to that.'

'What a shame.'

'Agreed.'

'We would have been neighbours.'

'Who?'

'You and I. Your Palazzo Malaspina sounds as though it would have been right next door to mine.'

'Next door to your what?'

'To my palazzo. On the Grand Canal. … I own one.'

'You do not.'

'The Palazzo Bolani. It's not an enormous palazzo, but it's a real palazzo. Much more than can be said of your grandmother the countess Malaspina's palazzo.'

'You like saying palazzo, don't you?'

'It's a fun word to say.'

'Why do *you* have a palazzo in Venice?'

'It was my wife's favourite place on earth. We used to holiday there.'

'Used to?'

'Have you ever lost somebody close to you, Anaïs?'

She stared soft-eyed at him. Anaïs had never lost anybody close to her, not at least to death. But she found that in these particular instances her soft-eyed stare led always to the assumption of the gravest of all possible conclusions.

'What was that quote again? It reminds me of her.'

'In memory of vanished hours so filled with beauty the consciousness of present loss oppresses. Exquisite hours, enveloped in light and silence, to have known them once is to have always a terrible standard of enjoyment. … I've always felt that I would end up in Venice. Do you ever feel things like that? And you know them because you feel them?'

'Not anymore. I felt things like that once and then my wife died. Her death stripped me of all illusions about the benevolence of the universe and the wisdom of our feelings.'

'Well this is getting *very* boring. Four more please, waiter.'

And when Anaïs was utterly mimosa-ed out they sauntered along the waterfront boulevard, she and Johnny both smiling down at the pavement, he occasionally turning to look at her in the hope that she would meet his gaze. He led her down a tiny alley which met the main road. Immediately as they joined the traffic they were stopped by a moaning lump of humanity. He crawled along, flat on his thin stomach, the shreds of plastic bag wooshing over the grime as he inched almost-elbow by almost-elbow ahead. He groaned and looked up at them again and Anaïs, two champagne bottles into her evening, averted her eyes and then buried them into Johnny's shoulder.

'What's the matter?'

'I can't look. It's awful.'

'It's… Yeah, it's awful. Come on,' and he put an arm around her and walked her on. They came to the rising plumes and halogen menus of a stretch of streetfood stalls. 'Are you all right?' Her head was still snuggled into his shoulder.

'Oh,' she moaned.

'Here look. Let's eat something.' He pointed to a cart piled high with toasted insect. He ordered from the smiling Thai woman and was handed and then waved at Anaïs a grilled chicken foot.

'What are you going to do with that?' said Anaïs, very suspicious.

'I'm going to eat it.'

'You are not! Don't you eat that!' she said, her eyes now wide open.

'Why not?' he said, holding up the claw and smiling. 'They're delicious.'

'They are not! They can't be.'

'No?' he said, moving the thing towards his mouth.

'John John, don't. Don't you eat that!'

'Look, here,' and he put a chicken claw between his teeth.

She gasped and shook her head. He bit off some flesh and chewed. 'Johnny, that's disgusting!'

'Yes it is. But you need cheering up.' He put another claw into his mouth and coughed and scrunched his face. 'Oh, it's so disgusting.' She took the thing from him with two of her own fingers and threw it onto the ground. 'Hey, I paid for that.'

'Come on!' she said, smiling again. 'Let's go home. Holy crap, is that a bag of Fanta?'

For a quarter of an hour they giggled at the Thai alphabet outside the fascist garudas of the Central Post Office. '*All* the letters look like owls,' said Anaïs, trying to find the letter he was pointing out to her. 'Except the safety pins. And the sperms. How do you say Hello again?'

'You say, Sawadee Ka.'

'I've heard them say it differently.'

'Sawadee Kaaaaa,' Johnny screeched.

'Ha ha,' she cackled. 'That's the one.'

'Your turn.'

'I'm not saying it.'

'Why not?'

'It sounds ridiculous.'

'It's fun, I promise.'

'Is it?' Johnny raised his eyebrows. Anaïs screeched, 'Sawadee Kaaaaaaaaa,' and cackled and sipped at the straw buried in her bag of green Fanta. Then she proceeded to say it to each Thai person they passed on their walk home. Then Johnny told her about the punishment for speaking ill of the royal family. For thirty minutes they spoke ill of it.

They stumbled, Anaïs with heels in hand, Johnny with Anaïs in hand, into the Shangri-La's lobby.

'I heard,' said Anaïs, giggling still as they lurched into an elevator, 'that the queen loves it even more than old Bummy-bowl. A right old slut she is. Where's Pookie? I want to pook her.' She laughed and exhaled joyfully as the elevator rose.

'We've passed my floor,' she said, squinting as she watched the numbers flash on and off overhead. 'I'm on the fifth floor. ... Are you getting out first? That's not very gentlemanly like of you. ... John John?'

'Yes?'

'Are you getting out first?' The doors opened at Johnny's floor and he held a thick arm across them. 'This isn't my floor.'

'I have champagne and peach puree in my room. Have you ever tried a Bellini?'

'You're a Bellini.'

'Come in for a drink.'

'I have tiredness.'

'Think of all the fun we could have.'

'I have plenty of funs in my room. No 'd'. Ha ha.'

'But my room is much nicer than yours.'

'Good for you.'

'Come in for a drink, Anaïs. Just one.'

She composed herself instantly and stood up straight. 'Not you too, Johnny.' She announced every word as though it were a sentence. 'You're better than that.'

'Better than what?'

'Than wanting, like everybody else, to make boom boom to me.'

'Who said anything about boom boom?'

She made serious her face and grunted him a laugh. '*You're* funny. Goodnight enough, Johnny. Now get out of the elevator. Press five. There's a good boy.' She leant on her front foot and pushed him into the corridor. 'Get out. Ha ha,' she cackled. 'Nighty night night.'

'I don't want to do this, John John.'

'Yes you do. You're doing swimmingly. The job's yours if you pull this off.'

'I don't want the job.'

'Of course you do.'

They were again at Sirocco atop State Tower. The sun had long set and a gibbous moon floated high in the sticky blackness. The circular bar was packed with tourists taking photographs of themselves. Lee Morgan played *Moment's Notice* across the terrace and out into the night. Every seat in the restaurant was occupied except for the two beside Johnny and Anaïs.

'It's *not* the right thing.'

'No? How do you know it's not?'

At midday in Angelini's Johnny briefed Anaïs on their dinner meeting. There had been no mention of his advance the night before but the memory of its rebuke had him obviously terse. He arrived early and ate alone and gave Anaïs the necessary facts and possible angles of persuasion as she waited for her pasta. He left before she finished eating. She knew for the first time which, of the two parties they were to meet with, Johnny—this evening she—was working for. She spent the afternoon in the sun, listening to Mick and Keith and *Heart Of Stone* from her phone and drinking pink gin by the larger of the pools.

A waiter brought Johnny his second whisky and what Johnny thought was Anaïs' second pink gin.

'I can *feel* that it's not right.'

'I told you about feelings. Especially not at work.'

And at the first landing there appeared Johnny's client. Dressed in primary colours, tall and with the florid complexion of a Belgian cloth merchant, Daan de Wilders was one of four in-house public relations managers for Verimar International Limited—a Singaporean agribusiness group recently voted for the twelfth consecutive year the world's least environmentally friendly company. He adjusted his horn-rimmed glasses and spotted Johnny's raised hand and came to shake it warmly. They had profited from one another for a very long time.

'This is Anaïs Spencer. She's going to run tonight for us. She's almost better at it than I am, Daan, so don't worry.'

'How do you do?' Daan sounded like an outdated robot.

And when Dionysus Tan, the t-shirted Malaysian representative of the World Wildlife Fund, appeared at the golden staircases Anaïs rose from her seat and accompanied him down to their table. 'First things first, whiskey or pink gin? Or something else? Wine?'

Dionysus said, 'Whiskey for me,' and Anaïs introduced him to the other two men. 'We were just discussing the best way to eat oysters.'

'I'm vegan,' said Dionysus.

'Ah. Well that I did not know. How long have you been one of those for?' She shook her head and waved her hand at the waiter at Dionysus' back. He turned quickly about with his tray of oysters and returned them to the dumbwaiter beyond the pine trees. Four waiters brought torches to enable them to read their menus. Anaïs chatted to de Wilders about the amazing new projects that Verimar had been undertaking all over the world— orphanages in Cambodia, schools in Burma, conservation parks in Kalimantan, primate rehabilitation centres in Vietnam. This Dionysus Tan could see right through.

'There are a thousand orang-utans left in Malaysian Borneo, Miss Spencer. We're *not* going to let Verimar cut this population in two. They've bought land over and over again, claiming to possess it in order to conserve it, and as soon as the issue is out of the papers they clear it. Here.' He threw onto the table a handful of polaroids. Each was an image of scorched earth, of geometrically perfect and entirely uninhabited plantation, of wounded or dying orang-utans, of baby apes in wheelbarrows. Anaïs rifled through them as a waiter brought what Johnny thought was her third pink gin. 'If the Malaysian population is cut in half by another Verimar plantation, pongo pygmaeus pygmaeus will be extinct within the next ten years. That is a fact. A statistical inevitability. Extinct. Gone forever. Five hundred are dying a year, Miss Spencer, out of a population of forty thousand. And then there's the pangolin. If we allow—'

'Are there penguins in Borneo?' said Anaïs. 'That wasn't in the brief was it?'

'The pangolin,' said Dionysus. 'The sunda pangolin.'

'I think you're saying it wrong. It's penguin.'

'No, the pangolin.'

'It's not panga-uin. It's penguin. With an *e*.'

'*Pan*golin. The pangolin. Not a penguin.'

'Like in Antarctica?'

'No. A pangolin.'

'What's a pangolin?'

'It's a scaly mammal.'

'Penguin's aren't mammals, man.'

'No, they're birds,' said Daan.

'Wait, are birds mammals?' said Anaïs.

'Pangolin,' said Dionysus, pronouncing each syllable clearly.

'No, it's penguin,' said Anaïs, repeating his slow diction. 'It's not pan-ga-uin. It's *pen*guin,' she said, blinking.

'They're a flightless seabird,' said Johnny.

'You're not understanding me,' said Dionysus. 'Pangolin. A scaly mammal. Here,' he said, and rifled through the polaroids. 'The sunda pangolin lives in Borneo and Thailand and they're critically endangered in both. If—'

'There are no penguins in Thailand are there?' said Anaïs. 'Wouldn't it be too hot?'

'Mr Tan,' said the Dutchman. 'Verimar International is entering a new era of corporate responsibility. Truly they are. They've already acknowledged the importance to humanity of the Bornean orangutan. You were at that press conference, I believe. And they have committed once and for all to sustainable palm oil production. No new rainforest clearing. They committed to that at the last roundtable discussion. Committed without reservation. You know what that means publicly. Verimar wants to purchase this land, from the Malaysian government, solely to ensure that the Bornean orangutan continues to thrive for all humanity. You need to believe me, Mr Tan. Distrust is unhealthy. Corporations can do more good in this world than any other group, certainly more than any government can do. Corporations alone have the money and the power and the will to keep this species alive.'

'Utter bullshit.' The heads at the table snapped to Anaïs.

'Beg your pardon, Miss Spencer?' said Johnny.

'What about their long-term investment strategy?'

'Miss Spencer?' said Mr Wilders, instantly uncomfortable.

'You're a lying bastard. Johnny, I know you can see this. He's the good guy and he's the bad guy. And the bad guy pays you more so you confuse the good guy into doing what the bad guy wants him to do. As clear as a shitty summer's day. Dionysus, I like your name, do *not* let people like *him* push you around. And *never* listen to what Dutch people have to say. Utterly godless. *He* wants to cut your monkey population in two so that they'll all be in zoos. Then they can do whatever the fuck they want with Malaysia and Indonesia and every fucking where. Their long term investment strategy literally contains the phrase "confinement of large Southeast Asian primates to zoos and rescue centres." You keep at it old cock, you're doing great work. And you…' she fumbled after another tirade but ended up simply waggling her index finger at Mr Wilders. 'Fucking Dutch! You sound deaf when you talk. And you!' she said to Johnny. 'The obligatory work of the only civilized country in Asia, my arse.' And she pushed her chair back from the table and fled across the mezzanine.

Johnny apologised frantically to Mr Wilders and Mr Tan and rushed to catch Anaïs at the elevators.

'What are you doing? Go away,' she said.

'What are *you* doing?'

'I want to go home.'

'You have no home, Anaïs.'

'You're so unspeakably boring.'

'Come and work for me. Come back to Melbourne. Tonight wasn't a normal business night. I never do environmental stuff. I hate it as well.'

'You don't do anything that's honourable, John John.'

'Neither do you,' he said, his voice rising with his surprise at the accusation's hypocrisy.

She became impatient for the elevator and opened the door to the stairwell.

'You're on the sixty-fourth floor.'

'You can accuse me of anything you like.'

She skipped down the first flight of steps, turned at the landing, and with her hand running over the painted-iron handrail descended manually the State Tower.

'That's not an accusation, Anaïs, you actually are on the sixty-fourth floor.' He followed after her.

'You may think that I do nothing honourable,' she called out to the vast empty column of the stairwell, 'but the men I associate with have too much money and they do nothing with it. I am the last person to enjoy all of this earth before it's gone. All of it! Mankind's sole legacy will be that he destroyed the very earth that gave him life.'

'I saw Interstellar too, Anaïs.'

'Murph!' she moaned. 'Muuurph! Mine will be the last generation metaphysically able to enjoy this world and only I am enjoying the whole thing.' She was shouting. 'People are always talking about how we live in a globalised world but who enjoys the entire globe, hm? Nobody. Their world is the commute from their boring houses to their boring jobs and back and that's all they ever see. I am enjoying God's earth before it is gone. The last to do so.'

'God, Anaïs? Really?'

'God.'

'Just come and work for me. Come home.'

'Australia is not my home.'

'Then where is?'

'I am a daughter bound to exile. Venice.'

'You've never been to Venice.'

'In the memory of vanished hours so filled with beauty the consciousness of present loss oppresses. Exquisite hours, enveloped in light and silen—'

'Do you even know what any of that means? Just because you've memorised it doesn't mean it means anything. Your youth is fading, Anaïs, fast, and your beauty with it.'

The sound of her footsteps upon the cold concrete slowed and shortly ceased. She stared up at the unsmoothed lath and plaster of the underside of the fifty-fourth floor's emergency staircase. Johnny stopped chasing her. He softened his tone. 'You have no tradable skill. No qualifications, no experience. What will you do in ten years' time?'

'So, so boring,' she said, slowly despairing. She kicked her feet out and continued without vigour her descent.

Johnny rounded the two flights of steps which Anaïs had on him. 'Your charm will have evaporated. You'll be tired of your own lies. Men won't be so ready to offer you suites in the Shangri-La Hotel. Think about what you're doing with your life, Anaïs. You were nearly killed by a Chinese people smuggler. Is that any way for a twenty-eight year old to be behaving?'

Johnny almost put his hands at her shoulders. 'So boring.' She shivered and closed her eyes. 'So, so, boring.'

'Go to Venice, Anaïs. I'll fly you there and you can stay in my palazzo. I don't for a second believe that you're a countess but I do believe that your lies come from real desires that you're too afraid to chase. You want to go to Venice, go to Venice.'

'I don't want to go to Venice with you, John John.'

'You are so self-obsessed. It won't be with me. I'm in Singapore for a month as of Saturday.'

'Why?'

'For work.'

'No, why me? Why fly *me* to Venice?'

'Why are you angry?'

'You know who I am. You know what I do. Why would you fly me to the other side of the world, to Venice?'

'*Because* I know who you are. Can a man not be kind?'

'Not without wanting something in return.'

'That's how you work, Anaïs. Not the rest of the world.'

'So boring you are. Boring, boring, boring.'

'People aren't as horrible as you think they are, Anaïs. You see them as things to be used, as empty. But everyone has goals and desires, regardless of how small or pathetic you think these might be. And a lot of them, and of this I know you take full advantage, are naturally very generous and want others to be happy. You'll be alone as long as you think everybody else is as selfish as you are, Anaïs.'

Twice she took a long breath in and huffed it all out. 'Bad John John,' she said. 'Bad, bad, boring John John.'

'Go and be happy, Anaïs. Go to Venice. Fall in love.'

EPISODE 3

Et In Arcadia Sunt.

I

Anaïs, in a navy and white striped dress which she had owned for six years but never worn, its long sleeves rolled up to just below her elbows, collar open, her hair in a low bun and loose at the sides of her face, stepped out from the halogen smog of the chain-stores onto the open landing of Santa Lucia station. The dress had been given to her in lieu of a declined jeep by the Emirati Sheik who had pursued her for most of the last year of what she would have termed, if ever she were forced to be so reflective upon her own life, her bland and certain normality. At first traumatic association had put the garment in abeyance; for the last two years it had been merely sequestered—through certain anticipation of one day traveling to its only befitting paradise—in the bottom of her suitcase.

And at last here she was.

Anaïs had never been told that one absolutely ought to arrive in Venice by boat. She had taken the train, on a track of weeds and freight containers and graffiti and shanty towns, from Milan. It was stopped in Mestre, in sight of the rail bridge; police dogs were brought on to sniff everybody's luggage as the underside of its thirty carriages were inspected. Anaïs' passport was rechecked by a kind-faced carabinieri. 'Sorry for the wait, signorina. But is a still eh… maybe a bomba.'

'Non c'é una problema.'

The sun was divinely warming on her lifted face. A church whose portico and slim green-leaden dome she did not yet know to be either classical or ugly greeted her from across the dull and swirling olive-green canal. Barges powered along like loaded buses beneath the flag of the European Union. The azzurro was dampened by long lacerations of white cloud, the electric lamp posts more attractive than the buildings opposite. She gulped. A great weight, long borne, ascended joyously from her shoulders. She breathed easier than she could remember ever having breathed. She in brown leather caged sandals walked the granite steps. A flock of Bangladeshis with their porter licences at their necks ran hand-drawn trolleys at her like rickshaws. She had used the flight, as well as to translate and memorise the phrases she knew would be essential to her sojourn, to study a map of the city. She knew better than most that the lost are the easiest prey, that the surest way to avoid being bothered in a new city was to appear always as though one knew precisely where one was going. She pulled out the handle of her ivory-white suitcase and joined the thundering herd of rolled luggage.

She passed overflowing garbage bins placarded with McDonald's and Burger King and Chinese restaurant advertisements; a long and sweaty line at the vaporetto ticket stall; huddles of Korean and Malaysian students stationary and spinning their maps around—and headed for Strada Nova.

Bangladeshis stood guard at the foot of the first bridge. They waved sticks around and yelled the foreign word, 'Selfie,' at her. She passed innumerable ATMs, a pair of tiny young Italian men pecking at one another's necks. Kaftaned Africans, handbags arranged on sheets at their feet, tried to get her attention with deep hoots of, 'Nice lady.' There were elephant trousers and heavy cameras dangling at chests, Bengals throwing squishy balls onto cardboard, and families chubby and despondent in matching fedoras. Bengals hawked sunglasses upon sheets at their feet, Africans belts, and there were man-buns and midget lesbians licking at ice cream cones and Bangladeshis selling fruit. Through this, the city which once counted its census by the number of its souls, Anaïs struggled to pass—a sludge of bum-bags and sunscreen, of mullets and mohawks, more West Africans selling more handbags, of Chinese handicraft shops and halal pizzerias, suitcases careening like wildebeest, mesh singlets and condom vending machines embedded into the very walls, tattooed arms and t-shirts, backpacks and little frontpacks and walking poles—the whole in-love rainbow of Venice's excited and ephemeral inhabitants.

She tried to overtake a dawdler on the left. Everybody seemed magically to spot a t-shirt they thought wonderful; she was pinned against a wall by French. She sped up to pass on the right; her new lane of Russian traffic was brought to a standstill by something shiny and unquestionably traditional and Venetian. She heard no Italian until she got fed up with this struggle and went into a gelateria.

'Buongiorno, signora,' said the silver-haired and swarthy man behind the high, curved ice-cream case.

'Buongiorno,' said Anaïs, almost yelling. She had discovered while practising on the aeroplane that there were fewer things more pleasurable than speaking Italian.

'Dimmi.'

She announced: 'Vorrei un cono con caffè.'

He stood erect and readied a cone and appeared to be tired as he said, 'Solo caffè?'

'Sì, solo caffè.'

And he reached down into the case and prepared a scoop. When he had transferred it into the cone he rose and said kindly, 'Where are you from?'

Anaïs did not hide her indignation. Her knack for impersonations, the result of two decades of practise, came most easily as a flair for accents. She had once pretended to be German for two days simply to see if she could get away with it. A Californian had for a week courted her under the assumption that she was from the North Shore of Massachusetts. Her English was taken from the affectations of Peter O'Toole and undetectable; her bogan especially flawless. But her Italian...

She protested. 'Ma, io sono una contessa.'

Her maiden Venetian stared at Anaïs with as blank a face as a Venetian is capable. She had spoken, though somewhat illogically, loudly and very clearly. He looked at once furious and merciful. 'Come?'

'Io sono una contessa,' and she smiled.

'Una contessa?'

'Sì. Una contessa.'

After a long stare he was able to accept with great sympathy that this young straniera perhaps *thought* that she was a contessa. 'Two euros, Contessa.'

And after an hour of labouring and toiling and wrong turns and stopping for gelato she reached the calle of peeling pink stucco and green mould, its bricks the colour and texture of pink froot loops, at whose end was the chipped and rotting green door which was the *porta terra* to the Palazzo Bolani.

The ground floor was dark and bare and of mud-covered stone. At the top of a modern iron staircase was a landing. Anaïs turned to the checkerboard floor of the *piano nobile*. She flicked a light switch and a chandelier came on and after warming up glowed. The floor was of pink and white marble, the room unfurnished save for a stone mantelpiece over a large fireplace. The walls were of egg-shell plaster crumbling around faded fragments of fresco painted by an incompetent follower of Tiepolo, once depicting the Banquet of Cleopatra, the Battle of The Nile, Wintering in Patrae, the Battle of Actium; around the chandelier rather more fragments survived of Octavian Triumphant.

It might have been the shabbiest room in all of Venice. Anaïs was in awe. 'Exquisite hours, enveloped in light and silence,' she repeated to herself, almost silently. She opened the green and white-striped blinds and sunlight streamed in and lit up the floating dust as flakes of gold. She stood upon the balcony and was simply disbelieving. The Bolani's façade was three doors down from the perfect early Gothic of the Ca' da Mosto. Its own front was unadorned thirteenth century, the *piano nobile* of pink stucco and three of the simplest windows in Italy. Boxes of daffodils upon a low balustrade of cast iron looked out to the arches of the Fabbriche Nuove. A crane and the Rialto Bridge and two bell towers to her left, bronze bollards below, an entire building gift-wrapped in grey scaffolding and Sansovino opposite, the red blinds and white arches of the Pescaria, the Grand Canal as far as her eyes could see. After seven years she had made it. 'In the memory of vanished hours so filled with beauty...' She knew barely a thing about the place. What she had known before her walk from the train station she had glimpsed in photographs. She knew neither how old was nor how glorious had been this prince of cities. She thought simply that it would be a place of exceeding beauty. '...Exquisite hours, enveloped in light and silence...' She had read not a single page of Ruskin. No guidebook on anywhere had ever been open in front of her. Knowledge she thought the great destroyer of all wonder, and wonder she was in Venice to do. Seven years of feeling, seven years of an intangible pull, a yearning, a kind of gravitational urge—fulfilled. Alone in a palazzo on the Grand Canal, almost precisely as ancient-feeling and as dilapidated as she had for so long imagined, Anaïs felt a sense of completion. '...To have known them once is to have always a terrible standard of enjoyment.'

Atop the second, marble, staircase were two bedrooms. Both were refurbished and had en suites with running hot water and marble basins and claw-foot tubs and rainfall showerheads. The walls were red damask, the chintz furniture of imitation gilt and claws. She opened her suitcase on the bed and to the bounce of Helen Forrest singing *Perfidia* showered.

Looking out again over the canal the wind lifted her curled hair and she closed her eyes. In Valentino white lace and coral-pink chiffon trousers she felt found. Quite easily she could have stood there on the balcony forever. She pictured the gondoliers bringing her food in order to give sustenance to her joy, the bringing in by a valet of the world's most comfortable chair, upon which she would bask until the season turned and she was forced to go inside to put on a jumper. But so much Venice to see. Found, she wanted to spend the first of her hopefully innumerable Venetian days getting lost again.

She returned to the calle and, knowing the direction of the Rialto, set off not really caring whether or not she reached it. She ducked into the first church to which she came. A dark and sombre chamber. She looked into the little wall-mounted font of cream marble and remembered that she was thirsty. There were three old women about—one praying, one lighting a candle, one watering the flowers—and a painting whose brilliance, even in its dark chapel, she marvelled at—the Greek inscription within the arch, the fig tree, the weedy rock, the hermit robed in persimmon, the gloriously bedecked bishop—signs and symbols obviously all whose place she did not know within a puzzle she could not solve. In a busy statued campo she turned onto a covered alleyway, then onto another, and then found herself back in the campo. Shortly she was before a wider street at whose end was a bridge. Stalls selling the same rubbish as she had seen on her walk to the palazzo. Then steps of soft white stone. Anaïs knew that she was ascending the Rialto. She strayed right and wondered which of the palazzi was hers then crossed to the left and saw for the first time in this city of unforgettable views that vista of sinking city and rising sea which nobody ever forgets.

The day was latening. The low sun cast beneath Anaïs' feet, along the canal, a shimmering yellow beam. The top floor windows of the palazzi burned orange with sunset. The restaurant lights came on beneath their maroon canopies. European Union flags swayed in the evening breeze. Water buses ploughed heavily up and down, stopping to load on more tourists, beeping as they set off. The water became a river of mercury, the gondolas ethereal silhouettes turning to slice through it; water taxis glided along with their Japanese passengers reaching their arms high and rotating as they filmed. The soft unpaintable tones of the houses in the low distance of the canal's bend burst across the early night as a veil of white peach. A lone gondolier was by chance left solitary in the quicksilver and the whole view was for a moment perfect. Twilight descended as a greying mist, the horizon soon seen as through a fog, and the night was lit only by the occasional flashes of the cameras which surrounded her.

Nobody but she had actually watched the setting down of the day. Most had poised their machines so that the shooter's head came between lens and panorama. Some had sticks to ensure a wider shot, some had tripods to ensure an unblurred. Anaïs lowered her elbows onto the cold balustrade and revelled. Her breaths had never been calmer. The canal below was practically silent. And she had an affinity for drowning out other people's enthusiasm, especially when most of it was in foreign languages.

'Do you believe in signs?' somebody said loudly and in English. Neither the voice nor the question registered. Then somebody grabbed Anaïs by the arms and turned her. 'Do you believe in signs?'

'You're shitting me.'

Stanley Felix was in pressed white trousers and a blue linen jacket. His tanned skin stuck out rather more in Venice than it had done in Bangladesh. And he was very happy to see her.

'I know you believe in signs, Anaïs. And in fate. This whole big city and I find you here. I've only been waiting here for two weeks. And you've turned up. I can't be apart from you. I don't care about your cover. I don't care that you're a Jew. I don't even have to talk to you. I just need to be in the same place as you. The energy that knowing that gives me! It makes me happy. So happy.'

Anaïs shrugged off his happy hands and rolled her eyes and stretched her jaw and returned her elbows to the stone balustrade.

'Isn't it beautiful? I've been here all day every day for the last two weeks. But it's still not as beautiful as you.'

'What are you doing here, Stan, you idiot?'

'I've come to be with you.'

'You have to go home.'

'I have no home.'

'Back to Bangladesh.'

'I quit my job.'

'You did not.'

'I did.'

'Stanley, you don't understand the nature of my profession. I've died four times in the last seven years, each time reborn with a new identity. I deal with very dangerous people. If I see you on the street, if you see me on the street, you *have* to turn and walk the other way. Do you understand? People are watching me. People who look for real patterns and real signs. If they see you more than once in my vicinity they'll know that you know me and then your life, your fingernails, your kneecaps, will be in serious danger.'

'I don't care about danger. I'd rather die a hundred times a day and be with you than to live anywhere without you.'

'That doesn't make any sense at all, you idiot. You're not immortal.'

'I need to see you.'

'Well you can't see me.'

'I want to take you out for dinner. Every night. The best restaurants.'

And Anaïs reconsidered. 'You can see me if I contact you. OK? Where are you staying?'

'At the Hotel Metropole. Can we have dinner? Tonight.'

'Not until I think it's safe, Stan. I'll contact you.'

'I can't wait.'

'I'm going that way now, Stanley. You *have* to go that way.'

And she left the lingering sunset behind and went down to the pescaria and was soon wondrously lost in the amber lights of San Polo. Osterias spilled out onto the alleys, loud with Italian and azure jackets and yellow trousers, lanterns bright amid thin lengths of speckled darkness. She spun in tiny dead-end piazzettas and followed the sound of cutlery clinking onto plates, of laughter around dark corners, opera wafting from high windows. The canals as black as roads were betrayed only by the occasional white lights of a hotel dock shimmering off their watery bends.

Soon the streets were empty and the shop-fronts shuttered and Anaïs had the whole silent city to herself. She found the Grand Canal, stared over its black waters, which seemed to transcend time, and turned around and, attempting to find it again from two alleys away, lost it. She crossed the same squares four times without recognising them, stared at two sides of the same church for an age without realising that they were the one building. When later, starving, she recrossed the Rialto she was the only person on it. She stumbled upon the little blush-pink church by the palazzo Bolani and was bewitched utterly by the time her head came to rest upon a silken pillow, and her newly innocent eyes closed.

II

She woke and wished there were somebody to prepare a breakfast for her on the balcony below. Instead she opened the bedroom window and watched the canalazzo come alive and glisten in the morning sun. Soon the smell of Italian coffee, deep and dark and strong, rose upon the breeze and she dressed and went to find some.

The calle was in shade and cool. At its end a tall figure stood perfectly centred, watching the hordes pass. Anaïs closed and locked the porta terra and both she and this figure turned towards the alley.

'For a member of every intelligence agency in the Western world you're *not* very difficult to track down.'

She closed her eyes and lowered her head and stormed furiously past Johnny Goodenough.

'Where are you going so angrily in the morning?'

She clenched her teeth. 'You lied to me.'

'I did not.'

'You said you wouldn't be here.'

'I said I wouldn't be here with you. And I'm not. I'm just... here. In a hotel like the rest of the tourists. The Bolani is yours. Do you like it?'

'Yes,' she said defiantly. 'Now where do you get coffee around here?'

'There's not a bad espresso in the city.'

'Why are you here?' Exhausted and famished in a white shirt with blue polka dots and a white skirt belted high at her waist Anaïs, clutching her purse and with her hair up, walked calmly over the centre of the Rialto with Johnny strolling beside her, his hands in the pockets of his royal blue linens. 'I cancelled all my business in Singapore.'

'That's not what I asked. Why are you here?'

'I want to get to know you.'

'You do know me. Now leave.'

'Don't push me away, Anaïs.'

'I'm not pushing you away, Johnny, because you're not anywhere near me. Nor will you ever be.'

131

'Does staying in my palazzo count for nothing?'

'No,' she warned. 'Don't you dare hold that over me. I would never have agreed to use it if I thought you'd hold it over me.'

'I won't crowd you while you're here. I'll give you space. But I want to make you happy. Will you have dinner with me?'

'So you can get me drunk and try to sleep with me again?'

They stepped out into the sunlight beside the Rio del Frari. Anaïs' feet slowed to a standstill. Her eyes pored over the bare brick of the church's façade, vast above the tourists reading maps before it. It seemed to dwarf even the immaculately blue sky. A gondola glided along the perfectly green rio. The square was aflutter with pigeons and people. The gothic baldachins, the pine trees, the simple volutions, the lancet windows, the campanile and its madonetta; the little white stone bridge, the covered well, the brightness of the sky. It was the closest Anaïs had been to real tears in seven years.

Neither of them spoke as they stood upon the bridge. She eased her feet down onto each of its eight shining steps and her neck craned. The arch and its fading fresco, the red and white marble of the rose window, the white mullions, the gabled portals of pink marble; the red umbrellas in the piazza, the covered well. As quaint and as cartoonish as a Disney princess' place of greatest happiness illustrated by Prout. Johnny watched her read in awe the Latin inscription on its southern wall, until she was distracted by the rising of some strangely welcome yelling.

Into the Campo dei Frari, walking backwards and orating to a slow-moving arc of Americans, Australians, an English couple and several pin-eyed Kiwis, there strutted in brogues, his arms gesticulating as he spoke almost in Anaïs' diminished accent, a smirking and rather dashing young man. His hair was dark and combed, his white oxford shirt rolled at the sleeves. His trousers were tailored to be looser than hose and, as though in a stage costume, the front of one leg matched the colour of the rear of the other. He strode in flashes of crimson and gold.

Those Venetians outside who could follow his English stopped whatever they were doing. Those inside the snack bars and gelati shops went to the doorways or to the open windows. So renowned had he become that several of those whose English was minimal had lately taken to studying it solely in order to be able to understand him. They too rushed outside to in order to catch what little they could.

'The Basilica dei Frari,' he announced, swinging an arm across its walls. 'The Frari Church. Santa Maria Gloriosa dei Frari, in full. Built by the Ferrari corporation in 1810 and dedicated to presumption. It's currently a Dominican church, which means it's owned by a guy called Domenic, who also happens to run a few Burger Kings. It used to be a Brandonian church, when Brandon owned it, and before that an Octavianan-anan. It is the only building in Venice which if you put your ear to its western wall you can hear the ocean. In 1971 Elizabeth Taylor paid to have the whole thing taken down, brick by brick, and shipped to Botswana and there rebuilt for her second wedding to Dick Van Dyke. Fearing that another reconstruction would damage her irreparably, Elizabeth Taylor was picked up by two helicopters and flown all they way back here and lowered down onto its original position. There are two McDonald's inside, one Ronald, one Old, and Michael Schumacher is in intensive care in the choir. And in case you were curious, the answer is Yes, there is a jungle cat in the bathroom and tinsel is *extremely* insulating. There are three pictures of Picasso.'

'Inside?' said one of the Americans, following his guide across to the square's well.

'No. Now, who can guess how many wishes have come true from coins tossed into this well?'

'Tin,' said one of the New Zealanders.

'Higher.'

'Uhlivven,' said another of them, causing his countrymen all to chortle and grin.

'A hundred?' said the Englishwoman.

'Closer. Three hundred and twenty-two wishes, have come true from coins thrown into this well. The Venetians first cottoned on that it had magical powers in the fifteenth century and the wishes remained small. They were a humble people. Nicer hair, a visit from Santa, a tasty crop of tomatoes. But by the early twentieth century people, Godless, had become unspeakably selfish and the wishes started to get out of hand. Raymond luxury yachts, tropical fish tanks filled with seahorses, Disneylands. Then after Mussolini came up from Rome and wished for Ethiopia the Venetian authorities sealed the well once and for all. Though the current mayor of Venice did say earlier this year that he'll open it again if Ed Sheeran is still popular in 2017, in order to wish for his assassination. Elephants…'

'*Anaïs*?' Johnny Goodenough had been trying to get her attention for some time.

'Hm?'

'Will you meet me for dinner?'

'Oh. Dinner, yes. Ummm… where?'

'Do you know where the Campo di San Silvestro is?'

'No,' she said, frustrated that he thought she had already so memorised the city.

'San Giovanni Crisostomo?'

'I have no idea what you just said.'

'It's a little pink church around the corner from the palazzo. You must have seen it.'

'At five. I'm starving.'

'Do you have a map?'

'God no.'

'How will you get home?'

'John John,' she said, most disappointed, and turned down a covered alley and spent the day lost in Dorsoduro. She spent her afternoon barely breathing as she rounded the Fondamenta Salute and looked upon that low and glorious seabedded picture—St Mark's campanile from the Dogana, those Byzantine domes and the Ducal Palace; San Giorgio Maggiore, a yacht and a green field of briccole, Giudecca.

She made it home for four-thirty and changed for dinner and by five was opposite Johnny in a cosy candlelit restaurant.

'You haven't quit your job have you?'

They sat in the window, Johnny facing out to the alleyway, Anaïs to the wooden bar and the bathrooms and the busy little kitchen.

'I've taken my holidays early.'

'Good. You really shouldn't be here.'

'Life is so short, Anaïs. Too short to not waste chasing you. No. Too short to waste not chasing you.'

'You're not chasing me, John John. You're buying me a meal and putting me up for a few nights.'

'I am chasing you. And I always get what I want.'

'Not this time, sport.'

Bread was brought to the table and Anaïs chomped and tore and woofed it down.

'Hungry?'

'Not especially. I've been in breadless countries for a month.'

Johnny ordered wine in impressive Italian. 'Have you got a list of things you want to see while you're here?'

'A list? John John, come on. I'm here to see Venice.'

'And what have you seen so far?'

'What do you mean?'

'Have you seen St. Mark's Square? The Doge's Palace? The Bridge of Sighs?'

'I don't know. I'm not a tourist.'

'Are you not?'

'No.'

'Well tomorrow make sure you do something cultural.'

'I am something cultural.'

'Is that a fact?'

'That's a fact.' She smiled a very satisfied smile and looked around the room.

'And if you need a tour guide…'

On the walls were modern black and white photographs of the city. Several older couples, mostly American, filled the restaurant, and two bright eyes among very tanned skin were watching her from above a menu at a table beside the kitchen. The menu was hurriedly raised.

'So will you please tell me something true about yourself, Anaïs?'

'Would you excuse me?' She put her napkin on the table and walked towards the bathrooms. She loomed close over the still-raised menu. It refused to budge. She slapped it away and lifted Stanley Felix by the arm out of his chair and into the back of the restaurant.

'What are you doing here?'

'Who's that?'

'What are you doing here?'

'I'm protecting you.'

'You need to leave.'

'I just ordered the duck.'

'Stanley, I know that the man with whom I am about to have dinner knows seven different types of martial art. How many do you know?' He hesitated to lie. 'Exactly. And if he finds out that you're watching him, what do you think he'll do to you, in the dark, empty alleyways of Venice? Who do you think he will ultimately end up throwing into the opaque, never-dredged waters of Venice?'

'I'll risk anything to keep you safe.'

'Me, Stanley. He will throw *me* into a canal. You watching us compromises *me*, not you.'

'I can have an army of Stanleys here in two days.'

'Bangladesh against Russia?'

'Russia?' he gasped.

'I am to take care of him when the time is right but until then I am very, very, undercover. You need to leave.'

'Are you sleeping with him?'

'Stanley, get out. Walk out now and go back to your hotel.'

'Is he a Jew as well?'

'Stanley Felix!'

'He is!'

'Shut up.'

'When can I see you?'

'Never again.' And she shoved him towards the front door. He lifted his jacket from his chair and as he passed her table he flicked over Johnny's water glass and apologised as he walked out.

They ate—Anaïs copiously—baby octopus and sardines with sweet onions, and scampi and mussels. Johnny walked Anaïs home. They ducked into a little gelato shop before the Rialto.

'Ho! La Contessa. Come va?' said the young man behind the freezer.

'Marco, buonasera.'

'Contessa?' said Johnny as they strolled across the bridge.

'I told you.'

'Why do you think you lie, Anaïs?'

'What makes you think I'm lying?'

'What then is truth?'

'Exactly. I *am* a countess, dispossessed.'

'And you've been to visit your palazzo Malaspina have you?'

'I've asked around. Nobody seems to remember where it was.'

'Not surprising. Why don't you ask them where the worker's museum is?'

'Gone too, apparently.'

'How inconvenient.' And Johnny veered into a little portico where a gondolier was waiting. Anaïs stopped halfway down the steps and Johnny smiled up at her in the lamplight and the gondolier sang softly, '*Buonasera, signorina, buonasera.*' Johnny offered her his hand.

'No,' she said adamantly.

'This is Massimo. Let's take a ride. The Grand Canal, on a gondola, in the moonlight. There's nothing else quite like it.'

'No,' she said, even more adamantly.

'What do you mean, No?'

'You're not chasing me, John John. Thank you for dinner. Good night.'

She watched the end of the calle as she opened the Bolani's door. Then from the balcony she watched the gondolas on the Canal in the moonlight until her eyes began to close.

She woke to striking bells and screeching seagulls and the hollers by which Venetians seemed to communicate. She searched the four floors of the house for a window through which she could see the calle but could find none. She peered through the keyhole of the front door for a few minutes. When no Goodenough-like figures were spotted she set out for coffee and some breakfast and was soon among the quiet splendour of Castello. Wandering, she emerged at the Riva degli Schiavoni and smiled in the morning sunshine and was elated.

Her stomach grumbled and she thought back onto last night's dinner. Soon she was imagining a champagne brunch of scampi and marinated eggplant, that baby octopus, artichoke, those sardines. A tiny hunched-over woman hobbled towards her, leaning low on a tiny walking stick. A kerchief covered her face and head and a tiny withered hand poked out and scanned from side to side as her voice begged for money in English. Then Anaïs found that quite by accident she was outside the Hotel Metropole. The lobby was darker than crimson, draped in brocade, was scattered with oriental lamps and satin cushions, displayed a reproduction of Gentile's Mehmed.

'Is Stanley Felix in his room?'

The receptionist scanned the pigeon-holes behind him. 'Sì, signora. He is in.'

'What's the best seafood restaurant in the city?'

'For seafood I would recommend La Bugiarda. It is over in San Polo but the food is amazing.'

'Could you call Signor Felix and tell him to meet me there at… What is the time? … At twelve.'

'There is a phone just around the corner, signora. Signor Felix is in room 601.'

'Better if you call him. And could you give him these instructions?' Anaïs filled two pages of a Metropole-branded notepad. 'And where is La Bugiarda on a map?'

Room 601's phone rang as Stanley stepped out of his morning shower. 'Hello?'

'Signor Felix, a woman has requested that you meet her for lunch at midday.'

'A blonde woman?'

'Yes. Very beautiful. She has left instruction for you.'

'What are they?'

The receptionist read from the notepad. 'She wrote, exit the 'otel and take sixteen-a steps to your left. The first person to pass you, knows who you are. Say to him, 'Pancake titties.' If he looks at you strangely that means the coast is clear. Then go to the tobacconists beside the tallest tower in the city…'

'Which is the tallest tower in the city?'

'Il Campanile di San Marco. The bell tower of Saint Mark. And ask the tobacconist for a pangolin. He will not understand what-a you mean but…'

'Ask him for a penguin?'

'Mm I don't know. It says a pangolin.' He spelt it.

'What's a pangolin?'

'I think is a… a scaly mammal.'

'So not a penguin?'

'No, it says pangolin.'

'Are you saying penguin, like the bird? I think it's meant to say penguin. Not pengauin. Penguin.'

'No, it definitely says a pangolin.' And he spelt it again. 'They are a different animals to penguin. Pangolin, pengauin. You see? Pengauin, pangolin. Pangolin, pengauin.'

Four glasses of prosecco and plates each of baby octopus, grilled eggplant and scampi in, and Stanley stopped running at the restaurant's closed door and stepped inside.

'You're *very* late.'

'I was trying to find the Somalian. I gave up and just came here.'

'You didn't find him?' she said, pretending to panic. 'You weren't followed were you?'

'I'm certain I wasn't. I was checking the whole time.'

'Oh you can't be certain, Stan! What have you done? At Russian spy school they spend four semesters teaching their spies how to follow someone without detection. Four semesters!'

'But I stole the suit from Ermenegildo Zegna, just like you said. Off the mannequin. There's no way they followed me after that. Do you like it? Can we eat? It's taken me three hours to get here. I'm starving.'

'Well I'm full now aren't I? You took too bloody long. Everything's been compromised. I need a walk. Would you like a sardine? They're not very nice,' and she ate the last one.

Stanley paid her bill and strolled after her along San Pantalon.

'And how are you enjoying Venice, Stan?'

'It's beautiful here.'

'Yes it is.'

'Not nearly as beautiful as you though.'

'Really?'

'I don't even care that you're a Jew. *That's* how beautiful I find you.'

'That's a very strange thing to say, Stan. Why do you so dislike them?'

'Jews? They're ruining the world.'

'Are they? All of them?'

'All of them. Together.'

'Just them?'

'Running it and ruining it. But I don't care that you're one. I'm in Venice and I'm with you…'

'You're not with me.'

'I'm next to you, and I'm free. You're what's been missing in my life all these years. Three ex-wives and not an ounce of love, and now love is all I can think about. You make me so happy. Love conquers everything, even Jews.'

Anaïs turned her head slowly and in bewilderment to Stanley Felix. Somebody called from inside a bacaro, 'Ciao, Contessa,' and Anaïs turned about and went back and waved and said,

'Ciao, Chiara.'

'What did they call you?'

'I'm a countess of Venice, Stan. From a very old family. It's the reason they use me on Venetian assignments. I have all the contacts.'

'You're incredible.'

They emerged from a covered walkway to the cramped splendour of the Frari and Stanley bought gelato. That young man from yesterday was back at the well. He was standing over his tour group, today's much younger than yesterday's and composed entirely of Americans and Canadians, all of them leaning down and with an ear at the well's iron cover.

'What can we hear?' said the young man.

'The ocean?' said one of them.

'Not the ocean. But water, certainly.'

'Bells?'

'No.'

'I can hear echoes.'

'You can. Echoes of joy. Screams. Beneath this iron cover is the world's longest waterslide.'

Anaïs smiled and shooshed Stanley and took her cone from him and stepped slowly towards the well.

'In ancient Venetian folklore it was said that this well was the entrance to the underworld. In 1492 Claudio Villa jumped in, hoping to be the first person to get all the way to the end, but he didn't take floaties. He drowned. The second expedition, led by an Englishman called Clark Griswold, lost their wristbands halfway through the day and weren't allowed back in. Several more inner-tube expeditions were undertaken in the centuries that followed, all of them kicked out for pushing in line. I don't know what you know about Italians but they are above all a sincere and believing people. Even today, every year twenty people are selected by lottery to be allowed to try the slide. It is said that nobody survives the journey, which takes about forty minutes and has six loop-de-loops, with their mental health intact. Every year a few people turn up all across the world claiming to have gotten to the end. They appear as homeless people, going on and on about equality and tolerance and so no sane person pays any attention to them. Anyway,' he yelled, and was followed across the campo. 'Here we have the Frari church.

Built in the twelfth century entirely out of sponge cake, it very soon rained and the monks had to rethink things. They tried regular cupcakes, the birds ate it, then liquorice, but it was too divisive, then gingerbread. Finally they decided, on the advice of the third little pig, on bricks and here it stands today, though the exterior is no longer covered with the original frescoes depicting scenes from the Life of Brian.'

He paused to allow his tourists to take in the building's façade. He looked around the campo and stopped instantly and at length upon Anaïs. She was smiling and he smiled back. She slowly shook her head and he nodded his and raised his eyebrows and recommenced.

'The Frari *is* open for visitors. You can go in and see the place where Robin Williams was sent by Jumanji for all those years. Twenty-six years he spent in the clerestory before Peter rolled a five. And there are a pair of pangolins in the nave if you—'

'Did you say there are penguins in the church?' said a mousy young Canadian.

'Pangolins. Two of them.'

'I think you're saying it wrong,' said her boyfriend. 'You're saying pengauin. It's *penguin*.'

The young man spelt it out for them.

'What's a pangolin?'

'It's a scaly mammal. Now, I do urge you to hold out for your visit until six o'clock on one of your days here, when there's a nightly performance by Cirque Du Soleil in the sacristy. If you would all follow me we'll head around the corner to the Scuola di San Rocco, where we'll see some paintings done by the real-life ancestors of Randy Quaid.' And they did.

'*Anaïs?*'

'Hm?'

'What are you doing for the rest of the afternoon?!'

'Oh. No, I have to meet the Serbian ambassador,' she said, impatient of his attention.

'That sounds so exciting.'

'It's not. He's a muppet and an imbecile and a pervert.'

'Oh. Do you want me to come with you and cover you? I'll be invisible.'

'How will you be invisible, Stan?'

'Uhhh…'

141

'Exactly. What a stupid thing to say. I would prefer it if you were invisible very far away from me. I do very, very, dangerous work, Stan. And I'm a Jew.'

'I know, stop reminding me. I'm not happy about it but I'm coming to accept it.'

'It's not an award, Stan. I am who I am.'

'And I am who I am, and who I am loves you who you are.'

'You're confusing me.'

'When can I see you next?'

'I'll get a message to you as soon as I can. Have an afternoon.'

'Be safe.'

And they stood facing one another in the campo, both expecting the other to leave first. Eventually Anaïs flicked her finger towards Stanley's rear and he said, 'Oh, I should go.'

'Yes.'

'Goodbye.'

Anaïs nodded impatiently.

'I love you.'

And she shook her head and Stanley backed away until he tripped over the bridge's first steps and fell onto his fingertips and hurried off around a corner.

She walked slowly home and ascended the steel stairs to the Bolani's *piano nobile* and stood again looking out onto the Canal. It was a bright mid-afternoon and warm. The pale colours of the houses, of the boats, of the water—puce and grey and asparagus—seemed brightly burning hues. Wakes shimmered and shadows soared long. Anaïs went upstairs to change and sat on the bed and slid off her shoes. Then the shower was turned on. No sound had ever seemed to her louder than did its gushing. She looked to the bathroom door. It was closed. In the corner between the dresser and the window was another, much larger and navy blue, suitcase. No piece of luggage had ever seemed so malevolent. The bathroom door, the vanity table—somebody else's make-up case. Anaïs unzipped it and opened it and inspected it with her fingertips. Nothing suspicious therein, though she handled the object like an improvised explosive device. She went to the suitcase and lifted its lid. Clothes as elegant as any she wore, though less fashionable. Then the shower was turned off. Terrifying silence, until the door within was slid open. Very shortly the bathroom door swung out and a

142

woman stepped, dripping wet, fully into the bedroom.

'Hello there,' she chimed, seemingly nothing more commonplace than her emergence from this of all bathrooms. She rubbed her long wet hair with a towel between her hands and crossed the room to put one hand into Anaïs'. 'Emma.' She was a decade older than Anaïs but just as slim, and on a slighter frame. Her cheekbones were full and through age pronounced and her skin was tight and mottled.

'Anaïs,' said Anaïs, slowly and almost as a question.

'I like your name.'

'Thank you.'

'What exactly are you doing here?'

'Thank you.'

'What are you doing here?'

'I'm staying here,' she said, though she was no longer certain of the fact.

'In my house?'

Anaïs could think of nothing to say that would not sound pathetic. Emma returned to the bathroom and turned on a hair dryer. She re-emerged, brushing her hair, without either of the towels. Her breasts sat perfectly upon her chest and nothing from her waist to her thighs sagged or even mildly hung. Her body, more than trim, was tight.

Anaïs averted her eyes and said nervously, 'Not umm… Not Johnny's palazzo? It's not Johnny's house?'

'Johnny Goodenough?'

'Yes.'

'You mean my husband? I'm sorry, did I only give you my first name? Emma Goodenough. No, I don't care for the surname, but tradition is tradition.'

'He umm… He told me that…'

'He what, darling?'

'He told me that ummm…'

'He told you I was dead, didn't he?'

'No.'

'That's the third time, the little shit. The whores annoy me, but it's just offensive telling you girls that I'm dead. He's a coward, a cheating lying coward. Where is he?'

'I have no idea.'

'Where is he?' she repeated, as though by this routine which she knew very well she would have to ask three times before receiving a truthful answer.

'I really don't know.'

'Where is he?' she concluded.

'I really haven't seen him today.'

'Is he at the Café Florian?'

'Honestly I don't know.'

'Is he at The Saracen? Just tell me where he is. I'll find him eventually whether you tell me or not. You've already further wrecked my crumbling home. At least make my life just a little bit easier for today. Where is he, darling?'

But only one other person knew where Johnny Goodenough was.

He was walking along a quiet street in Cannaregio. The day was latening and the shadows falling slowly over. He was deep in thought, trying to figure out how the hell he was going to get Anaïs to sleep with him. This one thought had preoccupied him now for a week. Deep in thought, that is, until Stanley Felix, astride scaffolding over the very same Cannaregio street and holding over his head a cinder block attached to a rope, mistimed the release of his very sizeable projectile. It swung down into the underpassage and missed Johnny's face by a foot. It hit the underside of the planks on which he was hunting. Thinking he must have at the very least stunned his prey, he leapt down onto the stones. He was surprised to find Johnny waiting with fists clenched. The two men took in fully one another's faces— Johnny's confused and Stanley's enraged—and the former knocked the latter in the jaw before the latter tackled Johnny into the wall. They proceeded to throw fists at one another until it became clear to Stanley that his was the losing battle. He simply could not land a punch. He backed away towards a wide canal and jumped onto the first boat that passed. Both his feet hit the bow at the same time and then instantly both his feet left the bow at the same time as he bounced backwards into the water, legs over head. Johnny brushed the brick dust from his jacket sleeves and returned to his conspiring.

Anaïs rolled her suitcase into the crimson lobby of the Hotel Metropole. Stanley Felix was out so she waited in the restaurant. When an hour later he arrived soaking wet she feigned distress and embraced him.

'Everything. Everything's been compromised. They nearly got me.'

'The Russian?'

'The Russians. They nearly got me. I got away. They stole my purse and now I can't use my locker at the train station. I've only got…' She checked her purse. '…eight euros.'

'Don't worry about money. I can take care of that. But you can't be seen with me. The Russian knows what I look like.'

'But where will I—. Wait, what?'

'The Russian. He knows what I look like.'

She became serious. 'How does he know what you look like?'

'That's not important.'

'Why are you soaking wet?'

'Acqua alta.'

'There isn't any. And you've got marks all over your face. Were you punched? Who punched you? Did the Russian punch you?'

'I fell over.'

'Stanley.'

'Nobody. I fell over on the street, honestly. And then I rolled into a canal. And then a boat ran me over. It's true.'

'You're a terrible liar.'

'No I'm not.'

'How much money do you have? I'm sorry to be so vulgar.'

'I suppose I have about a thousand euros in cash.'

'Israel thanks you. I'll get it all back to you with interest when I get back to Jerusalem.'

'All of it?'

'As much as you can spare.'

'So your meeting didn't go too well then?'

'Which meeting?'

'With the Slovenian ambassador.'

'Oh yes. No. Very counter-productive. I pissed him off royally. Then the Russians ransacked the embassy. I was lucky to get away.'

'You told me you were meeting with the Serbian ambassador.'

'Don't be foolish.'

'You did.'

'Trieste shares a border with Slovenia, not Serbia.'

'I know what you told me.'

'*I* know what *I* told you.' She looked to her left and then their right and then went to the restaurant's two entrances and peered furtively out before returning to Stanley. 'Can you have dinner with me?'

'Really?'

'Really.'

'I'd absolutely love to. Can we go for a gondola ride afterwards?'

'No. But I do need a room for tonight. Do they have one free here? And you can't know which one it is.'

'That was *un*believable,' said Anaïs, putting down her spoon after it had been unburdened of the last of the tiramisu. They were in La Bugiarda.

'Anaïs, are you sleeping with the Russian spy? I need to know.'

'Hm?'

'I know where he's staying.'

'You shouldn't know that, Stanley.'

'I followed you after your dinner and I followed him after he tried to get you into that gondola.' Anaïs stared at him, furious. 'Are you sleeping with him? Is he a Jew?'

'You are acting like a child.'

'He *is* a Jew. God-damn it. I hate them so much. Stealing my women and ruining the world. Is it because I'm not good-looking enough?' Anaïs had already thrown her napkin upon the table in warning. 'It is isn't it? I've been eating too well in Italy. I'll slim down. Or is it because his job is more interesting than mine? I'll become a spy too. I've got duel citizenship. British and American. I could—'

'Goodnight, Stanley.'

'Is he *really* rich? I'm rich too. You know that. How rich can he be? Is he Jewish rich?'

But she was already out the door. Stanley called for the bill so that he could chase after her. Anaïs chose the smallest alleys and the nearest turns in the opposite direction to that from which they had come. But it was no trouble for Johnny Goodenough.

He kept pace with her out of the restaurant and followed the sound of her platforms upon the stones. He caught her on the Riva Olio and said, 'Who was that?' She let out a muffled scream of pure frustration. 'Are you sleeping with him?' And another far less muffled scream which almost bloomed into a cackle.

'Who is he?' he called after her. 'You're seeing someone else. My wife told me.'

'Your dead wife?'

'Yes.'

'And how does she know what I'm up to?'

'She's the most conniving person I've ever come across. And that's saying a lot. Who is he?'

'He's just somebody I know.'

'And you're sleeping with him?'

Anaïs screeched and stormed down the steps and walked beneath the red columns of the pescaria.

'Is it because I'm not good-looking enough? Emma said I'm younger than him. How handsome is he? … Is he rich? I'm rich too. How rich can he be? … Does he own a palazzo?'

'Certainly not with his wife, no. … You lied to me, John John. You told a horrible, horrible lie, just so that you could sleep with me *Her death stripped me of all illusions about the benevolence of the universe*?' she said, slowly and sarcastically repeating his confessional. 'Please.'

'You do nothing but lie!'

'You knew all along that nothing I said was the truth. *We* laboured under the assumption that you *only* told the truth. That means you lied.'

'Equivocation.'

'Do you have any idea how embarrassing it was? I arrive home one afternoon and your dead wife is in the shower.'

'She said she didn't mind.'

'For me you idiot! Now stop following me. Stop right there.' She pointed at his feet. They were atop the Rialto.

He put his hands up and said, 'All right.'

'I'm going to bed now, Johnny.'

'I love you.'

'Shut up. I'm going to bed now and I don't want to be followed. If you see me again in Venice I want you to turn around and walk the other way. I am exactly where I want to be and I want to be left alone.'

'Where are you staying?'

'I'm not telling you.'

'I'm in the Hotel Metropole if you want to contact me.'

The evening's most forceful muffled scream. 'Go,' she ordered from behind clenched teeth. 'Turn around and walk away. I'm going to bed.'

And for thirty minutes she attempted to walk south in the hope of beating Johnny back to the hotel. When she made it to the riva she approached the Metropole slowly from the east and scoped out its entrance for her pursuers. Neither were about. She put her head down and hurried to cross the lobby to the telephone booth. She stood inside it with the door ajar for a few moments and then crept to the corner of reception to survey the restaurant. She found nobody present except the bemused receptionist, whom she asked for her key before going up to bed.

III

Anaïs sat on her windowsill six floors above the green of a thin canal—'*There's coming a day when the world shall melt away…*'—surrounded by the mauve damask and copper silk of her suite, leaning out to try to get a better view of San Giorgio Maggiore—'*No more tears, no pain, no woe, in this wicked world below…*'—and the white and blue sunshine of the fresh morning. Her hands were clasped below her bent knees; Hank Williams had been chanting and strumming the same song for a quarter of an hour. '*In this world of greed and hate will you wait till it's too late…*' The music faded in and out of her attention, fragments of its lyric bringing Anaïs back from the blue skies to her phone on the bed and into the suite. '*For he's coming someday to bear your soul away. Then will you be ready to go home?*'

Stanley Felix prepared to take his breakfast in the hotel restaurant. He read the news on his phone and sipped at his orange juice and left his bacon and eggs untouched when he spotted out of the corner of his eye Johnny Goodenough striding across the lobby.

It was one of Johnny's great Venetian pleasures to stroll to the Arsenale in the mornings before the tourists were loosed. It was quiet and open and the morning sun hit upon his face as he leaned on the wooden balustrade of the bridge and imagined before him the busiest industrial complex in the world. Had he known that that morning he would there be intercepted by his wife he would have gone on to the Biennale Gardens.

'What?' he yawned angrily, expecting to be epically nagged.

'Don't say it like that, darling. You say it as though you don't want to see me. I want to make things right between us. I want to have brunch with you. Meet me at eleven? In the Campo dei Frari?'

Though suspicious he agreed to do so.

'See that wasn't so hard,' and she smacked her lips together to sound a kiss and left.

A short time later, as he was struck in the back of the neck with an orange life preserver by Stanley Felix in his morning shorts, Johnny thought that as he fell he should probably look back up to the broken balustrade in order to see his assailant. Sure enough, there was Stanley Felix in his morning shorts holding an orange life preserver. Stanley let out a, 'Ha ha!' at his accomplishment as Johnny's back came floating up to the surface. He found a bounce in his step as he walked down the steps. There would have been far less of a bounce had he been able to see, two feet into the jade of the canal, Johnny's feet kicking him slowly towards the mossy steps which allowed his alarmingly hasty exit from the water. Stanley had never before attempted to kill somebody. He was finding little satisfaction in failing to do so. Indeed he was discovering it to be something of a frightening pursuit. But, he being in, as well as his morning shorts, his runners, and Johnny being in loafers, Stanley pulled quickly away and turned onto the Riva, where he was promptly called into a café by a striking brunette woman. She gestured for him to duck into the bathroom.

When Johnny had sprinted by, his wife told Stanley that it was safe to come out.

'Thank you.'

'But of course.'

'Who are you?'

Johnny checked his watch. It was three minutes to. He put his hands in his pockets and watched the morning crowd snake. His wife watched him through the window of the gelateria. Two minutes later Stanley Felix crossed the bridge and came to stand at Johnny's side. Johnny had spotted a particularly stare-worthy pair of cheeks and was watching them climb and fall as they went down a calle. Stanley checked his own watch and then watched some tourists get into a gondola to his right. The tight behind disappeared around the corner and Johnny turned and watched the embarkation of the gondola. Their heads moved in unison for a few turns, to the left and the length of the Frari, straight ahead to its façade, to the right and the bridge, straight ahead, left—until Johnny caught sight of a passing brunette's legs and followed them to the bridge. Then their four eyes met.

'You!' said Johnny Goodenough. Stanley's eyes popped open from fright. 'Why are you trying to kill me?'

'I'm going to kill you before you kill her,' and he grappled

Johnny at his shoulders and the two men pushed one another to and fro and side to side.

'Before I kill who?' said Johnny.

'I'm in love with her.'

'In love with who!?'

'You know who.'

'I don't know who,' said Johnny, finding the strength to break Stanley's hold on him. They stood aback from one another.

'You do know who,' said Stanley, panting.

'Who?' And then Johnny realised. He moaned in decrescendo: 'Anaïs.'

'You know her real name?' puffed Stanley.

'Anaïs,' said Johnny, tiring of it. 'And who do you think Anaïs actually is, old timer?'

'I can't tell you that. But I know who you are, Jew.'

'How about I give you a multiple choice? Do you think that Anaïs works for a – MI6, b – the CIA, or c – for Mossad?'

Stanled gasped. 'I have to warn her.' And he lunged to put Johnny in a headlock. Johnny struggled against it and threw punches at Stanley's gut. He was quickly able to invert the grip.

'Stop... trying... to kill me.'

'Never!'

'You two are pathetic.'

Doubled over, the men looked up from the pavement and saw black stilettos, long glistening legs, high khaki shorts, a white shirt, a popped collar, a loose ponytail—at last all of Emma Goodenough standing goddess-like before them.

'The Jew-wife,' said Stanley Felix.

She said, with a sympathy which smacked at the borders of patronisation, 'In love with a girl who's telling you she's a spy and trying to kill my husband, who is not one, in order to protect her. And you. Darling husband. Are in love with a girl because she reminds you of... of you.'

'I don't care who she is,' said Stanley, taking advantage of the lull in hostilities to again reverse the headlock. 'I love her!'

'So do I,' said Johnny, rising tall to lift Stanley from his feet. 'I'm sorry, honey, but I've fallen in love with her.'

'You'll never get her! She'll never love you. I saved her life.'

'So did I, Gandalf!'

'I'm not old! And you're a Jew! And a Russian.'

'Why do you keep calling me a Jew? I'm not Russian either.'

Then Anaïs entered the campo. She had come to catch that young man's fantastical tour. She found merely, together in this one glorious square, all the players in her present nightmare. Its supporting actress, immensely excited to see her, waved her over. 'You know there's only one way to settle this boys?'

They again paused their attempts to kill one another and, huffing, looked up at Emma. Shortly they both yelled, 'A duel!'

'You're idiots.'

'Venetian style!' yelled Johnny.

'Just you and me,' yelled Stanley.

'On gondolas!'

'Anaïs!' said Stanley, his excitement escaping through the blows which rained upon his torso.

'I love you!' said Johnny, taking a combo to the leg.

'*I* love you!'

Anaïs stood among blue and white bollards in a motoscafo which Emma Goodenough had moored outside the Palazzo Balbi.

'Men,' reflected Emma.

'Yep.'

And from the east, rowed down the Grand Canal by four men, there stood in a black gondola Stanley Felix holding an oar blade-up in his right hand. From the south there stood in a black gondola rowed at pace by four other men Johnny Goodenough. Tiny and pathetic figures in the picturesque distance, they had agreed that a run-up of a hundred and fifty metres would best enable them to reach what they were both shouting out to their drummers as ramming speed. They rapidly enlarged as they neared one another. Their helmsmen lined up the prow heads and both men widened their stance and readied their oars. They faltered as they came into clear view of the women, both thinking momentarily upon the consequences of a full-swung oar to the temple. But there was no backing out. Their Anaïs was watching. A thing as noble and as fair as she would love no coward, they both thought. Instantly they regained their resolve. Their boats glided quickly past one another and Johnny yelled out, 'Freedom!' and Stanley roared and yelled, 'Jew!' and they commenced their backswings at the same time, both men mistiming—the oar tips wooshed across their respective backs.

'Massimo, you get me closer!' Johnny yelled as his crew turned the boat about. They rose again from attack to ramming speed. 'Più vicino! … *Più vicino, Massimo!*'

The drummers amidships hastened their beaten pace and the prow heads were returned to parallel. Stanley yelled, 'You'll never have her!' as he readied his oar like a baseball bat. Johnny matched his stance and as the two men met he preempted Stanley's home run and brought his oar around and with its round end prodded him in the face. Stanley fell swiftly backwards into the canal and Johnny held his oar high. Surrounded by the resounding green of the canal and its thousand windows, he rejoiced. 'Yeah!' he yelled, as Massimo rowed him slowly over to the motoscafo. 'She's mine! … You're mine! … Anaïs, you're all—'

So ecstatic was he that he had ignored completely the fact that his very alive wife might be finding this whole tournament something rather more than offensive. She picked up a plastic oar from among the life jackets at her feet and serenely prodded her husband in the face. He was soon, for the first time in a decade of visiting his wife's most beloved city, swimming in the Grand Canal, and bleeding.

'Thank you, Massimo,' said Emma.

'Prego, signora.'

'I really am sorry,' said Anaïs.

'Oh you weren't to know, dear.'

Anaïs stepped up onto the jetty and wandered the pink bricks and mossy stucco of San Polo's high and cool alleys. For a time she was brought to an awed standstill by the most marvellously quaint canal that she had yet seen. A verdant and sunlit masterpiece, she followed the golden arrow of its antique russet sign to 'Tintoretto.' She soon, oblivious, ascended the steps of the Scuola di San Rocco and paid from Stanley Felix's money the entrance fee.

In a barely lit baroque hall which she could not comprehend— the chequered marble floor, the corinthian capitals, the carena di nave ceiling—she found vast paintings upon the walls. Anaïs knew very little about art. But looking up at that nearest the entrance, an Annunciation, at its white-robed angel, the host of cherubim, the fury of light in a band of darkness, the luminescent dove, the exposed bricks, the rumbling mess of timber, the virgin's Venetian bedroom—she could tell that there was just something about it. It could have been the most renowned painting in the world or the most derided. She loved it, instantly and completely. She was twenty minutes at its foot, staring up and, as so few do before paintings, thinking. She could not resolve the lambent riddle of its charm but was nevertheless bewitched. She passed by the Adoration and the Flight into Egypt and came to a Slaughter of the Innocents. She recognised there the same fury, the same sorrow, and joy, the depth of thought and feeling, the colour, the even brisker method. She was a further fifteen minutes before its lusting soldiers and topless mothers.

At the school's entrance that handsome tour guide nodded to the man behind the ticket window and the price list was swapped for another.

Anaïs turned and approached a Presentation At The Temple as a Scuola employee extended a metallic gate across the entrance to the upper hall. 'Closed for Restoration,' dangled as a sign at its centre. Then into the hall entered, orating, the young man and his tour. He had with him four Americans, three Australians, two English, and, his favourite, a pair of Japanese—all rushing to pay the illicit entry fee.

'Now despite the fact that the School of Saint Roch was only ever actually used for puppy classes, then as the model for Scrooge McDuck's money-pit, some of the paintings, as you'll see, are actually pretty good. Most of them are coloured in. And all of them contain hidden portraits of Woody Allen. And the backgammon,' he said, firmly to the Japanese couple. 'Backgammon?' he asked, and they nodded. 'I thought so. It took Tintoretto six days to paint the six paintings here in the lower hall. He went through fifty-five art smocks and ate forty-two kilograms of cheese and then afterwards he went on a motorbike trip across Thailand and wasn't to paint another thing until a young Danish girl asked him to do her fingernails. Donkeyfighting?' he asked of the Japanese. He pointed a finger at both of them and they, in their visors and large shoes, nodded and smiled and attempted to repeat his question as an answer.

'Darkufaity.'

'Exactly.' And he took the group through the story behind

each painting. 'You must understand that this was before the days of telephones or CCTV and back then, in the event of an evil baby home invasion led by a glow-in-the-dark chicken, most housewives cried out for the protection of angels. ... Here we have the world's first ever game of "Guess how many jelly beans are in the jelly-bean jar." ... This was just an orgy. Tintoretto loved them. He talks in his letters of a golden ratio, six women and two babies to every man. ... Here's a Santa Claus in judgment ... Fisherman three?' he asked the Japanese. 'Fisherman you motorcycle,' and they seemed not only to understand but to agree. 'This woman here took so much helium at a full moon party that she is actually floating away, while her friends, who she thinks are being boring because they all have girlfriends, attempt to keep her down. Tintoretto loved his native Thailand almost as much as he did his adopted Venice.'

He at last led them to the centre of the room and hushed his voice and turned his back to them. 'This room is the culmination of four centuries of Venetian art and so of its history. After the death of Tintoretto, he whose paintings you see upon these walls, all is decline and decadence and, for men with hearts, death and sorrow.' He looked over most of the room and came at last to stare at Anaïs. 'Richard Burton once said of this School and its paintings, (here he broke into loud impersonation) "In the memory of vanished hours so filled with beauty the consciousness of present loss oppresses. Exquisite hours, enveloped in light and silence, to have known them once is to have always a terrible standard of enjoyment." And I think I'll leave you with that.' He turned back to his tour group. 'I do hope you've enjoyed today. As you already know I don't charge for my tours but I do allow all my new students to donate whatever they think is fair. I'll be around for the next few minutes if any of you have any questions and I sincerely hope you all enjoy the rest of your time in Venice. Thank you.'

All lined up to thank him deeply and to donate, quickly to disperse. He took in the day's cash and spun around to say to Anaïs, who had crossed the hall to be close behind him, 'Salve.'

'You're a liar.'

He put his hands in his pockets and beamed. 'I know. Isn't it marvellous?'

'Did Richard Burton really say that about Venice?'

'Henry James wrote it, about this room.' The last of the boy's tour left and the metallic gate was refolded and the original price list restored. 'What's your name and why are you following me?'

'Following you?'

'I've seen you three days in a row.'

'Don't flatter yourself,' said Anaïs. 'Venice is a city full of coincidences.'

'In an ordered universe there are no such things as coincidences.'

'Is the universe ordered?'

'It had better be. Otherwise I've spent five years basing all my major life decisions on coincidences. I'm Octavian,' and he calmly extended his hand.

'That's not your name.'

'It is.'

'It is not. Come on!'

'Do you not like it?'

'No I really do.'

'Woah, easy! What's yours?'

'Anaïs.'

'Anaïs. ... I just made a small fortune, Anaïs. Let me take you to dinner.'

'Tonight?'

'Now.'

'It's two o'clock.'

'Have you not had a Venetian dinner?' Anaïs smiled. 'Shall we away?'

'Ciao, dottore!'

'Ciao, Paola,' returned this Octavian into a bacaro.

'A doctor?' said Anaïs.

'Some of them *may* think I'm a history professor.'

Anaïs pointed to the tiny orange-walled San Polo bar which they neared as they walked. 'Buongiorno, Contessa!' was called out from it.

'Buongiorno, Silvio! Tutto bene?'

'A countess?'

'Nothing more and nothing less.'

'And you speak Italian?'

'I once spent six months in a monastery in Rome having the

authenticity of my stigmata investigated.'

'And what did they conclude?'

'Divinely favoured, but no saint. Do you speak it?'

'I can speak Hungarian. And Mongolian. And Turkish.' His smile told her that he was itching to expound. 'All history is invasion. I thought I'd get a head start and learn the languages of the invaders, just in case.'

'And you have a history degree? No.'

'Molecular biology.'

'Mmm,' groaned Anaïs, bored.

'My team was the first to genetically engineer a mermaid.'

'I used to work as a mermaid!'

'At Disneyland?'

'All over the place. I owned a leg suit, a clamshell bra, prosthetic gills, algae-coloured glitter. I could hold my breath for seven minutes.'

'We almost caught a mermaid once.'

'On your genetics team?'

'When I was a merchant mariner. An able-bodied seaman. Do I still look able-bodied?' He pointed a fingertip to his chest. 'What do you think? I'm very insecure about it.'

She pondered and looked him up and down. 'Mmmm.' His wrinkled white oxford shirt was untucked over khaki trousers. 'You look competently-bodied.'

'Fair enough. She surfaced near the Cape of Good Hope,' he said in his intense Welsh sailor's accent. 'We went around the horn, all the way to Ceylon, and there lost sight of her.'

Two Spaniards had for ten minutes been standing on a not very picturesque bridge attempting to take of themselves and their children a photograph which captured the entire backdrop of glare, plain wall and ditchwater. Wife soon began imploring husband to just ask somebody to take it for them. He was very reluctant to do so, largely because he did not feel that in six months' time the photographs would mean anything. For once he had clinched the promotion he was sure he was about to get he could finally afford to keep a much nicer woman and to leave this hag with their doofus offspring. More photographs would simply be a hindrance to emotional progress. His present wife clicked her tongue and decided to just ask the next tourist who passed. 'I am sorry, please could you take for us a photo?'

'Yes!' said Octavian, smiling idiotically as he crossed the bridge without breaking stride.

'Have you *been* to the Andaman islands?' said Anaïs.

'Yes. Where are they?'

'In the Bay of Bengal. Next to Sri Lanka. Mermaid country. I was there with the last expedition to try to give them fire.'

'The mermaids?'

'The Andamanese.'

'Did they not have it?'

'They and the Tasmanian aborigines were the last people on earth not to. Now they're the only ones not to.'

'They didn't take it?'

'They shot me.'

'Where?'

'On the beach, as soon as we landed.'

'Where on your body?'

'Here, look,' and Anaïs pulled her collar across to show him her only chicken pox scar.

'Shot you with what?'

'A poison dart. I was hallucinating for a week, thought I was being ambushed by cave chickens.'

'I was demented from a cave chicken once!' he said, excited to be able to tell his cave chicken story. 'I ate one in Hanoi. Walking around for three days screeching at people that my name was Bob and that the answer was blowing in the wind.'

'What year was that?'

'Two thousand and ten.'

'The year I bought my first peacock,' said Anaïs.

'You owned a peacock?'

'My dear, every peacock owner knows that one never truly *owns* a peacock. They are immortal, and belong entirely to God.'

They walked through the pescaria. The young man who called himself Octavian led Anaïs to a traghetto landing.

'And in safekeeping a peacock one…' Her pause was the sole betrayal of her elation as they stepped down into a gondola and wafted across the Grand Canal in the perfect sunshine of a perfect afternoon in a perfect boat. 'Has to…' But she could not speak, so overtaken by the brief but entirely splendid boat ride was she.

'You were saying?'

'I was saying.'

'What were you saying?'

'I can't remember,' said Anaïs. 'Oh, yes! Did you know I'm the only known descendant of Robin Hood?'

'I didn't know that.'

'And Russell Crowe's my uncle. What are the chances?'

'*My* uncle's the world's biggest exporter of leopards.'

'I once spent a semester in a colony of lepers, in Hawaii. I was teaching them how to have higher self-esteem.'

'And Rex Harrison was my godfather.'

'I almost played Eliza Doolittle on Broadway.'

'Almost?'

'Rex Harrison was my godfather.'

'Yours too?'

'And the other cast members accused me of nepotism.'

'Nepotism, the curse of curses.'

'Is that Shakespeare?'

'No, it's my dad. He was a coiner.'

'He was a coiner?'

'Of phrases. For a living. None of us have had to work a day since he coined the phrase, "Cut off your nose to spite your face." We get royalties every time someone uses it. Do you know how he came up with it?'

'I don't.'

'He cut his nose off to spite his face.'

'What had he against it?'

'A knife.'

'Before he cut it.'

'Oh. Well he was fighting with hajjis in Fallujah and then his platoon was surrounded by the British. All homosexuals of course, so the Iraqis decided that rather than being molested by infidels that they would disfigure themselves.'

'And your dad did it too?'

'One must conform.'

'And he's dead now?'

'No, he's ugly.'

'That's quite a family you've got there. And while yours was running around exporting big cats and fighting the British mine were busy getting raped by Cossacks.'

'Wagner, Max! Totally irrational and crazy and absurd and, but

159

ah, I guess we keep going through it because… we need the eggs.'

They crossed a stone bridge to where the stencilled street sign overhead read, 'Fondamenta de la Misericordia.' Octavian pointed ahead to some empty chairs and he stopped at the doorway to a restaurant and let Anaïs enter before him.

'Buongiorno, Ottaviano,' said the ponytailed and moustachioed young man from behind the high bar.

'Ciao, Gio.'

It was a long dining hall furnished in dark wood. A high glass case with three shelves of metallic plates heaped with seafood and marinating vegetables ran into a small bar of steel taps flowing with wine and beer. Waiters and waitresses were pouring and making and delivering drinks, preparing platters, slicing and apportioning bread into baskets; old recordings of old jazz played softly from the back of the room.

Octavian ordered effortlessly in Italian and asked Anaïs if she wanted to grab the table outside. The entranceway, with a mosaic overhead of doves and waves and the humble name *Paradiso Perduto*, looked over a thin canal and faced a high wall of red brick. Octavian soon emerged into the quiet sunshine with two wine glasses of bright orange liquid and a skewered olive.

'What the hell is that?'

'Have you not had one? *How* long have you been here?'

'Four days.'

'And you're doing what here exactly? Are you a tourist heavily?'

'No,' she said, playfully disapproving of his insolence.

'And what brings you to Venice then?'

'I, Octavian, have always felt that I would end up here. And somehow I have, ended up here.'

'Is this the end?'

'Do you think it is?'

'How should I know? Taste that.'

She pushed the skewer back with her finger and drank. '*That's* amazing.' Astonished, she broke into a smile. Then she moaned with pleasure. 'That…' she sipped again. 'Oh. … It tastes like sunshine. You could drink that all day.'

'And so we shall,' he assured her.

'What's it called?'

'Spritz Aperol,' he said with a very attractive Italian accent.

From within was brought a large plate arrayed with every deliciousness that Anaïs had yet tasted from the lagoon. 'The fish and chips are cold,' she said, touching them with the backs of her fingers. Then she had some. '*That's* amazing. It's delicious.'

'You just ate mermaid tail.'

She cackled and then tucked into the grilled vegetables.

'All mermaid stories aside, you're in Venice why?'

'Why?'

'Yes. How did you come to be sitting at Paradise Lost?'

'Well you walked into that gallery today didn't you?'

'Not today. I mean how have you ended up here? What have you fled? All strangers who come to Venice have fled something. The city was founded by refugees. They fled the Germans. You've fled something, no? Or you were just in the area and you wandered across the rail bridge? Snuck past all the security? You know that's me?'

'What's you?'

'The terrorist threat to blow up the bridge.'

'That's you?'

'Anything to discourage them.'

'To discourage who?'

'The terrorists.'

'The terrorists?'

'Turks.'

'What?'

'Tourists, Anaïs.'

'And you're not a tourist?' Octavian shook his head. 'But you are a terrorist?'

'It is incumbent upon me. So come on then. Was your heart broken, Anaïs? Declare everything.'

'Everything?'

'Everything.'

'No.'

'All right then.'

'But...' And she began to mimic: 'Miss Spencer. As special gift of Cathay Pacific Airline we would rike to offer you flee upgrade for business crass today. Is that OK for you?'

EPISODE 4

Dare Not To Such Thoughts Aspire.

I

'So you see?,' said Anaïs, sliding with her teeth another olive from its orange-soaked skewer. 'Tossed by innumerable tempests and chased by idiots from every shore, I am at last in Venice.' Their plate had upon it only dyed oil and flakes of herb and eight, now nine, oliveless skewers.

'What time is it?' said Octavian.

'I have no idea.'

'I want to show you something.' He asked a waitress to hold their table for him. 'Certo, certo.' And then he set off down the street. 'Come come.' The sky was beginning to breathe colour. Dusk was rising. Octavian rushed ahead as they crossed one bridge and Anaïs came to his side at a second. She exhaled, long and softly, and was immediately relaxed. Across the bridge was a high red-brick church frosted with dripping white arches and finials. The water-stained stucco of the backs of the houses overlooking the canal had blushed to a deep pink. Little covered motor boats were moored along this delightful canal whose waters shone with the daffodil and tangerine and mauve of a sunset, repeated in reverse at the narrow and distant horizon up to an ecstatic blue and darkening firmament.

'Slow falls the eventide in Venice,' said Octavian.

Anaïs put her hands down onto the cold stone of the bridge and sighed inaudibly and they watched in silence until night set in.

Paradiso Perduto was full inside and out. Tables had been set up at the canal's edge and the space just inside the entrance, between the bar and the tables, was crammed with tourists waiting to be seated and with waiters yelling at them to make way. Benny Goodman and his Sextet had been turned up and

Octavian returned to the canalside with white wine.

'By the jug?' said Anaïs.

'By the jug.'

'Amazing.'

'Can you hear that?' Still standing, his arms were out at his sides and his fingers and foot and head were tapping to the music.

'What?'

'Honeysuckle Rose,' he smiled at her. She was enthralled by the joy he took in a song she had never heard. He poured their wines out as he danced and held his glass to hers. 'Salute.'

'Viva.'

'What's Viva?'

'That's how they say cheers in Brazil. To life.'

'You've been to Brazil?'

'I rode a motorbike from the mouth of the Amazon to Mexico City.'

'I rode one from Saigon to Constantinople.'

'And what was that like?'

'Hot.'

And they spent the evening recounting road trips that were more detailed, more fanciful, more elaborately structured than any epic ever invented, on the spot, by Homer, Swift, or Virgil. Before they had left the illegal gambling rings and presidential races of their first countries they had finished the first jug of wine and put in a standing order for a full one. By the time they were swapping notes of horror on Bangladesh they were hungry again and ordered another plate of cold fish and chips and fried scampi. The kitchen closed as Anaïs discovered a new species of flesh-eating capybara and Octavian ordered a tiramisu that again found Anaïs speechless. She found his narrative increasingly captivating. Drinks were cut off while Octavian was inferring from Attic fragments the heiroglyphs of an Azerbaijani river tribe, which, going by the slightness of the insult needed to send its warriors upstream to pee, he claimed was the country's most vindictive.

When she began to guess at the name of the Incan dwarf who plagued the desert of her payotic visions the two of them subsided into a crippling giggle and their road trips diffused to an end.

'So tell me,' said Octavian, returning to upright in his chair and sighing with the end of long laughter. 'What have you seen so far?'

'What have I seen?'

'In Venice.'

'I've seen a lot.'

'San Giovanni e Paolo?'

'I don't know.'

'San Pantalon?'

'No idea.'

'The Campo Santa Maria Formosa?'

'I really don't know. I've just been walking around.'

'But have you seen the Piazza San Marco?'

'That I definitely haven't seen.'

'Very good.'

'Why is that good?'

'There's no other time to see it than late at night, when it's empty. Will you meet me there?'

'When?'

'Now,' he said, as though there could only have been one answer.

'What do you mean now? Why don't you walk me there you idiot?'

'Meet me there,' he said, thrilled, and he sprung himself out of his chair and strode off down the street and leapt up and down the bridge and was gone before Anaïs could figure out if he was being serious or not. A waitress placed their bill on the table as her colleagues brought the outside tables in. Anaïs looked up at her, very shiny-eyed. 'I…' she said, looking to the bridge for Octavian's return. 'That little shit,' she said and eventually managed to pull her purse from her handbag. She then paid, albeit with someone else's money, her first restaurant bill in seven years. The ten spritz aperols and three jugs of wine were the first drinks for which she had paid in six.

She asked the waitress if she knew where the Piazza San Marco was.

'That way for two bridges, then you just I think follow the signs.'

At first she crept, expecting and hoping that Octavian would jump out from a doorway to scare her. After five minutes she hastened, following the black and yellow placards overhead for *S. Marco*. She came to a small retail neighbourhood devoid of people and wound her way along avenues of hideous and atrociously expensive fashion until she quite accidentally entered the arcade of an enormous piazza. At its end the blooming gables and heavy domes of the basilica rose like dark fire and mushroom cloud over the scaffolding which covered its façade. She stepped out from the gallery and had St Mark's square completely to herself. She edged forwards, spinning slowly around to take in the whole lovely view of white-lit arcades and dark and dirty arches.

'What do you think?' Octavian, entered from beneath the clocktower, called in Al Pacino's voice across the piazza.

'It's amazing,' she yelled.

'You like that word don't you?'

'Can you think of a better one, for Venice?'

'Exquisite.'

They met near the middle of the square.

'It's completely empty.'

'The terrorists are all in bed by ten o'clock. At night we have the whole city to ourselves.'

Anaïs ambled across the piazzetta, awed by the façade of the Ducal Palace, to the lagoon. Octavian explained the stories behind the statues of Saint Theodore and the Lion of Venice and Anaïs said, 'Will you walk me home?'

And as they strolled along the divinely empty riva to the Metropole:

'What are you doing tomorrow?'

'What should I be doing tomorrow?'

'Let me show you Venice.'

Anaïs nodded.

'I'll pick you up at eight.'

'AM?!'

'Too early?'

'Too early.'

'Eight-thirty?'

'Eleven.'

'Neither the damned nor dickheads rise before eight am. We'd have the whole city to ourselves. The day's over by eleven. There'll be terrorists everywhere.'

'I'm not getting up at eight-thirty.'

'Eleven?'

'Goodnight.'

'Goodnight.'

And she said to the night porter, adamantly and with a slight but obvious slur, 'Signore, please do not tell anybody which room I am in, not even Signor Felix, especially not Signor Felix, or Signor Johnny Goodenough, and don't tell them if I'm in or not. OK? Tell everyone who enquires of me that I am out.' And she hiccupped into the elevator. 'What was that?' she said, staring as the doors closed in front of her.

II

Late the next morning Anaïs phoned reception and asked after both the men whom she was avoiding. Neither were in. She walked the Metropole's red carpet in a sleeveless dress printed with orange Morris-like flowers and soft green vine leaf and stepped out into the blue sunshine of the Riva.

'Buongiorno, Principessa!' Octavian, with one foot on the bow of a motoscafo, the other on its driver's seat, opened his arms to her. He wore wayfarer sunglasses and a Gondolier's polo with its collar up and golden shorts.

'Good morning,' she said, standing over him at the water's edge. 'And I'm a countess, remember, not a princess.'

'Buongiorno, Contessa. Benvenuti a bordo *La Cenerentola.*' He offered her a hand and she hopped aboard. He reversed and pulled away and drove her, they both standing, slowly along the basin, past the lagoon façade of the Ducal Palace, to the mouth of the Grand Canal—guarded by peach-coloured palaces and the silvery dome and wildly robed saints of the Salute. He crossed through the water traffic to a little campo and moored the boat. 'First we wait.'

'We wait for what?'

'Do you see that little canal?' He pointed to the dark gap between a simple four-storeyed vermillion house and a later beige one. 'Just watch it.'

The faded green of the canalazzo lapped loudly at her feet. She watched it wrinkle and shimmer and swirl and could have done so for hours. A loud whir arose at their backs as a barge arrived to crane boxes of ice-creams and kegs of beers onto the bricks of the campo. Octavian clicked his tongue and pointed to the length of the square. Two white caravans were fenced off behind a wire fence wrapped with plastic hessian. They turned around just as an enormous barge bearing a huge green excavator ploughed slowly and loudly down the canal. Octavian moaned anxiously and said, 'Weapons of mass construction.' Soon the sun came into position. The dark canal opposite was slowly illuminated. The high walls of the palazzi became coloured and its waters went from black to glorious aquamarine. The façades looked like shining faces, thrust forward to catch the heat of the sun, and then an empty gondola floated slowly out.

'It's a city of miracles. Of astonishing glimpses of picturesque perfection.'

'But of no coincidences,' said Anaïs.

'Not a one. Come on.'

They crossed the Canal again and Octavian helped Anaïs up onto a traghetto landing. He hopped up after her and she turned at the top of the pier to wait for him.

'Your boat's floating away.'

'No it's not,' he said, very strangely, for it was.

'It is.'

'It's not.'

'I'm telling you, turn around, your boat is floating away.'

'It's not.'

'It is!' said Anaïs, almost yelling.

'It's not!' said Octavian, mimicking her frustration. He lowered his voice to cool the argument. 'It's not my boat.'

'It's not your boat?'

'No.'

'Then whose boat is it?'

'How should I know?'

'Did you steal it?'

'To steal would be to take and then to keep. As you can see,' he said, crossing a hand to his shoulder, 'I have not kept. Now, what do you know about Carpaccio?'

'Beef carpaccio?'

His face drooped. 'You're joking?' She shook her head. 'Bellini?'

'I had one of those the other day. I like them a lot. Anything with prosecco in it.'

'You're an idiot.'

'You're an idiot!'

'Today, only churches.'

'If you say so.'

'And I do.'

So they spent the afternoon treading truly the stones of Venice. They had neither map nor camera, and as bragging tutor and flippant student they strolled her tiniest alleys and sighed over her stillest canals, brushed with their feet the weed-grown cracks of her quietest campi, imbibed through whispered lessons her greatest paintings. He showed her Bellini in San Zaccaria and Carpaccio in the Scuola di San Giorgio and St Laurence in the Gesuiti. She touched things older than any she had ever even seen. They walked a long and virtually empty Cannaregio canal and Octavian quickly deciphered two voices ahead. 'You hear that?'

'What?'

'Those two.' In long denim shorts and black muscle shirts, with silver chains around their necks and trimmed fringes, two men hung their legs over the canal's edge and grumbled. 'Russians.'

'So?'

'I hate Russians.' They neared them and Octavian whispered. 'Run.'

'What?'

'Run. Until the next bridge. Cross it and go straight into the church. Go! Now!' and she quickened her steps. 'No, run!' he insisted, before pushing the two men into the water. He sprinted off and bounded across the bridge and waited for her inside the Madonna dell'Orto.

'I can't believe you did that!' she said, laughing.

'Russians,' he growled. 'They shoudn't be here any more than the Chinese. They can't appreciate beauty. They can own it or they can destroy it. They cannot appreciate it. Now...' As they caught their breath he explained to her the John The Baptist And Saints of Conegliano and then told her to look at the floor tiles and to tell him what she thought she found interesting about them as he walked her across to the altar. Then he told her to look up. 'This was Tintoretto's parish church. His house is just around the corner.'

'Who?'

'You're kidding me?' Anaïs winced and shook her head. 'The man who painted that,' said Octavian, pointing his finger to the full height of the Judgment. 'And the man who painted the Scuola di San Rocco.'

Both their necks were craned. 'Where we met?'

'Where we met,' he whispered. 'You know I sleep in there sometimes?'

'Can I tell you something?' she whispered.

'Anything.'

'I fall asleep looking at paintings too. I just don't like a lot of them. Especially the new ones.'

'Not while I'm looking at paintings. I mean overnight.'

'You sleep overnight there?'

'Upstairs there's an even amazinger hall that I don't show my tours. Did you go up there?'

'No.'

'Thirty of the best paintings in the world, all by Tintoretto. I sometimes have it as my bedroom.'

'Your bedroom?'

'Yeah. I sleep in there.'

'You do not.'

'I do.'

'How?'

'With my eyes closed. I make the scuola a lot of money with the tours. I have a key to the back door and sometimes I get the urge to sleep there among the paintings.'

'You're a liar.'

'Do you really think so?'

'This painting's confusing.'

'It's in a bad spot.'

And in the clear afternoon warmth they wandered back across Cannaregio and came to a small stone bridge which led to nowhere. It looked out to the long and distant curve of a wide canal, four-storeyed houses with candy cane moorings, and to the closer outer wall of a garden overflowing to the water with green. Bedsheets hung from high windows and little white flowers cascaded all around them in planter boxes. They sat on the bridge's edge and dangled their feet. Octavian pulled out his phone and put on some music. Old recordings of old jazz, slow songs with crisp cornets and weeping tenor saxophones, rose all around. They sat in silence for a time, staring out to the sea, watching the boats drift in, their wakes slapping at the foundations of the houses, and, when there were for long enough no disturbances, the rise and fall, the tiny crests, of the undisturbed lagoon.

'Do you think the music we listen to is the soundtrack to our lives?' Anaïs said nothing; Bessie Smith was singing *Baby Won't You Please Come Home*. 'Do you like jazz?'

'Almost nothing but.'

'Why?'

'*Why?*'

'Everyone who loves jazz has an answer to the question of Why Jazz.'

'It's the only music that celebrates the consolations of death, and laments the ultimate fate of love. It's real music played by real musicians, nothing's artificial, it's perfectly human. And it was done, out of spiritual wealth, for no money—they just did it. It was who they were.'

'You know,' said Octavian softly, leaning across to her. 'If you look straight ahead, and you can't see your own clothes, you've gone back in time.'

The elfin tinkling of a celeste rose into the air and Anaïs did as Octavian suggested and was soon too overwhelmed to reply. He was right. She saw their view in daguerrotype, eternally silent, the waters by absence of unrowed boats a perfect ashen looking-glass, the façades darkly stained with mould and sea air, their peeling stucco—all reflected in black and tin Manet strokes. A gondolier rowed beneath their feet, singing, and smiled. *Dear Old Southland* played between them and all Anaïs could hear was Louis' trumpet. 'I'm completely drunk.'

'From what? Have you been drinking?' said Octavian, himself groggy with invented wistfulness.

'On Venice.'

And as Sidney Bechet played the *Song of Songs* the sun lowered and the faces of the pink and red houses shone a bright warm yellow. Soon the sun was gone and they were in the cold blue of dusk. He turned to watch Anaïs. She was intoxicated still and perfectly serene. 'In two months in Venice this is the first sunset I've missed. ... Dinner?'

'Mmm,' she moaned, with heavy eyelids.

'Do you know where we're near?'

They dined by candlelight on hot and cold seafood and antipasti and drank aperol and valpolicella. A cool breeze blew in from the lagoon. The night was clear and the air cold, the stars everywhere like white sugar thrown across the sky. They filled in some of the gaps from their respective motorbike odysseys and discussed living in New York and Paris. Octavian descended briefly into waffling on about why he so loved Venice and then said, 'Shall I walk you home?'

'Already?'

'It's cold out here, no?'

'Can we take a really long way home?'

As they walked north, by the train station, and then down through Santa Croce to the Zattere, a blanket of warming cloud set in. They crossed the Academy bridge and there were no lights, even on the high buildings, save for the blinking of the water taxis. It began to spit and soon to drizzle. It picked up as they wandered the lower canals of San Marco. Shortly it broke into rain. Anaïs ran for a green awning lit by a hotel lobby. She and Octavian looked out across the Grand Canal, bombarded and dripping and breezy, silver-fogged, to the high dome of the Salute. Covered gondolas rocked gently around them, clunking against their wooden moorings. He stepped down onto a wooden landing and turned around and caught her eyes, now level with his. He looked into them and soon she gave an almost imperceptible nod. He returned it; they kissed. He tightened his arms around her and she moaned into his breathing mouth.

Late next morning he was again below the riva astride a motoscafo.

'Not yours either?'

'Do you have a bikini on?'

'Nope.'

'Go and get one.'

'I swim naked.'

He nodded at this peculiarity with childish excitement and sped her to the Lido. They baked on towels and ran their fingers across the sweaty smalls of one another's backs and swam in the cold ocean.

'You know I know nothing about you,' said Anaïs as they walked to get gelato.

'That is as it should be.'

'But you know everything about me.'

'Everything?'

'The important things.'

'I doubt that.'

'What are *you* doing in Venice? The truth. What have *you* fled?'

'The truth?' She nodded and he stared at her. Shortly he said, 'I lost somebody.'

'They died?'

'My wife.'

'Your *wife*?' she said, surprised and momentarily a little angry.

'Is that OK?'

'Why wouldn't it be?'

'I don't know.'

'And you lost her?'

'She was my brother's partner. A de facto thing. And she was very wealthy. Two years they were together and she wrote him into the will, but then she and I fell in love, in New York, and we ran away and got married. When my brother found out he killed her. Made it look like an accident thinking he would get all her money. But because I'd married her I was entitled to it. But then when it went to court her family got it all.'

'You're a bloody liar.'

'You keep saying that.'

'Your brother murdered your wife?'

He raised his eyebrows.

'I don't believe you.'

'No?'

'No,' she said, almost laughing. They strolled in sunglasses and with towels over their shoulders, back under the trees of the sunlit boulevard to the beige sand and waded again out into the water. 'And you're here now, lying to me, and to those poor tourists. Don't you want to do something great with your life?'

'I live in Venice. What could be greater?'

'You lie in Venice.'

'Is there a huge difference, between lying and living? At least I do it greatly.'

'Why don't you become a writer? Seems like a natural profession for a liar.'

'Oh I'm a writer.'

'Of what?'

'Of cover letters.'

'Of cover letters?'

'I write cover letters to literary agents in London and New York. Boring stories—sickly, sentimental, positive ones. Life discovery crap, affirmations, bright stories. Cover letters and their first chapters, and they *always* get accepted. Then I reply with a ridiculous reason as to why I'm not interested in representation *and I laugh*. It is amazing what these people will publish.'

'But you've not written anything of your own?'

'In art I'd pursue the naturalist ideal. The satirical grotesque. I would write to show how people *actually* are, today. Deceit, cruelty, stupidity, lukewarmness, jealousy, control. These are the powers that hold sway over humanity. I'd hold up a mirror to them and they would hate it. They're selfish, ungrateful, proud, and doomed. But there's no room for reflective art now, all art today must be refractive. You can't depict humankind as they really are, the story would be too sad. We're doomed, environmentally and spiritually, and people are secretly so aware of how miserable they are that they'll only read things that make them feel better about themselves. And that I'm afraid I cannot do.'

'Why don't you make them laugh?'

'Make 'em laugh,' he sang, 'Make 'em laugh! ... Theirs is an idiot laughter. Plus I'm not a female.'

'What does that have to do with anything?'

'The industry's run by women. Men don't read, because there's nothing for them to read. And they'll only let a castrated man publish a book.'

They headed back to the boat in the late afternoon and bought miniature bottles of prosecco and some ice from a supermarket. Anchored on the lagoon they drank through sunset. The towers and domes of Venice dropped to ochre and green and silver and Octavian took Anaïs again to the mouth of the Grand Canal and set the boat adrift and they dined, staring and smiling at one another, in a restaurant at the end of a long lantern-lit Dorsoduran calle. They crossed a nearby campo busy with students and late-night revellers and an enormous dog and Octavian asked Anaïs if she knew where she was.

'No idea.'

He told her to turn around and said that he was going to blindfold her. 'Do you trust me?'

'Yes, Aladdin.'

And she let him tie a white napkin over her eyes and he led her by the hand. They came to a silent lamplit canal and Octavian with an enormous key opened an ancient door and led Anaïs up two flights of steps and took her to the middle of the upper hall of the Scuola di San Rocco. Two hundred candles flickered on the mosaic floor; the gilt and bronze ceiling and the auburn wood glimmered. Octavian pressed play on his phone and Harry James echoed through the vast hall, his trumpet quivering and his orchestra lilting, and Octavian said, 'You can take it off now.'

Anaïs untied the napkin and nearly stopped breathing at the beauty of it all. She took in the size of the room, then one wall, then the ceiling, then all around her. She turned on the spot and looked at Octavian as though she were angry at him. She craned her neck and wandered, awed, beneath the enormous canvases whose strokes seemed to drip with manna. All she could manage to say was, 'Wow.'

'I told you I had this place as my bedroom,' he whispered.

'You weren't lying?'

He took her hand and walked her to the sala dell'Albergo. 'Now look at the floor. What can you tell me about the parquetry?'

He brought her across to its enormous doors and then told her to look up. There they stood before The Crucifixion. Her mouth, slightly ajar, slowly but steadily came to be agape. Moisture so welled at her lower eyelids that it pinched off into two drops and for the first time in seven years it could be said that Anaïs Spencer was crying.

'The greatest painting in the world by the greatest painter in the world.'

'Tintoretto?'

'Very good! This whole hall is him.' He again took on Richard Burton's voice. 'Before his greatest works you are conscious of a sudden evaporation of old doubts. I was never so utterly crushed to the earth before any human intellect as I was before Tintoretto. I must leave this picture to work its will on you; it is beyond all analysis and above all praise.' And he led her back into the main room and pulled the heavy doors closed behind them.

'Why are you closing them?'

'I wouldn't feel comfortable doing what we're about to do in front of him.'

'What are we about to do?'

'You tell me.'

And as Helen Forrest's voice descended across, '*You made me love you,*' Octavian put his arm at Anaïs' back and his hand to her cheek and kissed her and lowered her onto the white blanket beneath the Adam and Eve.

When they woke, white, gentle sunlight was lifting through the muslin curtains. Most of the candles flickered still and Anaïs and Octavian made love again and then left via the scuola's back door. They had coffee and lay in the grass outside San Trovaso, doing all those horrible things which only they can understand who are similarly enamoured of another human. He commandeered a motoscafo and they drifted down to the Riva and Anaïs changed and extracted her suitcase from her suite in the Metropole and they glided under the Rialto and passed the palazzo Bolani. He set the boat adrift outside the Ca d'Oro. He wheeled her suitcase onto Strada Nova and, holding hands, they were followed by Emma Goodenough across two bridges. She had been flirting with young Italian men at the outside tables of a trattoria. When she spied Anaïs Spencer being waited upon by a handsome young man she saw with excited eyes an unmissable opportunity.

Octavian led Anaïs beneath a stone archway into an overgrown garden. A short path led to a wooden door whose arched tympanum was draped with vine. He told her to wait there and walked ahead and disappeared around an invisible corner. Shortly the weed-covered tin door to Anaïs' right was making noises; then it was forced open. She stepped into an inner courtyard overgrown with ferns. Through this screen of temperate rainforest could be seen walls of thin brick and russet stucco stained white with salt, slim pointed windows and an arched door made of old glass encrusted with dirt. This Octavian struggled to pry open from its warped iron frame.

Anaïs crossed the threshold into a powder-white hall. The floor was white marble, the walls of sandy damask, the ornate ceiling sanded back to a thin film of plaster over red brick. From its centre sprung frazzled electrical wires where once hung a chandelier.

'You don't own this place?' said Anaïs, prematurely astonished by the idea.

'No.'

'Are you renting it?'

'No.' Octavian had his cheeky grin full across his face. Anaïs thought on the motoscafi in which she had been parading. 'So you're not rich?'

'I am very not rich.'

'Good.'

'Why is that good?'

They spent the day and the evening and most of the following morning in the little drawing room off this main room which Octavian was using as his bedroom.

'Do you want a coffee?' said Anaïs, sweaty and exhausted in a state nearing physical bliss.

'Mmmm,' moaned Octavian, three-quarters asleep.

'Where from?'

'Just... ahhhh... on the main street there. Right. I can't remember it's name. A golden place. Tell them it's for me and they'll let you take the cups away.' He stroked lazily at her back as she dressed. His luggage, a military-green duffle bag, was empty of clothing. A few wrinkled shirts hung from the backs of doors and chairs. There was a closed laptop surrounded by pens and notes and empty coffee cups upon an antique desk. Unframed miniature prints were pinned everywhere to the walls—Guardi, Tintoretto, Michelangelo, Delacroix, Caravaggio, Lippi, sketches by Ruskin, Hunt's Triumph of the Innocents. There were a few thin dog-eared paperbacks and socks and boxer shorts bunched into most of the corners.

In the full midday sun she wandered slowly, taking in from behind her sunglasses the faces of those who passed her and concluding that for once none of them could possibly be as happy as she was. At the white-façaded corner of a brick church she saw half a man's face. When she caught its eye this head snapped out of sight. She passed the little campo and looked to the solemn figure of its bronze statue and saw at its pedestal the same peering half a tanned face. It snapped out of view again. Anaïs strode over to it. Stanley Felix had the left side of his face pressed firmly against the creamy stone of the pedestal.

'What are you still doing here?' she snapped.

'Nothing.'

'Why are you holding your face against a statue?'

In one horrifying motion he turned his other cheek to Anaïs. Immediately a rat of a dog started yapping at him. Stanley Felix's hair, normally brushed elegantly back from his temple, now sprang from it like an old doll's pigtail. His left eye was pushed to a shut slit by black and green swelling and his left cheek puffed out as though his head were a balloon being squeezed from the other side. Anaïs jolted and then struggled to force herself to look at him. She let out a series of shocked groans. Only when he returned his face to the statue did the dog cease to bark, and Anaïs to gag.

'What the hell happened to you?'

'Why are you staying in that big palazzo?'

'What?'

'Who are you staying with? I know you're not a spy. The Jew-wife told me everything. You're a liar. Which means you're *not* a Jew. I knew it! Love prevails again, Anaïs. I love you. With no reservations at all now. I'm no longer repulsed by you.' With this last sentence he again pulled his cheek from the statue. The dog barked, fast and loud, and Anaïs averted in horror her eyes.

'You need to leave Venice, Stan.'

'Why?'

'First of all, you look absolutely terrifying.'

'The swelling will go down in a couple of days. You remember how good looking I am normally though. Don't you?'

'Put your head back against the statue. Thank you. I am in love with somebody.'

'You're what?'

'There's no point at all in you being here now.'

Made despondent by her confession, he slowly drew his face from the stone. The dog snapped into a concentrated frenzy which caused its owner to drag it from the square. 'You're in love?'

'Yes.'

'With the Jew?'

'Put your head against the stone!' Stanley peered at her sideways. 'Not with the Jew. Stop calling him that. And it's none of your business who I'm in love with.'

'You're in love with somebody else?'

'I'm in love with somebody else.'

'And it's not a lie?'

'It's not a lie.'

'Is he Jewish as well? They're conspiring to keep you from me aren't they?'

'I don't think he's a Jew, Stan. Not that that's important.'

'Maybe not to you. Is he good looking?'

'Stanley.'

'And rich too!?'

'Goodbye.'

He slowly drew his face from the stone and said, 'Goodbye?'

'Ah,' said Anaïs, blinking repeatedly to remove from her immediate memory the shadowed imprint of his contusions. 'Ah. God! Yes, this is goodbye, Stanley. I'm saying goodbye,' she said quickly. 'I'm sorry.'

And after wiping the pus from his bulbous eye, Stanley Felix hung his head low and joined the crowd of tourists following the signs for Rialto.

'Do you know what I just saw?'

'What?' said Octavian.

'On the front of a few bridges. A stencilled sign. "Anonymous Stateless Immigrants Pavilion".'

'Oh that, yes. No, not for us though. I've been to it, it's a modern art thing. For people who've abandoned their country and their people for another. Not for people who have neither.'

Anaïs dipped her chocolate cornettino into her coffee and said, 'What are we doing today?'

'I've left my favourite church for last,' said Octavian, rising. 'You shall be thoroughly blown away. But it's not time yet.'

'Not time?'

'The sun's still above it. You want it in front of it, setting, lighting the whole thing up in golden.'

Later they forced open the wooden shutters of the derelict *piano nobile* and straddled the low balustrade across its windows. Octavian was in khaki trousers and shirtless in the sunshine, Anaïs in camisole and denim shorts. They passed a bottle of prosecco around the columns and ate prosciutto and waved at the tourists who photographed them from the Ponte Pasqualigo. Art Blakey played Birdland loudly through his wireless speaker.

'I absolutely love it here,' sighed Anaïs.

Octavian sighed and said, 'Yep.'

She swigged and said, 'Why do you make your tours up?'

'It's fun. Fiction's always more interesting than the truth.'

'That is definitely not true.'

'Is it not?'

'I think only a boring person would say that.'

'I never claimed that I was interesting.'

'That's true, you didn't.'

'How about, fiction is more convenient then, than the truth.'

'That is a *very* suspicious thing to say. How deep is that canal?' Anaïs leaned out and looked down.

'I don't know actually. I've seen one drained before. It definitely looked deep enough.' He looked to either end for boats.

'Deep enough for what?'

And he stepped onto the balustrade and smiled at her and nodded and then dove into the jade water.

'Barely,' he called out, resurfacing with a profoundly attractive look on his face. 'Do not jump in.'

'The land was given to the Dominicans in the thirteenth century after the Doge dreamt that he saw white doves flying over it.' They came into view of Octavian's favourite bare façade, into view of the simple rose window, of Octavian's dearest door in all of Italy, his most perfect church in Venice. 'Inside are buried twenty-five kings of Venice. John Bellini is buried there, Pisani. And it has the skin of Bragadin, flayed alive by the Turks.' Then his excited steps slowed as his heart sank. Anaïs stepped up onto the Ponte Cavallo behind him and beheld what so deflated him. 'It's beautiful.' Scaffolding covered the entire right third of its façade. Half way down was an enormous billboard advertising a German car. Chipboard fencing covered in graffiti ran around the south-western corner. Octavian sidestepped to the Colleoni statue, his mouth open with fury and his eyes darting in disbelief, and found at the church's western corner another billboard advertising the same German car. 'No,' he whispered, disconsolate. 'Not here. No! No, no, no, no, no. Oh, God.'

'What?'

'What do you mean What?'

'It's beautiful. You said it's your favourite?'

'It's ruined. Completely ruined. Forever. A Volkswagen billboard? The Germans have invaded again. On San Giovanni e Paolo. San Zanipolo. This is more damage than the Turks could ever have done. More damage than Napoleon even. They've gone too far. They keep pushing me, and pushing me. Now I've got no choice.'

'Calm down, buddy. It's just a church.'

'It's not just a church, Anaïs. It's Venice. This church *is* Venice. More than St. Mark's. St. Mark's is tourist Venice. This is Venice Venice. Oh my prophetic soul. Anaïs, it's better to live somewhere you despise. It really is. I'm moving. Then you won't hate the world or the people in it as they all calmly conspire to destroy it.' His voice had loudened. 'They've destroyed it. Utterly. Venice is gone. It is no more.'

'You're being very dramatic.'

'You can't understand. Inside this church is the greatest lesson anybody could learn. It was taught to me by Ruskin. And it's been sold. For German gold. Venice and history are gone. They are no more. I don't know why I tried to pretend that they weren't in the first place.'

'They're not gone. You're still here. What about that guy?'

'I'll blow the place up. Better that it did not exist than that it suffers so false a fate.' And Octavian, mumbling dramatisms, wandered down to take in the scaffolding which covered the high round exterior of the southern chapels.

Beyond Colleoni's raised elbow, behind a green lamp post, Anaïs spotted, leering out at her, half a face. It too attempted to snap back from sight as soon as she eyed it. She crossed to the canal in a huff and, spotted, Johnny Goodenough took off and promptly slipped on an edge of wet marble and went face first into the murk of the canal. His head popped back up and he swam to the steps. He pulled himself out of the water and, in the general direction of the clump of seagrass draped over his shoulder, a small American child pointed and screamed and yelled, 'Monster!'

Anaïs pulled him by the wet arm to the shade of the alley.

'What the hell are you doing here? Ergh, what happened to your face?' She recoiled and could not breathe from disgust. 'Oh my God. Oh, turn your head that way.' His was in worse condition than Stanley's. His right ear was swollen to about the size of an adolescent's shoe and his cheek and forehead had become one knobbly surface of tie-dyed purple, black and blue.

'I love you, Anaïs,' he seemed to say, mumbling from the side of his mouth.

'Whats that?'

'I love you.'

'You don't love me Johnny, you are attracted to me.'

'I'm not. I love you.'

'You're not attracted to me?'

'No, I am! I am,' he moaned and mumbled. 'But I love you as well.'

'Stop saying that.'

She walked away from the campo, drawing him from Octavian and discovery.

'Who's the guy you're staying with?'

'What's that?'

'Who's the guy you're staying with?! Is he richer than me? Emma said he's younger than me. How much younger? Is he better looking than me? He can't be, can he?'

'Everybody's better looking than you right now. You look like a rotten leg of goat meat.'

Octavian's despondent head was lifted high as his eyes took in the full measure of the spoliation.

'Such a shame isn't it?' said Emma Goodenough, arrived to stand beside him.

'I just can't believe it.'

'I'll tell you what you won't believe.'

'You've only known him for four days,' Johnny pleaded from behind swollen lips.

'I told you about feeling things didn't I?'

'I have no feelings except for you.'

'What?'

'I have no feelings except for you.'

'Stop it with that crap. Johnny, I'm in love with Octavian.'

'Who the fuck is Octavian?' he growled with little differentiation of consonants.

'What?'

'Who the fuck is Octavian!?'

'Is her suitcase still packed?' said Emma, watching her husband gesticulate upon a bridge.

'Who's that?' said Octavian.

'What kind of stupid name is that?!'
'Hm?'
'What kind of stupid name is that?!!'
'I think it's a fantastic name.'
'And you're in love with him?'
'I'm in love with him,' she mumbled, mimicking him. She was once again entirely aloof.
'And not with me?'
'Nn-nn. Unfortunately not.'
'He *is* rich. He can't be richer than me though. I'm *really* rich. Like Jewish rich.'
'*Are* you Jewish?'
'Me? No. I'm just Jewish rich.'
'You're what sorry?'
'I'm just Jewish rich.'
'You're James Joyce's bitch?'
'I'm Jewish rich.'
'You're Jimmy Switch? Who's that?'
'No!'
'And it doesn't matter. I'm in love with Octavian.'
And, watched by his wife and Octavian, both of whom could only see the undestroyed side of his face, Johnny Goodenough at last accepted that Anaïs would not anytime soon be his. He cowered along the alley and waved goodbye to her.

'Do you *know* where Anaïs was staying before she was shacking up at your place?'
'At the Metropole.'
'And before that?'
'Why?'

III

'Possiamo sedire?' said Octavian to a balding Bangladeshi waiter at the Bar Foscarini.

'You are eat or you are drink?'

'Just for a drink.'

'These table here.'

Octavian pointed to the tables nearest the canal. 'Not those tables?'

'Those tables only for eat isn't it?'

'We might eat.'

'You are eat?'

'Maybe.'

'Sorry you must eat for front row isn't it.'

'What if your menu's a piece of shit? Hm? How about we sit and look at the menu then we decide whether or not we'll eat?'

'What was that about?' said Anaïs, easing into a silver plastic chair and watching the boats parade before the balustrade of bursting white petunias.

'Foreigners. And bloody look at that.' His teeth were clenched. A crane had been erected somewhere behind the Salute and several of the façades beside it were covered in opaque grey mesh. 'Cranes are the bane of my existence. Cranes and scaffolding. The two banes of my existence. Cranes and scaffolding, and tourists. Three. Three banes. My existence has three banes. Cranes and scaffolding and tourists. Ah, and foreigners,' he growled. 'God damn it. Four banes.'

'Could we get two spritz aperols?' Anaïs called over to the waiter, who was telling people where they could not sit.

'The four banes of my existence are cranes, scaffolding, tourists and foreigners. Agh,' he growled again. 'I hate so much.'

'Calm down.'

'Yep.'

'Did you like the last Batman?'

'What?'

'The one with Bane.'

'I haven't seen it.'

'I was wondering what would break first,' she said, covering her mouth and impersonating. 'Your spirit… or your body! … No? … What are we doing tonight?' she said, enthusing still.

His back was to the Academy bridge. Tourists crossed it en masse all at the same slow pace, as though they had been ordered to evacuate due to an impending Hollywood-sized disaster, only to be informed that on the other side of the bridge lay Acheron. His shoulder was to the canal and he stared from behind his sunglasses and spread his arms to rest them on chairbacks.

'Otty?'

'Do not call me that.'

'Do you have something amazing planned for us? … Hm?'

'Hm?' he said, turning to her.

'What amazingly fun thing are we doing tonight?'

'Oh I don't know yet. Let me think about it.'

'Are you *still* thinking about the church from yesterday?' she said, almost reprimanding him. He said nothing. 'Don't you think the church probably needed the money that the billboard brought in, for restorations?'

'That's the stupidest thing I've ever heard. There's no such thing as restoration. There is only destruction. You can't restore a church. You can only destroy it. Time must do its work. A church restored is a church empty.'

'Are you a Catholic?'

'My relationship with God is like Tolstoy's. He and I are two old bears in a cave.'

'So if you're a bear and you have nothing for us to do tonight can we stay in and eat pizza?'

He pursed his lips and rubbed the corner of his eyebrows with two fingers and a thumb.

'What's the matter?'

'Nothing.'

'Something's the matter.'

'Nothing is the matter.'

'Octavian.'

'Anaïs,' he droned back.

'Would you just tell me?'

'Tell you what?'

'What's the matter.'

'Nothing's the matter!'

'No need to snap.'

'I didn't snap.'

Anaïs raised her eyebrows and returned to her drink and the canal and Octavian turned again to his staring.

They sat in silence, for a few long minutes, until Anaïs upped and left the terrace and crossed the bridge. Octavian started after her but an arm was placed across his chest.

'You have not paid, isn't it? Pay you must.'

'Listen Yoda, she has my wallet. Let me go and get it and I'll come back to pay.'

'I know this trick, isn't it. Make her to come back or no leave till pay you. Call to her.'

'Lei ha il mio portafoglio, cretino nero, e il mio denaro. Hai capito? Lasciami passare, subito!'

And Octavian withdrew his erect finger from the waiter's face and strode up the wooden steps and caught Anaïs up as she rounded a corner. 'Quickly now. Didn't pay.'

'Really?'

'Nn-nn.'

She cackled and they hurried into the empty labyrinth of northern San Marco and then slowed to wander together. Back in Cannaregio they came to a piazza packed with journalists and lookers-on, all facing a middle-aged woman orating in Italian upon the steps before the closed doors of a round church, the eye of providence carved into its high tympanum.

'What's that all about?' said Anaïs.

Octavian listened until he caught the gist of the meeting. 'Umm... they only open the doors to this church once a year. ... It's been closed for two centuries. Once the Pope found out that nuns were performing illegal abortions inside he ordered it to be closed. ... But they say that the abortions still occur ... When a... when a member of the parish is in desperate need ... or the baby is the result of adultery. Yikes.' He turned to raise his eyebrows to Anaïs but she was gone. He looked around the piazza and could find her nowhere until he returned to his courtyard. 'Where'd you go?'

'I got bored.'

'Fair enough.'

'Do you want to go and watch the sunset?'

'No, not tonight.'

'No? Why not?'

'Eh, it wasn't hot enough today. And the weather's cold tomorrow. And there aren't any clouds in the sky. It won't be worth it.'

'Not even with me?' she said, pouting and putting her body against his.

'Don't,' he said, smiling.

'Don't what?'

'You want to go and watch the sunset?'

'Not if you don't want to.'

'I thought you wanted to stay in and eat pizza.'

'Yeah! Let's do that.'

Hers a consolatory excitement.

Anaïs' suitcase lay closed and unpacked beside the bookshelf that was doubling as a wardrobe. Octavian eyed it as he got onto the bed. He sat up and played with his phone and Anaïs crawled up the bed to have her face in front of his. She went to kiss him and he extended his lips mechanically to hers.

'It's just a church, Octavian. It's still standing.'

'It's not that,' he insisted.

'What is it then?'

'Shall I go and get dinner?'

'What?'

'What what?'

'What's the fucking matter? Everything was roses before that God-damned church and now you've gone cold.'

'I have not.'

'You fucking have.'

'I've gone cold then.' Anaïs clicked her tongue and rolled onto her back and exhaled through closed lips. Octavian sighed. 'The story you told me the night we met…'

'Mmm?'

'Was it the truth?'

'Nothing but the truth. Why?'

'No reason.'

'Well there must be a reason.'

'No there mustn't. I was just replaying it in my head. Some of the stuff I couldn't remember.'

'Like what?'

'I'm not thinking about it anymore. I'm going to get dinner.' He stood out of bed and watched her suitcase as he buttoned a shirt. Anaïs sighed and very shortly was eyeing it as well. 'Which way's the pizza place?'

'Why do you ask that?'

'I don't know. Just asking.'

'It's that way.'

'Towards the Rialto?'

'Yep. I'll be back in twenty minutes.'

'Mkay.'

'Mushrooms and salami?'

'Yep,' she said, and beyond the white entrance room the glass door fell heavily closed behind him.

Anaïs stared still at her suitcase. She breathed deeply. She was solemnising a decision she had already made, and delaying its execution. Shortly she went to the bathroom and repacked her make-up and her Essex House moisturiser, her Shangri-La toothbrush and her Metropole shampoo. She searched the bedroom for clothes that might have been thrown into a hidden corner. Finding none she knelt on her suitcase in order to zip it shut then pulled out its handle and rolled it across the bare white marble and out to the smooth stones of the street. The ferns of Octavian's squat courtyard swished softly in the evening breeze.

It was the hour of the setting of the sun, cool and blanketed in warm hues. A young woman, without legs, swinging slowly along on the tripod of her fists and severed torso, stopped at Anaïs' entrance to the street. She lifted a deformed hand and asked in English for some money. Anaïs stopped and closed her eyes and breathed in once, slowly, and then exhaled before setting off briskly with the flow of the crowd, most of it made of day-trippers headed, as was she, to the train station. She lifted her suitcase and scurried up and lumbered down bridges and as she neared a wide three-way intersection Octavian walked in from the perpendicular street and stopped at distance with a pizza box in hand. Anaïs and her suitcase halted. Staring into his eyes she soon remembered her decision and regained her resolve. She walked slowly towards him and then hastened to pass him. He sidestepped into her path.

'Where are you going?'

'You told me the pizza place was the other way.'

'I remembered another place. Seafood pizza. Where are you going?'

'It's my destiny, Octavian.'

'What's your destiny?'

'To keep moving. To be homeless. To live out of a suitcase. To wander.'

'I will set your suitcase on fire if you keep walking.'

'It's repeating itself again. It's all repeating itself. Yesterday morning everything was fine, and today you're a neurotic grumpy head case.'

'Why didn't you tell me about the palazzo Bolani?'

'I did tell you about it.'

'No you didn't. Not everything.'

'I did!'

'You're lying.'

'I'm not.'

'Who owns the palazzo Bolani, Anaïs? *Whose* palazzo did you stay in, for two nights? And whose wife caught you in it?' Anaïs lowered her head and set off through the wall of tourists, zigzagged her little white suitcase through pairs and trios and quartets of wretched simpleton and huddled mass and tempest-tossed homeless. Octavian lifted the pizza box overhead and side-stepped and strode after her. He cut her off between two trinket stalls. 'Did you tell me that John Goodenough has been here the whole time with you? Hm? That you were talking with him yesterday morning while I was in the *next street*?' He was almost yelling. 'You didn't tell me any of that, did you?' He leaned in and with a very cruel face said, 'Did you?'

'I was *arguing* with him yesterday, because I was telling him to leave Venice.'

'So you could jump on a train and go and meet up with him somewhere else?'

'No,' she said angrily.

'Then why? … Hm? Because you knew you'd get caught if you kept seeing each other?' Anaïs shook her head, slowly and furiously. 'Why?'

'Because I…' She stopped herself and set off again. He caught up to her at the foot of the Ponte delle Guglie and angrily helped an old lady with her shopping buggy. He lifted her beige wheeled contraption and ran it to the top of the steps. He put it down and stood over Anaïs.

'What were you going to say?'

'Nothing.'

'What were you going to say?! Why were you telling that very handsome man to leave Venice, Anaïs?'

'No.'

'What do you mean, no?'

She stared sternly at him and shook her head.

'Why?' he boomed.

'Because,' she boomed back.

'Because why?'

'Because I love you.'

And all motion zapped from his body. It quickly to returned as diffuse meanderings of his head and slow, deep breaths. The spires of Cannaregio canal were swamped with Spanish and English and the squealing of seagulls, her dark waters running with departing taxis.

'What did you say?'

'You heard me.'

'How can you say that when you're with one man one night and the next night you're with me?' He shrugged his shoulders, daring her to explain.

'I wasn't with him! I wasn't ever with him! I stayed in his palazzo for two nights, alone. He stayed in a hotel. His wife found me in the palazzo, alone. God I hate the word palazzo. He told me his wife was dead, so I had to move out. I never slept with Johnny Goodenough. I never went near him.'

'God I hate his name!'

'And he told me he wouldn't be here but he flew here anyway and I've been avoiding him ever since.'

'Over dinner, you avoided him?'

'I can't afford to eat, Octavian. I had to let him to buy me dinner or I didn't eat that day. Does that make you happy?'

'No. It doesn't. But you don't love me.'

'I do.'

'You're a liar.'

'So are you.'

'Exactly.'

'And?'

'You can't love me.'

'Why not?'

'Because.'

'Because why?'

'Because I love you too.' They both stared, frustrated and sideways, along the canal.

'Well there we are. Lah-di-dah.'

'I once promised a girl that I would love her forever, Anaïs. I promised her I would but I failed. I broke her heart. And I've been delinquent ever since. I can't love anyone again. I'll hurt you.'

'Then let me get past you.'

'No.'

'This is my destiny and I am a slave to it. Let me get past you.'

'You're not a slave, Anaïs, you're a liar.'

'So are you. I've been homeless for seven years. And all that time I've known that I would end up in Venice and I come here and I find you.'

'You found Venice.'

'In an ordered universe there are no coincidences, remember? I came to Venice to find you. Maybe after all I didn't know I would end up in Venice, but that my homelessness would end here, by finding you..'

'So what are you saying?'

'What are you saying? This is a confusing conversation.'

'What if we get married and you die within a year from cancer?'

'That's a horrible thing to say!'

'This is the heartache we're setting ourselves up for here.'

'Why?'

'Why? Because I'm about to be absolutely pummelled by tragedy. Very soon. I can feel it. I've never found anybody worth being good for, and so I've been bad. My scales of justice are stacked up like the counterweight to a trebuchet and this is just the kind of thing to loose the ropes and let the misery fly, all over everyone.'

'And?'

'What do you think, And? That's you, Anaïs.'

'What's me?'

'You're worth being good for.'

'I'm not. I'm really not.'

'You are.'

'You don't know anything about me.'

'I think I know more about you than any other person on

earth.'

'And I know nothing about you.'

'All you need to know is that…' His voice became his Richard Burton. 'When I love thee not, chaos is come again.'

She looked up at him from beneath her eyebrows. 'Have you been bad?'

'A little bit.'

'Me too.'

'So now what do we do?'

'I run. The same thing I've always done. I move so that I might one day find a home.'

'We start a home, Anaïs. We found one. We build a place just for us. You and me. Where we repose and where we're happy.'

'Here?'

'Not here. Venice is a fantasyland. I make enough money to feast, alone, but not to put a roof over our heads.'

'I don't have any money.'

'I have a little bit. And I can make more.'

'How?'

'The book.'

'What book?'

'The book. A novel. Almost finished. I write the cover letters in the evenings but in the mornings before my first tour I work on the book. It's hilarious.'

'What's it about?'

'Me.'

'Of course it is,' she said, half smiling, half blubbering.

'We move to London, I rewrite it in a month, we claim asylum for you, I send the book to an agent, they get back to me in a fortnight. We're rich by October and I am the scourge of princes. Now, do you love me?' She nodded. 'And do you trust me?' She shook her head. 'Really?' And shook it again.

'You're a liar.'

'So are you.'

'I've never met anybody worth not lying to.'

EPISODE 5

That Happy Shore.

I

They were joyfully inseparable through their last days in Venice—stopping in the warm sunshine of her bridges to luxuriate in her canalscapes, gliding between her churches to breathe upon her hidden paintings—damp and crumbling Veronese in San Sebastian, Titian high in the coldness of the Salute; blue and golden and russet afternoons at café tables with bellinis, at his laptop, planning their move to London. They settled, on the recommendation of an old friend of Octavian's and with the securing by that friend's father of a one bedroom flat there, on Battersea.

Inseparable that was, until the plain white arrow beside the searing-white words, 'All Other Passports.'

'I'll meet you in duty free?' Octavian kissed her loudly on the cheek and left her to alone descend a white spiral ramp into a hall packed with passengers. They shuffled all at a slug's pace in an enormous queue which snaked to a gloomy grove of pillboxes looking out from beneath the signs of 'UK Border.'

Surrounded by the nations Anaïs was instantly bored. She scanned the immigration officers and thought it strange that only a handful of them, and those the ageing and the waddling, appeared to be English. When eventually she made it to the front a uniformed and neat old man who reminded Anaïs of her grandmother sighed, 'Have you filled out your landing card, ma'am?'

'I have.'

'Good,' he said with kindly relief. 'Passport and landing card, number seven.'

Anaïs wheeled her little white suitcase up to the pillbox beneath the illuminated numeral. The young woman bunkered within had her hair completely covered by a wrap of black muslin. From this protruded the indigo-lined eyes and puffy cheeks of her face, its top lip darkened by hair almost to a moustache. Anaïs handed over her documents and saw on the tag upon her chest the name Isis.

'I like your name.'

'Thank you,' said the girl, kindly. 'What is the purpose of your visit to the UK, ma'am?'

'I've never been before. My grandfather lived here for most of his life. He was English, he flew Hurricanes in the Battle of Britain. I thought it was about time I saw where he lived.'

'And you got means to support yourself while you're 'ere do you?'

'Have I means?' She had reverted to her O'Toole, lengthening her syllables as delicately as she could.

'You've go' enough money?'

'Oh yes I'm very rich. My father left me a fortune when he died. He was in mining. Spanish copper.'

'And you're not gonna try and work 'ere are you?'

'Well I am a writer, and I *have* come to finish a book. Is that work?'

'Will you be get-in paid while you're 'ere?'

'I shan't be, no,' she said, delighted.

'That's fine. And what is your usual place of residence?'

'My usual place of residence?'

'Where's 'ome?'

'Where is home?'

'Yeah.'

'My home is a spiritual one.'

'Wha-?'

'Australia. I live in Australia. Where is your home?'

'And whereabouts in Australia are you from?'

'Melbourne.'

'And you're a wry-a there are you?'

'I am a writer there, yes.'

'And who do you know in the UK?'

'Not a soul.'

'And where will you be staying while you're 'ere?'

'Battersea, is it?'

'Ba-ersea. Very good. And,' said Isis, at last looking up from the passport, 'You have an onward flight booked ow o' the UK do you?'

'Not yet, no.'

'And why's that?'

'I do not know whither I shall fly next or when.'

'You know you can only stay in the UK for six months on this visa do you?'

'I do now. Thank you so much.'

And two stamps and Isis' signature were given her passport and Anaïs was dismissed with a thanks and waved on.

She walked the perpetually lit caverns of duty free and found Octavian in the blush and gold miasma of the fragrance section. His head was down, his nose held to a white strip of testing card. He breathed the thing in and held it away and turned his head slightly to stare into the distance.

From afar and in the few photographs which existed of him Octavian Hughe was plain looking. He possessed a few of the independent features of handsomeness, those adjectival catchphrases by which females describe their ideal man, but as a whole his looks were unexceptional. But when he talked, when he smiled, when the corners of that delighting mouth curled up and spoke their sugared words—to anybody he wished to persuade or to coax, into doing anything at all, he was irresistibly charming.

'Whatcha doing?' said Anaïs.

'Oh hello. Nothing. Just waiting for you. What took you so long?'

'The enormous queue. Interrogation by an Ethiopian called Isis. Why are you sniffing perfumes?'

'I sniffed the men's section. Felt a bit gay. Thought I'd come over and sniff the women's.'

'Your sense of smell is the closest part of your brain to the part that holds your memories. Did you know that?'

'I did know that.'

'No sense invokes nostalgia as strongly as does smell.'

'Is that a fact?'

'That's a fact.'

II

'You ready for this?' Octavian put the key into the dead lock.

'I'm ready,' she said, reassuring herself.

He turned it and pushed in the door. A carpeted hallway speckled with debris greeted them; a sideboard covered in letters addressed to two dozen different people and flyers for taxi cars and Chinese restaurants and halal butchers. At its end their home.

Octavian being without a credit score (and Anaïs not having heard of one), he had been able to secure the lease on 6A Freedom Street only by putting up six months' rent plus a bond—a fortune which had as near to emptied his three bank accounts as he was comfortable with. This Anaïs knew and accepted.

He gave her the keys and she without solemnity opened the front door.

A tiny carpeted entranceway with a pair of old running shoes; to their right an open and empty kitchen, white double doors, the view outside an encirclement of white paint, brown and sandy brick wall. A pine breakfast bar divided the kitchen in two, a large window looked over into the neighbour's backyard; a sink, an oven and stove and rangehood, a microwave, a combined refrigerator and freezer, blue cupboards above and below.

Anaïs rumbled her suitcase across the pine floorboards; Octavian threw his duffle bag into a corner. From the back doors the wooden balustrade of an unweeded terrace led down by brick steps to a garden skirted by a brick bed of dirt and weeds and detritus. The back wall was covered in strangling vines; from two dying trees were strung rotting strings of tiny lantern. Lattice heightened the brick wall of the closest neighbour's garden, it completely paved and littered with the enormous toys of young children and a clothesline. The garden descended again by red brick, to a wall against which rested a packed tent and pink camping chairs and black garbage bags full of metal rods. Here a glass door opened to the bedroom.

They took the house in in silence. Back across the kitchen a descending staircase and a doorway to a living room—its fireplace covered, an empty mantle and terracotta hearth, bare yellow walls, a black chandelier of imitation iron, a bay window with curtains of white muslin. Footsteps pounded upon the ceiling. Anaïs left her suitcase atop the carpeted staircase; they ducked as they descended. A large bathroom to the left, a white bathtub opposite a shower; their new bedroom to the right, long and looking up through the glass doors to the garden. Beside it, a small dark room with a wide window.

'Home,' said Anaïs, turning about in the bedroom to embrace Octavian.

'Home. Do you like it?'

'I love it. We'll put a rug in here. The bed there. There's heaps of cupboard space. I love that it leads out to the garden.'

Up the unweeded red bricks—a garden hose and grey paving slabs, various rusting tools and planter boxes and pots filled with mud and cigarette butts, all overgrown among the vegetation. It was cool and damp in the sunshine of late summer. They could see up into the kitchens of both neighbours. The garden was of a dead rose bush and creepers and climbers and weeds.

'I *like* the backyard,' said Octavian, embracing its decrepitude. 'See that?' He pointed to the little pink flowers cascading from the steps back up to the kitchen.

'And the moss on the bricks.'

'Think of what we could do with it.'

The refrigerator was empty and the drawers to the freezer frozen solid to their runners.

'What do we do now?' said Anaïs, never before having been in a room so completely devoid of the trappings and the suits of human habitation.

'Ikea?'

'Really?'

'Where else do you get cheap furniture? Think of all the stuff we need. A bed. A desk. And we can *not* spend very much money at all.'

The bus rides to Ikea took precisely as long as the flight from Venice. Inside they read the instructions on how to shop there and after two hours of doing laps of the place had selected— according to a tacitly agreed upon graph of price versus hideousness—a bed and a mattress and pillows and bedsheets, a desk and a chair, a bookshelf, and bar stools for the breakfast bar. 'Do we need plates?' said Anaïs before a shelf of them. 'We didn't look in the cupboards did we?' 'We can always get plates later.' 'We'll just have pizza for dinner if we don't have any,' and an electric kettle and a coffee machine and tea towels. 'Cutlery? Did you look in the drawers?' 'No. So pizza tonight and we'll check when we get home?' and a couch and cushions and cushion covers and a coffee table and another bookshelf for the living room and a clothes-horse and a toothbrush holder and a sponge attached to a handle which one filled with dishwashing liquid, and towels and a bathmat. 'Are you bored?' 'Yes,' said Octavian. Anaïs cackled. 'This *is* ridiculous. I think we're almost done though aren't we?' 'I should be writing.' 'Can you write when we get home?' 'I can only work in the mornings,' and a pizza cutter and ice cube trays with rounded bottoms and a screwdriver and a set of Allen keys and a hammer, a desk lamp and bedside table and a rug and a lamp for the bedside table and light bulbs and power boards. 'Do we need glassware? Wine glasses and stuff?' 'Yeah, I really don't know.' 'We'll drink from the bottle tonight?' 'Yes!' And toilet paper and candles and a rubbish bin and bin bags, 'Do we need a clock?' 'What for?' 'True,' and a chest of drawers and a dustpan and hand-broom and clothes hangers. It could not but be admitted that it was entirely convenient to have everything they needed in one place. They spent so much money that they were offered, if they signed up to 'The Ikea Family Club', a small wall-mounted television. Octavian accepted and had everything that would not fit into two big yellow bags delivered to their home.

As their first London dusk fell, beige and blustery, they were placing into their traditional resting places all that they had carried home with them. When their furniture arrived they ordered pizzas and Octavian played *Sidney Bechet et Claude Luter* from his speaker as they drank Soave from the bottle and put together the coffee table and bookshelf before the new couch. Then they assembled the bar stools in the kitchen and the desk and the chair and the bookshelf in Octavian's new study; and upon the jade rug which they unrolled in the bedroom they assembled the bedside table and the chest of drawers. And, at last, as Anaïs unpacked her suitcase and hung her clothing upon hangers and folded it into drawers and arranged her toiletries in the bottom shelf of the bathroom cabinet and put her toothbrush in a cup on the sink, their bed. They lifted onto it the mattress and fitted sheet and threw upon it the covered pillows and duvet before leaping onto it themselves, Octavian onto his back, Anaïs onto his chest. When their kissing broke Octavian said, 'I think we should do something before we go to bed.'

Still surprisingly excited by the whole day Anaïs smiled and said, 'What?'

The ivory-white suitcase which had carried for the last seven years across four continents every one of Anaïs Spencer's worldly possessions, and Octavian Hughe's military-green duffle, which had carried his across five, were emptied completely and laid down, in the yellow glow of an outdoor searchlight, upon the uneven paving stones of the garden of their new home.

Octavian offered Anaïs the can of lighter fluid. She doused the black lining of her suitcase. 'Matches,' and struck one and smiled at Octavian and with a whoomp their luggage became a pyre. They threaded their arms tightly around one another and watched.

'We're really doing this.'

Anaïs cackled. 'Yyyep.'

III

Anaïs woke to her whispered name.

'Anaïs… Anaïs, I'm going to work for the morning.'

'Mmm,' she moaned. She was immeasurably happy with her head upon Octavian's bare chest.

'I'll be done by midday.'

'Nkay.'

He slid out from underneath her and went into the room next door.

When she got out of bed she looked up into the garden and saw blue and sunshine. She put on torn black jeans and a white silk camisole and left the house as quietly as she could.

6A Freedom Street was possessed of few architectural subtleties. It was one partition in a row of identical partitions, all attached—an estate built at the turn of the twentieth century for the securing of happy, healthy homes and electric light for sober and industrious workmen and their large families. One end of the street was the bracken and chain-link fence of an overground railway line, loitered in by drunkards and drug dealers during the daytime and by drunkards and drug dealers and foxes during the night. At the other was a small park fenced off by sharply spiked iron railings and towered over by an enormous white and fading-blue toy of a residential tower. The park was intersected by a path of spongy ground which halved it—into a playground played upon by a mother and her seven veiled daughters and two differently abled sons, and parkland being dug up and spat upon by several monoplegic owners and their vicious dogs. Anaïs crossed the car park of the childishly ugly tower and came to a main road. Opposite was a halal butcher's shop surrounded by antique stores and salons for the grooming of dogs. Two estate agents' faced one another across a T-intersection and were overlooked by a scrolling billboard.

In the warming glow of morning she came to a wrought-iron entrance placarded as The Sun Gate. She passed beneath the concrete arch embedded in it and strolled along a wide boulevard of oak and cherry, their leaves rustling in the breeze which swirled about her. She put her cheek to the light and was rather content. There was dappled shade upon the asphalt and from the distance a woman jogged towards her with her elbows in tight. At pains to propel herself at her present speed, very quickly two waddling men overtook her. Then Anaïs felt an unnerving woosh at her elbow as a man sprinted past. At the bend was a distance of considerably more joggers, all being trailed by vastly more joggers. Soon she was unable to continue in a straight line. She dodged and weaved through swishing ponytail and flailing earphone cord. There were couples in matching outfits and women in long and loose sweaty t-shirts and men in tracksuit pants and black baseball caps and people with tiny backpacks and men with dogs anchored by rope to their waists and women in shiny puffy vests cradling French bulldogs. Then came the dog-people—a man wived to six pomeranians, a woman crawling on her belly to clean up after a dachsund, recounting in babytalk to their friends the adorable and immutable personalities of their four-legged soulmates. By the time Anaïs came to a tree-edged lake she was laughing uncontrollably. She turned off the footpath and watched the sweating Cruikshank parade from under a gazebo. An attractive young man in shirt and trousers came to stand beside her.

'How ridiculous is this!?' she said, laughing.

'What's ridiculous?' he said, immediately before pulling his trousers down over his running shoes and throwing his still-buttoned shirt onto the ground and jogging away as he stretched a sweatband about his forehead.

'That doesn'tt even make sense,' said Anaïs. 'What about your clothes?' she called, but he was gone, into the slobbering mess of enthusiasts.

'I've never seen so many people jogging before,' she said, smiling to Octavian. She was in the garden on one of the barstools, her feet upon the other, skimming through an Evelyn Waugh she had taken from Octavian's living-room bookshelf.

'I think it's supposed to be good for you.'

'God no.'

'You never tried it?'

'Jogging?' she laughed. 'What the hell for? I mean, how bored do you have to be? You should have seen them, Octavian! They were in fluorescent leggings, even the males, and shirts made out of God-knows-what. And they all have headphones in. How annoying must that be? One guy had a belt with tiny water bottles in it like a gay little Batman. People jog up and down on the spot at pedestrian crossings! How much fucking exercise do you lose if you wait for the red man to go green? Seriously. And the mothers push prams while they jog! Fun for the baby, going that fast. But *how fucking bored do you have to be*?'

'It's a nice park though?'

'Yeah, it's really lovely.'

'The sun's out again. Shall we have a drink?'

'And that sounds lovely too.'

With a bottle of prosecco they strolled happily beneath the old oaks. They passed a huge field of topless men and women recumbent upon their clothing (the sun had been out for almost ten minutes). They slowed to listen to the adoring reproach of a rolling lawn of people, speaking in English to the dogs, tongues to the children. Then they emerged onto the sunlit riverside, came into sight of the leaves of a willow tree dipped in brown water, the web of silken white beams rising from the Albert Bridge, its pylons like rods of gaudy frosted wedding cake, the Thames at full tide.

'Home,' said Octavian, failing to see the garbage floating in the brown mess or the joggers behind them.

'How was work?'

'I got *nothing* done.'

'Nothing?' said Anaïs, surprised.

'I wrote, but it was all rubbish. I can't write, or I can't be funny, unless I'm hungover. Deathly hungover.'

'Deathly hungover?' she said, already amused. 'Why?'

'I don't know. It's just something I discovered, accidentally. When I'm hungover I have this abandon and this detached cruelty towards everything that makes whatever I come up with hilarious. So I can sit and stare at the computer screen for four hours and write non-stop but nothing is any good unless I'm hungover and don't care, literally, if I died on the spot, so painfully atrocious is the hangover.'

'Can you write when you're drunk?'

'Not a word. As soon as alcohol touches my lips I'm lost to coherence. Work-wise.'

'And you have a book to finish?'

'It'll take me a fortnight.'

'So you need a fortnight of being completely drunk every night?'

'Epically drunk. Like, Roman Bacchanalia, Marc Antony screaming at Virginia Woolf drunk.'

Anaïs downed the remainder of her glass, repoured it, and downed that as well. 'Well you start tomorrow morning then.'

'God you're attractive.'

'Shut up and drink you wuss.'

'Did you just call me a wuss?'

They left the park and went into a pub whose doors were guarded by two plastic chained-up Great Danes.

'Due spritz aperol,' said Octavian to the barman, 'Two spritz aperol,' who made and presented them.

'Eighteen pounds.'

'What's that?'

'Eighteen.'

'*Eighteen pounds*!? … They're nine pounds each?'

'Mm hm,' he said, unmoved.

'These are two euros fifty.'

'Where?'

'In Italy.'

'You're not in Italy.'

'How can it be five times the price? You're two hours away.'

'Not by bicycle.'

'Did the ingredients come by bicycle? I mean that's thirty-five dollars! That's the weekly wage of a Vietnamese person. A Vietnamese person has to work for a whole week just to have two drinks?'

'If he wants to have them in this pub.'

Anaïs was at a table outside, looking up to the tollbooths of the bridge. 'Make it last. That was nine pounds.'

'Nine pounds? Why so expensive?'

'I have no idea.'

And they sat and drank as slowly as they could manage and then took the wine glasses and went to find a cheaper drink. They ended up with Picpoul in the park and soon the sun began to set over the bridge. Its lights slowly came on, golden between the burning pink and shimmering glaucous of the river and the streaks of red and straw and fading cobalt in the sky.

'Not at all a bad view. I know where I'll be of an evening.'

'Next to me?'

'No other place on earth,' he said. Octavian's voice deepened and his accent softened as he drank. Drunk, he rested on a brisk half-Welsh, half-My-Lord-Hamlet. 'And when at last this is done, shall we purchase another bottle? A bottle nother?'

'Are you not drunk enough?'

'My lady, I farely beel the lip of my tiver to be moist.'

'Oh God.'

They stood for a time looking out from the bridge over the London skyline, a blackness unmatched by the softness of the evening. 'This going to be a big adventure awfully is.'

'I do hope so,' said Anaïs.

'Hope builds as fast as knowledge can destroy.'

'What does that even mean?'

'If you do not know, madam, then I cannot tell you.'

'You're really annoying when you're drunk,' she informed him.

'*Who* is drunk,' he declared. 'Who!? All I'm tryin' to find out is what's the guy's name on first base. What's on second base. I'm not askin' ya who's on second. Who is on first. I don't know. He's on third, we're not talkin' about him.'

'Would you please shut up and kiss me.'

They walked into another pub. Barmats were being taken from the bar and thrown into the sink. A group of men and women swayed as they declared their love for one another in between making with their tongues immature noises and passes at the bar staff.

'How much is a beer?' said Octavian, frightened of the answer.

'Lager?'

'Please.'

'Four pounds is the cheapest.'

'Four pints of two pound lager then.'

'And we've already called last, so this'll be the last two for the night, yeah?'

They both leaned an elbow on the bar and Octavian put his cheek in his palm and his other hand around Anaïs. '*How* did you discover that you could only write when you're hungover?'

Octavian squinted. 'I wrote a book about a year ago I think, and I had to write the prologue last. So I finished the book and then went out and got quite drunk. I kicked a Porsche. And then the next morning I sat down to write the prologue, and I wrote it and spent the rest of the day trying to get rid of the hangover, and a week later I printed the manuscript out and the prologue was absolutely hilarious. Funniest part of the whole book. All I want to do is be funny, everything is a joke to me, you should know that about me. But I seriously thought that somebody else had written that prologue. It was perfect. And then when I started writing this one I tried a few ways to make it as funny as possible. There's so much thinking when you have to write, you lose most of what you're trying to do. Spontaneity flies out the window. Not good for comedy. But then every time I got drunk after a day's work, I mean really drunk, I would wake up and not think, just sit at the laptop and write and be furious. And it was always the best stuff. So that's how I discovered it.'

'You!' said a man who was being pushed towards the door by his friend. 'You! ... I fucking hate you.'

'Thank you,' said Octavian. 'Thank you so much.'

The man pointed a finger over his friend's shoulder. 'You're fucking Australian.'

'When I hear you speak... darling, I would rather be nothing else.'

'I fucking hate you.'

'You said that already.'

The man broke free from his friend's embrace and in his windowpane check shirt and blue jeans, in his hussar guards polo belt and blue suede loafers, with his finger very near to Octavian's face, he said again, 'I fucking hate you.'

'Come on, St. John,' said this person's forbearing friend, pulling him back towards the door by a grapple through his underarms. 'Sorry, mate.'

'Not at all, not at all. Remember my friend... Hatred is the anger of the weak.'

'What a wanker!' said St. John, his ankles scraping back across the floor. Then he was outside and crawling across the road.

Soon Anaïs and Octavian stumbled into their home. He fell face down into bed and she pulled off his shoes and socks and went to the kitchen and stared out over the quiet darkness of their garden and drank a glass of water.

At night an unease was returning to her, an urge to be elsewhere, anywhere else, and excitement at the thought of moving again. Standing there in her own kitchen she worked at dismissing the crippling lashes of what she was coming to accept as the necessary deprivations of accommodating herself to bland and certain normality. Long night afforded her a scope for dreaming which she was forcing herself to believe was no longer healthy. With some difficulty, at last only by thoughts of Octavian, she dismissed the revenant, hitherto abiding, destroyer of her happiness, and went to bed.

IV

Anaïs woke and was alone. Loud typing rattled from the next room. She spent the morning in the garden in one of Octavian's shirts pulling the larger weeds from between the paving stones and sweeping the dead leaves into corners; unchoking the rose bush of vine; pulling the black hessian from the garden bed and turning the dirt with a rusted hand fork.

When Octavian slid across the bedroom door Anaïs was wiping with a sponge the plastic garden chairs she had found stacked in a corner.

'How'd it go?'

'Marvellously,' he said, putting his arms around her. 'I am hilarious. The garden looks great.'

'I was thinking we'd go to a gardening store to get some flowers.'

'That sounds like a great idea,' said Octavian, nuzzling into her neck. 'I like you in this shirt.'

'Shall we go now? I'm done here.'

'Oh, I have to work.'

'Are you not finished?'

'I've finished writing for the day. But I still have to work out what happens tomorrow.'

'Oh. Umm… How long does that take?'

'I have no idea. I just go for a walk and then think and then whenever it breaks it breaks.'

'Should I go alone then?'

'If you want to. I just don't know when I'll be back.'

'Can't you do the story stuff later?'

'No, I have to do it while everything's fresh. My mind's racing. I've got the whole third act in my head.'

'All right,' she said, unhappily. 'Anything you want planted?'

'No. Tomatoes. No, they won't grow here. Ummm… No, just flowers. Pretty ones. Your favourites. I'll leave my card on the bench.' They kissed and he went back inside, calling, 'Don't spend too much money. It's just a garden.'

Anaïs walked around Battersea and eventually found a nursery. She read the plastic labels on the seedling boxes and, by the pictures on their front of the mature flowers and by what would survive the autumn, she selected those that would be their garden. She asked an employee what else she would need and had delivered what she could not carry home.

She spent the afternoon, the sun appearing for very brief moments through the cloud, digging and replanting and driving stakes and mulching and watering. She planted foxgloves and hollyhocks and rhododendrons, and lilies of the valley and chrysanthemums, and cabbage, rocket, and spinach. Soon she was scratching at the inside of her arms and under her chin and sneezing and having to blow her nose with toilet paper, for they had no tissues.

The sun went down and Anaïs went to the store and bought a bottle of Pinot Gris.

She sat in a garden chair and waited for Octavian to come home. The garden beds were neat and shining black with fresh soil and water, everywhere popping with green leaf and seedling. In the charcoal gloaming she put into an empty mulch bag all the seedling containers and swept again and went inside and called him. Rumbling sounded from his study. She found his phone flashing and vibrating on his desk. Her nostrils were red and sore from abrasion and her arms and neck were bumpy with a rash. She ran a bath and lit some candles and took a history of Byzantium with her into it. She fell asleep, to wake shivering when the water had gone cold. She reran the bath and warmed herself back up and went to bed alone.

She woke, alone, to the sound of splashing water and long loud groans of exorcism in the garden.

Octavian was in his boxer shorts holding the garden hose over his head. His eyes were closed and he shook his head in between painfully discharged moans.

'What happened to you last night?'

'Errrrrr,' he bleated. 'I have no idea.' He squeezed his eyes shut then popped them wide open again.

'What do you mean you have no idea?'

'God *damn* it feels good!' He dropped the hose and groaned again and breathed out long and slowly as though expelling smoke from his lungs. He shook his cheeks and neighed as a shiver ran through his body. He kissed Anaïs and said, 'To work!'

as he went into the bedroom to dry himself. He put on a shirt and was about to enter his study when Anaïs, having been greeted at the kitchen door by a life-sized yellow charging rhinoceros, screamed and put her hand to her chest and said, 'Jesus.'

'What's the matter?' said Octavian, coming up after her.

'What the hell is that?'

'What's what?'

'That,' she said, directing his attention as he came upstairs.

'Oh yes,' he said, walking the length of the imitation beast. 'Ha! I forgot about that.'

'Where did you get it from?'

'I have *no* idea.'

'You have no idea?'

'No, I never remember. Arthur was there.'

'Who's Arthur?'

'The guy who got us the house.'

'Were you in Battersea?'

'It took me a long time to walk home.'

'With the rhinoceros?'

'I think. No, I don't remember. Well I must have walked him home. But he's huge.'

'You really don't remember?'

'Uh-uh.'

'That's not good.'

'What's not good?'

'You don't remember what you do when you're drunk?'

'I remember the important things. I mustn't have done anything important. I did figure out the next bit of the story though. Can we name him?'

'That's such an excuse.'

'What's an excuse?'

'You can just do whatever you want and then claim you don't remember because you were drunk.'

'But what do you think I'm doing?'

'Anything. Especially when you're not coming home at night.'

'I did come home.'

'When?'

'I don't know what time. But I slept next to you. Or under you. I slunk out of bed when the sun came up. God, I feel like death!'

It's marvellous.'

'You're ridiculous.'

'Yep.'

'Do you like the garden?'

'What garden?'

'Our garden.'

He went to the window. 'Ooo. Looks delightful. Why are you scratching?'

'I'm allergic to something out there. Or everything out there. I had a bath to get rid of the itching but it just spread it. I had to drink a bottle of wine to get to sleep.'

'You poor thing.'

'Can we go to a home store when you're finished? We need pots and pans and stuff. And I was thinking we could paint the living room. I hate that yellow.'

He roared and said, 'I love painting! No, I've never painted before. Sounds like fun.'

'I'll see you at midday?'

'Wwwhat time is it?'

'Eight.'

'Midday… Yes. Half past. I'll be done by half-past.'

'And we can get rid of this thing?' She put her hand on the rhinoceros' spine.

'No! We name him. Billy!' Octavian stroked its forehead. 'Good boy, Billy. No, Agrippa! His name is Agrippa.'

'Bit big for the kitchen though, no?'

'Nnnn…'

And by two o'clock they were walking the aisles of another of the world's hundreds of thousands of warehouse-sized monuments to self-reliance and convenience.

'How about this one?' said Anaïs, pulling a hanging frying pan from a rack of hanging frying pans.

'Mm hm,' said Octavian, looking over the rim of a tumbler as he put it and its iced and watered whisky to his lips.

'You didn't even look at it.'

'It's a frying pan.'

'It's *our* frying pan.'

'Our frying pan?'

'Our frying pan.'

'*We* need frying pans not. It is merely *a* frying pan.'

'But in it shall all of our meals be fried.'

'Ha. Very good.' Octavian moved in to inspect the thing. 'It appears to have all the KPIs of a frying pan. Do you concur?'

'I concur. Now give me a kiss.' And as he did she knocked him gently on the head with their frying pan. 'Now what colour are we painting the living room?' They came to an aisle of swatches of colour and stood between two wide walls of beige squares. 'The kitchen's cream. I think we should stick with that.'

'Cream? But that simply won't do. I mean, what about… Oooh, this one. Moon Lily. Our living room should be the colour of moon lily. Don't you think? There aren't lilies on the moon though.'

'What about School Time? How is that a colour?'

'White Illusion. Who comes up with these names? I bet you they call themselves writers too. And I bet they make more money than I could ever dream of. Rainbow Mist. A rainbow's already the colour *of* mist. Rainbows don't have their own mist. A rainbow's mist would just make a bigger rainbow.'

'But it's next to Mirage Mist.'

'Mirage Mist,' he laughed. 'That's so stupid.'

'Sparkling Wine?'

'Please.'

'Ah!' said Anaïs. 'Chantilly lace. That's the colour we want.'

'Accolade!' said Octavian, pulling the swatch from the wall. 'I shall paint my living room the colour of Accolade. Make my very walls surfaces of honour, my cornices beams of award. Bassinet! What is a bassinet? For babies, no? Paper Aeroplane, Dove Wing. Wow.'

'Chantilly Lace. No objections, yes?'

'How could one object to Chantilly lace? What about Arctic Ice though? How is *that* the colour of arctic ice? Wouldn't arctic ice be blue? I mean has the namer of this colour been to the Arctic, seen with his own eyes ice which defies in its colour all of mankind's preconceptions about ice, returned after months of trekking and sledding and he gets home and declares, You fools! Arctic ice is not blue! *This* is the colour of Arctic Ice! … But it's almost the same colour as Miss Universe, and Mount Everest, and Phantom Dream! But here! Not blue! *This* is Arctic Ice!'

'Chantilly Lace then?'

'Not Sparkling Wine?'

'It's a bit plain. If it were Perrier jouet…'

'If indeed,' he said pointing a finger and his drink at her.

'Chantilly Lace?'

'For lack of a less ridiculous alternative, Chantilly Lace.'

And to Bunk Johnson and *Down By The Riverside* they drank Perrier jouet and painted their living room the colour of Chantilly lace. Half way across the ceiling Octavian, atop the stepladder, stopped his brush and leaned back and held his hands in the air and gave a long and feeble groan. 'I've got it!' he growled.

'You've got what?'

'I know what happens next.'

'Yes, you finish the ceiling.'

'No, he turns selfish, Anaïs!'

'Who turns selfish?'

'Spiridion.'

'Who the hell's Spiridion?'

'Playfair's sidekick. He becomes selfish in reaction to the clearly misplaced idealism of William Playfair, to whom he has so long looked up! He becomes selfish!' Octavian stepped off the ladder and made the motion of throwing something against the wall and then went and fetched his notebook and pen. 'I have to go out for a bit.'

'Where?'

'I have to work on this while it's fresh.'

'You told me you can't write when you're drunk.'

'I can't, but I can work. This is story stuff, it's different. I'll be back in a bit. I love you.'

'All right,' said Anaïs, unhappy but accepting of the fact that the young man with whom she had taken up might very well be erratic and not at all normal.

'You love me too?'

'Yep.'

'Hey!'

'What?'

'Say it like you mean it, kid.'

And she did and Octavian stepped out onto the street. The early evening was cool and threatened by rain. He set off down their street, rubbing at his forehead and swirling his hands in the air. Shortly he stopped to write in his little red notebook, its cover printed with the arches of the Ducal Palace. He scribbled for a time and said, 'Yes!' and then walked on, flailing his arms through the park and waving his pen around like the baton of a conductor. Again he stopped to write and then moaned with pleasure and said, 'Yes!' Increasingly he became euphoric. With his head down he turned at the main road and walked into a long metallic table resting on bluestone cobbles. 'Ow!' he said, and stood there for a time scribbling as fast as his hand could manage. He stopped to rest, was breathing heavily, and saw two people open a door just beyond another metallic table. To his left he saw that he was outside a pub. Into it he went, and sat at a barstool and said, 'Evening,' to the barmaid.

'Hello,' she said pleasantly in a pseudo-American accent. Surprised by the niceness of his voice, she smiled.

'A pint of lager. And a half for...' Octavian turned his ear to the empty barstool beside him. 'What is it?' He nodded a few times and then looked down at it. 'That's *not* your name! ... Really? ... All right then, fair enough.' And he turned to the barmaid and said, 'And a half for Caesar.'

Anaïs was woken by excited chatter in the kitchen. She checked her phone and found midnight.

'You're not, you silly man!' said Octavian, joyfully hollering. 'How could you possibly be?'

The kitchen lights were on and two coffee cups were on the breakfast bar. Octavian was alone on a stool in what Anaïs had accepted now was his uniform of blue oxford shirt and khaki trousers. He said to the other stool, 'If you expect me to believe *that* you're going to have to show me a photograph. You don't have any, do you? You do!? How naughty you are.'

'Octavian,' said Anaïs, a gentle voice in the strangeness.

'Anaïs! Lovely of you to join us! We're having a tea party.' He put his hand across his face and whispered, 'But *he's* drinking whisky.'

'Who's drinking whisky, Octavian?'

'Caesar is drinking whisky. Though we were drinking beer. I don't think he can handle his whisky to be honest. But we'll see.'

'Caesar?'

'Caesar!' growled Octavian. 'Ape... Not... Kill... Ape.'

'Caesar's drinking whisky?'

'Caesar bibitum whisky est, yes. He's a wicked little fellow. He almost got me into trouble at the pub. But look how small he is. I haven't brought it up, I'm too much of a gentleman, and he won't admit it, but…' Octavian whispered, 'I think he's me, only very small. He's been very good company. There's a lovely pub around the corner. The Duke of Monmouth. We met a Hungarian, only she spoke like an American. And he's telling me all about Japan. He's been, haven't you, Caesar? Do you want to go to Japan, Anaïs? It can't take that long to get there. Perhaps we'll see Tom Cruise. Or Tom Green! We could make Subway Monkey Hour 2. But Caesar said we shouldn't go in cherry blossom season because the bastards raise the prices. He called them bastards, not me. Though they killed your grandfather's brother, I told him that.'

'Come to bed, Octavian.'

'Yes I do think I should. Caesar was about to start speaking French. Loathsome stuff. You'll see yourself out? There's a good little chap.' Octavian gasped. 'Sorry, not little. Goodnight Caesar. Caesar!' He exhaled: 'Ape… not… kill… ape.' Octavian cackled and held his mouth wide open. 'Say goodnight, Anaïs.'

'Goodnight Anaïs.'

'Say goodnight Kevin.'

And next morning Octavian woke and groaned and swore and cursed Caesar as an imp. 'Oh my God!' he said when he attempted to roll over. 'Ape killed ape. This is deathly.' He stumbled into the shower and then went to work.

When Anaïs woke she made coffee and a small breakfast and found that she had nothing at all to do. Outside was overcast, grey and cool and imminently wet. The house was stiflingly silent; she thought she might go for a walk and explore London.

She crossed Albert Bridge and walked along a street called, Anaïs thought delightfully, The King's Road. She found nothing especial about the street except that it was crowded and that its nooks were flourishing of leprous homeless people. She passed an open lawn and there came a break in the cloud. At this new warmth she halted and put her cheek to the sun. Across the street she saw a store called Sweatshop. In its windows were pictures of joggers and running shoes and she shook her head and walked on. She went up to Sloane Square and beyond Harrod's was repulsed by Brompton Road and there turned about and walked home again.

She came in and drank some water and heard typing downstairs. When she emerged from the shower she found that it was ten minutes past midday and that the tapping had ceased. She knocked on Octavian's door. No answer came; she pushed it open and found the room empty but for his phone. She called out to him and was returned silence. 'God damn it,' she said and went back up to the kitchen. She washed the only dirty dish in the sink and looked out to the perfectly kempt young garden. She looked around the kitchen and blew a soft raspberry and took up the remote from the microwave and pointed it at the television that Octavian had mounted on the opposite wall.

On the lush green lawns of a country house, beneath the pole-pointed domes of a white pavilion, a dozen ageing or overweight people were attempting to outdo one another in the baking of a sponge cake.

'Sponge cake?' said Anaïs, and scrunched up her face. She sighed and looked to one side of the kitchen—a low and empty shelf between a radiator and a bare wall—and to the other, the same thing. 'Sponge cake,' she conceded, and walked to the store and bought a baking tin and sugar and flour and butter and desiccated coconut and cocoa powder. She preheated their oven, as her phone instructed her to, and when eventually her own sponge was baking she returned to staring across the room at the television.

An indistinguishable cast of polished turds, all wearing fake tan and eyeliner, male and female, talked to one another about their text messages and the gettings about of their reproductive organs. 'Ergh,' she said, repulsed, and changed the channel. A show about marriage, the couples soon revealed to have had their first sighting at the altar. 'Hm?' she said, and moved on. Bright lights and a loud audience of clapping simpletons, amazed beyond the capacity of Vitruvian man by a border collie able to walk for a time on its back legs, then by an obese Irish child in the getup of a Veronese dwarf dancing like a jacked-up half-Puerto Rican stripper. 'Aahh!' Anaïs screamed, and changed the channel. A house full of disabled people getting drunk and watching television with one another; two of them soaked a piece of cake in vodka in order to smear it over the mouth of a young man confined by cerebral palsy to a wheelchair. In his drunken stupor he induced again and again the machine which enabled

217

him to communicate to say, 'Fuck You,' as he slobbered and grinned and squawked.

Television had evolved since last Anaïs had watched it.

'What the fuck?' she said, and calmly took the screen from its brackets and flung it as a frisbee against the back wall of the garden. 'Octavian,' she growled. She checked on her sponge cake and found it to be ready. She sliced it and waited for it to cool. She spread one half with jam and then replaced its top and sliced the whole thing into fingers; dipped them in chocolate icing and rolled them in coconut. When the bench was full and all the mixing bowls and spatulas washed Octavian walked through the front door.

'Ape... not... kill... ape. What have *you* been doing?' he said, surprised at the spread upon the bench.

'Do you remember lamingtons?' she said, excited for them both. 'I made lamingtons.'

'Have you? Can I try one?'

'I haven't had one of these in seven years,' she said as they both took a bite. The cakes were distinguished immediately by their dryness.

'Do we have milk?' Octavian chased his mouthful with a swig from the bottle. 'Delicious,' he said, still trying to get the thing down.

'They're dry.'

'No!' said Octavian, smiling.

'They're dry. I've never baked before.'

'No?!'

'Shut up.'

'What?' he smiled.

'They're dry.'

'I like my lamingtons dry. I like all my cakes dry. To hell with moistness. Bring Octavian a barren cake.'

'Where have you been all day?'

'I've just been walking around, thinking. I think I was in Chelsea. I saw the house that Burne-Jones lived in. Do you remember I told you about him? And the house that Hilaire Belloc lived in and Percy Grainger and Oscar Wilde, and Rossetti.'

'All in the one house?'

'Different houses. They have little blue plaques on them. And I found the most amazing stained-glass windows.'

'Will you show them to me?'

'Of course.'

'Now?'

'Do you want to go and see them now?'

'I want to get out of the house and I want to spend the afternoon with you.'

'If you freeze the lamingtons and then defrost them they'll go soft.'

'Really?'

'Mm hm.' Anaïs opened the freezer door but could not pull any of the three shelves out, so frozen were they to its walls. 'Just leave the door open and put a towel down. That'll defrost it.'

'Have you started drinking yet?'

'I have not.'

'Do let's.'

And they rugged up and walked with prosecco to Sloane Square. She was humbled and awed and was briefly religious before the viridescent east window and its Elijah and Saint Ursula and its blue-winged angels. They walked to the Tate with another bottle and Octavian talked Anaïs through the pre-Raphaelites; they left before they became emotional. Fuelled by the bubbles of three more bottles they walked back through the sunset and caught its last glimmers upon the river from the park.

Anaïs vaguely remembered and Octavian completely forgot going into a pub for one last drink and there hearing from the Rioja-stained mouths of two hefty and tatty-haired women a cacophony of abuse towards men and some vitriolic interrogation about what constitutes a lady. A prissy blonde woman with dilated pupils who was certain that her husband did not love her hugged them at length. They were forced to overhear several celebrations of America's creeping universalization of marriage and the slobbering excitement of a conclave met to slur forth their marketing genius in aid of items of clothing endowed with an over-sized zipper. Before Octavian gave in to wanting to correct somebody's Shakespeare and before Anaïs gave in to wanting to point out everybody's pretentiousness, the young couple left and walked home.

Anaïs closed the freezer and in the morning woke to the sound of Octavian's inordinately loud typing.

She showered and went upstairs and attempted to open a freezer drawer so that she could have a lamington with her morning coffee. All three were again frozen solid to their surroundings. She ran hot water and threw cups of it at the freezer sides and then took a hammer to it. She sat on the floor and bashed away at the frost and ice and with claw and cheek scraped the shelves and the condenser coils until she could slide in and out all three drawers smoothly enough. She took her cake and her coffee into the garden and sat on a garden chair with a Henry James. The morning was largely one of cloud cover. Intermittent drizzle soaked the pages which Octavian had prescribed to her. As she spooned a soaked piece of lamington from her coffee mug a head popped up over the fence.

'Good morning,' said its hoarse voice. 'New neighbour are we? A few of us are having morning tea. Do you *want* to come and join us?'

Anaïs put her hair into a ponytail and put on her black jeans and some shoes and went round. The woman who belonged to the head Anaïs immediately recognised as a not unattractive feminist. Her sundress was unshapely and her hair straight and brown and untampered with and her face without makeup. She introduced herself as Clementine and said that it was lovely to have Anaïs as a neighbour. Anaïs was led through a house identical in layout to her own, every available wall and resting place littered with the paraphernalia of the spiritually wanting. There were books on every one of the Eastern and Southern and Northern religions and posters with slogans of positivity scrawled across sunrises and fields of feral horse. There were dream catchers and photographs of Spain and polaroids of Clementine beaming beside yogis and swamis and Peruvian shepherds. There were books on organic vegetables and the evils of meat and the many, many, narratives of lesbianism. All this on the few steps from the front door across the kitchen to the garden.

'Everyone this is Anaïs. I love your name.'

'Thank you. And I yours.'

'Just moved in next door. Yesterday?'

And so Anaïs was subjected to a sunless morning tea in the English garden of Clementine Flowerdew. She was introduced to Samuel and Tallulah Ilminster, neighbours on the other side, one of whose parents owned Europe's third most profitable environmental disaster recovery company, and to Emma Sheepring, Clementine's best friend and protégé—they both being deeply concerned with a unique trinity of vegetarianism, rebirthing and colonic irrigation. They ate vegan cupcakes flecked with gold dust and gluten-free cucumber sandwiches sprinkled with salt flown in from the Himalayas (not by Clementine personally, it was hilariously admitted) and drank Pimm's and lemonade. They told her everything that she should do in London while she still had the freedom ('before London Life gets you,' was the phrase they used). They told her she should go to Brixton Market, which was within walking distance, and to Borough Market and Portobello Road Market and Brick Lane Market and said that she should go to Notting Hill Carnival and Glastonbury Festival and Wilderness and Green Man and Freedom Festivals and that she should visit the Museum of Childhood and the Saatchi's exhibition on Death and they said that the Tate had one on about biomorphic abstraction and Anaïs said that she had been there but hadn't seen that one and they said that it had exhibitions on by Indian and Palestinian and Afro-Cuban artists that she absolutely could not miss. Then Clementine said that she and Emma and Tallulah all went to hot yoga on Wednesdays and Fridays and that they would love for her to come along.

'Oh no, yoga's ridiculous. Thank you though.'

'You what? How could you possibly think that?' said Clementine, gruffly.

'People go to yoga out of some kind of misplaced need for spirituality, no? If there's something wrong with your life don't put tights on and sit on a mat with a bunch of other people. Just stop doing the wrong thing. … No?'

'You don't know what you're talking about,' said Clementine.

'Probably not, no,' said Anaïs.

'So what does your boyfriend do?' said Emma, a delightfully buxom young woman.

'What does he do?'

'Yes.'

'He does a lot.'

'What's his job?' said Tallulah.

'Are they the same thing?'

'I like that,' said Emma.

'*Very* good point,' said Tallulah. 'We both used to be in finance.'

'I think maybe it's an English thing. In England, darling,' said Clementine, 'being in something is the same as doing something.'

'I'm not an idiot.'

'But you are Australian,' said Clementine.

'And new to England,' said Tallulah. '*We* were in finance and then we both decided that it wasn't making us happy. Didn't we?' George turned his nod, which began at his wife, to Anaïs. 'So now George's in banking and I'm taking fertility treatments and studying handbags. We're so happy now.'

'They're so happy now,' said Emma.

'We're so happy now,' said George, an ineffectually-chinned man. Anaïs detected in his assertion an affirmation. He looked at her with the eyes of a watched hostage forbidden to signal to an unknowing friend that he had at all been taken captive.

'That's lovely,' said Anaïs, her voice beginning high and falling.

'And we have such a lovely home,' said Tallulah.

'They have such a lovely home,' said Clementine.

'We have such a lovely home,' said George, and then nodded almost imperceptibly, once, to Anaïs.

'So *what* does your boyfriend do?' said Emma, still curious.

'He's a writer.'

'Oo, Clementine's a writer.'

'What does he write?' said Clementine.

'Novels.'

'How many has he had published?'

'He's just finishing the first one now.'

'Oh. So he's not a real writer,' said Clementine.

'Is he not?'

'How old is he?' said Emma.

'Twenty-nine.'

'And what was he doing before he was writing the novel?' said Clementine.

'He said that he was waiting for his genius to rise to the claims that he had been making for it.'

This amused them all. Shortly they began discussing the getting rid of all plastic from their lives. Then, as they compared life-kickstart workshops, Anaïs checked her watchless wrist and said,

'Octavian's just about to finish work I think. I'm going to get back and see if he wants to do any of that marvellous crap you told me about. Before London strangles me. Thank you so much for having me over, Clementine. You have such a lovely garden.'

'Anytime, dear,' she said and she got up to show Anaïs out.

'She has such a lovely garden,' said Tallulah.

'She has *such* a lovely garden,' said George.

'What have you two got on for the afternoon then?' said Emma as Anaïs ascended to the terrace.

'George's taken the day off. We're going to the fertility clinic and then we're just going to have a lazy one, aren't we George? We have to be happy for the day, that's what the fertility therapist said.'

A familiar silence reigned through the house. Anaïs checked the study. He was out again. She found a note on the kitchen bench telling her he had gone for a walk to work out some story stuff and that he would be back before dark. She breathed out her anger and called him again. She heard rumbling on his desk. With nothing at all to do she walked to Brixton.

It took an hour of strolling beside congestions of car traffic and streets devoid of people to get to the high street. There she discovered that Sweatshop was a franchise. Curious to see what they sold, she went in. There was a wall of nutritional supplements, racks of running hats and helmets, armbands for phones, wearable lights, t-shirts made out of God-knows-what and fluorescent leggings and tiny shorts and running gloves and running bras and running sunglasses. Satisfactorily perplexed, she crossed to the market. A London bus passed and from behind it a young girl, her face shining with tears, fell into Anaïs' arms. 'Help me!' she screamed.

'Hm?' said Anaïs.

'Help me! They's tryin' to circumcise me, in't they!?'

'Hm?' said Anaïs, her confusion rising. The girl rolled out of Anaïs' arms into those of the person beside her. 'Help me!' she wailed to an old man she did not know to be deaf. 'They's tryin' to circumcise me, in't they!?'

Immediately Anaïs was in the crowd of the marketplace. A gaunt and bearded man with one palm raised was shouting in a Caribbean accent from a street corner: 'Charity suffereth long, and is kind. Charity envieth not. Charity vaunteth not itself, is not puffed up. Charity rejoiceth in the truth. Allahu Akbar.'

Anaïs quickly discovered that Jamaica had a cuisine distinct enough to occupy the menus of entire restaurants. She strolled by polystyrene box upon polystyrene box of starchy fruit and tasteless root and rack upon rack of sock and stolen phone. There were strange and shrivelled carcasses hanging from hooks and a great deal of shouting; Algerian flags and a golden Chinese cat with a swinging arm. She walked into the quietest butcher's shop and said that she was making dinner and wanted something special.

She and the butcher were the only people in the stall. He, a towering West African, leaned over the glass counter and turned his head slightly to say quietly, 'Special special?'

At this strangely abrupt rise in mystery Anaïs became Blood-Diamond Rhodesian. 'What kind of special are we talking about here?' she said, matching his solemnity.

'Special meat we got goat.'

'Goat is not special where I come from my friend.'

'You African white girl?'

'Maybe I am. … TIA.'

'TIA too fucking right. So you want de special special huh?'

'How special are we talking my friend?'

The butcher looked deep into her eyes. 'I got bushmeat. Real real bushmeat. … Special special.'

'You want to give me Ebola my friend? I want *real* special.'

The butcher nodded and soon muttered, 'Reptile?' Anaïs shook her head. 'Fish?' And she shook it again and said, 'More special.'

'More special than fish? I think maybe you want this fish.'

Anaïs shook her head and said, 'Mammal.'

The butcher's eyes widened. 'You want mammal? Who you got comin' over for dinner girl? You got Yahya Jammeh comin' to your house? OK I get you mammal white girl.' He ducked through the plastic strips which led into the back of the shop. Shortly he returned with a tray covered by a tea towel. He waved Anaïs down to the end of the counter furthest from the street. 'You can't tell nooobody where you get dis. Not even that you *seen* this.'

'Of course not.'

Eventually, staring into her eyes, he pulled back the teatowel. A frozen forearm, severed clean, the hand untouched, skinned from the wrist down and obviously a chimpanzee's, rested upon the tray. Anaïs recoiled from the thing and put her hand over her mouth and, astonished and frightened said, 'No!'

When the butcher stopped laughing he smiled and said, 'Straight from Cameroon. No farm. Straight from of de jungle and onto your plate. But I hope you got *some* money. Not cheap the special special.'

'Can I tell you something?' They both raised their eyebrows and their faces neared again. 'I think I want *more* special.'

'More special than dis?' He pointed his forehead at her. 'Maybe I think you want the fish after all.'

'The fish?' The butcher nodded once. 'Is it... Is it mermaid?'

'Merman indeed.'

'How much does it cost?'

'What part of a fish do you want?'

Anaïs settled on, 'Thigh.'

'Thigh is expensive. I can give you cut off a thigh. Four-hundred.'

'Pounds?'

'Of course pounds. What you think, dalasi?'

'Show me your thigh, butcher.'

'You sure you not tell nobody where you seen dis?'

'Nooobody,' she said, and the man nodded and slowly rose to upright and covered the ape hand with the teatowel and went again into the back of the shop. Rather than sight butchered merman flesh Anaïs ran out of the stall and onto the cobblestones. When finally she was out of the cobblestone jungle she set off to walk home. Half way back she saw another Sweatshop and thought that, theoretically, an hour's walk would be a twenty minute jog.

'Wait till you see your butt in these,' said the salesgirl as Anaïs emerged from the changing rooms in fluorescent leggings and a shirt made out of God-knows-what.

She unpacked a Waitrose bag onto the breakfast bar and went to put a bag of blueberries into the freezer and found that she could not open any of the drawers. 'Are you fucking kidding me?' She wiggled the drawers by their handles and shimmied them and banged them. Still they would not unstick. So she

threw a cup of hot water at them and sat on the floor and took
again to the freezer shelves with a hammer until their kitchen was
covered in snow and sleet and meltwater. 'Octavian,' she called
out when she was done. She called his phone and followed the
sounds of its vibrating into his study. She huffed. A belt-sander
started upstairs.

Octavian walked into The Duke of Monmouth. He stopped in
its green high-ceilinged entranceway and scribbled for a time in
his Venetian notebook. He pocketed it and went to the bar.

'You're a writer,' declared a man who was already standing
there. Middle-aged and with shortly-cropped hair, in cargo shorts
and running shoes and a tattered green jumper with no shirt
underneath it, he had been for the last hour asking customers
their blood type and telling them his favourite part of The Last
Samurai. He stroked a wild and greying goatee as he watched
with roguish eyes Octavian taking notes.

'I am.'

'Me too. Where you from?'

'Why does nobody here ask where I'm going?'

'Good point, man. I like that. Don't ask me where I'm from,
but ask me where I am going,' he said, holding his beer glass in
the air. 'I give you a quote, you give me a quote. Jess, we'll have a
jaeger. What's your name mate?'

'Octavian.'

'Fucking cool name, man. You're Australian?'

'Allegedly.'

'All right! My whole family's in Australia. Do you want to hear
my Australian joke?'

'Probably not.'

'No, you won't like it. But I'll tell it to you anyway. What's the
best thing ever to come out of Australia?'

'What? … Lager,' he said to the barmaid.

'A boomerang. Do you know why? … Because it fucks off
back to where it came from.' This man waited for the rise he
wanted out of Octavian. He got none and started smiling. 'I'm
only joking, man. I love Australia. Like I said, my whole family's
in Australia. Right, two jaegers.'

'Sorry about him,' said the barmaid as the man raised his shot
glass and grinned and said, 'Do not ask me where I am from, I

will not tell you. But ask me where I am going and we will go together. Now what's yours?'

'What's my what?'

'Your quote.'

'You want a quote?'

'Go on. Something cool, something that makes you think.'

'A quote? All right.' Octavian raised his shot glass and said, 'To lost causes and forsaken beliefs. To unpopular names and impossible loyalties.'

The man's beady eyes shot open and he pointed at Octavian's chest. 'Did *you* write that?'

'No.'

'I fucking love that.' He repeated the abridgment and clinked his own against Octavian's shot glass and they drank. 'And who said it?'

'Dale Kerrigan.'

'You're in alone I see?' said the barmaid to Octavian.

'What do you mean?'

'Not like last time.'

'Have I been in here before? … Oh no.'

'You don't remember?'

'Uh-uh.'

'You sat at the bar and ordered a pint for yourself and then a half for your imaginary friend.'

'I did not.'

'Caesar. You kept saying, Ape not kill ape. I was like wwaaaa…. And then the two of you talked about ancient Israel for an hour.'

'Ancient Israel?' Jess nodded twice. 'Wow. Sorry about that.'

'No, it was my fault. I brought it up. You walked in and said to the whole place, Where are you going? And I said, Israel!'

'I got a joke for you.'

'No. Eric.'

'What, Jess?'

'Is it about Jews?' he said, grinning.

'Yeah maybe.'

'No.'

A young woman rifled through her handbag as she walked up to the bar. She said, 'Hi Eric,' to the man in the green jumper and kissed him on the cheek.

'Daisy, he's a writer,' said Eric, pointing over to Octavian as he hugged her.

'Oh, is he?'

'His name's Octavian *and* he's a writer *and* he's Australian.'

Daisy extended her hand and said, 'It's lovely to meet you.'

'And you.'

'I'm going to sit out in the beer garden. Should I have a drink with him? Eric, what do you think? Do you *want* to join me?'

Anaïs turned her butt and her new leggings to the mirror and slapped one of her cheeks. 'Hmm,' she said, approving.

The Duke of Monmouth's garden was small and brimming with flowers and bamboo and ivy. 'So how long have you been in London then?'

'Almost a week.'

'Wow! Fresh. Are you just traveling?'

'No I've moved here.'

'For a girl?' she said, slowly and with a cheeky grin. They sat in the intermittent sunshine on a long wooden table.

'To get a novel published.'

'Interesting.' Daisy appeared to be in her late thirties (cheap white wine was the chief cause of the lateness of the presumed decade), had thinning sandy blonde hair tied atop her head like a feral child and failed to conceal her fluorescent push-up bra. 'What kind of novel?'

'A very funny one.'

'Is it finished?'

'I finish the last scene tomorrow morning. After getting roaringly drunk tonight. Cheers.'

'Cheers. And you say it's funny?'

'The funniest novel you've ever read.'

'And you think you're funny then?'

'I know I'm funny.'

'What's it called?'

'*The Horrible And The Miserable.*'

'That doesn't sound like a funny book. What's the first line?'

'The first line?' Octavian straightened his back and took a sip from his beer and said, 'Like most men, William Playfair thought the world decadent, corrupt, immoral, and doomed, and could find nothing at all wrong with it.'

'Ooh,' she said, pursing her lips with approval. 'Still not funny though.'

'But it is witty.'

'And you back yourself?'

'Daisy, I'm the next big thing in literature. *Bridesmaids* made two hundred and eighty eight million dollars at the box office.' The statistic was slow and astounding from his mouth. '*The Hangover 2*, five hundred and eighty six million.'

'They're movies.'

'Yes, but! Imagine that everyone who saw those movies read one book. They didn't read books before, because books were boring, but now there's a book that's as funny as the idiotic films that they can quote by heart. My book. They read my book, because it's *that* funny. There are no novels written the same way that Judd Apatow makes films. And only I write novels as elegantly as Waugh and as hilariously as Todd Phillips. Once I can get an agent to see that, they'll see that every person who has ever seen *Anchorman* or watches *New Girl* will buy this novel. Because it's that funny.'

'Do you know what I do, Octavian?'

'What you do?'

'You're going to like this.'

'Why? What do you do?'

'I'm a literary agent.'

'You're not!'

'Mm hm.' And Daisy pulled from her purse her business card. 'Isn't this a beautiful coincidence?'

'In an ordered universe there are no coincidences. That is an interesting surname though.'

'Interesting? Why?'

'Trench-Hawe?'

'It's very English, darling. Hyphenated surnames get you everywhere. What's yours?'

'Hughe.'

'Octavian Hughe. Octavian,' she said, and then slid her hand up his leg and back again. 'If your book's any good I'm going to make you famous.'

'Uuuuummmm…' He cleared his throat and said, 'Do you want another drink?' and he downed the last of his pint.

Solemn angels genuflected on their high pedestals as Anaïs passed beneath a sky of menacing grey cloud. She was gliding, but for the thumping of her shoes against the asphalt and her breathing, silently, along a boulevard of arching bracken and flittering oak and dense bramble. She thought of nothing but the deadening rhythm of her feet beside the lawn and the sweat dripping from her eyebrows as she looked upon ivy-covered headstones and mossy, worn graves. She got lost for a time and soon realised she was doing laps of the place. When at last she found the gate at which she had entered she jogged home.

'Shit,' said Octavian, waiting for his drinks to be poured.

'Watch her, mate,' said Eric.

'Shit, shit, shit, shit, shit. Thank you.'

'Watch her,' said Jess, as she handed him Daisy's wine.

'I can tell. God damn it.' Outside he said, 'So who do you work for?'

'Ransom & Waterdown. One of the biggest agencies in Britain.'

'And you do what for them exactly?'

'I'm an agent. I have six authors and I'm building my list. And I have *no* funny novelists.'

'Because there *are* no funny novelists. Yet. All the funny people are vulgarising themselves behind microphones. What you people call funny novels are actually just lengthy collections of the diverting opinions of articulate housewives. I am *the* comedy novelist.'

'I think you should give me your number.'

'I am number one,' he said in a Russian accent. Daisy half-collapsed into laughter. 'Told you I was funny.'

'I think that you should give me your *phone* number. I live just opposite the pub. We don't *have* to be wasting all this time talking, you know?'

'What do you mean?'

'I mean we don't have to be wasting all this time talking, when we could be fucking.'

'Huh?'

'What?'

'That's a little bit vulgar, no?'

'You're Australian,' she scoffed.

'What does that mean? Wait, what *is* the time? Six? Shit. I've got goat meat in the oven. All right, I have to go. I have your number though, yes?' He held up her card. 'This is your personal number?'

'Yep.'

'And I'll call you?'

'You better. I'm going to make you famous. The book's finished, isn't it? As in polished, done, no more changes.'

'Except for the last scene.'

'I have my morning free tomorrow. Shall we do brunch and I'll look over the manuscript?'

'You're serious?'

'Can you email it to me tonight?'

'Definitely I can do that.'

'Well it's so lovely to have met you,' said Daisy. 'It's a shame you have to run so soon.' Then she put her arms around him and whispered in his ear. 'I promise you'll love how I make you feel. It's so early. Are you sure you don't want to come round? We'd have the whole night.'

And he pulled away from her and walked briskly inside. Octavian passed Eric, who asked him if he was leaving, and a podgy redheaded man alone at the bar talking to the barmaid about how many friends he had.

He was reading in the living room when Anaïs came sweating through the front door.

'Octavian?'

'In here.'

'Oh my God, Octavian. I almost bought chimp meat! I got offered chimp meat. The butchered forearm of a chimpanzee. Sitting right there, frozen on a tray in front of me.'

'Ape…' huffed Octavian.

'And I could have bought human!'

'Not…'

'We could have bought and eaten for dinner human flesh.'

'Kill…'

'In London.'

'…Ape.'

'Brixton is *awful.*' She leaned against the doorjamb. 'And among it all, English people just smiling and sipping lattes and

231

marvelling at what they think is diversity. I don't know what those horrible neighbours were going on about. I met the neighbours this morning, the next three houses that way, and they are all liars. All of them. They're not happy. They're just rich and they're trying to surround themselves with all the substitutes for happiness. One of them's writing a book and guess what it's called. Seriously.'

'Ape... not... kill... ape,' Octavian breathed up at her from the couch.

'Are you even listening to me?'

'Of course.'

'You're not. What did I just say?'

'You said... Ape... not... kill... ape.'

She glowered at him.

'I'm kidding. You told me to guess what the name of this woman's book is. What is it?'

'*The Path To Happiness.*'

'Wow. There is no path to happiness,' said Octavian as the Dark Knight. 'Happiness is the path.'

'What's that?'

'Some Buddhist crap I've always liked.'

'Oh, I wish I knew it when she came out with that title. Seriously, all four of them going on and on about London. How much they love London. Even though they said I should do all this crap before London gets me, they said, like it was a monster. And the yoga! God damn it! They would not shut up about yoga! God I hate yoga! If these people were happy they wouldn't be looking everywhere for Buddhist solutions to Christian problems. They're liars, Octavian. I could it see it in that man's eyes. He was terrified, but he was being made to lie. Not at gunpoint, but like there was this invisible bubble around everybody and they absolutely need it in order to live but simply to mention the bubble would make it disappear and they'd all die from the shock. Like it was the biggest possible outrage to admit that you don't like this expensive chimp-meat-filled cesspool that everybody pretends to fucking love called fucking London. This is why I left Melbourne. Nothing's sincere here.'

'Where have you been?'

'What do you mean?'

'Dressed like that.'

'Oh, I went jogging.'

'You what?' he laughed. 'Did you really?'

'Yep. And I did not enjoy it.'

'No?'

'Nn-nn. It is a fast way to see a city though.'

'So guess what?'

'What?'

'I've met someone.'

'What?'

'A literary agent.'

'You've met her?'

'What makes you think it's a female?'

'You said you met them.'

'I did.'

'Mm!'

'What!?'

'You mean you've met someone and now you're leaving me?'

'Hm? No. Why would you say that?'

'That's what "I've met someone" means.'

'No it doesn't, it means I've met someone. I've met a person. I met them at the pub, I met a literary agent. I met one.'

'But it's a woman?'

'Well yes, but what does that matter? Anaïs, this could be it. I could be in. An agent. I've fallen into it. I just went into a pub and a weird guy who looks like a gypsy Viking introduced me to a literary agent after telling me to go fuck myself. This is destiny. She's going to read the manuscript and see if she wants to take me on. I seriously could be in. Done. Published. Man of letters. Scourge of Princes.'

'They see fertility therapists, Octavian!'

'Who do?'

'The neighbours. And one of them said she studied handbags. What does that even mean?'

Octavian got up and put his arms around her. 'You really didn't like them, huh?'

'No,' she said, very grumpily.

'Shall we get them back?'

'Yes! How?'

'What movie do you think they would hate the most? Oo, I know.' And Octavian put his laptop on a garden chair and attached his speaker and turned both up to full volume and started *American Sniper* and he and Anaïs went out and were entirely intoxicated by the time they crossed Trafalgar square in the moonlight.

Anaïs woke alone and to silence. There was no typing and neither a running hose nor gasps of deathly hangover.

Octavian came home at eleven.

'Brunch?' said Anaïs when he told her where he had been.

'Daisy only had her morning free this week.'

'Who's Daisy!?'

'The agent I told you about.'

'Oh. The agent,' she said with derision.

'She loves the book! She said she couldn't stop laughing. She's in, she's taken me on. I have an agent. Not a week in London and I have a literary agent. Do you see? This was all meant to happen! All I have to do is finish the thing. She said, flat out, she's going to make me famous.'

'She's going to make you famous? Isn't an agent's job to make you rich? I don't like the sound of this at all.'

'Why not? She's lovely. She's a bit vulgar. But she's going to help me. Not a single person has helped me ever. I've literally never been helped.'

'And she knows about me?'

'Of course she knows about you! Why would you even ask that?' Anaïs raised her eyebrows and returned to dipping and rolling her lamingtons. 'Are you baking again?'

'I'm going to make, if it kills me, the most moistest lamingtons ever to be made moist.'

'Ha. All right, I have to get to work. I'm going to take a long shower and work myself up into an ecstasy and then finish this damn book. Today. It's happening, today!'

'What did you have for brunch?'

'Hm?'

'What did you have for brunch?'

'Why?'

'What did you have for brunch?' she said slowly. 'It's a simple question.'

'I had eggs florentine.'

'And what did Daisy have?'

'She had a gold-leaf cappuccino. Why?'

'What's a gold-leaf cappuccino?'

'A cappuccino with gold leaf flakes instead of chocolate.'

'You know we came home with swords last night.'

'*That's* what it was!' He lifted up his shirt to reveal a deep and long scratch. 'I could *not* figure out how this happened.'

'You're a horrible swordfighter.'

'I think you've had training.'

When the lamingtons were done Anaïs cleaned the kitchen to music (*...And some people thinkin' that the end is close by...*) and then could find nothing else to do. (*'Stead of learnin' to live they are learnin' to die.*) She looked out over the garden, at the shaded back wall opposite, at the cold wind turning the leaves. (*Let me die, in my footsteps...*) New and extreme idleness caused her to be reflective upon her own life. She thought at length about her time in Bangkok, of the warmth and the noise and the smell and the food, the air-conditioned lobby of the Shangri-La, tropical villas and howling monkeys and infinity pools, rufying Chinese people-smugglers with snake's blood vodka on rooftop bars overlooking The East.

Then she went for a jog, along the river, in blustery drizzle. She passed through a cemetery of nameless headstones and crossed two bridges.

Three hours later Octavian bounded back up the stairs. '*Madamina!*' he sang. '*Il catalogo è questo.* ... Guess what?'

'What?'

'Guess!'

'What?'

'It's fucking finished! *The Horrible And The Miserable* is done and done! I couldn't touch it again without lowering its incredibly incredible standard. It's perfect. As perfect as a work of comedic art can be. Not a word out of place. It carries its justification in every line. Light and excellent, swift and exact. Funnier than Apatow, as funny as Eastbound & Down. The Frat Pack novel. Let's get drunk!' Anaïs picked up one of the swords from the kitchen bench and threw it to Octavian. 'Oh yes?' he said.

'You have offended me, sir. I desire satisfaction.'

And she took a swipe and Octavian blocked it and took hold

of her wrist and pulled her in close and kissed her. Then he whisked her off her feet and cradled her and kissed her again and said, impersonating, 'I was wondering what would break first.'

'You *have* seen it?'

'Of course I've seen it! … Your spirit… or your body! … Now, let's go and join the English in England.'

At the first of their three local pubs they heard one side of a telephone conversation in which a young woman was complaining that she had turned up to the Swiss Alps to find that the boy had rented an Alfa Romeo after she had specifically told him she would only be driven around the Swiss Alps in a Jaguar. Among a hundred desperate pleas for more ketchup could be loudly heard a conversation about how interesting it had been growing up as the child of gay parents. Half way through a long two-sided lamentation about how difficult was writing website copy, they left.

At the second of their locals they were asked to down their swords, which they did, and they sat under the cover of an eave and listened to a table talk about how they were finally all allowed to meet after their cats had fallen asleep at the same time. One of them, a rotund and balding blonde, asked the table, at which her life-partner was sitting, when they all thought was the right time to start freezing their eggs. None could give a definitive answer. Then they all talked about how much of a blessing was childlessness and how cruel it was to be so selfish as to bring a child into this horrible, horrible world.

'There is no path to happiness,' Octavian said, 'happiness is the path.' He began to chant it with rising volume until they left.

In the Duke of Monmouth they laid their swords upon the bar and Octavian with beer faded into incoherence as the pub busied to full. There was a blowsy ginger with an upturned moustache sitting at the bar and talking to anybody around him who would listen about the International LGBT Travel Association and about Coca-Cola and the Conservative Party—his three biggest clients. To all who strayed into his web he concluded by telling them that what he was wearing was not a velvet tracksuit but in fact a Louis Vuitton. The attendees of an engagement party in the garden filed in and out, the males discussing which of the other guests they had slept with and at what stage of her rise to womanhood, the females the comparative income security over time of the guests that they had slept with or were considering marrying. Two of these men came to the bar and ordered drinks. One of them hung their head and was offered by his friend the consolation of, 'Don't *worry* mate, pussy's for the *end* of the night.' He rose to vigour and said, 'Yes! Let's go titty-hunting!' and off they went. Behind Octavian and Anaïs not less than six parties were eating burgers and drinking pints of coke and shouting about how much they hated Americans. Two girls from the engagement party came inside and sat at the bar in order to really break some matter down. One of them had a joker grin painted in Shiraz and the other empurpled teeth. Soon they asked the sweating Venezuelan barman to weigh in.

'*We* have a friend and did you know that she had never had an orgasm until another one of our friends who she was sleeping with stuck his finger in her bum, and she came instantly for the first time.'

The barman's blotchy face opened completely with amused shock. 'You should not be telling me this.'

'No, no, it's all right, she's a *very* good friend of ours. Actually you might know her, she comes in here all the time.'

'Her name's Daisy,' said the other friend.

'Wow,' said Octavian into his pint.

'What do *you* think?' the first girl said to Anaïs.

'I think I am going to the bathroom,' she said, and did.

'Whatever works,' said Octavian like a gruff Al Pacino. 'What are you all doing out there?' he managed to growl.

'Two of our friends just got engaged.'

'Mm. Lovely.'

'Is that a real sword?'

'It scratched me.'

'Where are you from?'

'He's Australian.'

'No,' said the other girl, as her male attendant arrived to put his arms around them both.

'We're just asking this man whether or not his sword was real.'

'Daisy that sounds dirty,' said Daisy, Daisy's friend.

'No it doesn't! It only sounds dirty if you say long. Or hard.'

'Are we having fun girls?' said Daisy's boyfriend, a lupine looking person with an obsessively maintained quiff of greasy blonde hair, and a long vermicular body, white scarf around the neck of his corduroy jacket.

'Too much fun.'

'He's Australian and he has a long hard sword,' said Daisy.

'I've seen you in here before haven't I?'

'I don't know,' said Octavian as John Wayne. 'Have ya?'

'I think I have, yeah. Why don't you fuck off back to Australia, mate?'

'Anaïs, door,' said Octavian, just as she returned from downstairs. 'Take the swords.'

'OK,' she chimed.

'Lord Gilbert,' Octavian announced. 'Baron of England by the grace of His Majesty King Henry the Second, did seize upon the person of a priest of the Holy Church and unlawfully held him in custody.' Octavian stood from the bar stool and thanked and apologised to the barman. 'Here we judge him damned with the devil and his fallen angels and all the reprobate,' he boomed. 'We cast him into the outer darkness, to eternal fire, and everlasting... pain.' And he punched the tall boy in the cheek, causing the face which he so adored to turn and fall onto the end of a table, from which it then bounced as he flopped onto the floor.

'I'm the third revelation!' growled Octavian, over and over as Daniel Plainview, pointing to himself as he backed out of the pub. '*I'm* the third revelation.' He cleared his throat and said to Anaïs, 'Let us to the bridge.'

'God, those people!' said Anaïs, wrapping her arms around his waist.

'I have a song for you.' And as they walked under the golden lights dancing across the Thames to Chelsea Octavian waved his sword and sang to the silvery waters, '*Adieu la vie...*'

'What are you doing?'

'*Adieu l'amour...*'

'Please stop singing.'

'*Adieu toutes les femmes!*' and he serenaded her with the *Chanson de Craonne* until they were in bed.

A week later Daisy Trench-Hawe had read Octavian's manuscript and wanted to meet him for a drink after work.

'You didn't tell me you had a girlfriend!' she said, very pleased to meet Anaïs.

'Did he not?' said Anaïs.

'It's so lovely to meet you! You're so beautiful! You look like that model. What's her name? Kate Upton.'

'Thank you,' said Anaïs, years ago tired of the comparison.

'Sorry it's taken me so long to get back to you. I don't normally have Tuesday-Wednesday-Thursday free. But my grief counsellor cancelled on me so I thought I'd use the opportunity. Now...'

'Grief counsellor?' said Octavian. 'Is everything all right?'

'Oh yeah,' said Daisy, dismissing his concern. 'I only see her because my joy counsellor thought I was getting too happy.'

'Your what?' said Anaïs.

'My joy counsellor. Ante.'

'What the hell's a joy counsellor?'

'Do they not have them in Australia? They're the best. They teach you how not to be selfless, not to be too humble. And she and my wealth counsellor work out of the same office so they work together.'

Anaïs said, 'Wow.'

'Anaïs,' said Octavian, warning her.

'Yes?' He raised his eyebrows to her. 'What is it my darling?' He said nothing. 'And you just have the three counselors do you?'

'*Anaïs.*'

'Just the three, yeah. I couldn't fit anymore into my schedule I don't think.'

'I'm going inside to get another drink. Anyone want one? No? Good.'

Daisy watched Anaïs leave. 'She's *so* lovely. Are you serious about her?'

As Anaïs rounded the bar a bald young man with gecko eyelids and a beard, his chief attainment in life the employing of other people to draw superheroes upon his skin, spun himself off a barstool and blocked her from passing between a wall and a large and very inconveniently placed green pole. He pointed and slurred and blinked: 'You're here with the Australian.'

'Am I?' said Anaïs, trying to sidestep him.

'And you're an Aussie too.' He leaned further in and spoke with viciousness. 'You're just a fucking convict. You're a fucking immigrant. You're no better to us than the Africans in Calais. Why don't you fuck off back to...'

And the tirade ceased only when Anaïs had circumvented the man and a swinging door closed behind her.

'Yes,' said Octavian, adamantly.

'Serious serious?'

'What's serious serious?'

Daisy reached a hand along the bench and put a finger onto his. 'I mean can you sneak out later and come over and fuck me?'

'Daisy!' said Octavian, bemused that she could be so persistently oblivious to the two-sided nature of human interaction. 'I love Anaïs.'

'So?'

'What do you mean, So?'

'So no?'

'You're going to be my agent, Daisy, not my mistress.'

'I could be your girlfriend couldn't I?'

'Anaïs is my girlfriend.'

'And do you love her?'

'Yes.'

'Do you really love her?'

'Daisy, I really love her.'

'Ohhhh,' said Daisy, her personality immediately and perplexingly forking off into a friend delighted for them both. She stood up and bent over to hug Octavian and said, 'I'm so glad to have a good male friend you know? Just platonic. Where there's no chance of sex or awkwardness. Just really good friends. I'm so happy for you both.' Then she whispered, 'If you change your mind you let me know. Oh, you're so beautiful,' she said loudly, returning to her seat as Anaïs returned to hers. 'Anaïs, I was just about to tell Octavian, I've taken the manuscript to a good friend of mine at Hackney Bromide. You know who they are of course?'

'Are they publishers?' said Anaïs.

'Yes, they're publishers,' said Octavian, almost snapping.

'All right. How do I know that?' said Anaïs.

'Yes they're publishers. Big. Huge. Global. They do Raul Lebre and Clementine Flowerdew and Jenna Jameson. They're huge. And I have a dear friend there, my best and oldest publishing friend and I've taken your book to her and she said… that she can't take it on because you don't have an SMP.'

Octavian stared at her. Soon he shook his head. 'What the fuck is an SMP?'

'A social media presence.'

'Wwwhat the fuck is that?'

'Well, my friend googled you, you see. And you don't have a website. And you don't have Facebook, which is bonkers, you're not on Instagram, you don't have Twitter, for a writer that's essential, you *have* to have Twitter, you don't have any Spotify playlists, you don't have a Nonsense account, no YouTube channel. Nothing.'

Anaïs interrupted. 'What does any of that have to do with being a novelist?'

'Anaïs,' said Octavian.

'What?'

Octavian moved his eyes over to Daisy and said, 'Daisy's talking.'

'I know she is.'

'Let her finish? … Go on.'

'Well you practically don't exist you see. And a publisher can't take you on if you don't exist. You need an SMP. Any aspiring author knows that. Nobody will buy your book if they don't know who you are. It's just for publicity it's absolutely essential. But… I can—'

'Publicity? Daisy, you want publicity? I fucking breathe publicity. See this? That's from a sword fight I don't remember having, in Trafalgar square. I have the political opinions of a Balkan shepherd. You want outrageous? I'll give you outrageous. I've been driven out by the husbands and jealous boyfriends of eleven different cities. I'll get you publicity. I am a bohemian citizen of the world, a hellraiser old school. And a comedian. I know more Shakespeare than Benedict Cumberbund and I never shut up about it. You want publicity I'll get you publicity. Front page of the newspapers, Daisy. You take the book back to your friend and you get it published and I will sell it for them.'

The glint in his eye that had enabled him not only to live but to thrive for the last four years without having worked a paid hour; the deeply-drawn flicker that had caused girl after girl to perceive in him an excitement that her home could not be without; that fiery glare that allowed him to live fundlessly the bounding life of a new Byron; the charm that had seduced models, actresses, dancers, therapists, lawyers, wives, milk maids, flight attendants, surfers, yogis, doctors, countesses, contadine, cittadine, Brazilians, Americans, Germans, Mexicans, Palestinians, Dutch-girls, Norwegians; that arrangement of wrinkled forehead and crow's feet, ignited by his ancient and unconquered soul—now won over his most prized quarry, a literary agent, this emotionally very puzzling English girl, Daisy Trench-Hawe.

'You're serious?'

'Deadly,' he said like the Dark Knight, and smouldered. 'Front page of the newspapers.'

'Is he serious?' Daisy said to Anaïs.

'Anaïs hasn't read the manuscript.'

'Have you not?' said Daisy.

'I'm not really a big reader.'

'Are you not?' said Daisy and turned to look at Octavian.

'But he's serious,' said Anaïs. 'He's not an aspiring novelist, he's a novelist. Just nobody else has discovered it yet. He's been waiting for his genius to rise to the claims that he makes for it and it has risen. He's there. At twenty-nine. You should be the person to discover it. It'll make your name.'

Anaïs and Octavian left The Duke of Monmouth hand precariously in hand.

'So how on earth are you going to get on the front page of the newspapers?'

'I'm going to get banned from France.'

EPISODE 6

To Return, And View The Cheerful Skies.

I

The Eurostar eased from its resting place and Anaïs and Octavian put their heads back against their seats in the mechanical quiet of the sparsely occupied carriage. Octavian took a bottle of water from the plastic bag which held all that they were taking with them to Paris and cracked its lid.

'Octavian, I don't like London.'

He drank calmly and returned the lid to the bottle. 'No?'

'No, I *hate* London.'

'Why?' he said, almost laughing at her vehemence.

'There's nothing here.'

'That is a big statement.'

'It's so boring. ... I have nothing to do all day, the weather's absolutely horrible. We're in the middle of summer and in two weeks the sun hasn't been out for longer than twenty minutes. There's no sun, there are no beaches, no swimming pools. It's unnatural for a human being not to be able to go swimming. This city's like an enormous artificial concrete dome after an apocalyptic drought, except it rains all the fucking time. There aren't even any hills. At least in Paris you get a nice view. It's just so boring!'

'We're having fun though aren't we?'

'But the place has no romance. It has less romance than Bangkok. And everything's so fucking expensive. You can't do a thing here without spending a fortune. We can't eat at restaurants, we can't go to the theatre. Tickets are literally hundreds of pounds. Drinks cost weekly wages for the rest of the world. We can't leave London because we don't have a car. During the day I've spent the day's budget as soon as I step out the front door.'

'But that'll all change when we have money.'

'And when will that be?'

'When the book is published and we're famous.'

'*We're* famous? I haven't lied in weeks, Octavian. There's just no fun to be had here. Do you remember how much fun we had in Venice? That's how much fun we should be having every day.'

'You have to be a bit more realistic, Anaïs. Venice is a fantasy world. We'd only just met.'

'"Be more realistic?" That's the most horrible thing I've ever heard. The streets are dead here. You leave the house at ten o'clock at night and what do you find? They're empty except for homeless people and staggering hooligans and cars. The gutters run with piss and vomit. They're dead. There's more life in the brambles of a cemetery than in the streets of London.'

'You've only been here for two weeks. Cities this big take time to get used to.'

'I knew I hated Bangladesh after eight seconds. That's a whole country.'

'Don't they say that to be tired of London is to be tired of life?'

'That is *complete* bullshit. I've seen that slogan plastered everywhere. It's a conspiracy. What it should say is, Whoever has retired from life lives in London. The place is an enormous geriatric community. Everybody's dead inside, and they've all committed suicide. Nobody's born dead inside, and they've all killed themselves and now they're walking around repeating the same slogans. "I love London. Don't you love London? That's so London. London life. Don't you just love London. That's so London." Life in London is not life at all, it's protracted death. They all *have* to live here to make money but rather than anybody own up to the fact that it's anodyne and dead they repeat the slogans of the whole industries that have sprung up just to keep people from moving elsewhere. Money is a lie and love of it a curse. The communists had the same thing, Octavian. *The party gives you everything. Liberty is preserved by obedience to the law.* And London has it only now they call it PR and marketing. Ask anybody who lives here, do you like London? They cannot rationally say yes. It's concrete and dirty and loud and full of tourists and foreigners. It has no romance whatsoever. It's always grey or raining, the food doesn't taste right even though it's extortionate. It's clogged with cars. It's flat. Everybody's either in a suit or homeless.'

A middle-aged woman in a pantsuit shooshed her. 'Somebody will hear you.'

'Good! Let everybody hear me. Stop lying to yourselves.'

'If you don't like it, leave.'

'If everybody left who didn't like London there wouldn't be a soul remaining on the banks of the Thames.'

'Anaïs, I've been working and we haven't got any money because of the house. That'll all change in a couple of weeks. The book is done. I won't have to spend my mornings in the study or my afternoons walking around or my nights getting drunk. I'm all yours now and we'll be rich soon.'

'I don't want to be rich!'

'Then what do you want? What is it you want, Mary? What do you want? Do you want the moon?'

'I want to be free. The people here are so fake. They're wretched and pompous.'

'Do you want to be free from me?'

'No, not from you,' she said, fatigued.

From Gare du Nord they took a metro to Madeleine.

'How long are we in Paris?'

'Until I get kicked out.'

'And where's the hotel?'

'There's the hotel.' Octavian pointed to the Hyatt Regency.

'Can we afford a room there?'

'Nope.'

'And?'

'And what? What do you mean?'

'I'm confused.'

'You're telling me, that the only known descendant of Robin Hood, she who once worked as a mermaid, Mossad's most feared operative, is confused?'

'Yes, she is,' said Anaïs, impatiently.

'Come on, Anaïs! Go and do your stuff.'

'Octavian, no. I just…'

'You just what, hm? Go in there and get us a room.'

'How?'

'Don't give me that! I know you know how. Go and do what you do. Do your thing liar girl.'

She reluctantly followed him into the sparkling white and copper lobby and took a few seconds to survey the place. Then Octavian watched and was utterly impressed as Anaïs in impeccable French told the receptionist that they had with them Israel's most respected travel writer and that he needed a room after theirs at the Shangri-La had been found to be infested with bed bugs and assured him that it would be of immeasurable value to the hotel's reputation to have Monsieur Ben-Gurion's upmost sympathy in light of the book he was writing in Russian and Hebrew on the great hotels of the world.

'Et est-ce que monsieur Ben-Gurion ont des bagages?'

'Non.'

And up in their elegantly simple suite Anaïs and Octavian made love.

'How are you going to get banned from France again?' she said, writhing upon the duvet.

Octavian went to the minibar and downed a bottle of beer and went into the bathroom. He soon emerged and downed another and turned to Anaïs and smiled, his face cleanly shaven but for a toothbrush moustache.

An hour and six bottles of beer later he was looking out across the Dôme des Invalides, at ease and meditating before the black marble and stupendous periwig of Vauban's tomb. He unbuttoned his shirt and handed it to Anaïs. He stood to attention, now in a t-shirt of three leopards couchant quartered with three fleur-de-lis, his wireless speaker hanging at his neck. He tapped at his phone; military trumpets blared out to call the whole baroque hall to attention. Then rose the slow stampeding of the *Pariser Einzugsmarsch*. Octavian slow-marched down the dome's steps and crossed the mezzanine and stepped up onto the marble balustrade. The Prussian horns blasted again before the parade rhythm returned, doubly loud. He unbuckled his belt and dropped his trousers and shyness soon left him. He shot a stream of fluid out across the room to splatter down upon the red quartzite scrolls of Napoleon's bilious casket. A few Asian tourists turned their filming phones towards him; the European ones grabbed the arms of their companions and whispered in his direction and strolled on to the sound of their audio guides. The guard at the metal detectors, looking up to the balustrade and

Octavian, closed his hands to make a clapping sound; he repeated the action, twice, and again, until he was joined by the guard beside him.

'Nothing!' said Octavian, throwing his arms in the air as he crossed the Pont Neuf. 'Not a warning, not a fine. They didn't even take the speaker off me!'

'I thought it was a good idea. I wish you would have warned me before you did it, but it was a good idea.'

'Applause!? How could they applaud? They're soldiers! What lowness of people are the French? I mean what do you have to do to get banned from fucking France?!'

There came, wailing towards them, a Japanese girl, her hands flapping at the sides of her miniskirt, her feet stomping as she neared. She collapsed into Anaïs' arms and howled, 'Nobody in Palis is Flench!'

'Hm?' said Anaïs, looking down at her.

'Palis is not so crean! Palis not so nice at all!' and she pulled herself from Anaïs' arms and fell into Octavian's.

'Nobody in Palis is Flench!' she wailed again. 'Palis is not so crean. Palis not nice at aaaaall!' and she rolled out of Octavian's arms and stepped up onto the low ledge of the pont and promptly jumped off.

'Woah,' said Octavian, calmly and with little interest.

'You know I know the mayor of Paris?' said Anaïs as they strolled on.

'You *know* him?'

'From when I lived here. We're good friends. I stayed in his suite in the Mandarin Oriental for three months.'

'Oh you stayed in his suite did you?'

'Not like that you idiot. Don't get jealous. I had dinner with him twice. I told him I was a Palestinian refugee and he sympathised. His mother was Algerian or something.'

'Do you really know him?'

'I do.'

'Why didn't you tell me? He'll ban me from France.'

'Will he?'

'After I'm through with him. Can you get him to have lunch with us?'

'Anaïs?'

It took Anaïs Spencer a few moments to realise precisely who had just passed them in the Parisian street and who had himself taken a few moments to remember her face. 'Anaïs?' he called after her again in three very distinct and very loud syllables.

'Harry Fuggle,' she exclaimed, amazed.

'Anaïs!'

'I haven't seen you since…'

'Since Hong Kong. You survived Uganda!' he said, elated for her. '*And* the cancer!'

'With bells on, old cock! Cancer's all gone. And Uganda's a lovely place really. I don't know what all the fuss is about. A paradise. This is Octavian, my black Ugandan friend.'

'How are you?' said Octavian in about the same accent as that butcher in Brixton.

'Yes, how do you do?' said Harry Fuggle, uncertain of him.

'What are you doing here?' said Anaïs. 'Are you on holiday?'

'No, no. I live here now. I got a transfer from the Fin Times to The Sun to be their Paris correspondent.'

'That's great!'

'No,' he said, reflecting.

'No?'

'No. I asked for the transfer so that I could follow my girlfriend here. Japanese. It was her dream to live in Paris.'

'Mmm?' said Anaïs, excitedly beckoning him to continue.

'She killed herself, a few hours after we got here.'

'Oh.'

'She thought Paris was going to be the most magical place on earth. She spent years dreaming about it. But then… Well, this is it, isn't it?'

'Well at least you must be enjoying the work more? More than the Financial Times? You said it was a bit boring.'

'No.'

'No?'

'No. Not much happens here that our papers care about. At the moment all the stories are up in Calais. The migrants. Hordes of them apparently. But the paper won't let me go because One Direction are visiting in a couple of days. Hopefully something happens with that.'

'I've got a story for you. We're about to be banned from France.'

'Are you?'

'He's a novelist. He's just been shortlisted for the Man Booker Prize. Don't let his idiotic African face fool you. He's quite smart. A renowned British novelist banned from France. What do you think? That'll get you something, no?'

'Is it an exclusive?'

'The story and the photos are yours, Harry. Octavian, give Harry your agent's details.'

'Hm?' said Octavian, then spoke to Anaïs in pseudo-Ugandan. 'Onde pankeh wendama. Ho ho! Lim a neh neh, tai mon nah. Ha! … There you are my friend,' he said, handing Harry Daisy's business card and clasping his hands between his own. 'I hope that we can do some good for my people.'

'For your people.' Harry's face jolted upon his neck for a few seconds. He was hesitating. Eventually he dared, with a finger subconsciously raised to his top lip, to ask: 'Who are your people?'

'You seem to know a lot of men in Paris,' said Octavian after they had farewelled Harry with the details and stipulations of tomorrow's exclusive.

'I know two. And one of them I knew from Hong Kong.'

'Mm.'

'Shut up.'

'Please don't tell me to shut up.'

'And tell me you're going to shave that moustache when we get back to the hotel.'

'I think I like it,' said Octavian, himself surprised.

'No you don't.'

'No, I really think I do!'

The sun shone splendidly on the golden sandstone of the Palais du Louvre. Anaïs and Octavian sat on metallic outdoor chairs at a gravel-floored restaurant beside a lawn of the Tuileries.

'That's him there.' Octavian pointed to the young man standing at attention in front of the sandstone reliefs. He raised a finger and the young man nodded. 'He's mine. When mayor what's-his-name…'

'Serendieu.'

'Whatever, goes to the bathroom, Pierre over there brings me a cream pie and I smash it into his fat French face. And your mate Harry Fuggle…' Octavian turned around to give Harry Fuggle a nod. 'Who you stayed with in Hong Kong for a week…' (He was sitting at the table beside theirs in sunglasses with his camera unlenscapped. He nodded, very seriously, back.) 'He takes some photographs and writes us a story and sends it to Daisy for amendment and—'

'He's here.' Anaïs gestured towards the path, along which was walking the mayor of Paris. Nicolas Serendieu was tall and sturdily built, middle aged, his combed hair showing no signs of thinning or greying. Octavian raised his eyebrows and said, 'What a knob. How do you say knob in French?'

Nicolas spoke to Anaïs in French until she introduced Octavian. 'It is very nice to meet you.'

'And you,' said Octavian.

He put his sunglasses on the table and crossed his legs precisely as were Octavian's. Octavian sensed that his trousers and shirt had become glaringly ordinary beside this fully grown man's impeccable suit. 'And how are you enjoying Paris?' he asked Octavian.

Octavian filled Nicolas' water glass and said, 'It's not an entirely awful place.'

'Do you not think so?'

'It has a cold beauty.'

'Interesting.'

'Do you not think so?'

'I ate it.'

'You ate it?'

'I hhhate it. Paris is a orrible place.'

'You're its mayor.'

'Oui, I ate it. Butter…' he admitted, 'but being ze mayor of Paris has many many perks. Many perks.'

'How many?'

'I am practically a king. And it is ze best step towards the presidency. Oh no. Sheet,' he said, turning his head suddenly away from the palace.

'What?' said Anaïs.

'No, it is nothing.' Nicolas put his sunglasses back on and held a covering hand at his forehead.

'What is it? Nick?'

'Nick?' said Octavian.

'You see zat woman who is talking with zat ozer woman.'

'The grandmas?' said Octavian.

'Yes. Ze ot one.'

'The hot one?'

'I am fucking her. Sheet.'

'Why is that so bad?' said Anaïs, almost laughing.

'Apart from the fact that she's a hundred.'

'Because I am fucking ze ozer one as well.'

'A double century.'

'Seventy-two ze ozer one,' smiled Nicolas. 'Pretty good for seventy-two, uh? And she is ze muzzer of my wife.'

'What?!' said Anaïs.

'Are you sleeping with your mother-in-law?' said Octavian.

'Amazing, uh?' he said, smiling with his eyes made huge.

'Nick,' said Anaïs, disapprovingly.

'Nick,' said Octavian, mocking her.

'I am sleeping wiss ma muzzer in law!' he said with excitement and saliva. 'Zis way I get to fuck not just ze muzzer of my children, I get to fuck ze muzzer of my children's muzzer as well! Ha ha.' He subsided into a cackle and rocked back and forth in his chair. 'And ze ozer one is the muzzer of my best friend! When I die I will go down as one of ze greatest muzzerfuckerz in ze history of France!'

'That's perverse,' said Octavian.

Nicholas Serendieu made a gurgling sound and drew back as wide a smile as he was capable. 'Fantastique, no?'

'No! That's seriously perverted, man. Even for a French person.'

'Yes, I am a great pervert!'

'You're a great pervert?' Octavian looked at Anaïs and pouted with amused confusion.

'All great men are perverts! And all French men are great. Zerefore we are all perverts. I sink you are a pervert too, Monsieur Octavian, no? Anaïs, is he a pervert ou non? You told me he was a writer. You want to be an artiste but you are not a pervert? Come on!'

Octavian widened his eyes very briefly and furrowed his brow and shook his head. 'No,' he said in the high voice which he reserved for returning quite obvious answers to foolish questions.

By now it was becoming clear to Nicolas that Octavian was not a pervert. 'You are not a pervert?' Nicolas suddenly became dour. 'Do you have somesing wrong with perverts?'

Octavian turned his head slightly and in one quick movement pouted and retracted his bottom lip.

'Please excuse me,' said the Frenchman, standing sternly and buttoning his jacket. He crossed the restaurant terrace and pulled out his phone and put it to his ear as he went inside.

Octavian searched for his waiter; he found him and nodded. 'You ready for zees?' he said to Anaïs as he turned to Harry Fuggle and nodded. Shortly a cream pie was put in front of him. He slid it under the table and rested it in his hand upon his knee. He was watching the restaurant's double doors when behind him a team of hideously armed gendarmes crossed the lawn. They calmly brought machine guns to rest a few inches from the back of his head.

'Uhhhhh,' said Anaïs, pointing up at the officers looming over their table.

'Lift up you ands,' said one of them.

Octavian turned his head and saw the inside of a gun barrel. 'Ahh. … Lift up my what?'

'You ands.'

'My ands? Do you mean you want me to say them louder? Or in a higher tone? How do you mean lift them up?'

'Octavian,' said Anaïs, sighing. 'Machine guns.'

'Mmm,' he growled. 'You want me to lift up my hands? All right.' And after putting the cream pie on the table he did.

'Monsieur Octavian,' said Nicolas, returned with his hands in his pockets. 'You are under arrest. And using ze powers given to me as mayor of Paris you are hereby banned from France for not being a pervert. Zis country 'as no place for people like you.'

Harry Fuggle stood from his chair and walked backwards as he snapped away with his camera.

'You will be escorted to ze Hôtel de Ville and put on a booce and sent back to England where you be long.'

In one frantic movement Anaïs picked up the cream pie and slammed it into Nicolas' face and smiled and laughed. Octavian cackled and widened his eyes with fresh adoration. 'Pudibond!' the mayor of Paris scowled as he wiped cream from his eyes.

Harry Fuggle began really to take photographs and was set after by a gendarme. He turned and sprinted away as Anaïs and Octavian were handcuffed and led across the Tuileries.

They spent the night in a dungeon beneath the Hôtel de Ville and were force-fed French food and made to listen to recordings of French people talking to one another about cheese. Before dawn they were walked to an underground carpark and shown at gunpoint into the back of a blue gendarmerie van. It wound up the carpark ramps and soon they were out of the city and riding along a highway. After a few hours the van slowed; soon the muffled conversation between the officers in the front seemed to become worried. The van stopped and the voices rose to a panic. Shortly one of them got out.

'That's not good,' said Anaïs.

'What's not good?'

'The road's blockaded.'

'Even for a police car?'

'I don't know.'

They listened to the whirring of muffled and unintelligible voices without. Then the driver's-side door opened and there was shouting and then a few thuds. The back door to the van was opened, by two West African men in ill-fitting gendarme uniforms.

'Where you are going?' one of them said to Octavian.

'England.'

'Good,' said the man, and waved a dozen of his accomplices over. They piled in to sit on the benches beside Anaïs and Octavian. The van's door was shut again and the front doors thudded closed. The clutch choked as it took off.

'So where is everybody from?' said Anaïs, wishing to break the ludicrous ice.

Twenty-four creamy white eyeballs moved to her.

'I am from Cameroon,' said one of them.

'Oh, Africa, lovely!'

'Me too.'

'And me.'

'I am from Eritrea.'

'I from Bangladesh isn't it?' said another, and was echoed by his four countrymen.

And there were a few Syrians.

'Well they all sound like lovely places,' said Anaïs. 'And you all want to go to England do you?'

'We go to England isn't it?'

'England...' said one of the hoodied Eritreans, pausing to dream, '...is a great country.' He breathed the words, and believed. 'In England is good life. In France is no good life.'

'And what about where you're from?' said Anaïs, addressing them as children.

'No good life at all.'

'Bangladesh horrible place, isn't it?'

'Well on that I can agree with you. But why don't you stay there and try to make those places better? Rather than going somewhere else that is already not that bad?'

'What can we do?'

'There is no work.'

'I had work,' said one of the Eritreans.

'He had work. But apart from that, there is no work.'

'And I am a doctor.'

'And Eritrea is full of poverty and disease.'

'There is no work.'

'And what makes you think there's a good life to be had in England?'

'In England is good life.'

'We read British newspapers.'

'I watch Great British Bake Off.'

'I want to eat Victoria sponge,' said another of the Eritreans, joyed by the thought.

'Britain is land of opportunity.'

'He who is tired of Lon-don, is tired of life.'

'Free housing,' said a Bangladeshi. 'In Bangladesh I no *have* house isn't it?'

'And education.'

'Was it you who said you were a doctor?' she asked, thrown by all the hoodies.

'N...H...S.'

'Buckingham Palace.'

'Win-stan Churchill.'

'Abraham will audition for X-Factor. He is a great singer and dancer.'

'Always he bring rain.'

'It is my *dream* to meet Simon Cowell,' said Abraham.

'Oh you poor fellows.'

And when Octavian found by his phone reception that he was again in England he knocked on the closed hatch which opened to the cab. It was slid open.

'Where exactly are we going?'

'Lond-on,' said the navigator.

'Land of opportunity,' said the driver, smiling.

'M&Ms world.'

'Win-stan Churchill.'

'Simon Cow-ell.'

'Could you take us to Victoria station?'

And when they pulled in and the rear door was opened and all of their van-mates had fled past the photographers out into the horrible city Octavian and Anaïs stepped out of the van and were ambushed by photojournalists. Daisy Trench-Hawe herded them into a waiting taxi.

'*So* ridic,' she said as their car eased through the journalists.

'So what?' said Octavian.

'Ridic.'

'What's that?'

'Ridiculous.'

'Why didn't you say ridiculous?' said Anaïs.

'It was fucking brilliant, Octavian. Here.' She handed him the day's *Sun*. It's second biggest headline, after '*Soldier Charged With Battlefield Murder*,' was Octavian's:

'*Author Banned From France. For Not Being A Pervert.*'

'You're trending on Facebook, Twitter, YouTube, BuzzFeed. I photoshopped that stupid moustache off your face. Your name's everywhere. Hackney-Bromide can't wait to meet you.'

'The publishers?'

'Pookie's read the newspapers and she's said she'll do the book. The cover's being designed, the launch and the release are already being prepared. She just wants a few minor adjustments and to meet you.'

'Adjustments?'

'Nothing major. You just have to take out some of the jokes.'

'Which jokes?' said Octavian, instantly suspicious.

'Well, Octavian, all the gay jokes, and the ethnic minority jokes and all the jokes about New Zealand.'

'Absolutely no way.'

'And the jokes about disabled people have to go as well, and all the people who talk with accents have to be changed, and the jokes about atheists and bestiality have got to go too.'

'No!'

Daisy warned Octavian with his own name.

'You're saying I have to take out all the jokes.'

'Just the offensive ones.'

'No joke is funny that is not offensive.'

'That's not true.'

'It is today. What do you want me to do? Write puns? This woman's a fat lesbian isn't she?'

'Octavian!' said Daisy.

'She is, she's huge, isn't she? It's all part of the FLA. The Fat Lesbian Ascendancy. Men being told what to do by women who have personal grievances against them. Real men are prosecuted today like recusants under Elizabeth.'

'No, she isn't fat, Octavian. She's lovely.' Aroused by his insolence, Daisy put her hand on his leg. 'So stop it, she's a very good friend of mine. Anaïs she can't wait to meet you too. I've told her all about how lovely you are. Pookie likes to have a close personal relationship with her authors. And that includes friends and partners.'

Anaïs looked at Octavian's leg and felt a sequence of emotions born hazily of fear and hatred. She looked at Daisy, who was smiling, and then at Octavian who had not brushed her hand off.

'Did you say Pookie?'

II

The polo at Sandhurst was a notoriously dull affair. There was no cheering and no applauding and nobody at all really watched the match. Sparsely littered on one side of the field—the other taken up by the spare rented horses and temporary pavilions of the partaking teams—were huddles of spectators with their backs to the game and a handful of disposable marquees begrudgingly occupied by the girlfriends and wives of those officers of the Royal Military Academy who had begged them to come and watch. Beneath one such marquee stood Anaïs Spencer, in a Bottega Veneta dress of orange Morris-like flowers and soft green vine leaf, and Octavian Hughe, clean-shaven in checked jacket and pink tie. Both were making chit-chat.

The sun shone lukewarmly upon that grand tower of red and beige brick, on the hallowed musty buildings which schooled those boys who as men had for decades been transplanted to the friendly nations of the earth, there to act as the opposing army in training exercises; where the descendants of real soldiers, guided by centuries of accumulated elegance, were taught how properly to observe through binoculars from a safe distance the journalists descending upon a valley to report on the plight of the civilian population being shelled there. A breeze blew greyly across the vast parade grounds, over which class after class practised proudly the lowering of the Union Jack from its hoist, the folding of the flag under which they served, its deportation—across that once boot-trodden square where young men learned to fight off cramp and itch as the politicians delivered their inoffensive orations; where the world's entitled were daily instructed on how with smallest possible show of displeasure an officer was to watch the raising of some other savage kleptocracy's flag in place of his own.

The canapés had been unpacked from their baskets and the bellinis had been mixed and Daisy Trench-Hawe laughed with Octavian and an enormous man whose name nobody could quite remember. Anaïs kept one eye on Octavian's frequently touched arm and one on the remarkably attractive Pookie Winkworth-Dumley, senior fiction editor at Hackney Bromide. Pookie was doe-eyed and tall and slim and had her shining black hair in a tight ponytail. Her dress was sleeveless, her arms soft-skinned and flab-free. She said her 'o's in a way which Anaïs found intangibly pleasant and had spent her twenties doing much the same thing as Anaïs, only upon fewer men and from India to the Middle East.

'I absolutely adore stories like that,' said Pookie when Anaïs had bridged the gap between Harry Fuggle in Hong Kong and Harry Fuggle in Paris. 'Your life sounds like a movie.'

'Well everybody's life is like a movie, don't you think? It's just a matter of whether or not you'd pay to go and see it.'

'Very true,' said Pookie, pleasantly amused. 'You don't have much of an accent do you?'

'Thank you. And you lived in Dubai as well?'

'For three years. I went to work for Reuters there and within six months I was being chased all over the place by an Al Qasimi. Didn't have to pay for a thing. He bought me a Jeep, would you believe that? I declined it of course, but I did get him to pay for me to stay in the Grand Hyatt while I was there. Saved a fortune. I still get their hand-soap shipped to me especially. Nothing else in the world smells so pleasant.'

'Your sense of smell is the closest part of your brain to the part that holds your memories. Did you know that?'

'I did know that. It is funny the hold that the past has over us isn't it?'

'Which Al Qasimi chased you?'

'Fahim. Why?'

Anaïs found this very diverting.

'What?'

'Did you ever meet Humaid?'

'His nephew?' said Pookie, surprised.

'Humaid bought *me* a jeep.'

'He did not!'

'And he put me up in the Waldorf Astoria for six months. I never went near him of course. Repulsive man. I was constantly ignoring my phone. God he wanted it. He offered me plastic surgery, horses, anything I wanted, just to hug me.'

Pookie said, 'Ha!' and laughed and sighed. 'You're *too* delightful. They are mad for us there aren't they?'

Lady Hannah Blink, one of Daisy Trench-Hawe's longest-suffering friends, snuck up on them with a tray of skewered prawns. 'It's *so* lovely to have you with us, Anaïs,' she said as Anaïs took one. 'I love your name.' Anaïs had never been among so many people who were so able to pronounce it.

'Oh it's so lovely to be here. You're all so nice.'

'Is that gold?' said Pookie, hovering a finger over the tray.

'King prawns and chorizo with a honey-soy and gold-dust glaze, yes.'

'Hannah makes the best canapés, Anaïs. But I can't eat gold, Hannah. I'm sorry. Or I won't. My father died from eating the stuff.'

Anaïs' eyes were long closed at the deliciousness of the things.

'Oh I'm sorry, I didn't know,' said Lady Blink.

'No, no,' said Pookie. 'You weren't to know. But he ate it all his life and at fifty the stuff had so clogged his insides that he just dropped dead.'

'I'm so sorry.'

'Not at all, darling.'

'Well I'll be back in a minute to top up your drinks.'

'And you've just moved to London?' said Pookie.

'A few weeks ago, yeah. I was in Venice before that. That's where Octavian and I met.'

'Oh, I love Venice. Especially in the spring. Were you there for the spring?'

'When's spring? I never know when the seasons are.'

Pookie's husband crossed the lawn from the college buildings and kissed hello all whom he knew. He was introduced to Octavian as Barnaby and by Pookie to Anaïs. The tall person whom Octavian had been deriding for the amusement of Daisy said to Barnaby, 'How about that tour old boy?' and Barnaby said, 'Absolutely,' and invited everyone to come along. Octavian said he would love to see the place. Anaïs and all the females except Daisy declined. As the foursome set off for the buildings the back of Daisy's head was thrown back with laughter and she leaned over and nudged Octavian.

'Powder the inside of our noses, ladies?' said Lady Hannah Crumble, who had known Lady Hannah Blink since first they had had a threesome together at university. 'Guests first,' and she handed Anaïs an opened pocket mirror. In the dish opposite the glass was a pile of white powder. Anaïs was proffered an antique snuff spoon.

'Is this cocaine?' said Anaïs.

'Don't be silly,' said Lady Blink as she refilled Anaïs' champagne glass with prosecco and peach puree. 'Of course it is.'

'I don't ahh… partake.'

'Do you not?' said Pookie, and reached the snuff spoon across and then sniffed at it hard and long.

For half an hour the girls talked very rapidly about a host of men and women, all unknown to Anaïs though apparently quite famous in England, with whom they had slept and who had slept with one another. Then came the topic of love of drink and who too suffered from it, then somebody they knew's resentment of childlessness and much laughter about a world-famous American actor's lust for young boys and those of their cousins who had succumbed to him, then a brief and excited comparing of notes about each of their joy counsellors. Soon all except Anaïs and Pookie were unconscious in the sunshine.

'And what about Octavian?' said Pookie as they watched him return, ambling, across the field. Daisy was chatting with Barnaby.

'What about him?'

'Where's he been for the last seven years?'

'I actually don't know.'

'Do you not?'

'I haven't asked him. He's been travelling for five years, I know that.'

'Are you too afraid to ask?'

To this Anaïs made no answer. 'How was it?' she called as he neared the marquee.

'They have amazing stained glass windows in one of the chapels.'

Barnaby kissed Pookie on the mouth and said that he had to be off. Daisy joined her friends in the sunshine and that tall person in whom nobody was interested took off his shoes and in preposterous socks reclined beside her.

'You know, Octavian, I could put a word in for you at MI6 if you'd like. My cousin does something for them. He won't tell me what, but he's been there for years now. I'm sure his word would count for something.'

'Why would I want you to have a word to MI6 for me?' he

said, smiling with ignorance.

'Your charming girlfriend was just telling me that you'd applied for a job with them. Good sport I say.'

'Oh did she? Well, my darling girlfriend is sometimes a little inventive with biographical details. I have not applied for a job at MI6.'

'Oh. Understood,' said Pookie and winked at him.

'No really I haven't.'

'Though I do keep saying that he should, don't I? He's so good at accents and foreign languages. And he's super fit.'

'Though not as fit as you. Anaïs has taken up jogging, Pookie, haven't you?'

Anaïs smiled dryly at Octavian and said, 'I'm in a foreign land and entirely without my friends. And my boyfriend spends so much of his time with his imaginary ones that I just have so much spare time.'

'Which unforeign land did you have friends in, darling?'

'Are you drunk?'

'No. Are you?'

'Octavian, Anaïs was just telling me about her travels. Aren't her stories hilarious?'

'Pookie, I want to talk to you about this final edit.'

'I thought Daisy spoke to you.'

'She did.'

'Octavian, I really like the book. It made me laugh. But I'm *not* one of the people who are going to pay to read it. We, and now you, make money off a very new world. And we are all an integral part in trying to build an even newer one, where we make even more money. And that world is a world where being gay is no longer hilarious. Do you understand? A world where the way Asian people talk is not an impetus to derisory immitation. A world where Islam is a beautiful faith that we should all embrace. Why? Because we need all the gay Chinese muslims to be good consumers. And if we're making fun of them they won't join us, will they? They'll join ISIS. That's *our* civilizing mission.'

'And what then *am* I allowed to make fun of?'

'That's for you to find out. You're the writer.'

'Christianity?'

'No, Christianity's scary, it's not funny.'

'What about a book whose main character has lost his religion, and his country has been overrun by very lovely foreigners, and he's lost all desire to have a family or to go on living.'

'A superhero?'

'Pookie, can I tell you what I foresee? How I work? What I'm working towards?'

'Please.'

'Well, Australia is half way between Britain and America. Culturally as well as geographically, yes? The world's two dominant English-speaking cultures. And what Australia should be doing is creating a synthesis out of these two cultures. Taking the best from both nations and from both cultures. The elegance and tradition of British civilization and the honesty and individual narratives of the American Empire. The elegant novel is English, the comedy film American. Mastery of the language is English, fun and lack of pompousness American. Imagine the synthesis, Pookie! Imagine what we *could* be creating.'

And here, half way through his damp screed, Anaïs realised precisely why Octavian was waffling and so frequently using the word 'culture'. His eyes had changed from their enchanting electric blue to be predominantly black, so enormous were his pupils.

Daisy Trench-Hawe stirred from her stupor and crawled silently to a picnic basket. She slid from it a bottle of vodka, took four plastic shot glasses and tried to wake her co-slumberers before putting one into each of their hands. 'Where's the cocaine?' she said, waving an arm at Pookie. 'Pookie,' she groaned. 'Pookie! Octavian! *Anaïs*! Oh, Anaïs, it's so nice to have you here. Really, we love having you. You're so beautiful. Isn't she beautiful, Pookie? She looks like that girl from Wolf of Wall Street. What's her name? Maggie Something. Octavian, I'm *so* glad to have a good male friend. Platonic, you know? We can just talk. Oh,' she said, sighing and lowering her head and letting her bottom lip hang in between sips of vodka. Hooves thudded behind her as the ponies galloped hard into one another. Daisy's head jolted up and in the voice whose sickliness was normally reserved for the supplicating of managers who had just banned her from their establishment she said, 'Partying is such sweet sorrow.'

'I want to go,' said Anaïs.

'Do you really?' said Octavian.

263

'Yes.'

'You don't do you? Come on.'

'What do you mean, Come on? I want to go home.'

'No you don't,' he said in decrescendo, as though she were being playful.

'Yes, I do.'

And as Daisy threw up on the M3 motorway a police car flashed its lights at Octavian and he pulled her car over.

'And you're insured to drive this vehicle?' said the officer.

'Not to the best of my knowledge.' He pointed at Daisy's mouth—it being wide open and her eyes quite closed—in the back seat. 'It's her car. She drove us to the polo and then she got far too drunk and we had no other way of getting home, so I'm just driving her car back to London.'

'And she's your girlfriend is she?'

'No,' said Anaïs, standing beside them.

'Are you aware that it's illegal to drive a motor vehicle in Britain without insurance?'

'I'm sure she's insured. And I'm sure the car's insured.'

'Not how it works I'm afraid. Is there anything you want to retrieve from the vehicle before it's towed?'

'Towed?'

'All the details on how to retrieve the vehicle are on the back of this form here. You'll receive the fine in the mail within the month.'

'A fine? How much is the fine?'

'Mohammed,' called the officer to his partner.

'Yeah, Shuvie?'

'How much is the fine for driving a vehicle without insurance?'

'Three hundred and thir-ee pounds.'

'*Three hundred and thirty pounds*?!'

'If you do need to get anything out of the vehicle before it's taken, any valuables, anything else you need, best get it now, because here's the tow-truck.' A Rastafarian pulled in from the motorway and leaned out of the window to measure his reversal towards Daisy's car.

Octavian was breath-tested and then he and Anaïs pulled Daisy from the back seat. Once the officers were vaguely certain that she might eventually be returned to consciousness they allowed them to lay her in the weeds. The breeze blew in flecks of drizzle which soon became sheets of rain upon the wind. Anaïs and Octavian were alone on the asphalt of the motorway, huddled between a ditch of bracken and six lanes of endless, speeding traffic.

'Son,' said Octavian.

'What?' she said, her arms folded and her neck pulled into her shoulders.

'We are pilgrims in an unholy land.'

III

Octavian struggled for two weeks with extracting from *The Horrible And The Miserable* all the jokes which Pookie Winkworth-Dumley thought retarded the building of that vastly more profitable world which she and her income-bracket were attempting to build. He considered the list of underidable topics, which she emailed him, objectively to be one of the most amusing documents in the history of comedy. It was like a Magna Carta to him, and would have been to every man and woman who had been possessed of a sense of humour in the whole century of comedic work which led up to the preemptive censorship of his debut novel. As he worked his way through the manuscript, turning William Playfair into the superhero that his publisher wanted of him, as he reread his jokes under the glaring light of Pookie's post-post-post-postmodernism he felt old and fusty, as though at the age of twenty-nine he were a grandfather railing about the dangers of Popery to a dildo store full of gaysians.

Anaïs woke to his growls and his swearing and to the scribbling out of whole pages with his pen. She rolled onto her side and pulled the duvet over her shoulder and instantly recoiled from the bed, cupping her breast. 'Oooh,' she groaned, pressing her hand against it. She got up and showered and went upstairs to make breakfast.

She found in the cupboards only a torn crust of bread and resorted to the freezer in order to procure her morning toast. Not one of its three drawers would open. She turned once again to the sink and threw some hot water upon the frozen façade and took the hammer from the drawer and once again began chipping away. She sat cross-legged and hacked at the over-frozen railings of the middle drawer and when she could slide it in and out easily enough she stood and threw up into it.

'What the hell?' she said, and put the whole drawer in the sink and ran hot water.

She went to the fridge and took a punnet of strawberries and a tub of yoghurt. The closing door swung into her other breast. She doubled over in pain and then stood in the kitchen for a time, her hands pressing at her breasts, testing at which point of pressure they began so badly to ache. Only a gentle nudge was needed. 'Shit,' she said, and went to the supermarket and bought bread and a pregnancy test. 'Shit, shit, shit, shit, shit.'

'If bottom line shows up, negative,' she read and summarized to the bathroom mirror. 'If bottom *and* top line show up, positive.'

Three minutes later only the top line had shown up.

'What the fuck does that mean?'

And from a more expensive supermarket she purchased one of each of the eleven pregnancy tests which they sold.

All top lines and all pink bars showed up and all absorbent tips changed colour. Her sense of future sounded like the struck bell of a carnival strength-tester. Sitting upon the toilet she put her head in her hands and tried to assess fully the situation. Surrounded by instructional leaflets and open boxes of thin cardboard and the plastic rods which foretold of her prison house she rotated her fingers at her temples and soon decided to bin everything. She tied the plastic bag shut and threw it onto the street.

She returned to the breakfast bar and pushed her hands at its edge and hung her head. She hit random on her phone's music player and a frantically picked acoustic guitar began. The cupboards of their home now brimmed with the ingredients necessary for the making of lamingtons. She had attempted them four times, each moister than the last. A haunting trill of a voice began to cry out. Soon Anaïs snapped—she took up a spatula and readied a mixing bowl and into it poured out her sugar and her vanilla. '*Your daddy is, a handsome devil...*' She tapped an egg once at the edge of the bowl, tapped it twice, then crushed the thing utterly. '*He's got a chain, five miles long...*' She picked out the shell from the sugar and then took up another and tapped it at the bowl's lip. '*And on every link, a heart does dangle...*' It remained defiantly intact until the action of her wrist rose to destroy it. She clenched her fist and took a deep breath and washed her hand. '*Of another maid...*' as she loomed over the mixing bowl with her knuckles on the countertop. '*...He's loved and wronged.*' Miss Baez strummed her last chord and the study door opened and closed.

Octavian sang as he bounded up the stairs: '*Questo o quella, per me pari sono, a quant'altre d'intorno, d'intorno mi vedo. ...* Anaïs, I figured it out! Are you all right? What's the matter?'

She lifted her head. 'What?'

'What's the matter?'

'Nothing, I'm fine. What did you figure out?'

'The jokes. I don't have to get rid of them at all. I just have to reverse them and then put a key in the middle of the book, like a sign that tells people that everything is to be read as reversed. So all the liberals will think I'm making fun of the people they think are ridiculous, and they'll become my champions, but all the smart people will see the key and theirs will be all the pleasure of the dissident, plus the hilarity. What's the matter?'

'I feel ill,' she said into the nascent sponge cake.

'What kind of ill? Stomach ill?'

'You ready?'

'Am I ready? For what? Is this the mail?' He shuffled through the letters on the bench and soon dropped all but one. 'This is it,' he said, suddenly animated. 'Anaïs, do you know what this is? This is it. This is the first dollar I've ever made from writing. This is it! And you know what?' He opened the envelope and unfolded and read from its single sheet of paper. He exhaled its words. 'Please find enclosed a cheque for the sum of five… thousand… pounds.' He closed his eyes at the figure and breathed heavily and slowly and smiled and shivered. 'Ah,' he moaned, and tilted his head back and looked to the heavens. 'Five thousand pounds. Ten thousand dollars.' He might have just come from six hours in a hammam, so euphoric was he. 'Oh,' he moaned, simply happy.

'Octavian.'

'Mmm?' he said, delirious-eyed.

'I'm pregnant.'

'Mmm,' he continued. 'Wait, what? Huh?' He quickly recovered from his bewilderment. 'What did you say?'

She stared across the kitchen at him and clenched her teeth and dropped her head back down to the mixing bowl. She exhaled: 'I am pregnant.'

The last vestiges of Octavian's insensibility changed to keen attention. 'Really?' Then he was excited. He rounded the kitchen island and lifted Anaïs up by her waist and beheld her. 'You're really pregnant?'

'I'm really pregnant.'

'You're not lying?' he smiled.

'No,' she said, sternly impatient of his playfulness.

'That's amazing! This is amazing!' He kissed her and looked into her despondent eyes and kissed her again.

'You don't mind?' she said blankly.

'Mind? What do you mean mind? Why would I mind? How could I mind? Your boyfriend's a writer, his girlfriend is a gorgeous pregnant woman with whom he is completely in love. We have to celebrate. No! I'll bank the cheque first. Then we can see the balance on a screen and then we *really* have the money. Rich and a family! You have a kid now, you need money.'

'*We* have a kid.'

'*We* have a kid, and we have money. I'm going to the bank. I'll send you the screenshot from my phone. Holy crap. I love you.'

'Yes, I love you too.'

'Yeah? You do?' he said, crouching to look up into her eyes.

'I really do.'

'What's the matter?'

'This is a lot to take in.'

'It is a lot to take in. But think of it this way. We're rich. And we're famous. Nothing matters anymore. Everything's easy. I'm writer famous, so nobody knows what my face looks like, we won't be hounded by photographers or fans, but my name will get us everywhere. We're rich,' he said, the notion again rising to fully sink in. 'And famous and a family, Anaïs! We have a home and a family and money.' He lifted her shirt and kissed her stomach and then kissed her lips again.

'I'll be back in half an hour. We'll celebrate, yes? We'll go out for lunch. The biggest fanciest restaurant with the tiniest most tasteless portions in the world. Sound good?'

'Sounds good.'

And Octavian took the letter and the cheque stapled to it and went out. Shortly Anaïs sliced off some butter and put it in the microwave. When the machine dinged she set it aside to let it cool and went to the back doors and stood in the cold wind upon the porch and looked down over the grey garden. Then sounded the squawking noise which was their doorbell.

Anaïs was greeted at the front door by a woman shorter than herself in a strapless top. She had kind eyes and did her eyelashes well and her hair was curled and blonde.

'Hi,' they both said, Anaïs with curiosity, the young woman with apology.

'Hi,' said the woman again. 'Does umm… Does Octavian live here?'

'He does.'

'Ah.'

'Why?'

'Ah. No, no reason. I just wanted to have a word with him.'

'About what?'

'It's not important. You're umm… You're his girlfriend?'

Anaïs took the woman in more completely. Shortly it became alarmingly obvious as to why she had pressed the doorbell of the home of Octavian Hughe before midday. Her strapless top was in fact a dress; she was in platform shoes and had an oddly protruding belly which she cupped with one hand and caressed with the other.

Anaïs felt the sudden return of the urge to throw up. She ran inside and into the kitchen sink did.

Octavian came excitedly home and found at the barstools in his kitchen a sight which he had definitely not ever anticipated seeing. Very rapidly did his enthusiasm become dessicate.

'K….' The consonant diminished into a throaty hiss.

'Kate,' said Anaïs, reminding Octavian of her name. 'Kate is pregnant.'

'So are you!' said Octavian. 'So is Anaïs,' he said, moving his finger from Kate to his girlfriend.

'Mmm!' said Anaïs with a furiously patronising rise and fall. 'Kate, is pregnant with your child.'

'Ah.' Octavian clicked his tongue six times, quickly and to his own rhythm. 'So are you. So is Anaïs.'

'Mmm,' said Anaïs, pulsing her eyes open, feigning elation at Octavian's solving of her little puzzle. 'We've had a lovely little chat. She was telling me all about Canada. I've never been. She said you didn't like it there very much though. Thought it was too boring. She even told me what you said to her when you left. "It's not you. It's Canada.".'

'And you've come here to tell my girlfriend that you're pregnant? No.'

'Daisy,' said Anaïs, 'told Kate that you lived here alone. Isn't that nice of her?'

'Did she really?'

'She must like me so much. They're such a lovely people, the English. Sorry, Kate. I'm sure you're marvellous.'

'How do you know Daisy?'

'Publishing's a small world,' said Kate, spitefully in her weak Northern accent.

'And you're back in England because... You...'

'I'm back in England to get rid of the baby. I'm not keeping it, I've already booked the appointment. I came to see what you were doing with yourself. I heard about the book and I thought I'd drop by. After all, you did kind of tell me that you loved me. Aaaand that you'd come and rescue me when the book was published. But I can see that you're thriving. Anaïs, it was so nice to meet you. Octavian does not know how lucky he is. Trust me.' Dismounted from the barstool she said goodbye to Octavian and left their home.

'What... the... fuck?' said Anaïs.

'What?'

'What do you mean, What?'

'What?! What did I do?'

'What did you do?!' Anaïs said, slowly and tensely, 'How many women do you think you might have impregnated in the last three months? Octavian?'

'That's not a fair question.'

'Is it not a fair question? I do think I should know. I have to make sure I have enough coffee in the cupboard for them when they *drop by*.'

'I'm sorry she came here, Anaïs. Really I am. I didn't even know she was in England.'

'Well come on then. Give me a roundabout estimate. Two, three? Well we already know it's two. Four, five? Five girls currently carrying your unborn children? Stop me when I've gone too high. Octavian? No? When *seven* have had morning tea here I can stop expecting pregnant women to knock on the door, with your unborn children?'

'Anaïs.'

'What?'

'She doesn't know that that child's mine. Seriously, Kate's a tramp. I met her through a friend who only warned me about her after we'd already started seeing each other. And I stayed with her because I thought she might be able to help me with the book, and because I needed a place to stay in Toronto.'

'And that makes it better does it?'

'Doesn't it?'

'No, it does not.'

'You've done as much.'

'*I have not,*' she said as though she were tearing the words apart. 'I hadn't slept with anybody for over a year before I met you.'

'Bull. Shit.'

'No, not bullshit. Now, come on, tell me, how many girls in the world are currently under the impression that you love them and are on your way to rescue them? Hm?'

'I was about to be homeless, Anaïs. I told her I loved her. It was a bad move. I admit that. But I had no other choice.'

'How many are there?' she repeated slowly, impatiently. 'Come on.'

'How many what?'

'How many Kates? How many girls are currently under the impression that you love them?'

'That's not a fair question to ask.'

'Is it not? Oh I'm sorry. But I do want to know. I do think that you actually love me, so I'll be fine with it. But I want to know. I can tell you how many men are currently in love with me.'

'Go on.'

'You want to know? Eleven.'

'It's only Kate, Anaïs.'

'Are you sure about that? What if you were drunk when you told the others and you don't remember?'

'It's only Kate. And she told me she'd already had an abortion anyway. Her womb probably has a flusher on it.' Anaïs' mouth shot open with shock. 'The doctor'll just have to pull a string, it'll be like a big bag of water hanging from a helicopter, just…' He pulled a closed fist towards himself as though he were untying a knot then both his hands fell down as he made the wooshing sound of a deluge loosed upon the ground. 'Maybe they'll use her womb to extinguish a forest fire.' And he repeated his animated procedure. 'No? Nothing? Anaïs, the kid's not mine. I'm certain of it.'

Thinking her top and bottom jaw had separated as far as they could, Octavian was very surprised to watch them continue to distance. Anaïs' eyebrows dropped towards her nose. Quickly it became apparent that she was furious. She breathed like an exhausted bear; shortly her face drooped as her heaving eased and she looked off into the distance of the kitchen wall and appeared to be sad. She took her house keys from the bench and wiped a forming tear from her eye and walked out.

'Anaïs,' said Octavian, and he let her leave.

He was sitting at the kitchen bench at his laptop when four hours later she came home.

'Anaïs, I'm sorry. If Kate's baby's mine, then it was absolutely a mistake. I'm sorry you had to know about it.'

'I don't care about that, Octavian.'

'Then what is it?'

'It's nothing. Can we forget about it?'

'I'm sorry she came to the house, to our home. Really I am. I had no idea she was going to do that and that's a huge invasion of our privacy, of your privacy. I honestly didn't know she was even in England. If I'd have known she was here I would have contacted her to tell her about you. She's obviously crazy, no? I mean who would do that? Clearly she came here just to tell me about the baby. There's no way she had to come here to have an abortion, right? I mean I'm sure there's a doctor in Canada who's capable of dropping a baby from a dunk tank.'

'There!'

'What?'

'Why do you have to make jokes like that?'

'Jokes like what? I always make jokes. That's what I do.'

'Abortion's not funny.'

'Is it not?'

'No it's not!'

'You don't find it just a little bit funny? What about—'

'It's not funny!'

'Are you people protective of your unborn babies or something? I didn't know that. Like collectively? I didn't know you had communal pride with other pregnant women. She's going to flush *her* unborn foetus down the toilet, not ours.'

'Octavian!'

'What?!'

'Shut up!' and Anaïs began to cry.

'What the fuck is the matter with you?' said Octavian, suppressing his yelling and moving in to hold her. '*What* is the matter, Anais? I'm sorry for making jokes. … What's the matter?'

She cried into his chest and he circled her back with his palm. When she had ceased to sob and was merely huffing Octavian said, 'Anaïs, what is it? Please tell me.'

'It's nothing.'

'What is it? What's the matter? … I want to know.' She rocked her forehead against his chest. 'I want to know everything about you, Anaïs. I love you so much. … Please tell me what's wrong.'

And so Anaïs Spencer began, slowly, to tell for the first time in seven years the story of her last year of bland and certain normality. She told of finding out from her best friend that her boyfriend was cheating on her with their other best friend, and of choosing Dubai and work as a flight attendant as her place and method of escape. She told of finding out in between demonstrations of how to use the inflatable emergency landing slide and chanting, 'Ice, slice, swizzle stick!' that her medical showed that she was pregnant, and of having to fly back to Melbourne because her chosen course was in the UAE punishable by death. She told him how she had flown home without telling a single soul, not even her parents, and that it was the loneliest most horrible thing she had ever done, and that she ever since had been running not only from the shame, but from the shame of feeling ashamed. She told him about the flight back, spent mostly in tears, and of the recommencement of her training in the desert. She told him how at her graduation party she and the other Western girls were from the distance of a private booth each selected by the sons of fattened sheikhs and how she was pursued by one of them from Lagos to Islamabad to Kuala Lumpur and back before finally he attempted to rape her in the private room of a Dubai nightclub whose security company he owned. She detailed the large sum of money he paid for her silence and recounted how that money had begun to run out three years into her wandering and how she had never once told a lie before then.

'Octavian, this isn't working.'

'What's not working?'

'This.'

'Us?'

'I need to get out of here. I need to get out of London.'

'Do you really hate it?'

'I really, really, hate it. The people are awful, the weather. It's what the weather must be like in purgatory. It's never extreme, it's never great, it's just weather. You can always walk around outside but you can never enjoy it. And the people! They really are genuinely wretched and pompous. Half of them are addicted to alcohol and half of them are addicted to cocaine and the rest are addicted to both. All they talk about is money or sex. I can just feel it, Octavian, and I trust my feelings. This place is a graveyard. And when I feel something I know that it's true. There's no excitement here. Nothing's old. It's meant to be an ancient place but everything's hideously new. But not the good new. Not the "Wow, that's amazing," new. Just: "Oh, that's new." Concept and fusion restaurants and pop-up shops new. Moving from Bangkok to here was just moving from one circumference of concrete afterbirth to another. I'd prefer to be in Bangladesh before here. At least that was interesting. I'm a wanderer, Octavian. Call it a disorder if you want, call me defective. But I am so, so bored here. I just don't care about vegan cupcakes, or television, or listening to other people talk about television. I don't care about jogging or craft ale or brunch or having an outdoor setting or a freezer that won't fucking open. I don't care about fucking lamingtons! I don't care about having a house. My home is a spiritual one and on God's earth I am destined to wander. An Arab seeking her cup of cold water in the desert, just like you said. I want to buy a motorbike, Octavian. And I want to ride it from Saigon to Constantinople. Do you remember, in Venice? I want to live dangerously. I want to fire a machine gun again. I want to lie. I want to conquer. I'd prefer to be dead than domesticated. I want to be at war with wealth and with boredom and with the people who are ignoring the fact that our world's going to end within the century and that their lives are mediocre and sad and dull compared to what they *could* be. What everybody else *could* be, that's what I want to be. I want to shake the dust of this crummy little town off my feet and see the world! Picture what's out there and then picture this, look around. White sand beaches, coconuts, water the colour of warmth and happiness. Please let's get out of here. You're a writer now, can't we be the scourge of princes from anywhere in the world? We're mobile. We came to London, we got a home, you got published. It's done. We accomplished everything we set out to do. Now let's burn the home and take the writing with us.'

Octavian, numbed by the truth of Anaïs' voyage, had slowly been reintoxicated by her incitement. Feeling gradually returned to his body, to his fingers, at last to his heart. He let loose the tension in his neck and gave a warmed smile. 'We'll have to buy new luggage.'

Hesperia named of old.

The loose strumming of an acoustic guitar was joined by a lazy piano, and soon by the rest of The Stones—'*Well we all need... someone... we can* lean *on...*'—resounding all from the speakers hidden in the palm thatch overhead.

'So we're laughing, we're bleeding, we're drunk as scallops, and we're in the alleys of Casablanca, you know, we don't know where the hell we're goin'! Then around the corner come these Polish legionnaires. They know the streets, we don't. But it's three of us, three of them, it's a fair scallop of a fight, right? I grab a wooden pole that's holding up a tarp roof and I, I bust it over my knee and give the other half to my buddy, and we're standin' there, you know, like we're ready for a hundred-mile-an-hour pitch, like a batter at plate, and me and my buddies we just grit our scallops and wait. And just then, in the nick of time, two MPs with long scallops, *long* scallops, drive up behind the Legionnaires, and they, "You boys need a hand?" they say. The Legionnaires, they just, hands straight into their pockets. Surrender. They knew.'

'My *Lord*, that is a story!' said Larry, his white moustache twitching. 'Moon, can you get us three more pina coladas? Oh look, Jerry, there's Bob. Bob, come here, you gotta hear this.' Bob, in white tube socks and sandals and long khaki shorts, was called in and waved over from ascending from the beach to the hotel. He ducked beneath the ceiling fans of the bar and came to put a hand at Anaïs' bamboo barstool. 'Make that four pina coladas would you, Moon?' said Larry.

'I was gonna grab a bite to eat before we go into town to get those massages you talked about,' said Bob. 'What do I gotta hear?'

'Bob, this is Anaïs. Her grandfather was a, a medic under Patton. She's tellin' us his old war stories. But she's doing it in his accent, Bob. He was from the North Shore.'

'My third wife was from Gloucester.'

'That's what I told her! Go on, hun.'

'These pina coladas are in-credible, Moon. So, guys, you've heard of the Kasserine Pass?'

'Sure,' said Jerry, the sweatiest of the three. His *333*-branded singlet was soaked through. 'Patton defeats Rommel.'

'So we're bringin' the wounded back to the field hospital, you know, Battle of Kasserine Pass, the field hospital's fifteen miles to the rear, down through cliffs. We load some guys in. We're under fire the entire time. And the white cross on the top of the truck is supposed to protect us, right? Are you kidding!?' said Anaïs, leaning in precisely as her grandfather used to do when telling this story. 'We just drove around with a huge scallop on our roof like a target! They could spot us from all around. So I'm drivin' like a race car driver up these scallopy mountain roads and down the pass and all of a sudden we see a German fighter plane in the rear-view mirror. My buddy says, "He won't shoot us, we're an ambulance." But I'm not so sure. Then he lines up directly behind us, screaming fast too, and I slam on the brakes and we both leap out of the cab. I swear I could see the eyes white as scallops and a smile on the face of that Kraut pilot as his bullets cut the truck in half, just like a scallop. All the wounded got the bullets. No survivors.'

'In-credible!' said Bob, amazed behind a wedge of pineapple and a toothpick umbrella. 'Where'd you meet this girl, Larry?'

'Oh, these stories do make me miss him.'

'And now tell us, what was the incident you were gonna tell us about when you first sat down?'

'No, I'm too ashamed even to bring it up, Larry.'

'Come on, lady, we're all friends here. Moon get us four shots o' somethin' would ya? What do you wanna drink, Anaïs?'

'Do you know how to make a slippery scallop?' Moon looked sideways and pursed his lips. Shortly he shook his head at Anaïs. 'No. All right then, how about just vodkas?'

'Five shots of vodka Moon, you have one too. So come on. Tell us what happened.'

'Are you sure, Larry? I don't want to impose.'

'Impose? You're keepin' three old fellas entertained here.'

'All right then. Well, Larry, so I was intending to stay in Vietnam just for two weeks, you know. I told you why I left, I was living in Paris and I just wanted to get away from all the Muslims after what happened. And so I arrived late last night and my taxi driver puts all my stuff in his scallop, what you call a trunk, and then he drove off, Jerry. He drove off! My purse, my phone, my passport, all my scallops, all my clothes. Gone.'

'You're kidding me?' said Bob, quite astonished.

'Did you call the police?' said Larry.

'My hotel called them, but what could they do? I didn't have his name, his driver number, his licence plate. Nothing. They just laughed. Then when my hotel realised I didn't have a scallop to my name to pay them they wouldn't let me stay there. I had to sleep on the beach last night. Thank God it's so hot here. I can't even pay for this pina colada, Larry. I really couldn't afford a single scallop in the world.'

Sipping at his own pina colada in the furthest corner of Mango bar, a young man with lengthening hair, his shirtless back to Anaïs and her audience, was clearly eavesdropping. He shook his head with admiration.

'Now, Anaïs, don't you worry about a thing.'

'What could you mean, Larry?' said Anaïs, concentrating on the ocular conveyance of hopelessness.

'Don't you worry about the pina coladas, and don't you worry about your hotel, either. No granddaughter of no World War Two vet's gonna go homeless while we're around. How about we put y'up for a few nights?'

'No, Larry, please. That's—'

'Here! This is a real nice hotel. Real nice. Just until you can get your bank to send you another card or whatnot. Thuy,' said Larry, waving over the young woman standing behind a lectern at the bar's entrance. 'Thuy this is a very good friend of ours, Anaïs. I want you to put her in a room for four nights. Is four nights OK do you think?'

'No, Bob, that's way too much,' said Anaïs, tilting and shaking her head.

'Non-sense! It's nothin'. What's four nights' accommodation in a hotel in Vietnam to three old millionaires, hm? Thuy, do you have any suites available?'

'Suite 514 is free, Mr Hickenlooper, for you if you like.'

'And there y'are.'

'Hickenlooper? That's such a lovely surname. I knew I liked you guys. Bob, Jerry, am I right in accepting accommodation from this old scallop? I mean, how much of an old scallop is he, really?'

The young eavesdropper nodded and slurped up the last of his cocktail and shook his head again. He stood and turned, a smiling baby in a halter at his chest, and walked to the door. As Octavian, grinning with a light beard and anomalously large sunglasses at his face, passed Anaïs he looked to the thatched roof and said quickly, 'You win, wrap it up,' and he left.

'Well just don't go accepting anything else from him now, will you?' said Jerry.

'And make sure you see your drinks being poured!' said Bob, and all present laughed.

'Now do you need any cash to see you through?' said Jerry.

'No,' said Anaïs, exhaling. 'Thank you so much. A friend of a friend's already given me just a little bit. Street food it'll be for me, but that's fine, I like the food here. Oh, you guys are so nice. Thank you so much, really. I'll see you around, won't I? You're sure you're all right to pay for the drinks?'

'Don't be absurd, young lady,' said Larry. 'Of course we're paying for the drinks.'

'Shall I come down from suite 514 tomorrow to tell you some more stories?'

'And we'll call it even,' said Jerry.

'I say that's more than ample repayment,' said Bob.

'Shall we say midday?' said Larry.

'We shall,' said Anaïs, and hugged and kissed on the cheek all three Texans.

She put her sunglasses on—crashing cymbals and hooting and, *Bleed it alright... You can bleed all over me!*—as she stepped onto the terracotta terrace between the resort's two pools. Behind her an unspoilt blue panorama—a vast strip of topaz ocean, the highest and widest burst of hot, cloudless, azure. She rounded the larger pool—shimmering, ultramarine-tiled—and ascended to the lobby. It too was high and wide, and quiet, adorned with a podium of spice baskets and fruit crates and local handicrafts, floored with grey concrete, and immaculately air-conditioned. Beyond two sets of automatic glass doors Octavian was sitting on their motorbike—a white and so far reliable Honda Win—with his toes resting on the ground and their son at his chest.

'Well that took you long enough.'

'You try saying scallop thirty times in a normal conversation, let alone in a conversation about World War Two! That was tough. I think, what, twenty-two minutes? That's impressive.'

'It was most impressive, yes. A suite too, that's pretty good.'

She poked him in the shoulder blade and said, 'And your turn after Thursday. Ha!' and she leaned up to kiss his cheek.

'You on?'

Anaïs readied her feet on the pegs and put her arms at Octavian's stomach. 'Yep.'

'You ready, Agrippa?' Octavian put his finger to their baby's palm and Agrippa's tiny fingers closed around it. 'Yeah you are. To Byzantium? No, we'll see, won't we little man? How 'bout the beach? Yeah!' he said, ga-ga-ing excitedly. 'You want to go to the beach? You *love* the beach don't you? All right, we ready?'

He tapped at his phone and from the speaker taped to the speedometer a band of American angels began rejoicing in a capella; they strummed guitars and whacked a snare drum and then an alto voice gently wailed: *'This is the way… I always dreamed it would be…'*

Agrippa looked up at his father and smiled and bounced his arms and flapped his fingers and giggled *'The way that it is, oh oh, when you are holding me…'* Octavian started the bike and rode from beneath the palm-shade of the resort's drive out into the scorching sunshine.

'…And I can't explain, oh no, the way I'm feeling inside. You look at me, we kiss and then, I close my eyes and here it comes again…

> *I can hear music,*
> *I can hear music.*
> *The sound of the city, baby, seems to disappear.*
> *Oh-o and, I can hear music,*
> *Sweet, sweet music,*
> *Whenever you touch me, baby,*
> *Whenever you're near.'*

Made in the USA
Charleston, SC
20 February 2016